To Iona

It was evening when we came to Chilitenango

Passing through the towns we saw gangs of men outside all-night bars lit by the blue light of televisions. We heard snatches of shouting and gunshots and explosions, jittery dance music on transistor radios, smelt the hot fat from roadside fry-ups in car hubcaps, tortillas and chili and beans. Then as we climbed up higher into the mountains, through the dustclouds left by the truck ahead we saw dense forests, wooden shacks with corrugated iron roofs, bare electric bulbs clouded with mosquitoes. On occasion, out of the villages and in the silence between the grind of the truck gears, we would hear the cry of some nightbird. And through the drifts of red dust thin figures would lurch towards us, faces would appear, and they seemed like the faces of people we knew, family or old friends we had forgotten, poorly clothed, tired, their lips not moving though we heard their voices. We were sleeping, dreaming, dreaming of adventure, and our dreams were disturbed by voices and cries and all and none of them true. And we had no certain knowledge of why we were in that country or where we should go after

1

It was evening when they came to Chilitenango.

The red dust powdered the wheels of the truck and hung in slow drifts behind. Crammed in amongst the others, the four volunteers lurched awkwardly, grabbing at the slatted sides. Some of the village women drew their headscarves across their faces against the dust, but also to hide their smiles.

'The gringos thrash about like saplings,' said a younger man. An older one reminded him they were guests.

Three of the English students stood taller than any of the men. Only Lucy was their height. The women eyed her fair hair sidelong as if they would cut if off and flee with it. Bury it under a stone like treasure. The men could hardly look at the fairskinned fairhaired girl, it made them so sad with longing.

The potato truck pitched and came to a halt outside a low white building, brakelines hissing.

'Here's us!' said the fat gringo with curly hair. The truck had no steps. He sat on the boards and dropped. The other three had brought rucksacks but he had a suitcase. An enormous glossy black suitcase with retractable wheels. A man slid it down to him.

'I thank you, peasant!' he said in English.

The others followed. The fairhaired girl Lucy, the older Caitlin with an Ulster accent, and the tall one, Nicholas, reserved and eager and boyish all at once.

'*Gracias*,' they said.

'*Adios*,' said a few of the men gravely, raising their straw hats.

The truck ground away up the hill, bleared dusty headlights

skimming the darkness of the forest. The four waved after it. The tired men and women did not look back again.

'No buffet trolley either,' said the boy with curly hair. 'Useless. Sorry, my name's Bridge by the way.'

'Bridge?' said Caitlin.

'Yep.'

'What's that short for, Bridget?'

'Very droll. It's just Bridge. An old family name.' He held out his hand quaintly. 'Bridge Kynaston.'

Caitlin shook it. 'Quite a name.'

'Distinguished, isn't it?' He shook Nicholas's and Lucy's hands too, terribly old-fashioned. He didn't seem to be worried about a thing.

He tried to pop out the wheels on his suitcase and the whole thing opened up in the road. They helped him repack.

'You've brought a yellow corduroy suit,' Nicholas couldn't help observing.

'So I have. Along with anti-fungal powder and a plentiful supply of condoms.'

'But a *corduroy suit*. In the tropics.'

'And yellow,' said Caitlin. 'So very yellow.'

Lucy had a hand over her mouth. Nicholas was grinning from ear to ear.

'Well,' said Bridge. 'I thought it might be just the thing to dazzle the natives.'

He had flown in from a beach in the Caribbean, and was studying marine biology. They told him they had already spent a week in the capital here learning Spanish. Nicholas had backpacked around for a month before that - Nicaragua, Guatemala, Belize - and he and Lucy were doing medicine. Caitlin was working with orphans.

'What'll you be doing here exactly?' asked Caitlin.

'Iguanas and turtles,' he said. 'They really need me. To be honest, I don't know how they've survived two hundred million years without me.'

They stood and surveyed that quiet evening valley. It was magical.

'Well, what an adventure!' said Nicholas softly, looking round at them.

'Let's hope so,' said Caitlin.

A man emerged from the building. 'You're very late.'

'The truck broke down,' said Caitlin. 'Not our fault.'

The man grunted. 'Come with me.'

They arrived at Caitlin's homestay first.

'Enjoy the craic,' said Bridge.

'See you tomorrow.'

Then Lucy's. The man gestured up a broad rust-red track, potholed as if recently bombed, and across a wild meadow. A parakeet screeched in the trees and a single paraffin lantern shone through the dusk from the window of a whitewashed cottage half hidden behind banana leaves. Lucy was slow to move.

'I'll take it,' said Nicholas.

She looked at him eagerly. 'You sure?'

'Nice and quiet.'

'Not quiet,' said the man. 'Four children. Three boys.'

'Well ...' He started up the track.

'You other two then, in the village.'

Bridge eyed Lucy. 'Cool.'

2

The mother was standing in the doorway of the cottage when he came across the meadow. He saw a female figure, a red headscarf, and then she was gone inside. He was instantly mobbed by seven or eight boys, swarming up out of the long grass like insects. One began to climb him like a tree.

'Hello! Hello! Where are you from?'

'England.'

'England! Manchester United!'

He counted again. No, there were three. Just seemed like seven or eight. The smallest climbed highest, the other two clung to an arm each, so that he moved slowly through the long grass as if in a dream.

'My name is Héctor,' piped the smallest, holding his hair.

Nicholas tried to detach him. 'Hello Héctor.'

'I'm four.'

'Hey!' called a man's voice, then some rapid Spanish he couldn't follow. The boy climbed off him, reluctant as a monkey from a fruitful tree. They led him captive to the cottage doorway. A man stood there with a straw hat in his left hand. He had a moustache and wrinkled eyes and was a head shorter than Nicholas. He held out his hand.

'*Buenas tardes*,' he said softly. '*Bienvenido.*'

They shook.

Nicholas never heard him raise his voice again.

His Spanish was still rudimentary, but it was enough. The people in the villages spoke sparingly.

The woman pushed a plate in front of him. The man took his rucksack. In the kitchen was an adobe wood-oven and a wooden table and two plastic chairs. The family had eaten much earlier. They stood and watched in silence while he ate by lanternlight, the lantern half hidden by moths, chickens pecking in the doorway. There was rice and beans and chili and fried plantain and an egg. It was very good. When he had finished the woman took his plate and immediately began to spoon more onto it.

He cradled his belly in meek protest. 'No, really....'

She paused.

'Yes,' said the man.

'Eat eat eat!' cried Héctor with vicarious excitement, dancing about.

'Héctor,' said the father.

He agreed to a little more.

The father was José, she was Maria. Joseph and Mary. Even the national airport was called Jesucristo airport. José was wiry, calm, capable, laconic, early or mid thirties he guessed. José answered his children's endless questions thoughtfully, fingering the seashell amulet he wore around his neck.

She must have been early twenties. And four children already. She might have started at fifteen. Slim and pretty, with an upturned nose and her dark hair falling down from under her headscarf and her dark eyes. Her expression was serene until she smiled, when she looked girlish and mischievous. Nearby there lived Maria's mother, Abuelita, a wizened ancient of nearly seventy, who had had Maria when she was over forty, a miracle child. Abuelita said she would only die when she had seen her youngest grandchild safely married. The three boys were Alejandro, Jaime and Héctor, and the little girl with her beaded pig-tails and wide watchful eyes, the second youngest, shyest of them all, was Lala. Eulalia.

'This will be your room,' said José.

It was the bigger of two bedrooms. The other was a

dormitory for the children.

'But where will you sleep?'

José gestured to the floor of the kitchen. He looked embarrassed.

'This is not right,' said Nicholas.

'Yes,' said José.

'The bedroom fell down!' said Héctor.

'Héctor,' said his father warningly. He looked at Nicholas and tried to smile but his eyes were filled with shame. 'A cow came by,' he said, and made a rubbing motion with his hip. 'The wall came straight down.'

'Ploof!' said Héctor. 'Like Joshua and his trumpet!'

'But you can't sleep on the floor,' said Nicholas.

'Please,' said José, pleading and a little more stern. 'We have prepared it for you.'

'I've got a hammock and everything, look. I've slept all round Central America in it for the past –'

'Please,' said José. 'This is your room.'

'I beg you,' said Nicholas. 'It would make me very unhappy to take your room and leave you sleeping on the floor.'

Maria was behind him. She said, 'José. If the guest would prefer to sleep in his hammock it is not for us to say no to him.'

'I will help you rebuild the other room,' said Nicholas. 'I promise. Then we can all have rooms.'

'*Aie*,' said José. 'That damned cow.'

He helped Nicholas put up his hammock under the trees. The boys hindered. Héctor took his mosquito net and wore it like a cloak and vanished into the forest making a noise like a trumpet. José said nothing. Héctor reappeared a while later.

Nicholas asked, 'Are there mosquitoes up here?'

José said, 'No-o.'

It meant, not really. Not like in the rainy season, or down on the coast. Not to complain of.

José admired the hammock very much, as they lashed the webbing straps around the second trunk. Was it English?

'Made in Canada,' said Nicholas.

'Ah. Canada,' said José, voice reverent. 'Of course. And you will be warm enough? It is cold before dawn.'

'I'll be fine.' He showed him his sleeping bag.

José gave a little bow of his head. 'Sleep well sir,' he said.

Nicholas hung the mosquito net over his hammock – he wasn't a medical student for nothing. There were other exotics around as well as malaria. Dengue, Chagas, Chinkugunya, Japanese encephalitis, and this lively newcomer, Zika. He hung up his rucksack from the tree and brushed his teeth and rinsed his mouth from his water bottle and spat into the grass. He opened a side pocket of his rucksack and took out a plastic tube of probiotic pills and stared at them and then put them back. His gut flora would just have to get tropical.

He lay on his back in the hammock and smiled and the stars twinkled beyond the mesh between the giant nodding leaves. Phosphorescence in a fisherman's black net. The leaves whispered amongst themselves, rubbing their hands, benignly conspiring. Boys' high voices came from within, and then Maria's and they fell silent. *Los humildes*, the city people called them. The humble.

Then they started up again. He half-heard what they were saying, guessed the rest. The adults were more muffled, but he could tell they were smiling from their voices. Outside there was a gringo in a hammock, come to work for Papa! Their very own volunteer! He was so tall. He had been up in an aeroplane. Did he have a machine gun in his rucksack? They thought so. Was he a millionaire? They thought so too. All gringos were.

'But why is he asleep outside?' That was the little girl's voice. 'Why doesn't he come in here with us, where it's warm?'

Then silence reigned but for the bats in the rafters, the

9

hawk wasps burrowing in the earth floor, hiding paralysed locusts for their breakfast.

Nicholas's heart beat fast. He couldn't sleep either. Every night they rose up to meet him again, the indescribable cold years of his childhood, never to be escaped or forgotten. Then years bent over books, staring at screens, sponging up anatomy, pathology, pharmacology. Austere joy. And now this, here. This other world. How was it possible? Burning from the inside. Lying back in a hammock in a village under the stars of Central America. How could he sleep when already falling in love?

3

Eulalia lay snuggled against Héctor. It was very cold at night now. Christmas seemed like ages ago already. The stars were icy teeth biting through the night sky and everyone in the village went to bed early except the Men Who Drank.

Once she had walked right up to the head of the valley after dark with Papa. He held her hand all the way but it was still frightening. Huge green eyes watched them from the forest. Things stirred among the leaves. If he had lost her on that dark track.... She quivered and stretched under the blanket, her feet cold. Yeto mumbled.

Papa had said that sometimes when you stood at the head of the valley after dark and looked away to the southwest you could see burning lava coming down out of the moonlit clouds on Santa Ana, the clouds' underbellies red with the fire below. He said that beyond Santa Ana ran the great cordillera of volcanoes that were the backbone of the country, and they went all the way down to South America and the unimaginable snowcapped Andes.

Snow didn't taste of anything and it made your fingers fall off if you held it too long. She longed to see it.

Old Jorge from the village said he had once crossed the Andes on a llama, leather panniers bulging with Inca silver and gold, but a wicked woman had stolen it all from him and broken his heart in two. But Abuelita said Old Jorge was a wicked storyteller and had been since he was a grubby boy and was not to be trusted. Papa said perhaps Grandma and Old Jorge had courted once when they were young, a hundred years ago, and her heart was still bitter against him. Grandma

11

gave a dry little laugh and said that even as a young girl she had more sense than to look at that rascal Jorge Rodriguez MacLellan.

Next after Santa Ana was San Miguel and then San Salvador, always throwing up orange lava and a guide for sailors at night. Papa said that the sailors blessed the volcano and called it the Lighthouse of the Pacific. And sometimes on very still nights, the moon on the mountains, a mighty column of smoke rose straight up from San Salvador to heaven, lit up grey and ghostly like the cloudy pillar that led the children of Israel when they were lost in the wilderness.

4

The night was cold in the mountains in the dry season, but then the sun came up fast over the forested ridge to the east and in minutes he was perspiring in his sleeping bag and it was too hot to stay in his hammock.

He and José sat on the step and Maria brought them each a cup of coffee. It wasn't real coffee.

José nodded. 'Roasted maize,' he said.

Nicholas drank again. 'It tastes good. But you grow coffee? In this country?'

'Of course. Then they sell it.' He raised his arm. 'El Norte.'

'Ah. To gringos!'

José grinned. 'To gringos. Lots of money.'

'But you have had real coffee?'

'If you work on the fincas. The plantations.' José glanced over his shoulder to see if Maria was near then murmured, 'Or in the city. You cannot buy it here, but when I have been to the city. Then sometimes I buy myself a cup of American coffee. It is very good.' He looked down and scuffed the ground. 'But I feel ashamed. We have no money, and the children have never tasted chocolate.'

He felt ashamed even as he said it. He did not want to sound as if he was begging, wringing the gringo's heart for more dollars. There were parents who taught their children to run after gringos in the street, to beg. A wretched thing. He did not want to be misunderstood.

Nicholas said he could have brought chocolate with him.

José looked sidelong at him and said, 'Better never to taste chocolate than taste it only once.'

13

He rolled a cigarette out of a husk of maize and proffered it. Nicholas shook his head.

'You don't smoke?'

'No.'

José smoked with great enjoyment. Nicholas nodded at the seashell amulet around his neck and said, 'We're a long way from the sea.'

'This? Ah, this was what – this was what my wife gave me in the early days.' And he looked down, blushing visibly. 'Now you're embarrassing me!'

'Sorry,' said Nicholas. They both laughed.

The boys came near them, to watch the gringo, to learn how to be men. And the little girl Eulalia, shy of him both a stranger and a man. Shy but rapt, standing against the doorpost halfeaten by beetles, hung with an armadillo shell for luck, peeping out from under her cropped fringe, silent and fascinated.

Héctor threw grasshalms at him.

'No Yeto,' said José softly. 'Be respectful of our guest.'

He blew out a long bugle of smoke that hung in the still morning air. Héctor dashed it away with his hand, the smoke ghost, and trod on Nicholas's feet and gargoyled into his face from six inches away. Nicholas tickled him under his arms and he melted to the ground.

'Will the children annoy you?' said José.

'No,' he laughed. 'Well... only a bit.'

'You have children?' said José.

'No.'

'How many brothers, sisters?'

He looked down at the wriggling four-year-old larva between his feet. It was OK to say so, so soon. They were used to death here, not surprised by it. He said, 'I did have a sister but she died young.'

'Ay.' José nearly added in sympathy that he had lost another daughter himself, Rosalia, she lay in the cemetery now. But he held his tongue. It might sound almost boastful.

As if competing in grief. Instead he said, 'Your families in England are small?'

'Yes. Small things.'

Nicholas finished his coffee and went over to his rucksack. Héctor followed him. No ants in there yet, but give it time. All the children watched closely to see him get out his machine-gun and show Papa, but he only took out a photograph, and then remembered the present he had brought. A miniature of Scotch whisky in a handsome presentation carton. Emblazoned with gamebird couchant and mistwreathed ancestral castle, most aristocratic of cardboard tubelets.

Suddenly it looked utterly ridiculous to him.

But José took it in silence and called Maria. She came and took it like something holy.

'You are very kind. It is very beautiful.'

He was so embarrassed by it now. So paltry a thing. Already he realized they would never drink it.

She took it inside and set it on the stone ledge in the kitchen beside the fresh forest lilies in a can and the picture of the Virgin.

Nicholas sat beside José again. José nodded at the photograph he'd brought out of his rucksack. 'What was her name?'

'Lizzie. Elizabeth.'

The children looked over his shoulder. They saw a girl with long straight hair, an uncertain smile.

José said, 'She was gentle.'

He put the photograph back in his shirt pocket.

'She died because you are from a poor family? Because-' Then he stopped because he was asking too many questions. But the guest did not resent the impertinence of the question. He was not offended, a modest boy.

He gave a strange smile. 'You could say my family was poor. But not in the same way that people are poor in this country.'

José nodded. 'Not so poor.'

15

'No. Not hungry, for instance.'

'But you have done well, to come from England and study so hard and to become a doctor. Your parents must have worked very hard to send you to school.'

'Well,' said Nicholas, 'my parents paid for me. But in England it's free for everyone to go to school.'

José was astonished. 'How is this?'

Nicholas thought. 'It is a rich country really,' he said. 'A very rich country.'

José pondered, then said again gently, 'But your parents must be very proud of you. You will miss them while you are here.'

Nicholas nudged the giggling Héctor with his foot and Maria called from within that the tortillas were hot and they stood and Nicholas said 'Yes' and they went in.

After breakfast he walked down the track towards the centre of the straggling village, a mile or so, pressing his shirtsleeve to his forehead to swab the sweat. The sky was a burning blue and there were chestnut cows in lush meadows and a brilliantly-coloured bird arrowing into the trees, scarlet and gold and an elegant trailing tail. Some children paddled in a stream by the track. They held their hands up to him, fingers splayed.

'Hiya!'

'Hiya!' he said. 'Manchester United!'

They stared at him with dark round eyes. Evidently intelligence of Old Trafford's celebrated ballmeisters had not yet penetrated to all in these remoter parts. He grinned and walked on. There were children everywhere, bare and grubby, and no noise in all that country louder than their splashes and cries.

5

I t was his first sight of the village in daylight. A dusty square, a whitewashed church with worn steps up, an old woman sitting crosslegged at the top of the steps selling oranges on a rug. Schoolchildren coming out of tumbledown huts so neat and tidy in white shirts and blue shorts or skirts and plastic rucksacks, waiting quietly for the bus down to the nearby town of Santo Domingo. Men on horseback with bare machetes slung from their saddles leaving to work in the fields or the forest. A drunk man sitting propped up against the sidewall, hat over his head. Several dogs lounging in the street, getting up wearily and moving out of the way when the village bus came wheezing through. Every square inch of the bus was painted as gaudily as a Hindu temple, and she even had a name: the Little Virgin of Suyapa, according to the sunstrip across the top of her cracked windscreen. The children climbed aboard and the Little Virgin wheezed away down the valley.

He wanted to ride into town on the bus painted like a temple. He wanted to go to school with the children and learn what they learned. He wanted to ride into the forest with the horsemen with their machetes. He wanted it all.

The other volunteers were already at the aid office. Bridge looked stricken.

Nicholas asked, 'How's your homestay?'

'Rank. Worse than school. The shower's only cold water and you have to shit in, like, a *bucket.*'

'Outrageous.'

'You got a shower?' said Caitlin with her sardonic Irish lilt.

'Cold.'

She raised her eyebrows. 'Maybe you should've volunteered to help turtles in Surrey or somewhere. Or Kensington.'

'Dah.'

She wasn't giving up. 'Why d'you come out here anyway? What d'you expect to get out of it if you're already moaning?'

Bridge said, 'My hope for this year away is to come back a better, more serious, more committed person, with a deep empathy for the disadvantaged peoples of the world.' He nodded. 'Plus, ideally, experience of a coke-fuelled threesome with a couple of dirty blonde beach bunnies from Oz.'

Even Caitlin laughed. 'You're disgusting.'

'Yet somehow loveable,' said Bridge.

'What about you guys,' she said.

'Well ... the same,' stammered Nicholas. 'I mean not the beach bunny thing, but, you know ... to help people. Make them better if we can, learn about stuff. As much as we can do.'

Caitlin smiled. This boy scout with his fine straight nose and blue eyes and his floppy side-parting hair that really needed an update. She wondered if he carried a Swiss Army knife.

He saw her smiling and grinned as well. 'Yeah, well. No doubt I've got a lot to learn.'

'Has anyone else noticed we don't get a signal *anywhere?*' said Lucy.

'Isn't it great?' said Nicholas.

'No mobile, nothing. The only thing we've got apparently is an internet café down in Santo Domingo, a bus ride away, run by a mad evangelical.'

'The Jesus Christ Died for my Sins Internet Café,' said Nicholas. 'I saw that as we came through.'

'Are you serious?'

18

'Serious.'

'I'm just not going to last here,' said Bridge. 'I need certain standards.'

'I agree,' said Caitlin. 'Honestly, you might as well leave now.'

'I just might,' he said.

The style of management at the aid office was not pro-active. The sole employee was the man who had met them last night in the dark and led them to their homestays: a plump, shiny, lethargic man called Tumax, according to the brass nameplate proudly displayed on his desk. It was Maya for Tomás. He was interested mainly in his large bag of cheesy nachos and his very small television, which was showing football. He had no idea about the orphanage Caitlin was supposed to be going to as a psychotherapist. Bridge's vocation for marine biology was a mystery too, and led to a confused exchange.

'Working with iguanas up in the bio-reserve here,' he tried to explain. 'Then turtles. Down on the coast.'

'Turtles?' said Tumax, hand suspended between bag and mouth.

'Yes.'

'What are you going to do with turtles?'

'Help them breed. Save them from being hunted and eaten. From dying out.'

Tumax looked baffled. Couldn't turtles breed by themselves? Hadn't they always? The thought of a man helping a turtle to breed conjured images in his mind that were frankly obscene. And anyhow, hunting and eating turtles seemed to him quite a good way of *using them up*. He crammed another couple of nachos into his mouth and them mumbled through the crumbs, 'Turtles are down on the coast. No turtles here. This is mountain and forest.'

'Yes,' said Bridge patiently, 'I know that. It's iguanas here.'

The clinic wouldn't be open for a few days either, and the

sacks of cement and the sand still hadn't arrived for building projects. They would have to occupy themselves. Tumax reached for his can of Coke as a full stop to the conversation. The other three turned away but Nicholas said,

'Have you tried to phone them about the cement?'

'Yes. I phoned them yesterday, the day before.'

'What do they say?'

Tumax was irritated now. He wanted his Coke and a nap. 'They said it will come.'

'But when?'

'I do not know. Mañana. When it comes.'

'And none has come already?'

'What?'

'Come on Nick,' said Caitlin.

'You are sure no cement or sand has come already?'

'Yes I am sure,' said Tumax. 'Go and do your other work, help them in the fields. Go and grind some corn. I will tell you when it comes.'

'I hope so. We can't build without it.'

Tumax drained his can and set it back on the desk and rubbed his shiny nose and concentrated on the television and waited for the gringos to go.

'You gave him a bit of hard time there,' said Caitlin.

'He gives us a hard time,' said Nicholas. 'And the villagers.'

'How d'you mean?'

'That cement has already come and gone.'

'How the hell do you know that?'

'The poor always steal from the poor.'

'Jesus, that's a bit bigoted.'

Nicholas said nothing. Round the side of the aid building the grass lay flattened and grey with traces of recent cement dust.

Caitlin was saying, 'Just because we're in some really underdeveloped country, you think you see corruption

20

everywhere, everyone on the take, just because they're poorer than you, and maybe a different colour. That's an awful attitude. It's really going to prevent you from getting the most out of this experience.'

Nicholas said nothing.

'You really need to open your mind,' said Caitlin. 'And get over yourself.'

She strode off towards the town to find the internet cafe, tall and determined and bony.

Bridge said, 'Well, let's hook up in the bar tonight. But maybe not the Irish witch.'

'Oh she's all right. Maybe she's got a point.'

'Bloody Mary,' said Bridge.

Nicholas walked back up the long red track, red dust powdering his boots. He felt disappointed at Tumax's indifference, frustrated that it left him with nothing useful to do.

A few minutes later he passed an old man in a straw hat and woollen shawl - in this heat - walking with a stick, his hands and wrists cramped with arthritis. A big silver crucifix on a brown shoelace round his neck. Bowlegged trotting gait, ancient face segmented and cracked like the sunbaked mud of a dried riverbed, lips almost purple, shy black eyes. That interior gaze. What worlds were there?

Nicholas wondered if he would ever understand, wondered about the shallowness of exotic and farflung travels. Maybe you don't really encounter different peoples, don't come to understand different ways of living and believing. Maybe you just stare, and photograph, and go home travel-arrogant but no wiser.

He touched the brim of his hat to this veteran of the mountains and said *Buenas tardes*. The old man didn't acknowledge him nor did he smile. Some of the older Indians, he'd read, still refused to acknowledge white people at all, refused to believe they were real. A bad dream that would pass away in time.

Caitlin would admire that!

Someone was ringing the church bell. So beautiful a day, his spirits rose again. The sun in the blue sky, rust-red earth and green grass, the cows fat and velvety in the meadow. The cows stopped chewing and stared at him, considering him thoughtfully as he passed before them. A foot-long lizard crossed the track ahead. The maize fattened and yellowed in the fields of the village of Chilitenango and all down the lovely Valley of San Antonio de las Flores.

6

A little further on and out of sight, the old man Pedro Xom stopped, head bowed, and touched the crucifix at his throat. He was old and sour. That tall young gringo had passed him by like a cool sweet breeze, swinging his arms loose-shouldered, smiling at the world, young as the morning sun. Only the young are beautiful. Crackling with eager energy and longing, life all before them like a broad white road. Pedro should have greeted the friendly young man, sour old goat that he was. Men are many.

Pedro Xom had been out walking since early morning. How could you know the land but by walking it? The sun still slanting low through the leaves, brazen on his neck between hat and shawl, a burning and a blessing. He had seen the first people stirring in the valley below. A cockerel, an old man's laboured morning piss, leaning against his cottage wall. Who is it that burns and blesses in one breath? Reigns over the volcanoes, fattens the maize, hears the lizard's footfall. God the sun.

You plough us, Lord, in the morning and in the evening, flawed in the furrow, sown in solemn sadness. Red earth is dumb. The nights are long now, the moon burns cold on the mountain. The gringos keep coming to help us, the young gringos. My people are fools. Our kingdom washed away in the rain generations ago. In the milpas the maize hangs her head in perpetual prayer for the maize that lives and dies. The nights are long but the promised days are endless.

7

Eulalia was worried about her puppy, El Pipón. He hadn't had his breakfast this morning, and he wasn't called Potbelly for nothing. Instead he lay unmoving by the watertrough, looking up at her with sorrowful eyes that made her heart ache.

'Don't worry yourself,' said Mama. 'Puppies are very strong, like babies.'

Eulalia was doubtful. People in the village were always burying babies. The cemetery was full of babies' graves and plastic pots of flowers. And she would be so sad if El Pipón died, she would weep and wail beside his grave in the cemetery daily, and all the village would weep to hear of her mighty sorrow. She dwelt on that image for a while. But then she did so want El Pipón to live, especially until next Christmas, which was *ages* away, because Abuelita had told her that the animals talked to each other on Christmas Eve, and she wanted to spy on him. Cunningly though, she would make him think that *she was asleep first*.

'I don't believe it,' said Héctor.

'Don't believe what?'

'About the animals on Christmas Eve.'

'You don't believe anything any more.'

'That's because I've been told too many wrong things,' said Héctor darkly.

'He's just eaten something,' said Papa when he came back from the maizefield.

'What like?'

'Something disgusting. A dead mouse.'

Eulalia stroked the stricken puppy and he eyed her mournfully.

'Puppies are always eating disgusting things,' said Papa. 'So are small boys. Look at Héctor.'

Héctor said, 'What?'

'We found him once,' said Papa, 'lying fast asleep on the doorstep with half an alligator hanging out of his mouth. He'd tried to swallow it whole.'

Héctor laughed until he nearly choked. Eulalia didn't laugh. It was still very worrying. El Pipón always ate his breakfast. Quite often twice.

'Next week is the Fiesta of Francisco Morazán,' said Papa. 'Then we will all eat too much.'

'Who was he?' said Eulalia sulkily. Papa was trying to change the subject.

'Don't you remember last year?'

She shook her head. There were a lot of fiestas in the village. The Fiesta of the Oranges, the Fiesta of the Doughnuts, the Fiesta of the Lost Lamb of Sabanagrande, the Fiesta of Candelaria, when the women wore palm leaf hats decorated with long bands of moss and yellow chichita berries. But Mama said all the fiestas were really just excuses for the young people to romance each other, and the men to neglect their fields and get drunk.

Papa rolled a cigarette, carefully folding over the square of crackly maize husk and putting the end in his mouth and leaning inside to take a smouldering stick off the oven. He lit and inhaled deeply and breathed out again.

He said, 'Francisco Morazán united all the small countries of Central America into one great country. So we should stand strong together, and not be pushed around by greater countries.'

Eulalia stroked the ominous gurgling drum of El Pipón's belly.

'The People were very grateful, and then they forgot they were grateful and shot him. And then they put up statues of him everywhere, and hailed him as the Great Liberator.'

'That's stupid.'

'What they did to Jesus, if you think about it.' He crinkled his eyes and gazed away to the blue Cuchumatanes, where the coffee grew, and the foothills of the Sierra Madre, and lonely Mount Pacayala.

He was wearing that funny crinkly smile of his.

'Is it funny?' she said. 'About Francisco Morazán?'

He blew out thin smoke and laid his hand on her head. 'Not really. More sad and funny mixed. Life is like that, niña.'

Then he said, 'Look, here comes our guest Nicholas. He's a doctor. Ask him about El Pipón.'

And there was the tall, blue-eyed young Englishman coming striding over the meadow.

'Go on,' said Jaime, seeing her shyness.

She hesitated, sucking on one of her pigtails. The gringo started talking to Papa about cement or something. *Cement!* Even as El Pipón lay dying beside the watertrough! Grown ups were so odd.

Feeling prickly with shyness, she crept near and let go of her pigtail. 'Please *señor*,' she whispered, knowing Jaime was laughing at her behind.

The two men carried on talking high above her.

'Please *señor* ...' Hardly able to believe what she was doing, she reached out and touched his hand. He was very tall and blue-eyed and nice-looking and it only made her more nervous.

Nicholas felt something tickling him and looked down.

'Please *señ* ...' - she could hardly hear her own voice - 'my puppy is sick.'

The English doctor looked grave. 'Well then, we shall have to examine him. How long has he been sick?' And he took her by the hand, his hand even bigger than Papa's, and she led him to El Pipón.

Nicholas knelt down and laid his hand on the toxic little

drum of the puppy's swollen belly. He diagnosed advanced abdominal distension. '*Distensioné abdominalio*, ah, *advancado*,' he pronounced in creative Spanish.

Her eyes were very wide. 'Is it serious?'

'Hm.' He coughed and laid his ear on the puppy's hot flank. El Pipón raised his head and made a half-hearted attempt to lick him, his pink tongue the size of a thumbnail, and then gave up and lay flat again. Nicholas knelt upright. The boys were gathered round too now, fascinated and jealous.

'*Cardico-thoracico fuerte y normale*,' he said. 'He has a good strong heart.'

'He eats lots,' said Eulalia. 'Insects and everything. Even bees.'

'Ah well, that's why. You clearly look after him very well.'

She looked down. She wasn't sure she did really. El Pipón was always in trouble, even more than Héctor.

'I pronounce that he requires – a purgative. *Un purgativo*.'

The children were crowding around him so closely now that José had to tug them back. '*Purgante?*'

'*Si, exactamente. Purgante.*'

He sent Eulalia to ask her Mama for a cup of cold cooking oil. Soon he had the grossly bloated puppy lying on his back, clamped between his knees, while he poured the oil down his pink little gullet. A minute later El Pipón arched and vomited, and very soon after he shat copiously beside the watertrough. He turned and sniffed it, considered eating it again, thought better of it, bounded joyously around Eulalia's bare feet, and then the children chased him yapping into the meadow.

Nicholas took a bucket of water from the trough and sluiced the puppy's effluvia into the ditch.

'*Que malo*,' said José. 'Some animal?'

Nicholas grimaced. How to describe, *in Spanish*, that fetid green stew El Pipón had brought up? Rotting seaweed and sodden hair, bilious foam and nameless tissue, and the tiny bones of some woodland innocent swallowed whole.

He said, 'A bit of a nightmare.'

José laughed and laid his hand on Nicholas's thin shoulder. '*Amigo*,' he said. 'You are a brother to us all.' Then glancing sidelong he saw the sudden brightness in the boy's eyes and turned and went inside and left him his dignity.

José put his arms around a startled Maria and kissed her dark hair in his expansive sympathy and said, 'This guest is going to be all right.'

8

'To work,' said José. 'Always work.'

But no cement, no schoolhouse to build, no clinic open for another week. What else could they do?

'We can still build,' said José. 'You can help us. We will repair the *bodega*. The storehouse for the beans and maize. And then we will rebuild the side room for you to sleep in.'

'You don't have to, honestly. I like sleeping in my hammock.'

'We will rebuild it,' repeated José with a firm nod.

So he and Nicholas and Alejandro and Jaime went into the forest to cut saplings, José examining and choosing each one with care. He cut three or four with the machete and then Nicholas tried. They all laughed.

'Here,' said José, looping his fingers round Nicholas's wrist. 'All here. Let the blade fall.'

They cut thirty or forty saplings and carried them back to the cottage in relays, the boys trumpeting. Maria brought them *atole* and they gulped it down. Héctor said he was still hungry. Maria said he must wait.

There was a wall behind the cottage, remnant of the previous storehouse destroyed in the rainy season. The forest and the rain and the insects devoured everything, nothing endured. They tore it down in clouds of ochre dust and cleared the site. Then they poured bucket after bucket of water from the stream over the red earth until José could start driving the strongest poles into the ground. He showed them how to interweave the thinner poles and hammer them down tight with a block of wood.

When they went for more water, Uncle Uberto was at the door. He had a big domed bald head and sleepy eyes.

'*Olá*,' he said, eyeing Nicholas.

'Our guest,' said José.

Uberto nodded and chewed thoughtfully and then said, 'They have heard gunfire in the next valley.'

Maria was standing in the doorway drying her hands on her apron. She looked at José.

José hummed. 'Someone hunting.'

Crickets chirruped. Eulalia pulled El Pipón's tail. Uncle Uberto said, 'Since when did hunters use machine guns?'

José stood abruptly and drained his cup. 'Come. There's work to do.'

José and the boys passed the spade between them and took turns to dig out a trench nearby. Eulalia and Héctor ran back and forth bringing pails of water and pouring them into the trench, then jumped in and trod the earth into a dense ooze. Before long Héctor was covered in mud from head to toe, hair plastered down like a clay wig.

Then they brought up dry grass from the side of the track, Eulalia saying to be careful of the grasshoppers where they chopped the grass, but the boys paid no attention. It made them feel grown-up to shrug and say the world was made that way. They mixed in the grass and then scooped up handfuls of the daub and slapped them into the new laid saplings.

Then they went down to the stream to wash off the mud. The children wiggled their toes dry in the sun. When they walked back, Eulalia whispered to him,

'Is it all right? About the machine guns?'

Nicholas said, 'I'm sure it is. If there is any danger we will hear about it.'

'Then who was it?'

'Just some hunters. Come on, let's help Papa.'

'He's not your Papa.'

'José.'

'Anyway, you just called him a potato. He's not Pápa, it's Papá.'

'I'm so sorry. I didn't mean to call your father a potato.'

She took his hand shyly.

'How old are you, Eulalia?'

'You can call me Lala if you like.'

'Lala.'

'Nearly seven.'

'So you're six.'

'I'm nearly seven,' she said doggedly.

'OK, you're nearly seven.'

'Are you an orphan?'

He laughed. 'No!'

'But you haven't any brothers and sisters?'

They were back at the cottage. Mama called out to her not to annoy the guest.

'No, I haven't any brothers or sisters.'

Eulalia released his hand and went to hover in the doorway, twisting back and forth at the waist, chewing on her pigtail, looking in at Mama, trying to think of more to say. She liked looking at his blue eyes so much. But she didn't just want to talk rubbish like Héctor. Then she said, 'Do you like being here?'

'Yes.' He stepped up and laid his hand on her head like Papa did. 'I like it very much.'

After lunch he drowsed in his hammock until the children all wanted a go in it and he clambered out again. And Eulalia had thought of more conversation.

She said, 'A man got shot in San Martín a week ago, Papa said.'

'Oh dear.'

'It hurts like mad to get shot. But it doesn't have to kill you. If you go to the doctor.'

'No. But it can still do a lot of damage. That's why it hurts. To tell us not to get shot.'

'This man didn't *want* to get shot,' she explained carefully, as if to a simpleton.

'No. No, I don't imagine he did.'

'What does liver do?'

'Liver? Er, it purifies the blood.'

'Kidneys are for wee.'

'That's correct.'

'But you can eat kidneys. I've eaten calves' kidneys. Mama cooked them. Even though they're for wee.'

'People eat a lot of funny things.'

'Not as funny as El Pipón. Does it hurt a calf to get shot as much as a person?'

'Er - yes and no.'

She looked unimpressed.

'I mean, I think the pain is the same for the calf as for us, but then people also have lots of fears about what is going to happen next. I don't think a calf does. When I see people who are hurt or sick, they're also worried about infection, worried about dying, about their families. Knowing that they will die one day.'

'Don't calves?'

'Not in the same way, I don't think.'

'Are you sure?'

They sat in pensive and sceptical silence awhile. Then he said, 'Lala, the truth is, when children ask grown-ups questions, very often the grown-ups don't know the answers. Often they just pretend they do.'

'I know that,' she said, leaning against him and laying her head against his arm by way of commiseration. They sat peacefully in the sunshine, falling asleep.

Now that they were over their first shyness the children would not leave him alone. The boys sat with him whenever he rested, so that he would not be lonely. Héctor liked climbing him, and Eulalia's enormous dark eyes lingered on him with such wonder and adoration - Doctor Nicholas, He Who Had

Saved El Pipón - it made Maria smile. He must be exhausted, poor boy.

When he murmured that he might go down to the village tonight for a beer with the other volunteers, she smiled and said, 'Of course, of course.'

'Do not drink too much beer,' said José gravely. 'Do not shame us.'

'I won't.'

Maria flicked him with her cloth. 'He is only joking, Doctor Nicholas. Pay him no notice.'

'Or fall asleep in the road walking home,' said José, 'like one of our own people. Then we will have to come and carry you. Do not be a burden to us.'

'And if you meet a jaguar in the dark,' said Alejandro, 'make a loud noise like a monkey.'

'And always remember,' said José, 'the wise saying of ours. The day the old lady disappears is the day the jaguar shits grey hair.'

'Oh you are a rude man!' scolded Maria, flicking him much harder with her cloth this time. 'Rude and ridiculous. Go and drink your beer, Doctor Nicholas. You have worked very hard and been,' she gestured discreetly at the four children clustered close around him even now, 'very patient.'

José said, 'Do you have a light to see your way back? There's no moon till dawn.'

He showed them his wind-up torch. The children were fascinated. When he went home he would leave it with them. *Home*. The word was a blank to him. Then he raised his hand and walked quickly away. In just three months he would walk away for the last time.

9

He came to the dirt road down to the village and there was a car there, a jeep, facing towards him with the engine running. Headlights boring into the smoky dusk. Two men in the front, windows down. They seemed to be surveying the country, then they looked at him hard. He went at a stroll, trying to look as much as possible like a mild, vague and harmless gringo.

The driver was in military uniform, a young blankfaced soldier, and in the passenger seat was a handsome moustachioed man of forty or so, in immaculate white shirt, a gold watch on his wrist. He nodded and said without greeting, jerking his head,

'Where are you from?'

He grinned, diffident, deferential, and said in exaggeratedly halting Spanish, 'Inglésh. Ingle-terra.'

'*Inglaterra* eh? Far from home.' The man's voice was strong and authoritative and he rolled his r's with relish. 'A volunteer? How long are you here?'

'Three months. More or less.'

'More or less. Yes.' He smiled. 'You are walking to the village?'

'Yes. Just for a beer.'

'For a beer. But it is dangerous.'

'In the village?'

'Everywhere. There are thieves, violent men. It is always dangerous. Be careful, my friend.'

'Thank you, yes.'

The handsome moustachioed man said sharply, 'Look at me.' Because Nicholas' gaze was wandering vaguely around.

34

They looked into each other's eyes and Nicholas saw something very dangerous there. The man said, 'I think you should leave. All of you volunteers should. This is no place for you. It will only bring you to grief.'

He gave a respectful little bow and said again, absurdly, 'Thank you, yes,' because he couldn't think of anything better. Then he walked on, pretending to glance off nervously now and then into the forest for the shapes of thieves and violent men. Absolutely resolved now not to leave this place. He had come here because it might bring him to danger and to grief.

The jeep's engine continued to thrum and then after he was round the corner he heard it move forward and turn and come back past him in a spew of dust.

He would not tell the others, the volunteers. Better not to worry them. Are you all right? they would ask. I'm fine. How far and fast we fell. I'm fine now though. I mean to be better now.

He walked on down towards the village, and found Caitlin's homestay under the trees.

A dumpy unsmiling woman answered then called into the house. Caitlin appeared a couple of minutes later with wet hair.

'You choose your time. I was just in the shower.'

'We're having a beer.'

'I'll get some money. Wait there.'

The bar was no more than a square of beaten earth beneath the open sky, a bare plot between Wilbur's Supermercado and a single storey house. There were three white plastic chairs and a fridge, interior light gone. A cable of dim lightbulbs was strung through a hole into the house. The fridge contained a dozen bottles of local beer. There was a stall like a hotdog stand, behind which Henrietta, the proud proprietress, wearing bright red lipstick and a bobble hat with earflaps and

35

numerous layers against the winter cold of the mountains, stood and squawked like a macaw and urged them to eat more of her *tamales*.

Bridge and Lucy were there when they arrived.

'Have a chair,' said Bridge.

Caitlin sat. Nicholas said he was happy to stand, but Henrietta brought him another chair, insisted.

'You are my guest! It will make me happy.'

She shoved him down into it and returned in triumph to her stall. Two other men arrived, one older, one younger, and stood before her drinking tiny shots of rum.

Bridge beamed around. 'Charming, simply charming. Reminds me very much of a delightful little gastropub we know of in the Chilterns. At weekends, Daphne and I used to pop into my old MG Roadster, and we'd motor off....'

Nicholas surveyed him as he chattered on, a ceaseless flow of nonsense, eyes bright. Under his fleece he wore a green t shirt emblazoned with a giant marijuana leaf and the motto Fuk Da Feds.

Nicholas nodded at it. 'Are you sure that's wise?'

Bridge stopped talking for a moment, pulled his t shirt out at the hem and stared down. 'It's in English,' he said.

'Up to a point.'

'You think I'll get into trouble?'

'It's inevitable.'

Nicholas got up and went over to the fridge and got a Coke and a beer and went over to Henrietta and paid her the eighty *centavos*. She smiled broadly, flashing goldcapped teeth, and urged more *tamales* on him.

'A tall fellow like you!' she shouted. 'You must eat more!'

He bought two and offered one round and Bridge took it. He gave Caitlin the beer.

'Cholera here we come!' said Bridge, cramming his mouth.

Lucy had been down to Santo Domingo that afternoon on the bus. It was called El Titánico, which seemed a little ominous. It had a sunstrip with the slogan, *Yo manejo, Dios conduce*. I drive, God guides. People carried live chickens in baskets, one man brought aboard a goat on a rope which ate the remains of a seat cover. Children ran along behind and caught up and jumped aboard El Titánico as she progressed along the narrow mountain road at her stately walking pace.

Lucy said, 'They sold fresh tortillas wrapped in cloths and antibiotics. Out of a plastic bag. *Antibioticos!*' she mimicked. '*Bueno salud!* People bought them by the strip.'

'Did you see what they were?' asked Nicholas.

'Amoxicillin,' she said. 'Generic. Cheap as chips. They probably take them for their colds.'

'We are so doomed,' said Caitlin. 'Aren't we?'

'On a number of levels,' said Nicholas.

'Chin chin!' said Bridge, tipping back his third bottle.

Then Lucy said she'd checked the Foreign Office website in an internet cafe. No change, but there was something about the presidential election being contested.

'If there was any problem we'd be whisked out in no time,' said Caitlin. 'Avoid embarrassment if nothing else.'

'Anyway we wouldn't be targets,' said Lucy, 'even if there was another banana republic coup. Would we?'

'You could always charm them with your ukulele,' said Bridge.

'You brought a ukulele?' said Nicholas.

Lucy gave an embarrassed smile. 'Thought I might busk a bit.'

'More *tamales*!' squawked Henrietta. 'You need to eat, my volunteers! Keep strong!'

'My dad said it was all about drugs here anyway,' said Lucy. 'Nothing to do with left and right any more. They're even growing cocaine here now. Nearer to the American and European markets. It's like, globalization.'

Caitlin said, 'And didn't you read, the day we flew in there was a bag left on a bus in Santa Cruz. Inside they found the severed heads of two policemen.' She shook her head.

'Fucking Americans.'

'Was it Americans who killed the policemen?' said Nicholas.

She ignored him. 'They have a saying here in Central America apparently. So far from God, so near the USA.'

'I read that too,' said Bridge. 'In my *Lonely Planet*.'

Caitlin looked sour. 'Anyhow you'd have to be pretty stupid to get into drugs over here.'

'Funny you should say that,' said Bridge.

They regarded him. 'What?' said Caitlin, eyes narrow.

He backed off instantly. 'I just said, funny-'

'What've you done?'

'Nothing.'

A one-eyed cat leaned its threadbare hank of body against the wall and rubbed and yawned and stared at him, its one eye cold with fathomless disbelief.

'Tell us,' said Caitlin.

'Nothing. Just ... Jesus, it's like being back at school. It's just, I met this guy in the square when I was having a cig. And we got talking, and ... you know.'

'We know what?'

'There's plenty around. Coca-Cola, as it were.'

'You could be a drugs mule back to the UK,' suggested Caitlin. 'With your cherubic looks. If you fail your next turtle exams.'

He took up the idea enthusiastically, just to annoy her. 'Fifty thousand quid a kilo! Imagine if you could get just one kilo back home in your luggage. Like a bag of sugar. No more student loan!'

Nicholas was longing to be away from them already. He didn't dislike them but they were so clever and knowing, knowing everything and believing nothing, so overflowing with irony and sarcasm, so very modern. He wanted to be back with José and Maria and the children, away from the plump, preposterous Bridge Kynaston with his yellow corduroy suit. And Caitlin the Psychotherapist, unimaginative and hardworking, determined and literal-minded. And sweet-natured, pale-skinned Lucy, with her ukulele, here mainly because she thought she *ought* to be here – he wanted to be away from her too.

But he stuck it out and did the usual medical student bonding thing with her, swapping horror stories and arrogant surgeon anecdotes. He was feeling restless, unconsciously drumming his feet when Caitlin asked them about their homestays. Nicholas talked about his with such fondness his drumming feet slowed.

'Daughter eh?' said Bridge. 'Hot Latina babe.'

His voice rose. 'She's *six*.'

'Ah well.' He swigged and grinned. 'Give her a few years.'

Nicholas's drumming feet stopped. 'Don't talk like that.'

'You know the natives start young in these parts. I read somewhere that no one here even seems to know what the age of consent *is*.' He grinned suddenly. 'This guy comes home to find his girlfriend in tears, packing her bags. He says, What's up? She says, You're a *paedophile*. He says, That's an awfully big word for a six year old!'

Nicholas was suddenly on his feet, his chair scuttling backwards across the earth like a white plastic crab, shouting with wild indignation, 'How can you say that? How can you make a joke about that?' Clutching his fists by his sides, with his carefully rolled-up shirtsleeves and floppy hair and fine straight nose, he looked like an irate boy scout, a preposterous figure born out of his time.

Bridge made the mistake of laughing, while looking puzzled at the same time, and jovially telling him to fuck off. Then Nicholas strode at him, shouting right in his face.

Bridge stood to meet him and they both tripped clumsily over his chair. Caitlin swore afterwards that she heard Bridge's head clonk on the ground like an empty coconut shell. Lucy was screaming and Caitlin was trying to pull Nicholas away but he was made of steel cables, face white and fixed, gripping on to Bridge and still shouting at him.

39

Eventually the two men came over from the stall, unhurried. The younger one took him by the arms and the other knelt beside him and rapped him hard on the elbow joint, sending his arm into nervous spasm. They had seen fights before. This one was very poor. They pulled the two gringos apart.

'Calm yourselves,' said the older man.

Bridge was dusty and shaken but not much hurt. Nicholas looked far worse, staring and trembling violently. Lucy was shaken too, and Caitlin was yelling in Nicholas's face, 'Stupid, stupid, stupid ... You're supposed to be a bloody doctor, here to help, not beating people up...!'

The older man held his hand up to her and spoke quietly.

Bridge held his hands up too. 'I'm sorry man. I didn't mean to, like … Just my sense of humour.'

Nicholas was in a daze and didn't say a word. The older man faced him. 'Hey. *Amigo.*' He held him tight again by his upper arms, looking straight into his staring eyes. 'Walk home,' he said slowly. 'Breathe slow. You still have trouble in your heart.'

Bridge shook his head. 'Jesus. How did *he* ever get into medical school? Scary. I'm not having him looking at my testicles.'

'Leave him alone,' said Lucy. 'I think he's got some really complicated thing with his family.'

'Then he shouldn't be out here. This is a psycho little country enough as it is.'

'Just leave him alone. He's OK.'

'Yeah. Till he attacks one of his *patients*.'

10

He did not even know where he was as he walked. Someone passed him, drunkenly raising a bottle. He was in a dark cave, bats cried out under the trees. A muddy river. Police helicopter overhead, churning the night air. A boy on a bunkbed, bare soiled mattress, buttons imprinting his back. Sister above him sobbing, adult laughter in the next room. Adult laughter the most terrifying sound of all. His father in a wheelchair, not speaking. Not speaking for years. Except to say sometimes, gin on his breath, 'You're a fool, Nicholas.' Or, 'You're a disgrace to the family.' Or sometimes with wet-lipped relish. 'Unstable as water, you shall not excel.'

The sound of shouting in the hallway, the sound of someone coming up the stairs. *Growling like a bear* – could that be right? Broken childhood memories. And worse than the memories, the empty plains, the vast steppelands of his childhood when he could remember nothing at all.

He crouched down beside a low stone, arms around his knees, rocking unsteadily.

His father always wore his tie with a small tight knot. His mother's haggard look and shaking hands. There was a dead mouse in the grand piano, trapped under the strings like prison bars, slowly decaying. No one cleaned it out. It was difficult to bring friends home. Although there was plenty of room in that cavernous house with its vast entrance hall tiled in ox-blood tiles, its seven damp bedrooms, the ivy growing up inside the smeared windows. The tangled gardens, the moss-grown pathways, the rhododendrons always dripping rain. Perpetual November.

But let us not dwell, we are not there, we are here. We are here, in a sunny country now. Let us concentrate on the world around us and with a tremendous effort of will pretend to be sane.

Here, and an old man on the path up ahead, coming down towards him. The inner voice died. He was Nicholas, Nicholas Palmer. Here it was going to be different.

Old grandfather made up of wrinkles and threads, cave breath, bats' eyes. He stopped and raised his hat. '*Buenas noches.*'

'*Buenas noches.*'

'Are you drunk?'

'No, not drunk.'

'Are you lost?'

Nicholas shivered at him.

The old man looked back stiffly over his shoulder. 'There is nothing up there but the mountains. Where is your house?'

He said nothing, face sweating and stricken, tongue and heart locked up.

But Pedro Xom knew him. He was the young gringo who had passed him by, the guest of José Silvestre Chacach and his family. What was wrong with him, crouching and sweating here? Some fever. Surely he was sick. Lord, why do you send us these young gringos with their soft and eager hearts, looking for redemption among us? This is a hard country even for us. Send us good seedcorn and send us land. Not these shivering travellers on a darkening road. Not these lost children.

'Turn around,' he said, rapping his stick. 'Walk with me.'

They walked together very slowly, saying nothing. Once the old man stopped and pointed his stick into the undergrowth. There was a faint rustling then silence. '*Un tépi,*' said the old man. A tapir.

They walked on. He breathed very slowly, parasympathetic, diaphragm up, down. It was physically impossible to have a panic attack if you controlled your breathing. Spelt his name backwards. The sum of the digits in any multiple of nine is nine: check. Do not look back up to those terrible mountains. Try not to look back. He was Nicholas. A third year medical student, on elective in Central America. In the middle of the night, in the jungle, half mad himself, with a mad old tapir-fancier for a guide. Situation normal, all fucked up.

A little further on the old man stopped again and pointed upward. An awkward pause.

'The moon,' said Nicholas patiently.

'The moon, yes. But in truth it is not the moon. It is a miracle without a name.'

Nicholas stared up at the moon, shivering, irritated, standing beside this crazed old shaman or curandero.

The old man beside him said quietly, 'There is no resistance. There is no other help.'

He lay quietly back in his hammock, hardly daring to move, and the stars glared down. Arclights of the cosmic Gestapo! He gasped out a sort of laugh. They hurt his eyes. They dredged out the past. It was always cold in his father's room – 'the library' - lined with silent books that turned their dusty backs.

His father's son. But he would make his father proud of him yet, from beyond the grave. He would be a doctor, a respected man of achievement. He was five thousand miles away now from that house of lost children.

Maria awoke in the night to hear an eerie moaning that chilled her. She shook José but he mumbled and didn't wake. She turned on her back staring up into the darkness, praying that it wouldn't come again. Then it came again.

Could she persuade herself that it was some wounded animal in the forest? No she could not. It was much nearer. It came again, then a cry. She knew who it was.

43

Palms sweating, upper lip damp, she got up off the mattress and tied a thin blanket around her waist over her shift. None of the children had woken. She went to the door.

Nicholas was woken by his own cry: the usual. The usual creatures of his innerscapes and nightmares. Children running crying down a lonely road. A thorn tree stuck with severed hands. A man with the head of a bear or a bull. A man rising up out of the sea, his eyes blazing silver, and when he opened his mouth he vomited forth silver light, which meant the end of the world.

He did as he always did and stood ready to fight. But first he had to claw at the zip of the mosquito net. He pulled it back and slid out, standing there in the moonlight in striped boxer shorts, shaking, ridiculous. There was a woman there, white shift and a patterned Indian blanket around her slim waist - Maria - and he stepped forward and held her very tightly. Then she drew away.

'Perhaps you ate something bad.'

With one hand he reached back and grabbed the edge of the hammock. 'Like the puppy.' He managed a faint smile. 'I'm all right. I'm sorry. Just a bad dream. Nothing bad I ate.' He was already turning back to his hammock.

Maria said, 'This is a different country for you.'

'Yes,' he said, 'that's it. A different country.'

Lying on her back, she did not go to sleep for a long time. Her thoughts were like wild goats.

He tried to sleep too. But the inevitable tide of memories, the polluted, drowning tide, tumbling with flotsam and rags and foul remnants....

And he had bitterly betrayed himself there in the bar with the boy Bridge, it was true: failed to meet his own standards. Now he was here, lying in a hammock. Was it really only his second night here? It felt like he had been here for so long already. There were cloud forests, volcanoes, a mountain stream, a family. There were things of wonder. Orion was right overhead at these latitudes, look, and the moon, which wasn't really the moon, but a miracle without a name. There was no other help.

And he was going to be a doctor, a paediatrician he hoped. People would trust him, admire him, need him. He was not weak because of what he had seen and known but strong, stronger because of it.

'One thing you may never be very good at,' his counsellor had smiled - beautiful, well-spoken, kind - 'is relaxing.'

Try now though. Let all the other things go. All that was far away now, many thousands of miles away and years ago, in another world, another life. A different country.

11

In the morning Eulalia slept quite late, although she hadn't been at all tired the night before, and only really woke up when her mother came and stood right over her and sang in her funny shrill wake-up voice which wasn't her normal voice at all but as shrill as a parakeet that has eaten too many ripe coffee beans and gone loony.

Then her mother said in another voice, low and spooky,

'Wake now, mistress slug-a-bed,
Lazy bones and sleepy head,
If the goblins find you sleeping,
There'll be certain cause for weeping.'

She got up and went out to the forest, looking warily for goblins and child stealers lurking behind trees. Why did Mama say things to frighten her if she loved her? All the birds were singing in the morning sun. That one was called a tody motmot and that one was a pygmy tyrant. Papa used to smile his funny smile and say there were a lot of those in this country. And that one was a sabrewing, and that one was called a potoo. And cruising above them all, she could hear the laughing falcon. He killed other birds and ate them for breakfast.

There were other things to look out for too, so many other things to worry about. There were fer-de-lance snakes and man-eating spiders and enormous millipedes and ghostly *nahuales*. There were trees that wept sap that could blind you if you slept under them, and the guarumo tree always full of yellow biting ants, and the *quaunacaztli* tree with its fruit shaped like human ears, and the *guachipotzl* which sang in the

46

night with an eerie high pitched song. And on certain nights there was a moon so round and bright that it blinded the animals in the fields and cracked the trunks of the mahogany trees.

Then there was the *Cenicero*, a little sprite who ate ash from old woodfires. He was a grey thin sad little sprite, very meek and quiet and not too scary really. But then there was also the *Duende*, a little man covered from head to toe in long grey hair, who cut off your thumbs while you slept because he didn't have any himself. Worst of all was the *Cisimico*, a huge and hairy creature of the forest, who never made a sound, but stole women away into the treetops. But Papa said that was just a sloth.

Papa said that the sloth moved so slowly that algae grew in its fur, and was so lazy that it never bothered to climb carefully down from the tree it sat in, but simply rolled itself into a ball and dropped to the ground. A hundred feet! Papa said it was too lazy even to hurt itself. Mama said that it reminded her of Uncle Uberto.

Eulalia laughed to herself as she was coming back and then she saw a man lying in the road. Was he dead? She watched him for a bit from behind a tree but then she could see his chest going up and down which meant he wasn't dead, he was probably drunk. She came back and told Mama and Mama made her wash her hands at the water trough and then she had her tortillas hot and delicious off the ovenstone and cratered with crinkly craters like a full moon. She had some beans and cuajada cheese and an orange, and her fingernails turned orange and smelt of orange, and Héctor came and stole a bit of her peel so he could cut it and turn it inside out and put it in his mouth to make it look like he had great yellow horse teeth and he could run down and scare the smaller children by the pond.

Doctor Nicholas was eating his breakfast at the kitchen table. Mama had cooked him some eggs. Mama was always cooking him eggs.

Then Yolanda came over with her baby, and Eulalia was thrilled when Yolanda let her hold it, though Yolanda carried on holding it as well. It was a tiny baby. Yolanda was a cousin of Mama's and had had her baby too young and without a husband. It was called a 'Carnival Baby' or a 'Child of the Air'.

When Yolanda had gone, Eulalia said, 'I would like a Carnival Baby, Mama.'

Doctor Nicholas laughed at this and spluttered over his eggs. Eulalia looked at him indignantly.

'Certainly not,' said Mama. 'You find a husband first.'

'But I don't want a husband.'

'You will.'

'Why will I? Many husbands are given over to drink.'

Mama and Dr Nicholas *both* laughed at this. She was clearly being very funny today.

'Because,' said Mama, looking serious again, 'every day for Yolanda is a struggle, and she may yet have to give her baby up for adoption.'

'What's that?'

'She hands her baby over to people in the city for money, and they send the baby to be brought up in the *Estados Unidos*.'

Eulalia had never heard anything so terrible.

'Well then,' said Mama. 'No Carnival Babies for you.'

'The baby,' said Nicholas after Eulalia had gone outside to play with El Pipón. He still felt shy and embarrassed after that brief, dreamlike episode last night beside his hammock. But he had to ask. 'Was she born early?'

Maria was sweeping the wood ash out of the oven for spreading on the vegetable patch. She looked round and nodded. 'Do you think she looks unwell?'

He didn't want to say anything. 'She could bring her down to the clinic for a check up.'

Maria stopped sweeping and sighed. 'I know she should. The baby is not strong. But she is ashamed. And without a husband there is no money to pay for medicines. It is a bad situation.'

'I don't know if she needs medicines. Maybe just a better diet. Will the father not marry her?'

'He may yet. Let us hope so. He is only a boy himself and he is probably afraid of what has happened. But a baby receives life from a mother, strength from a father, we say here.'

12

Word had come through that today the clinic was open. Dr Hércules Menendez had returned from the city.

'We'll finish the *bodega*,' said José.

'You're better off without me,' said Nicholas.

'No,' smiled José gently. 'Don't think that.'

'Why are you going? said Eulalia.

'To work in the clinic.'

'Don't you want to work here?'

'It's only in the daytime. It's what I'm trained to do, make people better.'

'And puppies.'

'People and puppies, yes. I don't think I'm much good at building *bodegas*.'

'I think you're very good,' she said crossly, and turned inside.

Her mother smiled. 'Here,' she said. 'Take this to Abuelita.'

Eulalia took the cup of maize coffee and stepped outside again.

She never ceased to wonder at how much coffee Abuelita drank, because she was so old and shrunken. She was over sixty years old, mama's mama, she had had mama already quite old, and wasn't very well and was very wizened like a lizard and slept a lot in the day and then shuffled about at night and was very kind and hardly ever told her off. Usually just waggled her forefinger and came out with strange old sayings that were so wise they sometimes made no sense at all. A recent one was,

'Today is but tomorrow's yesterday.'

And when two foolish men in the village had fallen out with each other about a cow, Abuelita said,

'Ah well, two buttocks cannot avoid friction.'

Now she stirred in her chair where she had been dozing in the sun. She smacked her thin lips. She loved her coffee though she hardly ate anything.

After she had taken a sip she said the sun was very hot today. She said this every day. She nodded. 'Very hot,' she said. She always wore at least three shawls, sometimes more.

Eulalia told her that El Pipón and the Baby of Yolanda were now curled up asleep side by side on a blanket inside.

Abuelita sipped more coffee. 'That is because the little one does not yet know it is a human being.'

Eulalia looked unconvinced.

Abuelita nodded. 'You are not born a human being. You must become one. It is the great work of life.' Her old eyes crinkled. 'You think digging weeds in the maizefield makes you ache? Tch. Growing into a human being - take it from me, niña - that's the biggest ache of all.'

Nicholas was getting ready to leave for work, after breakfast, packing two rolled tortillas in paper into the top pocket of his rucksack, when Eulalia suddenly took his hand. He snatched it away and stared at her, as if miles away. Her eyes glazed. Maria saw it all, mixing limewater with maize flour. Lala hanging her head like a small sunflower in the rain.

Maria kneaded the flour. This English boy was strange, but he was one who tried hard. Lala adored him. And children were rarely wrong. Look at him there, patiently taking her small left hand again in his right. Checking the time on his watch, but secretively, so that Lala would not see.

He was the only gringo that Maria had ever talked with properly, the first ever to stay in their home, for a bewildering eight dollars a week. Just to eat their food and to hang his hammock beneath the trees! They must rebuild that room soon. She had heard that eight dollars was little to a white. But this Nicholas did not seem like a rich man to her, he had not the carelessness. He had only two shirts, one blue and one a faded red, and he folded his few clothes neatly at night and he always finished everything on his plate.

She was glad she had cleaned the house for a whole day before he arrived, removed every last cobweb, dead fly, wiped down every wall, swept every corner, scrubbed the step, and hauled the rugs and the mattresses outside and beaten them in the sun until the sweat poured from her and she went to the river to bathe. She returned still wringing out her long dark hair that José so loved.

He had squinted around and said the gringo would never notice.

'Of course he won't,' she said, 'he is a boy. That is not why I do it.'

'There is a man,' Eulalia was telling Nicholas now, clutching his hand very firmly so he couldn't snatch it away again. 'Lying down in the road.' She pointed away towards the village. 'He's a husband and he's drunk too much rum.'

Nicholas shook his head and tutted.

Héctor, observing him closely, tutted and shook his head as well.

Eulalia said, 'The sun is coming up and he hasn't a hat. And he's snoring. You can't go to the clinic now. You must be a doctor to him.'

'Hm. You think when the sun comes up his brains will boil and bubble in his head? Like a boiled egg?'

She looked anxious. 'Is that what happens?'

'I'm afraid so. Speaking as a doctor.' He surreptitiously checked his watch again. 'Well then. Let us quickly go and look at him. Then I must go on to the clinic.'

Eulalia scowled.

'I want to come too!' said Héctor.

'He's my drunk, I found him,' said Eulalia.

They began to squabble, then José said, 'Héctor, I need you to help me in the forest. Man's work.'

Reluctant but persuaded, he went with his father.

And Maria watched the other two head off down the track towards the road hand in hand, Nicholas tall and silent, Lala's chattering voice fading birdlike down the valley.

José already knew what their guest Doctor Nicholas and Lala would find there in the road, and was ashamed of it. The drunk would be one of those men of the village who sometimes surrendered to the impulse of self-ruin and took a plastic carton of homemade cane spirit and reeled into the village and drank until they fell over and lay all night in the dust. Drank to escape their hungry children always scabbed and sick and sometimes too tired to cry, their tired wives, their listless daughters, and the scab or the blight on the potato leaves, the caterpillars and cutworms and weevils, the rots and pests and plagues that threatened every crop, every year. And the all-night rustle of the beetle-infested thatch, and the contempt of being an *Indio*, and the dry soil blowing away and half the seedlings withering never to grow to green...

José rolled a cigarette and watched his fore-destined youngest son already drawing the lightest saplings into a bale.

People of the highlands hacking with their chipped machetes and dragging with their clumsy hoes at the poor dust like so many insects generation after generation, rising and falling and then buried nameless in the earth beneath the uncaring unblinking all-seeing eye of the sun forever.

The drunk lay twisted and grotesque as a car crash victim, one dead arm thrown across his own face. Eyes screwed up in pain even in his sleep and straw hat long since lost.

'Is he dead?' said Eulalia.

Nicholas laid his forefinger lightly on the man's wrist and took his pulse, just to be sure. Quite lively. 90bpm or so. He was fine. Wrecked, atrociously dehydrated, but fine.

'He's alive,' he said. 'But what can we do? He wouldn't say thank you if we woke him up.'

'We should build him some shade over his head.'

The sun was higher in the sky by the minute, burning with gold tropical menace.

'More building. I don't know how good I am it at.'

She twisted her fingers. 'Look, with some banana leaves.'

They found three sticks and he tied them into a tripod using strands of strangler vine from the edge of the forest.

'Twist them all up first like Papa,' she said.

He twisted them a few times and they came strong enough, and he bound the tripod firmly and set it over the drunkard's head. Then they hung banana leaves around it, tied to the sticks by the stem. The drunkard's flushed face lay in darkness.

'If there's a wind the leaves will soon blow away.'

'There won't be,' said Eulalia. 'And then when he wakes up he won't have a head like a boiled egg. And also he'll think someone has stopped specially in the road and been kind to him.'

'Which they have. And he'll never know who.'

'He'll think it was the Blessed Virgin.'

'Really?'

'Or Jesus.'

He saw that she believed it wide-eyed already. She could already see the Virgin walking along in her heavenblue robe, bare feet dusted with the same red earth as hers, kneeling and laying the leaves with a mother's smile over the head of the prodigal rumsoaked son.

13

Caitlin and Nicholas were first at the aid building. Locked and bolted, no Tumax there, and still no cement.

Caitlin didn't bother with good mornings. She said, 'You're not going to apologize to corduroy boy are you?'

'I will, I will. I'm sorry.'

'The Psycho Doctor, Bridge already calls you.'

Nicholas looked lost.

'But seriously, calm down. You didn't go round starting fights back at med school did you?'

He didn't answer. Although it was true that he had not yet run amok down the hospital corridors, armed with scalpel and proctoscope and his plethora of unresolved issues....

They set off walking down to the clinic building.

'Anyhow you're not a psychopath,' said Caitlin. 'Even if your response to Bridge was *inappropriate*, as we say.'

'Thank you so much.'

'Psychopaths don't do guilt or remorse, for one thing, they only fake it. I'd say you do quite a lot.'

'How perceptive you must be,' he said.

'I heard you spent your summer vac going to Auschwitz. On your own.'

'So?'

'You walked quite a lot of the way. Got the train to Berlin or something, and then walked the rest.'

'How word gets around.'

'But quite austere. For a holiday.'

'It wasn't a holiday,' he snapped. 'Though I realize it would have been more *normal* if I'd spent a month in Ibiza, guzzling ketamine and getting pubic lice.'

She laughed. 'Don't you go on holidays?'

He didn't answer. Instead he told her about the long walk out of East Berlin, hitching a lift at times but no public transport – that had been his resolution – and then the flat plains of Poland, the Tatras mountains rising snowcapped to the south, and the road to Auschwitz-Birkenau....

'How amazing,' she said, sounding fatuous even to herself.

She saw him striding lean and serious, this tousle-haired and solitary backpacker schoolboy, eager as some young idealist from the nineteen thirties heading off to fight in the Spanish Civil War.

The clinic was locked, just like the aid building. They sat and waited. He read a book. He was always reading.

'I thought medics didn't read,' she said. 'Didn't have the time.'

'Yet here I am,' he said, not looking up but smiling slightly. 'Reading.'

End of conversation.

So they sat and he read on a sunbaked hillside in Central America, surrounded by high and forested mountains. Forming up below them at the side of the track was a small crowd, increasing by the minute. Patient *campesinos* in white cotton, men in straw hats, women in pink headscarves, children and snotnosed infants. Staring at these two outlandish gringos, the woman in trousers quite unashamed, with expressionless compulsion.

'How come it's so tiring being stared at?' said Caitlin.

A monstrous orange hibiscus flower hung nearby, a butterfly the size of her palm. The clinic behind them a wooden shack with shutters.

She said, 'I went into the market in town early this morning, for the Friday market, and there was this smell of fresh corn bread and flowers, raw meat, mud and drains and flies and skinny dogs. I like to think I'm tough and I nearly fainted. Lucy's right. It *is* exhausting in this country. But not in a bad way. Overwhelming – like India. No?'

'Sorry, what?'

Then an old 4x4 pulled up nearby and Doctor Hércules Menendez eased out and down from the cab and stood before them, scowling from beneath thick grey eyebrows.

'*Americanos*, eh?'

'*Ingleses.*'

He tested their Spanish. 'You have learnt a little,' he said grudgingly. 'Now all you have to do is learn a little Ch'orti' Maya, a little Garifuna for the coast. And stop th-th-th-ing. The peasants will laugh at you. Though they'll laugh at you anyway. And speak more lazily, like you're about to fall asleep. The national style. Now come and admire the magnificent range of colourful diseases our country can boast of. I tell you, once you've seen the size of some of our intestinal worms, you will never watch a horror film again. Or maybe you will never go to church again. It affects different people in different ways.'

Dr Hércules Menendez was morbidly obese and smoked thirty local strength cigarettes a day. He had breathing difficulties at the best of times. When he delivered an entire speech, or laughed, his lips turned blue with cyanosis.

Disdaining a white coat, he worked voluntarily and erratically in the highland villages wearing a densely ruched and crumpled dark blue suit, white shirt with top button undone, and every day the same garish floral tie, well loosened around the folds of his neck. He wore fancy two-tone cream and chocolate shoes, one of which bore an indelible rust-coloured stain suggesting old blood. He was doubtful about life and contemptuous of death, sweaty, pungent, wheezy and imperturbable.

Caitlin said she was a psychotherapist, not a medic, but was it OK for her to sit in? She'd studied pharmacology. Lucy, the other medic, was in town, having intensive Spanish lessons.

'Meanwhile,' she said, 'I'm supposed to be working at an orphanage somewhere in this department, but haven't been told which one yet.'

'Report to any of them,' said Dr Menendez. 'They'll have you.'

'But they won't know I'm coming. And what about checks and paperwork and stuff?'

'Paperwork?' he chortled. 'Checks?' He found this very funny. 'And you are a psychologist?'

'Psychotherapist, yes.'

'You are a student of psyche, the human soul?'

'Well, we –'

'Very funny,' he said. 'That's very funny. There's plenty of work for you in my country. Meanwhile any volunteer help is welcome. Now then. This is the clinic, and here is what we have.'

He unlocked the clinic and they surveyed the contents. A table, a chair, a cupboard with some equipment: stethoscopes, spatulas, a carton of disposable latex gloves, iron and vitamin C pills, worm medicines, laxatives, 'use by 12/2011'.

A small man was standing outside the door of the cabin, seeming bleached in the white sunlight, hovering, straw hat in hand. 'Please –'

'Open at nine a.m.!' said Dr Hércules, rapping his gold watch that had long since ceased to work and not turning round. 'Meanwhile give yourself up to prayer!'

The man stepped away again.

'The peasants are accustomed to waiting,' he said. He shouted out of the door at another. 'You: wear a hat! You've less hair on top than you think.'

He collapsed back into the solitary chair and regained his breath. Lit a cigarette. Examined the blue tinge to his fingertips unimpressed.

'Now,' he said. 'I do not care what you have been told back in England by your venerable medical school, no doubt founded by St Luke himself.' He seemed to have decided that Caitlin was an honorary medical student for today. 'Nor what your in-country co-ordinator here has told you. Whatever it is will be scandalously optimistic. Here we do not have successes, only greater or lesser failures. We keep someone alive a few years longer, but Death claims them sooner or later. Remember He is always with us.'

He jerked his thumb over his shoulder into the corner of the cabin, as if they should see there the cloaked figure, the scythe and the gaunt and patient grin.

'He is always standing behind you, smirking at your paltry efforts. Bestowing upon you deceitful and unhelpful emotions. Making your hand shake, sprinkling microbes down upon that juicy open wound as guests sprinkle flower petals and maize seed upon the bride and groom at a wedding. But marriages are temporary, Death is permanent, and Love is not as strong as Death. Remember.'

Personifications of Death played little part in medical teaching in twenty-first century Britain. Nicholas found it quite refreshing.

Dr Hércules Menendez flicked his halfsmoked cigarette still smouldering to the wooden floor without bothering to stub it. A fine plume arose from between the dry boards.

'Now, beware of your homestay too. Treat yourself first, treat any insect bites immediately. A bite on the face may mean Chagas. And do not get bitten by a dog: just don't. Tuberculosis is not uncommon here, viral as well as pulmonary, a real little bastard. Stomach bugs and dysentery you know all about, but still, boil everything to hell and back. Peasant life is picturesque but filthy, you only have to look at them. They have no concept of germs. You have to explain again every time. They are very sceptical that anything exists which they can't see, unless of course it's spirits and ghosts and the little dwarf who lives in the forest and steals away their virgins.

'So. How *are* your homestays?'

They told him. Nicholas said that the children were so thin, but seemed energetic enough. And an unmarried girl called Yolanda, a cousin, had had a baby that looked dangerously underweight.

'There's never enough food for them,' said Dr Hércules, 'especially protein. And they all have worms.

'Do you sleep in the house?'

Caitlin did, but used a net. Nicholas said he was just outside in a hammock, but used a net too.

'Use it every night, always.' He sighed. 'Most of the people here are ill most of the time. That's the truth. But treat what you can, and don't go about diagnosing complex diseases to show how clever you are. You're still under your own ethical and professional rules out here. What's the phrase?'

'To recognize and work within the limits of our competence', said Caitlin.

'There you are then. Look at me: smoker, fat as a hog, wheezy, distended chest. So I have emphysema. What if you suspect the same of the fellow in your homestay? The peasants smoke heavily, it is one of the few pleasures they can afford. You tell him what you suspect? You can treat his emphysema? No. It is incurable anyway, as you know. Do not diagnose what you cannot cure. It is mere cruelty. The peasants live with pain and sickness all their lives.

'Remember, after Haiti, this is the poorest country in the Western hemisphere. Not the rich West. Not England.'

14

Their first case was the small man at the door. '*Dolor de estómago.*' Blood in his stools? He didn't think so. Dr Hércules Menendez told him to look carefully and come back if there was blood or mucus. Temperature? Normal. He prodded his stomach, told him to rest and drink plenty of clean water. If he still had problems next week he could have worm medicine.

'*Por lombrices*?' said the man doubtfully.

'*Si. Lombrices.*' Dr Hércules rolled his eyes at his assistants. '*Lombrices* also means earthworms. They know nothing. Guts full of parasites, heads full of ignorance.'

'*Antibióticos*?' murmured the man.

They said it was not necessary, and he went away with his head bowed, hat held to his chest, as if ashamed that they had denied him *antibióticos* because he wasn't worthy of them.

Next was a young mother and little boy of three or four. Caitlin took an oral temperature. Nearly 44.

'Ah no,' said Dr Hércules, emitting a sharper wheeze that might have been laughter. 'That thermometer lies like a priest. Here.'

Better. His temperature now nudged 39.

'The temperature will kill the sickness in him,' he told the young mother. 'Do not be afraid. Give him lots of clean water to drink. Boiled. A little salt and a banana.'

He gave her paracetamol to use if he seemed worse and instructed her as to the dose. She couldn't read. He made her repeat back to him the dose. She did so, humiliation plain on her face. He told her to come back again if the boy became much worse. The woman nodded and walked slowly away.

Caitlin watched the woman go, barefoot and slight, graceful sway and weary. She said, 'How does she carry a three year old child like that?'

'She is stronger than you,' said Dr Hércules.

'Is there really only the one thermometer here?' said Nicholas.

'No, two,' he said. 'But this one you need to subtract around 5C to get a correct reading. Don't worry. Next week we're having a full operating theatre installed. Though don't get me started on the NGOs. They who talk of *the vertical and horizontal integration of resources*, but never send enough kerosene for the refrigerators. They define health as "complete physical, psychological and social wellbeing", an insane definition. Do you know anyone who is healthy, by that definition? We all have our blemishes! We all have our psychological scars and social ulcerations!'

Nicholas grinned.

Caitlin was getting impatient. 'But even a digital thermometer only costs a fiver now. I mean, seven or eight dollars. Surely –'

'Things go missing in this country with great frequency,' said Dr Hércules. 'Not just boxes of medical aid donated by our rich saviours overseas. Entire roads through the jungle can vanish. I once worked in a place where they swore a village in the neighbouring valley had disappeared overnight. Never seen again. Mind you, this was back in the eighties. Many things disappeared in the eighties. Mostly people.' He lit another cigarette. 'Another time, one of the logging companies might stumble upon a lost city in the jungle, an entire new civilization perhaps, but they will quickly bulldoze it and cover it up, so as not to let it interfere with their profitable business of exporting mahogany to China.'

Nicholas said, 'In the capital nobody seemed to know the names of the streets. I was in the capital for a couple of days before I came here, and I'd ask people for directions. They'd say things like, "Well, it used to be called the Street of the Flowers, but now I think it's called the Street of the President," and they'd shrug. "*No sé*.""

'*No sé*.' Dr Hércules smiled. 'The national motto. In this country, nothing is certain and nobody knows anything. And by the way, before long you will also have your first encounter with … I do not know the English word. *Brujería*.'

They looked blank.

'*Brujas*. How do you say? Maledictions upon people.'

'Ah, witchcraft,' said Caitlin.

'As an atheist, not to mention a cynic, I know it is all dung of course. Which makes it doubly irritating for me that it works, all the way to the grave. What I call the placebo effect in negative. You like that?' Dr Hércules was scowling with extra intensity now. Surely this meant amusement. 'I do not imagine you have training in your medical school on how to deal with witchcraft?'

'We learn how to deal with different belief systems,' said Caitlin. 'People opposed to drugs and blood transfusions and so on.'

'Hm. It is very strong here. Mothers take their infants to the *curandero* first, us last. By which time said infant is often half-poisoned and near dead.'

They saw more stomach upsets, a little girl with a badly swollen foot from a thorn which did merit antibiotics and saltwater bathing three times a day. Another little girl with a deformed foot for whom they could do nothing. Nicholas told her that in his country, it was believed that people with a foot like hers would have good luck in life. She stared at him.

'Her mother brings her back every month or so,' said Dr Hércules. 'Always the same. She has great faith in the advance of medical science.'

Nicholas and Caitlin sat outside for their lunch of tortillas and boiled eggs and oranges in the shade of a huge old ceiba tree, the one with buttresses like small mountain ranges. It was very hot and they felt drained. Dr Hércules had stayed inside.

Caitlin said quietly that his manner, his attitude, his treatment of his patients was terrible: arrogant, paternalistic, condescending, barely listening to them, and worst sin of all, talking over their heads to the two of them.

'We-ell,' said Nicholas. 'Yeah. But he loves them really. That must help.'

Caitlin snorted.

There was a dustcloud down the track and a painful grinding of gears, and then a filthy old pick-up truck came slowly past. The driver drove one-handed in the local manner, swerving frequently. In the other hand he held a megaphone through which he shouted as he drove past the clinic.

'Deviants! Ignorant men! Turn from your wickedness and live!'

Dr Hércules appeared in the doorway, and gave the driver a dignified wave.

'Fools of Satan! Beware of false idols! I am the Way, the Truth and the Life, said the Lord Jesus. Not your test tubes and drugs!' The truck veered hard left, hit an embankment and bucked violently, rolled back and regained the strait path. 'Your filthiness is in your skirts! Woe unto you, O Israel! All wisdom is but folly to the wisdom of God!'

The remainder of the sermon was lost to them as the truck's engine roared out in righteous wrath and the preacher vanished in a pillar of dust.

Dr Hércules relished his boiled egg even more, ate with even more slow delectation, as he felt the burning curiosity of his two young disciples.

'Who was that?' asked Caitlin.

He smiled with a mouthful of egg, eyes twinkling. Finally he swallowed. Gasped for breath. Even his peristaltic muscles were packing up these days.

'Alfonso the Simple,' he said.

They waited. He took out his handkerchief, also floral,

matching his skewed tie, and mopped his brow and his mouth.

'Sounds like something out of Cervantes, does he not? But you have not read old Cervantes. You are bright young people of Science, what need have you of such things? Alfonso the Simple is an Evangelical, and he believes that what we do here is the work of the devil. Also he hasn't forgiven me for doing all the ironing.'

'Ironing?'

'Yes. In the evening I like to do ironing. It calms me. But there is never enough of my own to do, so I take in ironing from the villages. I do not charge. But nothing is simple in this world, especially doing good. It used to be Alfonso's wife who did the ironing and pressing for the village, so now I have made her unemployed and she's furious with me. You give your old clothes to charities in England, yes?'

They nodded.

'To be distributed among the poor of countries like this? Promptly putting local clothes makers and menders out of work.'

Caitlin began to argue, but Dr Hércules talked over her. 'Anyway,' he said, 'Alfonso the Simple. Twice I have caught him in here pulling up the floorboards. He is convinced that we perform abortions, and bury the foetuses under the floor. He has the zeal of the recent convert. There is a great war over the souls of the peasants, some being claimed by the Catholic Church, but more now by the North American evangelicals. Only a year ago Alfonso the Simple went into an American evangelical church in the city by mistake, and saw what fine shoes and shiny watches they wore and what dazzling teeth they had. Surely they were blessed by God. The next day he came back from town tottering under a sack full of evangelical pamphlets printed in Tennessee. One was called *The Wrath of the Lord*, I remember, and another was called *God's Love for Israel*.

'Alfonso said that he no longer believed in the saints or the Blessed Virgin but only in the Lord Jesus, and soon they would see it from his teeth. Everyone was very puzzled. Since then two more of his teeth have fallen out, but Alfonso remains steadfast in his new faith. I understand that this is called cognitive dissonance. When he is not daily haranguing unbelievers through his megaphone, he sings choruses. You can hear him coming round the corner like a cow with a bell. *Jesús, Jesús, Jesús es mi Salvador!*

'And down in Santo Domingo you may have seen the Jesus Christ Died for my Sins Internet Café? And also the hardware store, The Blood of Redemption Ferreteria? There's a notice in the window offering a free machete with every copy of the Gospels purchased. Or is it the other way around?

'And then there are all the American sophisticates and the Europeans like yourselves, agnostics and liberals and sceptics, who love to sneer at the American evangelicals and discourse about the evil that they do in such innocent and unspoilt countries such as this.

'And such is my imperishable love of contrariety that I nod and say sarcastically to them, Ah yes, those terrible Bible-reading evangelicals! With their extensive vaccination programmes, their warm and kindly homes for AIDS orphans, that awful way they fought to abolish the slave trade back in the nineteenth century. What a stupid and terrible people!

'But enough. Here comes another eager and credulous young person of Science to help redeem our doomed and colourful country.

15

It was Lucy to report that Bridge had gone off to town for the afternoon, as it was nearly the weekend.

'Why am I not surprised?' said Caitlin.

'He said that manual labour wasn't really his thing, he was only really any good at turtles. Ideally on a nice sunny beach.'

But she looked anxious. She said, 'And he got on the net this morning. He looked at the CNN website and it said the president had been thrown out in a coup.'

Dr Hércules beamed at her. 'My dear, he was thrown out two days ago. The day you arrived, in fact! Lovely timing. Gossip travels faster than radio waves, you know.'

'Isn't that ... isn't that a problem?' said Caitlin.

'Not at all. Ignore it. A coup is not news, it is un-news.'

Lucy said, 'Also there was lots of shooting down at a palm oil plantation on the coast. Military and protestors. Several people killed, lots injured.'

'Ditto,' said Dr Hércules. 'A daily occurrence. Pay it no attention. And isn't this why you eager young white persons come to countries like this isn't it? To find hardship and poverty and suffering, and therefore redemption? You used to turn to Christ to redeem you from your sins. Now you have matured beyond all that primitiveness, you turn to black and brown people instead. You worshipped a Jewish child, now you worship a little black child. You make your pilgrimage to Africa or Latin America instead of Jerusalem. No? With a little pilgrim's icon of Saint Nelson Mandela sewn close to your hearts, perhaps? Upon your Che Guevara t shirt?'

Nicholas shook his head and laughed.

'You need not worry about anything political in my country,' said Dr Hércules. 'The closest our peace-loving and fantastically idle country ever came to full-scale revolution was back in 1954, and never again since – although no fewer than three of our presidents since then have ended their days in the asylum for the clinically insane. But as for revolution: let our obstreperous neighbours bomb and shoot each other. We have not the energy for such nonsense. In 1954 however there was the Great Banana Strike, and a handful of students who had studied in Paris came excitably to the fore and led a crowd from the docks up to the National Congress, shouting for democracy and workers' rights.

'As they passed through the streets, however, their numbers dwindled. Some of the marchers were distracted by the whorehouses of the lovely Santa Ana district, some by the delicious smell of roasting coffee in the alleys of the Mercado San Isidro.... When the plump, bearded student leader arrived at the Congress building, he turned to find his vast army of ideologically awakened proletariat had shrunk to just eight men, and three of them had only tagged along under the misapprehension that there was free drink involved. He said something about "ignorant backstreet guttersnipes", at which they pulled his beard, rolled him in the gutter, peed on him and then ran off to back to the banana docks to tell their workmates and have a jolly good laugh.

'My people's understanding of politics and economics has not evolved one iota since then. Given the choice between one chocolate today or three chocolates tomorrow, they will cry with one voice and without hesitation, Three chocolates today! At which the weary and despairing master of ceremonies will have to stop and explain all over again, No, listen, there are only two options. *Either* you can have… But he will never get to the end because by then a fight will have broken out over a whore.

'You should never have any faith in the common people. That way madness lies.'

Impatient as ever with Dr Hércules's embroidered digressions and self-delighting pessimism, Caitlin said, 'Did Bridge get anything in his email?'

Lucy shook her head. 'Not a word. Nor from the in-country co-ordinator. And the Foreign Office advice page hasn't updated. Just, exercise caution, high crime rate blah di blah di blah –'

'The *highest* crime rate,' said Dr Hércules proudly. 'Our national football team may be a perennial embarrassment, but we can now boast the highest official murder rate in the world!'

Caitlin headed off and Nicholas stayed on with Lucy. She was still worried her Spanish wasn't good enough, but Nicholas told her hand signals were wonderful things.

Later in the afternoon a man came to them with a deformed chest and breathing difficulties. Nicholas sat him in the chair and probed his ribs. The man remained expressionless. He asked him to take his shirt off and tried not to gasp. The man's whole rib cage was caved in. He listened to his heart and lungs. Heartbeat strong enough but breathing laboured and constricted, not surprisingly.

'How did this happen? Were you born like this?'

'A bull charged me in the field. Now every day I am sick.'

'You mean that you vomit?'

'Yes. Sometimes twice a day.'

'This will need an operation.'

Behind him he was aware of Dr Hércules stirring. He cursed himself.

'When did this happen?' he asked.

The man frowned. 'You mean the bull?'

'Yes.'

'About … twenty years ago.'

There was a stunned silence. Then Lucy asked to listen to him. She stepped away. The man sat in silence.

'I'm sorry,' said Nicholas. 'There's nothing we can do here.'

The man looked up at him. 'No?' His Spanish was imperfect, his first language was Ch'orti'. 'I come a long way, when I hear that there are doctors here who will look at me for no money. I have no money.'

Nicholas shook his head. 'I'm sorry. We can't help you here.'

'It is my chest,' said the man. 'Many of my bones were broken.'

There was an agony of silence. Why were they here? What were doctors for in this helpless country but to tell sick and broken people that they were sick and broken, and send them on their way?

The man went away. Lucy took off the stethoscope and wiped the bulb and laid it back in the cupboard and turned her back on it.

'You said the correct thing,' said Dr Hércules. 'What use explaining to the poor bastard about reconstructive surgery? He wouldn't even be able to say it, let alone pay for it.'

Lucy stepped outside.

A few moments later Dr Hércules told Nicholas to go and find her.

'You understood all that OK?' he said.

She turned to him and nodded and said, 'Sorry. I've seen worse things than that in London, I know. A child die of meningitis, another with one of the worst cases of rickets in about a century. It's just –' she indicated the clinic – 'knowing that guy would be fine elsewhere. In another country. Just this abject little country, there's nothing we can do.'

'You sound like it's the country's fault.'

No. I...' She blew out, a wisp of her blonde hair floated. 'I can feel myself starting to hate it here though. Which is horrible.'

After a while he said, 'It's like Dr Hércules warned us. I think back home, people expect perfect health, at least until seventy or more. Here they don't. They expect life to be painful. Look at all the crucified bleeding Jesuses we saw in the churches our first week here. We hated them but they worship them.'

Lucy said, 'But it wouldn't be hard to get his ribs fixed in the UK. Hardly even classed as reconstructive surgery. They just need re-setting and time to mend. And there he is, throwing up twice a day, all his life. And in constant pain too I presume.'

'He'll never go to the city hospital, he's Indian, and he hasn't got any money.'

'We could give him the money! Start an appeal!'

'I still don't think he'd go to the city. But we can keep trying.'

She was tearful again, hating the country, hating herself for it, hating them for being … *los humildes*.

16

Tropical dark came down. Dr Hércules lit the kerosene lamp and extravagant moths mobbed it softly. He saw two more patients together, husband and wife.

Nicholas told Lucy to go down to the bar for a beer. Bridge would be there by now, talking cheerful drivel. He'd be down soon.

Her blonde hair faded in the dusk. She was so middle-class, so well-spoken, so kind and hopeful. But there was no danger to her on that darkening track to the village. Not here. Not yet. He stood a while longer, hearing Dr Hércules's quiet and steady wheeze as he worked, taking a blood sample from the woman's thumb. She remained expressionless.

The crickets and frogs rattled and croaked, the grackles cried out. The volcanoes burned deep in their crimson hearts and cast giant pyramid shadows over the valleys and the lives of *los humildes*.

Dr Hércules had switched on his torch and was turning down the wheel on the kerosene lamp when they heard the engine of a jeep. He switched off his torch and kept his finger and thumb on the wheel, ready to kill the light. He looked uncharacteristically hesitant. Nicholas backed up against the wall.

The jeep spewed to a halt, engine still running. One man ran across in front of the white headlights and pulled the door open and then two hobbled back, the driver and another leaning on him heavily, arm around his neck.

'*Olé* and alleluia,' said Dr Hércules. 'Overtime.'

He switched on the lamp again full and they came into the

cabin and the wounded man fell back in the chair, sweating heavily. He had two or three bloodsoaked bandannas wrapped around his throat and jaw.

Dr Hércules went to the cupboard and tossed Nicholas a pair of latex gloves.

The wounded wore jeans and a dark t shirt, his companion likewise, with a straw cowboy hat pushed back on a cord around his grimy throat. His companion could not speak. They had no guns.

'This isn't A and E,' said Dr Hércules. 'You need to go to town.'

The wounded man was no older than Nicholas, twenty one or two. His skin and his lips were already pale from blood loss.

'It is impossible in this light,' said Dr Hércules. 'There is nothing –'

The other man instantly returned to the jeep and turned it round so the headlights blazed into the cabin.

Nicholas took the man's pulse. Fast and fluttering. Dr Hércules began to ease off the bloodsoaked bandannas around his jaw. The man's jeans were spotted with more blood. Only then did Nicholas see the blood welling darkly from a neat bullet hole in his shoulder.

Dr Hércules said, 'I suppose I do not waste my breath – I am short of it already – asking who shot you?'

No answer. Instead the other man said, 'The bullet is still in his shoulder. Get it out. He will not scream.'

Dr Hércules snorted. 'Too many cowboy films,' he said. 'The bullet's the least of his problems. Men can walk around for years with bullets inside them. It's the blood loss that'll kill him.'

'Pulse rate 130bpm,' said Nicholas. It was very bad. The man in the chair looked up at him pleading, more than ever a boy. Then suddenly he sat up and tore the bandannas free altogether and they saw his jaw had been all but shot away. Something fell wet to the floor and there were shards of teeth and bone hanging loose where his chin had been. His saliva drooled down. Nicholas could see his tongue lolling. His companion groaned. Nicholas had to force himself not to grimace or step back or look away.

'We can do nothing,' said Dr Hércules, raising his voice, reaching for the bandages.

'Do as you can,' said the other man.

'He needs to go to town. To the hospital. Or he will die.'

The man shook his head. 'Here.'

So they bandaged up his shattered jaw afresh with gauze and bandages as best they could, though only surgery could make sense of such a mess. They put a pad on the shoulder wound and Nicholas pressed firmly, waiting for the blood flow to stop or at least slow. But immediately his comrade pulled the wounded man to his feet again.

'Leave him!' ordered Dr Hércules. 'Or he will die!'

But short of physically preventing him, there was nothing they could do. The wounded man was hauled out of the cabin barely conscious now, and the two staggered to the jeep.

'Hospital! Do not have a death on your conscience!'

They never said another word. The jeep's engine raced and it pulled tightly around and sped up away into the mountains.

After a while Dr Hércules said, 'I am sorry. You are all right?'

Nicholas nodded, trying not to look shaken. It really was going to be an experience here.

'I do not suppose you see many gunshot wounds in England.'

'You'd be surprised,' he said, trying for a nonchalant drawl. 'They're getting quite fashionable nowadays.'

They washed down the chair and swabbed the floor as well as they could in the dim lamplight, and peeled off their gloves and threw them in the flip-top bin and washed their hands again and rubbed them with sanitizer. Once again Dr Hércules switched on his torch and then switched off the kerosene lamp. They walked slowly down to his car.

'He's going to die, isn't he?' said Nicholas

Dr Hércules nodded. 'I think so, yes. We will never know. But I do not see how he will live until morning. Do not tell your friends about this.'

'I won't.'

'You know how dramatic it would sound. What a thing to boast of.'

'I know.'

They got in and slammed the doors shut. Dr Hércules indicated the inside lock. Nicholas looked quizzical. Dr Hércules nodded. They both switched their inside locks and Dr Hércules turned the key in the ignition and drove sedately down towards the village.

'Do you think we're still OK here?' said Nicholas. 'We volunteers?'

'OK? In this country?' He wheezed mirthfully. 'Don't be ridiculous. Nothing is OK in this country. But if I think your lives are in imminent danger I will advise you of it. They are not yet.'

After a while Nicholas said, 'Were those men from the gangs?' *Narcotraficantes*? Or ... insurgents?'

'Or private security. Or army in plain clothes. Or hired assassins, or the enforcers of some big landowner.' Dr Hércules shrugged. 'Or perhaps the driver fellow himself shot the other for sodomizing his mule. We will never know.'

They came to the village square. Boys were playing football in the dust in near darkness except for the mean string of bare lightbulbs across one corner. Dr Hércules switched off the engine. Dustmotes revolved and insects danced in the beams of the headlights. He turned them off and they sat in darkness. Dr Hércules had more to say.

He lit a cigarette and unlocked his door and pushed it half open.

'It is not clear to me how much your medical school in London really knows. Or your in-country co-ordinator. Of course they stand to make money by organizing volunteers, homestays, work programmes. And where there is money there is corruption.' He exhaled. 'How much do you think you have paid for your homestay?'

'Thirty US dollars a week.'

'Your family will be receiving much less than this.'

'Are you sure?'

He nodded.

Nicholas felt an instant surge of indignation. Dr Hércules raised his hand.

'Do not do anything,' he said. 'If you ask your family they will be humiliated. And if you protest to anyone else, your family will receive nothing at all. Learn. This is how it is.'

Nicholas sat tight and motionless.

'Only a month ago,' said Dr Hércules, 'driving out here from the city, outside Dulce Nombre, I stopped to relieve myself. In a ditch nearby there were three dead bodies, freshly killed. At least they had not been mutilated. What did I do? Like a good doctor, first I relieved myself, at a respectful distance. You cannot hope to be an objective man of science with a full bladder. Then I returned to the dead, handkerchief to my nose. Flies were feasting plentifully, laying their eggs in eyes and ears. Nevertheless I got down into the ditch with the dead. It was not so bad. Not so bad to be down in a ditch with the dead. Good practice for later, since it is where we will all end up before long.

'I took their pulses. In the nineteen eighties, when the army massacred whole villages in the highlands, there were stories of people, especially children, surviving for a day or more under a pile of dead bodies and then crawling free. Little children. Because the bullets from the machine guns had gone over their heads. But there in the ditch they were all dead – except me. Nearly dead.'

He paused. 'Why am I telling you this?' he wondered aloud, examining splayed pudgy fingers and blue fingernails. Then he twisted his bulk a little in his seat.

'You have come to a terrible country,' he said. 'Sixty two generals and only two decent hospitals. The strange thing is,

you will fall in love with it.' He looked hard at Nicholas.
'Especially you.'

17

Lucy and Bridge were both drunk in the bar. They had sourced a bottle of Cuban rum and Henrietta was selling them cola. Caitlin was on beer. Bridge immediately came over to him, bright-faced.

'Want a rum, mate?'

'Just a Coke, thanks.'

Bridge grinned and went over to Henrietta for another Coke and a plastic cup. Sorted. Easy as that.

Nicholas examined the rum bottle and deliberately spilled a little over his fingernails where there was still some dried blood and wiped it off on his jeans. The appearance of the dying man seemed a scene of horror to him now and he had to make sure he kept very calm.

Bridge said, 'I still think things are getting dodgy here.'

'I miss my mum!' wailed Lucy.

'I think things have always been dodgy here,' said Nicholas.

'Does the Doc think we're still OK?' said Caitlin. 'Did he say?'

'In his roundabout way – yeah, he thought we were OK. There's still some point in us being here.'

Bridge said he had spoken to his lot back home and they said they were monitoring the situation very closely, plus keeping in touch daily with the British Consulate in the capital. Despite the coup, they reckoned everything was pretty stable and no cause for alarm.

'Plus,' he said, 'there's a load of American Peace Corps just in the next town. They'd soon hear of anything.'

Then Lucy's phone buzzed and she said joyfully that it was

a call from her mum and she went off to sit on the bench in the square under the lights. She talked for half an hour and came back tearful and happy.

'Did you see that guy come up to me?'

They hadn't.

'Offered me ten dollars for an hour! Thought I might be a *puta*! He should be so lucky.'

'That's why we're here!' cried Bridge, triumphantly vindicated. 'Because life back home is so comfortable. We're dying of boredom!'

'You think so?' said Nicholas.

'Fuck yeah. England's just old and grey and tired. Don't you think?'

'No,' he said, 'I think it's all getting really interesting again. I mean, in our lifetimes, the English will become a minority in England, with large parts of it Muslim.'

There was an embarrassed silence, then Bridge said, 'Christ, now who's being provocative? You sound like UKIP or something.'

Nicholas laughed. 'People always say that. But it's only demographics. Maths. And then Africa's current 1 billion will be approaching 3 billion by around 2050, and a lot of them will be wanting to come and live in Europe too. That's going to be *really* interesting. What will we do? What will be the right thing to do – if we really care so much about developing countries?'

He excused himself and went for a pee round the back.

Lucy whispered apologetically, 'I think he's spent a lot of time on his own.'

They went back in a group, dropping Lucy first, right at the door, then Bridge, then Caitlin.

'You're OK going up there on your own?' she said.

'I think I'll make it,' said Nicholas, winding up his torch.

'Beware of any Muslims hiding behind trees.'

'Will do.'

'Machetes glinting in the moonlight.'

'Thanks.'

'You don't get a mobile signal up there do you?'

'Happily not.'

'But you get one in the village?'

He nodded.

'You can always borrow mine if you want to phone your family or anything. I'm on a really cheap rate.'

'Ta.' He smiled and walked on. 'See you tomorrow.'

18

The last time he spoke to his mother was some six weeks before. He tried to phone home but of course the line was dead due to unpaid bills.

Her latest address was a damp cottage on a country estate. Windows mildewed and bleared or resignedly boarded, door peeling grey scurf in the sun.

Garden gate gone. Garden! Path through waist-high ragwort, a variety of mammalian ordure. He pulled the iron bell-chain. Then a long, long wait, a welcome time for reflection and sweet remembrance of things past. He waited so long, he took out his book to read. *The Great Gatsby*. It was all about re-inventing yourself.

Then the chains on hell's gate began their infernal rattle, one after the other fumbled and wrenched, and then the face like a collapsed soufflé, the stupid stare, the flash of resentful recognition. And then the protecting veils of delusion and denial as she turned away, stumbling back up the hallway.

'Come in darling, I'll put the kettle on. You haven't got any fags on you have you?'

He shut the door behind him and locked it carefully and fastened all three chains. For the dead certainly return, and mostly when the living sleep.

Telling her about going to Central America on medical elective. He might as well have told the cat. Her eyes watery and wandering, breathing stertorous, breath of the grave. Telly on maximum, batteries gone on the remote, searching for the volume. Only disconnect! He stood waiting while she made the tea, stumbling, hacking, man's check shirt and baggy corduroys, the kitchen filled with bottles and binbags, landfill and floodwrack. My mother's post-apocalyptic kitchen.

He took his black tea.

'Thank you Mother.'

'*Mother*?' she said. 'Bloody hell.'

They repaired to the drawing-room for *conversazione*. He saw that she still took *Country Life* and *The Field*, which was almost funny.

Three dolls on the sagging sofa, its underbelly scraping the floor. Lizzie's dolls. His mother kept them for reasons of deluded sentiment. Two stared vacantly at the television, stunned by the violence of its volume. The third lay face down. It could not be blamed. Much of the house bare of furniture otherwise, and every last carpet gone. Surely not sold? Who, even the most charmed connoisseur of stained and mottled broadloom and drugget, who would buy?

He knelt in front of the TV and managed to find a volume pad to turn it down.

'So,' she said, staring at it. It was a programme about dream homes. 'How've you been Nicky darling? Is life simply thrilling?'

He began to deliver his script. Her eyes wandered from the television and then she started talking over him. The bastards had cut the phone off again, she didn't know why. Sometimes she thought they were bugging her. The fridge was making a terrible noise. He didn't have... He couldn't ... could he? He shook his head. Her eyes narrowed. The old meanness beneath the helplessness.

She had liked him better when he was as messed up as her and they shared the companionship of failure. But she said nothing, shaking tea over her own hands, confusedly hating him. His neat clothes, his quiet determination, his refusal to suffer or to inherit suffering. Coming here to remind her of everything, her rubbish self, stirring the cesspit under her nose. Why did he come here anyway? To jeer at her that he had left her, he had gone far away from her now. America did he say? Bugger America. Look at him, glancing around the

room. Well what if it did need a clean? Just because he was so
… *composed*. Well let him look. What did she care.

Someone rolled over in bed upstairs.

'What's that to you?' she snapped.

He had said nothing. And troublesome to ask his name, she
might not know him that well, the new gentleman of the
house.

'Who are you anyway?' she snarled with sudden violence,
her lips dark and twisted like some rotten fruit.

He said nothing. It was an interesting question.

He listened to the fridge, diagnosed that it was terminal.
Considered explaining about heat exchangers then thought
better of it. Washed up the mugs, but after brief consideration
decided against attempting any further cleaning. Better to
leave it to the emergency services.

He drove down to the nearby mini supermarket in the
village, and came back with two bags: UHT milk, bread,
bananas, apples, some tins of tuna – nothing that needed
cooking – plus washing-up liquid and toothpaste. Surely even
she couldn't sell those for gin?

She took the bags, saying, 'I knew you wouldn't buy me
any fags.'

'Student grant won't cover it.'

'I swear you were fathered by a Jew.'

They sat again, watching a bit about farmhouses in Devon.
'Oh that one's nice,' said his mother. She nodded
thoughtfully.

There were many things they didn't talk about. His medical
studies. The past. Family… The list of unmentionables was
long, and recalling them might have caused awkwardness.

'Are you ill?' she said suddenly.

'Ill? No. Do I –'

'You look ill.'

Coming from her this was really very funny.

Then there was more noise from upstairs. The gentleman

of the house was getting up now, waddling across the bedroom, yawning and scratching his testicles. Though Nicholas had long since learned considerable self-control, this was enough to signal the break-up of the delightful tea party. He looked at his watch. He had managed nearly an hour and a half here, with the shopping trip. That wasn't bad, all things considered.

'You sure you can't lend me fifty quid?' she said.

It was the word *lend* which made him smile. He shouldn't have.

'You always were a tight bastard. Just like your father.'

'No,' he said. 'I am nothing like my father.'

'You cunt.'

It was hard to know what she really thought or felt any more. Perhaps she didn't know herself, so how could he? He just did his usual thing of staying entirely calm, saying goodbye, still smiling.

She said, 'Don't bother coming again.'

She often said that by way of farewell. She might have meant it or she might not. Or possibly both. He got in the car and drove down the chalk track across the field. Only when he was out of the gate onto the lane did he pull in and switch off the engine and lay his arms across the wheel and rest his forehead on his arms a while.

19

The next day Nicholas and Lucy were on their own. Dr Hércules had to go back to the city to work at the hospital.

'Even though it's a Saturday,' he grumbled. 'Germs and diseases don't have weekends off.

'And any cases that are beyond you,' he said, looking pointedly at Nicholas, 'Send 'em to the city hospital. Be very firm: you're just a clinic. They must go to the town - and so must I. A man must eat.' He caressed his belly fondly. 'I must have good red wine from Argentina, and steak, in a restaurant. If I eat another of these peasant tortillas, my health will be ruined. If only I could visit my sweet, laughing, twenty-two year old mistress tonight as well.'

Nicholas coughed. 'Why can't you? Late shift?'

He smacked his fist into his palm. 'Because I don't *have* such a mistress, damn it! How can that be? Eh? Look at me! With my wealth, charm and astonishing physical beauty, how can that be?'

And wheezing with mirth he was gone.

Bridge was gone too: to the beach.

'The beach? For the turtles?'

Caitlin said, 'I don't think it's for the turtles. He got a text from some mates who've come over from the Bay Islands. He wants to try kite surfing.' She shook her head. 'He is a bit of a twat.'

'But that makes us feel morally superior, doesn't it? Which is nice.'

She laughed.

But Bridge hadn't the fixedness of character to make

enemies. Laughing with his big greedy shiny face, his shock of curly hair, his entertaining lies. He said he had seen a dragonfly in the forest with a metre wingspan. He said he slept with three different girls in a single night in Cancún. That his father was a multi-millionaire art dealer. Liar, gossip, cheat, coward and fantasist. How could they not like him?

They saw a five year old girl with serious anaemia. She was flour pale, her lips, her gums, even her inner eyelids. Most serious of all, a heart murmur.

'Probably hookworm.'

Lucy took a blood sample and she had a haemoglobin count of three. It should have been eleven.

She said, 'At home she'd be straight in for a blood transfusion. Here she's still walking about, probably still helping her mother wash the clothes and make the tortillas.'

'You're doing a Dr Hércules.'

She looked puzzled.

'Talking over the heads of the patients.'

'Sorry.'

Nicholas asked in Spanish, 'Do you work?'

The little girl nodded tiredly.

'Go to school?'

'Sometimes.'

They gave the mother worm medicine, iron tablets, vitamins and Incaparina, a powdered protein supplement.

'It's good if you can wear shoes,' they told the little girl. 'When you run about. Even just sandals. They will stop the worms entering in through the soles of your feet and making you ill again.'

And they told the mother to give her the pills one a day, with food, and let the little girl rest as much as possible. They must come again soon for another blood test.

'It is not possible,' said the mother very quietly, looking down. 'We are very far away. In the mountains.'

There were various cases: an old injury beyond their power to treat, a cut that needed cleaning and some stitches, a tetanus jab. After lunch there were worms, worms, anaemia, worms. An early case of leishmaniasis caused by sandflies. A young mother with a noisy toddler. Nicholas heard her say,

'Quiet, or the gringos will give you an injection!'

And then near the end of the day, when they were feeling tired and longing for Sunday, a girl with a baby: it was Yolanda, Maria's cousin. The baby girl looked suddenly much worse than when Nicholas had glimpsed her at the cottage and he felt very anxious. He should have done something. *Why had he not done something?* Why had he not said something to Maria, or tried to get Dr Hércules to visit her? Why had he not tried to get the girl Yolanda to visit the clinic earlier? How could he have just left it, have *done nothing...*

'What is her name?'

The girl's voice was almost inaudible.

'Clara?' repeated Nicholas.

She nodded.

The baby's skin was shiny and blotched, eyes sunken, apathetic. Her skin wrinkled at a pinch and did not spring back, and the fontanel on her head was depressed.

'When did she last urinate?'

'I don't know,' said Yolanda. 'Very little.'

Lucy tried not to let the girl's passivity anger her.

The girl stroked her baby's head continuously. The baby's lips were split and she emitted the faintest whimpers. Nicholas cradled the heavy head in his right hand. Hair as fine as silk thread, but with the russet tinge of severe malnutrition. He thought of the pitchpine children's coffins in the windows of the undertakers in the city. One of the first things he had seen when he came to this country.

He opened the baby's mouth and there were white curds of thrush on her tongue. The girl's eyes were dark with pain.

'How old is she?'

'About five months,' said Yolanda.

They weighed the baby very gently, already horrified at her deathly lightness as they laid her in the scales. She weighed eleven pounds. It was hardly possible. She needed urgent IV, which they did not have.

Nicholas said, 'Can we phone Dr Menendez?'

'What can he do?'

'We have to do something.'

The girl began to weep in silence. She knew, as they talked over her head.

'She's malnourished,' said Nicholas. '*Malnourished*. No more.'

'We can try to get her rehydrated, then go down to the village for a signal.'

The girl looked at them, stroking the silken hair. Her baby's listless eyes still on her, only her. Her little one, Clara, who was to die. Then she said, 'I want to take her home.'

'No, please, wait,' said Nicholas desperately. 'Just wait. We will not be very long. We need to go and talk to the doctor, Dr Hércules Menendez. Please wait for us. We will give you some medicine for your baby while we are gone.'

They showed her how to spoon the homemade electrolyte mix into the baby's mouth, a teaspoon at a time. It was the clinic's homebrew, a mix of boiled water, the juice of an orange, a tablespoon of sugar, pinch of salt and pinch of soda.

But it dribbled out of the side of the baby's mouth again. She hadn't the strength to swallow. She needed an IV urgently.

'We will not be very long,' said Nicholas again. 'Please wait for us.'

They raced down into the village. Lucy got a signal, they rang Dr Hércules, went to answerphone, left a hurried message. He rang back almost immediately, listened, said they had done well.

'Try to keep the baby hydrated whatever you do, and insist the mother must go into town. Her baby must have intensive care. Bring her to this hospital. I'll get her in somehow.'

When they got back to the clinic, Yolanda was standing outside with her baby Clara in her arms and a youth only a little older standing beside her. Human trinity, all too human. Others crowded close and were silent and some of the women caressed the girl, tributaries bringing no gifts but themselves, and Yolanda was softly weeping and they knew, they knew.

Nicholas looked at the baby. Her face had a blueish tinge, the shadows of the trees. He touched the girl on the arm and she raised the small blanket that covered her. The baby's chest no longer moved. He felt for a pulse, horrified that the tiny wrist might break between his fingers, and then again at the neck. There was nothing.

Dutifully he and Lucy both went inside the clinic to get their stethoscopes. But there was no point them both listening. It only prolonged it.

'You do it,' said Lucy.

He placed the cup on the baby's chest. There were faint sighings and gurglings, sometimes like the pattering of tiny feet. Heard through a stethoscope, death was anything but silent. But there was no heartbeat. There was plenty of life, microbial life, now spreading out from the digestive system and colonising the body. Countless billions of microscopic lives. But there was no human life.

Tears streamed down the parents' cheeks. They made no sound. The boy who had not wanted to marry Yolanda or be a father was now holding her hand. A grackle laughed in a treetop and then fell silent. Nightfall was only an hour off. Nobody spoke a word.

The quiet ended with a pick-up truck revving down the road.

Nicholas asked, 'How will you get home?'

The young father said, 'Perhaps a truck.'

Nicholas ran down the road to the pick-up truck and waved it down.

'I want you to give my friends a lift. I will pay you twenty dollars.'

The man regarded him blankly. 'How far?'

'Not very far.'

'Thirty dollars.'

He shook his head. 'Twenty.'

'Let me see the money.'

He gave him ten dollars. 'Another ten when we arrive at the house.'

The man folded the note and put it in his shirt pocket. 'Get in.'

The boy and girl got into the truck with the baby. Nicholas got out, but the boy said, 'Please come too.'

Nicholas and Lucy looked uncertain.

'Please.'

Lucy nodded. They told the last few people that the clinic was now closing for the day but would be open again tomorrow. Nobody complained. Some said, 'Of course, of course.' They locked the cabin and Nicholas pocketed the key and some of the men raised their hats in farewell. They went in the back of the truck with the boy and the girl and the baby.

'San Luis,' said the boy, leaning forward and pointing up into the mountains. The driver grunted.

The boy held out his hand. 'My name is Miguel.'

They all said their names.

Nicholas sat well back again.

The baby lay in her mother's arms. Where was she now? Where was she? Was that it? Was that the end? The parents stared up ahead. Both younger than him, patient even now, without complaint. What did they know that he didn't? Or were they just tired? He gauged each breath, each swallow, his chest like he'd been charged by a bull. Twenty years ago.

Lucy's eyes were bright. There were no other cars or trucks on that quiet dust road into the mountains.

20

The boy Miguel signalled to the driver near the top of a hill and there was a cluster of thatched huts amid the trees.

'We will walk from here.'

The young couple got down and the boy said to the driver, 'Thank you sir, you are very kind. May God go with you.'

Then he looked up at Lucy and Nicholas and they got down too. The young mother embraced Lucy, the baby between them, as if it were she who needed the comfort. The father shook Nicholas's hand again and then they began to walk up the path to their hut.

The driver said, 'You don't want a lift back?'

Miguel on the path turned around, face streaked with tears, and said to the two volunteers with immaculate politeness, 'Please. Come.'

Nicholas gave the driver the other ten dollars and he turned the truck around and drove away down the hill into the dusk. The moon was already over the jagged mountains. Up ahead, the couple were going into their hut and the people were gathering to meet them, to be with them.

More and more people arrived. How did they know? They sat in front of the hut. Women lit rushlights and lanterns, others brought food fresh and cooked. Lucy and Nicholas could not speak for sadness and the sense of privilege, except to say thank you, thank you. Nicholas wondered if José and Maria might come as well. It was possible.

Chairs were brought for them, for it was well known that gringos were frightened of sitting on the ground, while people sat on the ground or squatted against the log walls of the hut, hands clasped before their lined faces. Plates were given to them while the people ate from the common bowls with their fingers. The esteemed guests, the foreign doctors, who had cared for the lost baby of Miguel and Yolanda.

People talked low and murmurous. After a time the door of the hut was opened and they went inside and on a table with burning candles around her lay the baby in her finest clothes. Her cheeks had been reddened with the juice of hibiscus petals. The table was covered with a fresh white cloth and her russet-tinged hair was combed and there was a crown of white flowers around her head. On a bed in the corner of the room lay a little boy and girl, fast asleep.

A man wiped his mouth and stepped up beside the table and said, 'Brother and sisters, let us pray.

'*Our Father who art in heaven, hallowed be thy name...*'

The two knelt with the others, trying to remember the old words, suddenly embarrassed and bewildered by their own unbelief. Yet now of all times, a dead baby lying before them, their unbelief ought to make sense. The grainy dirt floor pitted their knees. The darkening forest bowed over them.

The man said, 'God is with us.'

Afterwards they found places for the honoured guests to sleep, with bedding and blankets. So that they should not feel alone, two men would sleep on the floor beside Nicholas, and two young girls in the room with Lucy. Two families slept in a single room to make it possible. A man took Nicholas gently by the hand and said that in the morning they would walk with them back down the valley to Chilitenango. It was not a problem.

Nicholas lay wondering where the young mother and father had got the money for the tablecloth and the baby clothes and the candles. Then he thought, From the neighbours. One brought a baby's white gown, one brought a white candle, another another. One by one they all came.

In the morning they were given fresh tortillas to take with them, and the mother and father came to say goodbye. The mother embraced Lucy again and the father shook Nicholas's hand. He said that they thanked them from the depths of their hearts. He said,

'We are sorry we have no gifts to give you. But we are thankful to you more than we can say.'

Nicholas shook his hand very hard, holding on tight.

Then they set off down the dust track and the long walk back to Chilitenango, and five men walked with them in earnest silence, so that they should not feel dishonoured or alone. After an hour or more of walking they found a truck to give them a lift onward, and even then the five men wanted to come with them. But they insisted that there was no need.

'Thank you.'

'Truly, thank you.'

The church bell was tolling in the village, and even though it was Sunday there was a group of people outside the clinic, waiting in the morning sunlight, as always, and laid at the door outside were gifts. Freshly baked tortillas in corn leaves and some eggs wrapped likewise and those tiny sweet red bananas called lady's fingers.

'I'm sorry,' said Nicholas, holding his arms up helplessly, 'but today the clinic is closed.'

The people looked on, some nodding solemnly.

'Nick,' said Lucy behind him.

'Please,' he said, sounding faintly desperate.

The people bowed their heads and began to shuffle away. One woman glanced back and smiled.

Lucy had opened the clinic anyway.

'What are you *doing*?'

'Come inside,' she said.

They stepped into the cool shade, the smell of wooden boards and disinfectant, and she shut the door behind them.

'They're not wanting treatment,' she said. 'They just came

to say thank you to us. They must have got news of last night.'

She turned away from him and retied her ponytail with a hairband. Then she said, 'I don't think I can take much more of this. All this gratitude.'

'Me neither,' he said.

'Kind of different to back home isn't it?'

'Kind of.' He nudged the chair with his foot to turn it round and sit. Lucy opened the door a crack and looked out.

'Come on,' she said, 'let's sit outside. Coast's clear.'

They sat on the grassy slope in the hot sun, haloed in sleepy flies.

'Hey,' said Lucy. 'You OK?'

'I should have *done* something. I could have...'

'How?'

'The mother is a cousin of the mother at my homestay. Yolanda. They're all family.'

'I'm sorry – but I don't see what difference that makes.'

'I saw the baby a few days ago. I should have *done* something.'

Lucy put her hand on his shoulder. 'Come on,' she said. 'We did all we could. It wasn't much, but it was all we could do. You know the golden rule. On to the next one. Keep doing what we can.'

He continued to stare at the ground.

'I know,' she said. 'Let's go to the church.'

'What?'

She got up. 'Let's go to church. Valuable anthropological experience.'

So, slightly bewildered by their own decision, they walked down to the church where the bell was just slowing and stopping. Cautiously and shyly, they went in. There were candles and incense and a man with a Spanish guitar, and women in bright dresses and cardigans and pink headscarves. The church was as cool as a cave, the crucified wooden Christ was mournful and remote, eyes lifted to heaven.

They stumbled through the singing, half a line behind, and

knelt when everyone knelt, and when the priest raised his hand and pronounced God's blessing on them all, they were glad they had come.

Nicholas was dreading going back to the cottage. But when he came in sight of the cottage that evening as the sun was already low and shining in his eyes, Maria saw him and stood and when he came closer there were tears in her eyes.

'We heard what you did, you and the other doctor.' She looked so sad – for *him*, and for Lucy. 'You did so well.'

'I am just sorry we didn't...'

'No,' said Maria, very firmly. 'That baby was never well. It was a bitter shame. Perhaps she should have been adopted at once.'

And lost her parents, her village, her language, her country, thought Nicholas. And held on to her life.

'Now she is in the hands of God,' said Maria. 'And that is the truth.'

Nicholas didn't know if it was the truth. But then he thought of the baby lying there in her crown of white flowers, surrounded by candles, and he didn't know if it wasn't the truth either. Or maybe it wasn't for him to say whether it was the truth or not.

When José returned a little later, walking tiredly out of the Sunday evening twilight, he was even more laconic. He shook Nicholas's hand and said, '*Hombre*,' and then he took off his hat and sat down to his supper of rice and beans.

On the return of Dr Hércules on Monday morning, they told him about the baby, the young mother and father, the gifts.

He listened attentively, studying his fingernails, and then said, 'You did very well.' His voice was sincere for once.

'You think so?'

'I do. I am proud of you both.'

'Back home,' said Nicholas, 'there'd probably be a lawyer on the case by now, and those parents would be suing us.'

95

Dr Hércules could hear the defensiveness in the young man's voice and understood it. He said gently, 'I think it would be easier for the peasants to understand ... quantum physics, than the idea of suing someone who had tried to heal your child.'

21

They were attending to an elderly woman with terrible breath and carious teeth, explaining that she really needed a dentist, in the town, when a jeep drew up sharply outside. The waiting people retired right back under the trees.

Two men got out, one in jungle camouflage, the other older, handsome, mustachioed. Nicholas knew them at once.

Dr Hércules pretended not to notice them and began to reach for his mirror.

'Good morning to you all,' said the middle-aged man, removing his smart red-banded hat. Handsome moustache, deep commanding voice, crisp white shirt, fine upright figure, politely removing his sunglasses.

'Good morning Colonel,' said Dr Hércules.

Nicholas saw Lucy looking even more interested when rank was mentioned. And now that he was standing before them, in daylight, he – the colonel - was indeed a magnificent figure. A little over medium height, but proud bearing and presence made him seem taller. Jet black hair combed back, thick glossy black moustache, manly jaw and chin thrust forward. A powerful build beneath the immaculate white shirt, with cuffs folded back showing big, thickly veined hands, powerful wrists and forearms.

'A moment with you please,' said the colonel.

Dr Hércules looked up, sighed, apologized to the old woman, told her to rinse her mouth out with salt water, laid down his angled mirror, asked the two volunteers to give them a moment.

They sat under the ceiba tree.

'What's going on?' whispered Lucy. 'And who is *he?*'

He looked back. The colonel was talking, gesturing politely but firmly, the doctor listening with absolute neutrality.

'He is *so* alpha male,' said Lucy. 'Caitlin would have loved this.'

Nicholas took out his book and started to read.

They left after five minutes. The colonel touched the peak of his hat to Lucy and gave her a flashing smile. She waved back.

'Marvellous,' said Nicholas, not looking up.

Dr Hércules had a different perspective. 'The scum,' he said softly. 'The scum.'

They had never heard him so sincere.

'Is there a problem?'

'Nothing that a bit of civil war and genocide won't fix.' He scowled at them. 'Apparently we should be more judicious about whom we treat.'

'Were they threatening?'

There was a long silence while he lit a cigarette, smoked, held his hand up to prevent the next patient approaching outside. Finally he said,

'I think you should be ready to leave. I know you've been here all of a few days, but –'

'Oh, everyone's telling us that now.'

'Ssh Nick,' said Lucy. 'Do you really think that, Dr Menendez?'

'There is no danger to you, but you should be ready. Not just yet, but at short notice. I do not think you will stay the whole three months. I am sorry. This country is built on volcanoes.'

But for a few more days the sunny winter days and cold starlit nights passed peacefully. Nicholas worked on at the clinic with Lucy – who now kept her bag packed and with her at all times just in case.

José was embarrassed that he still hadn't found time to finish the new room for Nicholas to sleep in. But Nicholas insisted that he was fine in his hammock.

'Anyway, how will you find the time? You do twelve-hour days as it is.'

José grinned ruefully. 'More than that, as we start harvesting and storing.'

'Well then. I like sleeping out, honestly. I can see the stars.'

In spare hours he loved walking the long forest paths round the village for mile upon mile. Most of all he loved to be with the family – *his* family. He played football with the boys, and when El Pipón punctured the ball he went down to the town with Jaime and Héctor and bought another.

He was happy to sit long with Abuelita and drink coffee and try to answer her questions about life in England. Did they have coffee there? Real coffee? He said yes. Were they decent Christians? He said yes to that too, surmising that she would be upset to hear otherwise. 'Very decent,' he said, 'very devout.' Had Americans truly walked upon the moon? He smiled and shook his head and said, to cheer her,

'A lot of people think it was all a hoax.'

Abuelita gave her dry little laugh. 'I knew it!' she said, and her skeleton fists drummed a triumphant tattoo on her blanketed knees. 'I always thought it was a tall story. Men walking on the moon indeed. What fools do they take us for?'

He had more conversations with Eulalia about puppies, teeth, stars, dwarves in the forest, beards, cheese, cows, bats, dinosaurs and bad men. They watched Héctor feed the hens.

He threw down corn for them and they came running. One hen limped sadly behind the rest. Héctor picked it up squawking and set it down with the others. A fat brown hen turned and pecked the limping hen. Héctor kicked the fat brown hen. Social justice is always difficult.

When he was at the clinic, even when he was hard at work and concentrating, he found himself missing the family.

Whether playing with the boys or talking to Abuelita or Lala, he was often aware of Maria watching him with a smile, quickly turning away if she thought he realized. It was more than a week after he had held her tightly to him in his nightmare that their eyes even met again. He came back from the clinic after a good day – no deaths, two definite triumphs, a young mother who had finally got the idea of sterilizing a baby bottle – at full stride and confident and hungry and tanned, with the brief tropical sunset making him glow across the meadow and his hunted stricken look quite gone, and he saw her looking at him and smiled and she smiled back, eyes meeting.

He took two photos of the family with his mobile, once as photographer and then, after fiddling with the settings, once on ten-second timer with him in as well.

'Run! Run!' screamed the children as he ran to join them.

Afterwards they all crowded round the tiny screen and peered and then laughed and Maria held her hands to her mouth. Not the best photos he had ever taken, but then again the best.

His next afternoon off, he took his phone down to the Jesus Christ Died for my Sins Internet Café, and asked the proprietor if he could print them out. The proprietor stared at the phone and the files and then said it was possible.

'Come back later.'

He came back after an hour and a bad coffee and collected the two 6x4 photos, hazy and overlit but acceptable. After a moment's consideration he dropped the first one in the bin, and kept the other one of him among the family.

Maria was washing Jaime down when he came back. He looked annoyed to be seen getting a scrub from his mum at his age. She looked so pretty and so tired. She always looked tired, pretty but tired, cooking and cleaning and washing for four children, and her apron so proudly, scrupulously clean: what washing that must have taken, down by the river, the stains of tomatoes and maize oil scrubbed out in the cold mountain stream, reddening the skin of her slim brown hands. Her crouched by the river, her hair falling forward from her headscarf in a shining bird's wing of dark hair ...

He smiled then at the memory of a ridiculous dream he had had just last night. There were arrows in the sky, and he had put his arms around her. The arrows hissed down and stuck in his arms like hypodermic needles, but she was unhurt.

In any spare moments she was tending the pumpkins and the squashes, the chillies and the peppers in the tiny kitchen garden, watering, weeding, hoeing. Feeding the chickens, collecting the eggs, getting a ride in a truck and taking any that they could spare down to the town of Santo Domingo to sell in the market when they needed extra cash. They always needed extra cash. It was time Héctor had his first pair of trainers. Once he might have had leather sandals made for him by his father, as José's father had made for him: a piece of cow leather with a thong. But that tradition was over.

Héctor had gone barefoot so far, but Nicholas had told them gently about hookworm and other parasites. He wished he could pay for the trainers himself. A child-sized pair from China, down in the market in Santo Domingo, sold for 320 centavos: around eight US dollars. But José and Maria would not like him to pay, they would prefer to pay themselves. And to earn eight dollars to buy Héctor's first trainers, Maria would have to sell ten dozen eggs. A lot of eggs.

He watched her. She worked every hour of daylight, twelve hours a day, every single day of the year. No Sundays, no holidays. No expectation that anything would ever be different.

He wished he could do more to help. He could cook dinner one night, and he could mend clothes, sew on buttons. He had taught himself. But it was impossible. She would be ashamed not to provide for the honoured guest.

On impulse he went up to her and handed her the photo of the family without a word. She wiped her hands dry on her apron and took it and was very touched.

'And you are so tall!' she exclaimed.

'I think I was standing on a hump.'

'But you should have a copy too.'

'I'll get a reprint next time I'm in the village, don't worry.'

'Here.' She handed the precious image back to him. 'Go and put it on the shelf in the kitchen where it will not fade.'

He stepped inside the cool cottage stooping and went over to the whitewashed shelf. There was the miniature of whisky he had brought them as a present, still untouched. He propped the photo up behind the little plaster statuette of the Virgin, but did not let it go. Turned away... The Virgin wobbled and fell face first towards the floor but he knelt and managed to catch her in time. Set her back on the shelf. Set the photo behind her again, letting go of it this time. Wiped the sweat off his upper lip. If he had let her break...

He stepped outside again. She was still scrubbing Jaime vigorously.

'Where is Lala?' he said casually.

'She and Yeto are just down the road somewhere. Didn't you see them?'

'No.'

'Or in the forest.'

He pulled a face at Jaime and then said, 'I'll go and look for them.'

'They'll be fine. They live half their lives in the forest.'

'Well. I'll go anyway.'

He went away down the hill, mid afternoon, burning sky, the sun's metallic stare. That colonel. And the feeling that something dark was about to fall from the bright sky, and it

102

was not his dark past rearing up behind him this time to cast its shadow, but something as real and hard as that bright sun.

22

They were playing in the forest up on the ridge when they first heard the trucks.

They were running round the old ceiba tree up there, jumping over its huge hollow buttresses and drumming their feet against them to bring the monkeys. Eulalia said that was what the monkeys did to summon all the monkeys of the forest to a council. And when all the monkeys were gathered together, the leader would light a fire in the centre of the circle and they would all sit and talk.

'Monkeys don't light fires,' said Héctor.

Eulalia nodded solemnly. She didn't actually say anything because it was wrong to tell lies. But she nodded with great solemnity, since she had just imparted a profound secret to her little brother. Even though it was a lie, strictly speaking.

Héctor regarded her. She was such a *liar*.

That was when they heard the trucks.

They looked at each other.

'Wait, Yeto.'

But he was already off and running down the mountainside through the trees. He loved the sound of engines. One day when Papa was rich they were going to have a truck of their own.

'One day,' Papa used to say. 'When we strike oil in the maizefield.'

The noise of the truck engines got louder. They were coming up the road from Santo Domingo. Maybe it was a whole column of volunteers in their white jeeps coming with biscuits. Tall blue-eyed blancos, with red peeling noses like the bark of the tourist tree, and very scruffily dressed though they were rich.

She peered through the leaves. Where was Héctor? Dogs were barking up in the village. Billows of red dust along the road. Then she could see them. They weren't white jeeps full of biscuits, they were green trucks full of soldiers.

Héctor was standing down by the side of the road, saluting.

The soldiers in the open trucks wore wet handkerchiefs over their mouths and noses because of the dust, and had rifles propped up between their knees. At the head of the column of trucks was an open jeep with a white symbol on the door, and a driver wearing dark glasses, and in the passenger seat a handsome officer with gold braid on his shoulders. Behind them was another soldier sitting behind a machine gun that swivelled. That soldier watched Eulalia as she came down out of the forest but he didn't swivel his gun. She looked at the ground, pretending not to see him watching her.

'Aha, my good little soldier!' cried the handsome officer, seeing Héctor standing there saluting. He made the jeep stop, and all five or six trucks stopped behind him. Stopped, just to look at Yeto saluting!

He would be awful tonight. He would be *odious*.

'A whole column of soldiers stopped to salute me, Papa!' he would declare at the top of his voice, marching in and out of the cottage amongst the chickens.

Little idiot. Marching around rattling his empty plastic bottle on the end of a stick, his favourite toy. Eulalia stopped beside him and grasped his other hand firmly in hers. Héctor didn't even notice her there, his face shining up at the handsome officer.

The handsome officer gripped the top of the windscreen and stood up in the jeep. He smiled broadly and saluted him back with a tremendous sweep of his hand.

Héctor looked like he would burst.

The officer spoke the fine Spanish of the city. Eulalia

pictured him riding a fine white horse, and leading great parades through the plazas of the capital at the head of thousands of horsemen. Afterwards he would drink coffee with his friend the President and they would tell each other jokes.

The officer was saying, 'You will soon join the army, my brave!' His voice was strong and manly. 'Fight alongside us against the guerrillas and the insurgents!'

Héctor nodded happily.

Eulalia squeezed his hand hard, but he had already left the world of mothers and sisters for the world of men. She looked up properly at the officer now, shielding her eyes from the sun.

'Ah, and you have a beautiful sister too!'

Héctor nodded happily again, still saluting. Eulalia could have slapped him.

'Enchanted, *señorita*!'

Eulalia stared back.

One of the soldiers in the nearest truck said a badword.

The officer sat down again. 'Farewell, my little soldier! Farewell, my lovely *señorita*!'

The jeep and the trucks rolled off. The soldiers in the trucks looked down at them as they went past and said things amongst themselves and laughed. Héctor waved goodbye with his free hand.

'He was a colonel,' he said softly.

She held on to him until the column had vanished round the corner, then she let him go and carried on up the road in their wake. Héctor came trotting along behind, riding upon his snow-white charger, waving his gleaming sword high in the air and then sweeping it down through the swathes of his cowardly foes.

She was thirsty. But you could only drink from the stream above the village, not below it, or you had to go to the toilet for three days.

'Come *on* Yeto,' she said crossly over her shoulder.

'What?' he said. 'What?'

Little idiot.

He cantered after her, swinging his sword. She was just cross because she would never be a soldier like him because she was only a girl.

They came up the road and round the bend where the road grew very steep up to the church and could hear the truck engines just round the corner. Héctor started climbing over his favourite rocks there which meant you didn't have to go right round the bend in the road, though it took just as long and you often grazed your knees and got tiny stones stuck in the palm of your hand. When you brushed them off they left little white dents. Eulalia placed her hands on her hips and looked up at him climbing and sighed with exasperation, and then followed him up the rocks.

When they came over the top of the rocks they saw the trucks had slowed almost to a crawl up the steep slope beyond, their engines roaring.

'The soldiers will have to get out and push,' said Héctor.

As if he knows all about soldiers and trucks, thought Eulalia.

Then he said, 'Look!'

One of the soldiers was standing up in the back, wobbling slightly on the moving slope of the truckbed, and his comrades were cheering and shouting out.

'It's a guerrilla bird!'

'Shoot the badword!'

Then he raised his gun and there was a terrific bang and he had fired wildly into the heart of the forest beyond the church. Lots of birds rose up from the treetops crying and he raised his gun again to shoot them all.

'Guerrilla birds!'

Then the truck stopped suddenly and he gave a lurch, and his gun clattered to the metal floor of the truck. His comrades jeered.

A few moments later the colonel came striding round the back, his face dark and ferocious.

The children pressed themselves down into the dust behind the rock. They shouldn't be here now.

The waiting trucks creaked on the steep slope. The colonel ordered the soldier down. The soldier was pale as the colonel was dark. He fumbled coming down the little metal ladder at the back, trying to carry his gun.

'Leave your gun!' roared the colonel.

Eulalia was very afraid, she couldn't swallow, her mouth was full of dust. She didn't want to look, she kept looking. Héctor's eyes were as wide as an owl's.

The soldier came down the little ladder carefully until the colonel reached out and seized his shirtcollar and dragged him to the ground. The soldier reeled and stood. The colonel fixed him with his black eyes and undid his pistol holster. The soldier cowered. The colonel took out his pistol. Eulalia's heart was thumping the ground beneath her. Then the colonel turned the pistol round very quickly and lashed out and struck the soldier a terrific blow across the side of his head with the handle. The soldier never made a noise, just turned a bit and then collapsed into the dust. The colonel kept looking down at him, very briskly putting his pistol back in his holster and clipping it in again. Then he looked up and signalled to two more soldiers in the truck to pull their comrade back up the ladder. He turned smartly on his heels and marched back to his jeep.

The two soldiers pulled the fallen soldier up the ladder like a potato sack. Near the top the wounded man started to mumble something and roll his head around. Then his voice was drowned out by the big engines roaring up as the trucks once more began to climb the steep slope to the village.

The children waited terrified for a long time. Finally Eulalia whispered, 'I hope they go away soon.'

For some reason this made them both laugh. They got up and scrambled down to the road. Héctor pointed in the dust.

'Is that real blood?'

Eulalia looked. 'No.'

He stared a bit longer, then he looked away into the trees. 'Where did the bullet go?' And he started walking off into the forest. 'No, leave it, Yeto,' she said.

But he was in a trance. She followed him. They wandered dreamily around the edge of the forest, and then they found a dead bird.

'What a shot!' said Héctor. 'He must be a *marksman*.'

'A what?'

He squatted down beside the dead bird and picked it up with both hands.

It was a guardabarranca – a guardian of the ravine. It was one of the luckiest birds of all, Abuelita said. Its song protected the whole valley. A riot of colours, ruddy and blue and green with a fierce turquoise streak above the eyes, and an amazing tail. It was a beautiful singer, its song an excited trill, rising, getting faster and faster. It sang by streams and rivers, it loved water.

Its long slim tail feathers with their strange tips stuck out one side and its head hung limp over the other side of Héctor's hands, though its eyes still looked bright and alive. Eulalia wasn't sure the soldier had shot it. It might have died anyway, or been killed by a snake or something. She told him to lay it back down on the ground. It would melt away there, be eaten by the ants. And somewhere else in the forest, another guardabarranca would struggle up out of the mud and shake its wings and fly.

23

'The church bell is ringing,' she said.

'What?'

'Why are they ringing it now?'

'And why did they shoot it?' asked Héctor, puffing at her side, still worrying about the guardabarranca.

'Those soldiers would shoot anything,' said Eulalia. 'They would shoot a quetzal if they saw it.'

'But why?'

'I don't know, Yeto, stop asking me. Ask them, ask your friends the soldiers.'

Héctor stopped. 'Would they shoot Jesús?' He looked horrified at his own question.

Eulalia nodded.

Héctor looked torn. Wasn't Héctor the name of one of Jesús's disciples? It said in the Bible, he was Jesús's closest friend and most trusted soldier in their battles, he wept by far the loudest when Jesús died and he was the strongest too and always stood by him in his battles with the Romans in the Garden of Olives.

As they came near the village, a single truck passed them going back the other way. They looked after it, and through the billows of dust, Eulalia saw the village priest sitting in the back, between two soldiers. His long, solemn, bearded face.

He gave her her first communion, and she wore a white dress and carried a basket of white flowers and wore a wreath of jasmine on her head that was called a chaplet. Héctor hadn't had his first communion yet. She pictured him in a white dress, wearing a wreath of jasmine on his head, and laughed out loud.

Nicholas was coming down the road when the column of trucks went past him. He stared sourly and the soldiers stared back. Country boys, callused hands on their rifles, broad watchful Maya faces. Then in a stupid atavistic moment he gave a sarcastic Nazi salute. The trucks went on.

Yob. How was that going to help? He walked on, scorning himself, and then ahead a lean young man in glasses came out of a barn where he'd been sheltering. Avoiding the trucks. He addressed him abruptly.

'You work at the clinic?'

'I do.'

'Stay. Do not leave here. You cannot leave.'

'And you are?'

'I come from the city. Do not leave here.'

And then the young man turned and ran back down the road towards the houses.

Eulalia cried out, 'Dr Nicholas!' and ran to him.

He detached her from his legs and then led them both off the road. 'Let's go through the forest.'

'I want to see the soldiers again,' said Héctor.

'I'm tired,' said Lala. 'It's tiring walking through the forest. And thirsty.'

He pulled his water bottle from his cargo pocket and handed it to her. 'Come on. I want to show you something.'

'What?'

He had no idea. 'A secret.'

They followed a wide dirt road into the forest leading away north east. And then it topped out and started descending again, and Nicholas realized it was heading back down into the next valley. The children were complaining. He gave them the last of his water.

'We should find a Jesús Cane,' said Héctor.

'What's that?'

'A cane that grows in the forest that's full of water. You

111

can drink from it. Papa showed us.'

'Is everything in this country named after Jesús?'

Héctor looked at him woodenly. 'No.'

'Come on. This way.'

'Are you sure?'

Leading off left from the dirt road was a narrow singletrack footpath. Through the trees he could see that it curved gently back on them. It must return to the village. There was nowhere else for it to go. One of the old footpaths that mad moonstruck shaman used in his wanderings, like the paths he was discovering for himself round about. But this one was new to him. Either they took it, or they would have to turn around and retrace their steps. The children were tired but it wasn't that far, only half an hour, and he had a compass on his sports watch.

'Come on,' he said jovially.

They still looked doubtful.

'Trust me, I'm a doctor.'

They followed him down the narrow path, deeper into the forest, bare brown legs brushed by spear grass and ferns. He'd have them wash tonight. God knew what ticks and parasites clung to those delicate fronds.

Then the path divided. Logically if they kept taking the left-hand path, they couldn't go wrong.

The path grew more and more overgrown, and then disappeared altogether.

'Damn.'

Both children looked worried.

'Sorry children. Don't be afraid. I promise I'll make it up to you.'

'What is it?'

'I've made a stupid mistake. I think we'll have to go back and round.'

'What, all the way back to the road?'

'But that's *miles*!'

'Truly, sorry. But this path has disappeared. Look.'

And the sun only has a couple of hours left, he could have added but didn't.

'Come on, turn around and let's get going. I'll tell you a story.'

'What about?'

'About ... a gnu.'

'You're making it up.'

'That's the idea with a story.'

'What's a gnu?'

'Well. Deep in the heart of darkest Africa...' Then he stopped again. There was a large patch of sunlight over to the right, in the heart of the forest. A clearing. Maybe a remote cabin. Maybe a way through after all.

'Hang on, wait here. I just want to go and see –'

'No, don't leave us!' they wailed.

So they came with him, through undergrowth often over their heads.

It wasn't a clearing. It was a crash site. There was a long ploughed furrow through the trees, and then the remains of a white twin-prop plane at the far end, dug in right under the canopy.

'Stay here this time. I mean it. I'm just going over there. Don't move.'

'But you said you had a secret to show us!' they protested.

'Yes, but – I didn't mean this secret. There's another one, later on. Now just stay here.'

They stood waiting. So much had happened today already, and now this. A plane crash! Near their village!

Under the canopy a dark green tunnel had been driven through the undergrowth, eerie and strewn with white fragments, a tailboard with lettering on it, shreds of stuff. And then at the end there was the small white tube of the plane with its wings torn cut off as if by some giant. Surely someone must have

113

heard it?

He glanced upwards – in smashes at this speed, anything could have happened. He had seen car crash victims. But no, no bodies hanging from branches, backs snapped in half, leaves below them dripping.

Nearby a bird or a monkey hooted.

He came to the plane with breathing shallow, stepping silently, mind racing. The fuselage was tilted up on its nose, the windscreen smashed and bloodied, and several yards out in front, a dead man kneeling as if in prayer, his skull flattened.

He heard something behind him.

It was the two of them, staring in fascinated horror.

'I told you to *stay back*.'

'Is he dead?' said Héctor.

Lala suddenly burst into tears. Nicholas gave her a hug. 'It's OK, it's OK. It was an accident.'

'He's got a flat head,' said Héctor. 'And lots of ants on him. Are they eating him?'

'Shush. Now stay back. I mean it.'

He went over and checked the man, ludicrously. You'd have to be pretty comatose to let ants do that to you.

He came back to the wingless fuselage. Spilling out of its ruptured belly were grey plastic crates, and spilling out of one of them in turn were neat black plastic packets, about the size of bags of sugar. He knelt on one knee and tugged at one, but they were bound in thick industrial plastic. He hunted around and found a stick and stabbed it in. Pulled it free. White powder came dribbling from the hole.

'What's that?' said Héctor.

'Medicine,' he said.

Héctor looked doubtful. 'Should we take it back to the village?'

'Let's leave it for now, and come back another time. No one will know it's here.'

That much was true at least. An overhead spotter might see

the gouge through the forest, but it could be anything. The plane itself would be hard to find unless they had sent a last message or had gps tracking.

'What about the man?'

'He – he's not really here. Only his body. It'll be buried later. We'll tell someone. Come on, we've a long way to go.'

'Has he gone to heaven?'

'If he's been a good man. Now go on.'

Eulalia, still drying her eyes, said, 'I hope he has been a good man.'

'Me too. Tell me – seriously – have you seen a dead person before?'

They both nodded solemnly. He didn't ask any more. Perhaps a family member. This wasn't England, after all, and death wasn't hidden here, nor sterilized, nor denied its place at the table. Death was garnished and decorated, wept over and solemnly celebrated. The baby Clara with her hibiscus-rosy cheeks, lying among the candles ... And that meant maybe what the children had seen today wasn't as traumatic for them as it might have been. It was so hard to judge.

They began to retrace their steps. He wondered what would happen if the army ants found the medicine.

But it was the other lot who were after it. The soldiers and their dapper moustachioed colonel. Now he knew why they were here.

Somehow he would have to think of a way of making sure the children didn't tell anyone what they'd seen. A four year old and a six year old – keeping a secret.

Very quickly, as the children went on ahead, he snatched up one of the packets and slipped it in his bag. The children were silent and tired as they walked, and his mind raced.

He could go into Santo Domingo. Buy an ancient Toyota pick-up for three hundred dollars. Wait until darkness, drive back to the crash site. Headlights off, just use a torch, drive very slowly. Load up. It would take him no more than an hour or two. And then, and then... Hide the truck. A lock-up somewhere maybe. Go to Santa Cruz. Find a dealer on a street corner. Demand to meet his supplier. Demand to meet *his* supplier. There would surely be a 50% chance he would be killed along the way. Why should they pay him? Why not just take the drugs and kill him? Gangs like the Mara Salvatrucha killed people for looking at them. But if it worked – if he sold it on, and wasn't killed in the process – he might come back to the Valley of San Antonio de las Flores with, what, a hundred thousand dollars? Sold on the streets of LA or London, it must be worth five million. But still, a hundred thousand. And say, José, Maria, here: I have something for you. This is for you. All of it. To buy yourself a farm.

The thought burned into him. It was a fever dream and he dreamed it all the way back. It was dark by the time they arrived, they'd been walking for over two hours and the children were exhausted. They came along the dirt road, and then along the track, that broad rust-red track, potholed as if recently bombed, and across a wild meadow. A single paraffin lantern shone through the dusk from the window of a whitewashed cottage half hidden behind banana leaves, and he thought I can't. It would be pollution.

24

It was while they were in the forest that the trucks had pulled up in the village square. The soldiers dismounted and orders were sent for the church bell to be rung, and for everyone in the nearby houses and fields to assemble in the square. José came very slowly, furious. Mama hurried the boys.

'What are they going to do to us?' asked Jaime.

'Nothing my pet, they will just want to address us.'

Alejandro suggested they should run and hide in the forest, but Mama said it would be all right. They had done nothing wrong.

They waited under the burning sun. The soldiers lined up with their guns and the colonel stood very still in front of them, waiting for the people to stand orderly and silent. Pedro Xom stood at the front of the people, looking down. He was praying, his fingertips lightly on the silver crucifix round his neck. He remembered how it was thirty years ago well enough. The sky was very blue and there was no wind and the sweat trickled down. Then the colonel suddenly shouted, right in Pedro Xom's face,

'Look at me! Look me in the face like a man!'

It was terrible to shout right in the face of a man. Pedro Xom was one of the oldest and wisest men in the valley, he would never look directly at you, it was not the people's way. It was wrong to look into someone else's eyes and soul. Only an idiot bared his soul to the world. You might as well leave your seedcorn out in the rain.

But now Pedro Xom raised his head as commanded and returned the colonel look for look. He knew how to meet with *Ladinos*.

The colonel stepped back and turned, and holding a short black stick behind him, he began to stride back and forth before the people, like a general reviewing his troops.

He stopped, and raised his head, and jutted out his manly jaw.

'People of Chilitenango, you have been infected by traitors and rebels. You and all the native people of this department. Treachery and rebellion flourish in these valleys like poisonous weeds. In a land that should be sanctified by Law and Liberty.

'You who live here in this lovely valley, the Valley of St Anthony of the Flowers, blessed in every conceivable way by the merciful Hand of God – there have spread among you ideas of sedition and subversion!

'That this country is still owned and run by the Fourteen Families – a ridiculous error! As if we were still living in colonial times, and governed from Old Spain! Or that our President, the Father of our beloved country, is no more than a thief and a bully. And that the ruling class are all thieves and bullies, swindlers and fraudsters, and you will always be poor unless you demand more power for yourselves. Do you truly believe this nonsense?'

They said nothing. Shuffled, looked at the ground. He spoke to them as if they were children. And yet he spoke very finely, with the unmistakable note of a man born to command. Then suddenly his voice became gentle.

'You do not understand. You are fine, strong people, but yours is not the business of government. Yours is to till the earth, and to raise your families, to reverence God, and to obey the law of the land. And reject this spirit of restlessness and hatred.'

At this, a few of the bolder men murmured in soft protest. But the colonel nodded his head.

'Yes, I say!'

And he dashed his black stick splendidly to the ground.

'Have you not heard that the Lord Jesus commanded

obedience to Caesar, to worldly powers? Do you even understand such complex matters? No, you do not. But remember that your President, the Father of our country, watches over you like a great eagle. His eyes see all, and he defends his beloved people, and we live safe and secure under the shadow of his mighty wings.'

Some of the men stood straighter at these magnificent words, and set their shoulders back and raised their chins. Old Jorge looked sidelong and tried to catch José's eye, but could not. Old Jorge had a strong desire to pee, and a stronger desire still to pee on the colonel's gleaming boots.

'Yes, like a mighty eagle he flies over the mountains and forests of our land,' said the colonel, swiftly retrieving his stick from the dust where he had so manfully dashed it, and striding back and forth. 'He sees all and understands all – El Padre, El Jefe, El General, call him what you will. We, you and I, we are all humble people in his shadow.

'Ludicrous learning and foolish notions from foreign lands, of such things as *self-determination*, and *distributism*, and *globalization* ... These ideas will do you – will do *us* – no good at all. Do you even understand these words?'

He pointed his stick at one old man who was grinning lop-sidedly.

'You, old man, is it *self-determination* that you dream of each night? Or a storeroom full of maize and a pretty young wife?'

The man smiled his lopsided smile and said nothing, and some of the people laughed.

'Now listen to me,' said the colonel. 'All the valleys round about, all of this department and the next, are seething with bandits and guerrillas. They call themselves freedom fighters, liberators of the people, but they are no more than drug smugglers and cut-throats. All they seek is women and dollars. They have no noble dream for this country. They are the scum of the earth. I could show you photographs of the things they have done, to villages like this ... Photographs of women, children … But for your peace of mind I will not.'

Jaime gripped Maria's hand and looked up at her, but Maria looked straight ahead.

'I will not show you these photographs. They would haunt your dreams and become your nightmares for the rest of your lives. But remember, we who bear the burden of government upon our shoulders, we have seen these photographs, nay, we have seen such things in reality. And we must bear upon our shoulders and in our hearts the great weight of sorrow that these atrocities bring us. Now do you understand? The great responsibility that we take upon ourselves, the great weight that the Father of our Country bears, for your sakes, and for the sake of Law and Liberty? Understand only this, and then give thanks to God that you live in a country so benevolently governed and so fiercely protected against such evildoers. Then return to your little fields, and your work, and the love and comfort of your families.'

The people shuffled, and some nodded.

'And leave us, the armed forces, to defend you against these scavengers and wolves. For make no mistake' – he raised his arms now, his voice grew louder – 'we will fight and we will die to protect you, and perish if need be beneath the sacred ensign of liberty! Then my bones and those of my heroic men shall find their only sepulchre in the earth of our beloved country, while our spirits proud and free shall soar aloft!'

At these ringing words, many of the people gave a great cheer and threw their hats in the air.

The colonel now held his arms wide, benevolently, like a priest at the end of the mass, giving his final blessing. The people fell quiet again.

'Be content, good people, here in your beautiful Valley of the Flowers. And any knowledge that you may have of seditionists, communists and *narcotraficantes*, you must be sure to communicate it to us in future. Trust us, and co-operate with us, and all will go well with you. We are your great

120

protectors.'

He nodded once more, looking keenly over them all.

There was a profound silence as his words hung in the air. And then one thin, quavering voice said,

'I have just one question for you, Sir.'

It was Abuelita, very small and ancient in her black woollen shawl.

The colonel jutted his chin at her. 'Speak, woman. You need have no fear.'

'I have no fear. My question is: Who will protect us from you?'

There was silence in the square, and then the colonel said, 'You clearly have no idea what you are saying.'

'No, I have a very good idea. I have lived a long time.'

'Your wits are gone. Have a care.'

But Grandma's voice only grew louder, so all the people could hear.

'Why should I care? Look at me! I am old woman. I care only for my family and my blood.'

The colonel turned his back on her as if she no longer existed and stood before the people again.

'Remember what I say, good people. For we cannot turn a blind eye to cut-throats and law-breakers for ever.'

After the visit of the soldiers and the strange speech of the colonel, the people went back to their homes, darkness climbing swiftly up over the eastern mountains and over the valley. Women laid more wood on the hearthfires that had burned low all day so that they blazed up warmly again and gave comfort. But winter was coming to an end, and the wood they had dried and stored was running low.

25

When Nicholas and Eulalia and Héctor came back up the track to the cottage in the darkness, they found José and the boys and some other men gathered around a fire in the brazier, drinking coffee and talking about the day.

There was Uncle Uberto among them, José's brother, and wily Old Jorge. Now they beckoned Nicholas to join them, and Mama told the protesting younger children they must go to bed. They looked exhausted from the long walk but they begged to stay up a few minutes more and Mama relented.

They sat on the worn cottage step, Eulalia and Nicholas and Héctor, a pyramid silhouetted against the light of the kerosene lamp in the kitchen. Moths flew about and the night was alive with bats and beetles. The scent of nightflowers descended around them in a veil, sweet forest jasmine and the clove-like scent of the raintrees.

Things rustled and called in the dark treetops, and the men were talking about the colonel's speech.

Eulalia nudged Nicholas. 'You still haven't told us the secret.'

'What?'

'In the forest. You said you were going to show us a secret, but then we came to the crashed aeroplane and you said *that* wasn't the secret, and you still had another one to show us.'

He smiled at her dogged childish determination. 'Well, the secret is...'

He racked his brains. He was very tired, almost as much as the children. And they had witnessed something terrible today, even if it wasn't their first dead body. What was worse, he didn't think he could tell José and Maria about it, because he felt instinctively that it would be dangerous for them to know about the plane.

Then again, young children were unlikely to keep quiet about things. It was so hard to know. He would sleep on it.

'*Tell* me,' said Eulalia, bumping her head against his arm with impatience.

'OK. The secret is.' He swiped his hair back out of his eyes. 'Not everything matters as much as you think.'

He knew as soon as he'd said it that it was a pathetic idea of a secret for a six year old. Eulalia looked up at him with a look of such button-nosed scorn that he pulled a comically apologetic face. She didn't laugh.

And then she said very solemnly,

'Well I think *everything matters.*'

Uncle Uberto was saying, 'That, that colonel though, he spoke very well.'

'A very fancy speaker indeed,' said Papa.

Eulalia knew from the way her father said this that he didn't mean exactly what he said and she grinned at him. He saw her then, and winked back. Jaime, her oldest brother, scowled at her. This was men's talk.

'You should be in bed,' he said, trying to sound gruff. Jaime was eight.

Uncle Uberto said, 'A splendid, a splendid speech.'

Uncle Uberto always said the first word or two of every sentence twice. Mama said it was to give his brain time to catch up with his tongue.

Uncle Uberto had a round kindly face and round eyes. He had never found himself a wife, being too timid to take on that tremendous burden, nor had children, which was a shame and a disgrace. Mama said that was just because he was bone idle, and preferred to sleep in long after sunrise, and in the evening eat other people's food and drink their coffee, rather than go to the effort of bringing children into the world.

Uncle Uberto said he had never heard such a speech, and

it had given him food for thought. Was it all true? About those terrible atrocities? Yet the colonel was no fool, certainly.

'But then,' said Old Jorge with his almost toothless smile, 'neither are we.'

When he was younger Old Jorge ran the mule train down to the Pacific coast, where it was always hot and steamy and they grew prawns for the Chinese. Eulalia pictured a mule train as a train full of mules, all looking out of the windows, some wearing sunhats. Old Jorge's full name was Jorge Rodriguez MacLellan, owing to one of his grandfathers being from a country called Scotland a long time ago. He was old but very thin like most of the men in the village, for smoking numerous little corn-husk cigarettes all day long kept him in excellent trim. He used to walk twenty miles in six or seven hours over the harsh mountains to the coast, sometimes more, trotting alongside his mules with little padding steps in his sandals made out of old car tyres, chewing dark tobacco mixed with lime juice.

It was a grave conversation. Some of the men said that it was the army itself that committed such atrocities, disguised as guerrillas. Others said that they were no true guerrillas, just criminals, sometimes disguising themselves as the army, and some said that both the army and the guerrillas made their money and bought their weapons by transporting cocaine and kidnapped girls for the Mexicans, and there was nothing to choose between two evils. Was it not well-known that the army had committed many atrocities before, and indeed, during the Disappearances a generation ago, had slaughtered whole villages in the southern parts of the country?

Somehow they must try and find out the truth.

'It, it is important to keep up with the way the world is going,' said Uncle Uberto.

'On the contrary,' said José, blowing out a thin stream of smoke, 'it is important *not* to keep up with the way the world is going.'

'And was that it?' asked Nicholas quietly. 'The speech,

they arrested the priest, and then went? Nothing more?'

José raised his forefinger. 'After the speech, they gave us instructions about obtaining land licences from the city, from the national land registry. At the cost of two hundred dollars per time. And then we who had remained silent became very angry, because we saw this was a trick, because some of us would struggle even to find two hundred dollars, and so lose our land. Some began to argue furiously with the colonel, until eventually they were threatened with arrest. The colonel said they would be put in the trucks and taken away to the city.'

At last Nicholas said, 'What will you do?'

Another man said, 'They will come back sooner or later. And the People must be ready to fight, whether you want to or not.'

José snorted. 'Don't be ridiculous. We are not soldiers. We have no guns. And we have done no wrong.'

The younger man said angrily, 'There is not one honest man in our country's government, or army, or police force! And they always want more and more. Greed is never satisfied. I think the land licences are just some ploy. I think they want this valley for themselves.'

'This valley is our valley!' said Uncle Uberto. 'We have been here since before history was written.'

'And we will get our land licences, as the colonel instructed,' said José. 'Somehow we will find the money for them. And then we will be secure.'

'That's a fool's dream,' said the younger man, his voice sharp. 'You could say the departments of Gracias a Dios, the jungles of Mosquitia, belong to the Indian tribes who have lived there since before history was written. But if you go out on the road east to Olancho, coming the other way you see nothing but truck after truck bringing out mahogany, teak, rosewood. They are selling the jungle itself! Selling it off to the Chinese bit by bit, like all the rest of our country. Mountain by mountain and forest by forest. In return the Chinese build a few roads, a few bridges, and then go and leave us with nothing. Not a tree standing. Just a land of starvation and dust.

'How can the few thousand Indians of Mosquitia, some of them who still carry bows and arrows, defend themselves against the power of China? Meanwhile our own rulers, having razed every forest and worked out every mine, will have gone to live in Miami or Los Angeles. Where none of us will be allowed to follow after, remember, because we are *illegals*!'

There was a grave silence and then Old Jorge said, 'You are passionate and young, and you speak well and have many answers.'

'You are mocking me,' said the younger man.

Old Jorge inclined his head.

'But in this and neighbouring departments, whole villages are on the move, hiding in the mountains, cold, frightened and hungry. They have heard of massacres. I don't know if these massacres are real or made up, to frighten people, or who is supposed to have committed them. And nor do you.' He gulped back his coffee and emptied the dregs on the ground and set it down. He said, 'For five hundred years we have been an oppressed and humiliated people.'

José said sharply, 'For five hundred years, we have worked these fields and valleys in peace.' He looked down and rubbed his palms on his jeans and said more quietly, 'No doubt much like before the Spanish came, under the old Kings. I don't believe the ancient Kings and the Lords of the Maya cared so much about our happiness either. We were always just peasants to them. It is Mother Corn who feeds us, not the government, nor was it the ancient Kings before that, nor will it ever be some bloody revolution. Let us be, young one. We have troubles and dangers enough.'

The group was silent a while. José Silvestre Chacach was no fool. Then he said,

'Nicholas, our guest from England. You are more educated than we are. What do you say?'

The other men waited politely. He was the young doctor who had tried to save the baby of Miguel Paíz and his girl Yolanda. He sat there now peacefully on the cottage doorstep with two sleeping children.

He wondered whether to tell them about the plane crash. There was money. But he still thought it would be poison to them, somehow. He said,

'I am more educated in medicine, that's all. The rest is very complicated. It is not for me to say. But it's probably safer if there are foreigners around, who might report back to their countries. It's just possible our being here, the volunteer doctors, may be of help. But...' He shrugged, feeling so helpless. 'I don't know. Has anyone spoken to Dr Hércules Menendez?'

'A bit late now,' said Old Jorge.

'What?'

Old Jorge looked surprised he didn't know. 'Dr Hércules was taken to hospital this afternoon. In the town.'

'In Santo Domingo?'

'I believe.'

'What was the matter with him?'

'I don't know. I heard this from my friend.'

Nicholas looked at his watch. It was only just after eight p.m. now. Lucy was supposed to have been working this afternoon.

He stood up and went over to his rucksack and found his wind-up torch and checked it. The night was bright so far but it might cloud over.

'Where are you going?' asked José.

'I want to go down to ask the other volunteer about Dr Hércules. She's in the village.'

'You can't go at night.'

He shook his head. 'I'll be fine, don't worry. I won't be long.'

'It's half an hour into the village.'

He grinned. 'Quicker if you run.'

He ran and then jogged all the way. He passed no one. It was only a mile or so and he was there in ten minutes, drenched in sweat. He knocked on the door and the mother came and then Lucy, sleepy already.

'Nicholas. You look hot.'

'So what's happened to Dr Hércules?'

'Hm? Nothing. What are you on about?'

'Weren't you working this afternoon?'

She was waking up now. 'No, he sent me home. What is it?'

'How come he sent you home?'

'He kept looking at his watch, and then about two he said he was expecting a visitor and he'd rather see him on his own, and I could have the afternoon off. I sat and read all afternoon back here and got sunburnt, *duh*, and went to bed early with a rehydration tab. Sorry ... what?'

Nicholas pulled up his t shirt to swab his face. 'I just heard he was taken to hospital this afternoon. In town.'

'Shit. Why?'

'They didn't know. That was all they heard.'

'God.'

They stood awkwardly for a while and then she asked if he wanted to come in.

'I'm all right. Some of the men are up at the house having coffee and stuff. It's pretty interesting.'

'It's getting wobbly though isn't it? Being here?'

This country is built on volcanoes.

'I think it is a bit,' he said. 'We may not be here much longer. OK, I'll go into town tomorrow and find the hospital. We may be panicking about nothing.'

'I'll come with you. Call on me tomorrow. Shit. You're quite worried, aren't you?'

'I am a bit.'

'It'll be OK. Call on me tomorrow.'

'OK I will.'

'You're going to walk back in the dark?'

128

'I'm going to run!'

She laughed. 'Mind the armadillos.'

'Yup. Incidentally, did you know that the only other place that the leprosy bacterium, *mycobacterium leprae,* can colonize apart from the human body, is the foot-pad of an armadillo?'

'Delightful. I'll bear it in mind. Here, have some water.'

He took her bottle. 'Just a swig.'

'And do be careful.'

He gulped. 'Cheers.'

The men were so impressed that he had been to the village and back in that time that they slapped him on the back and said he was an *hombre* and called for more coffee.

'I think perhaps we should have some *chicha*,' said Uncle Uberto thoughtfully. 'It's been a troublesome day.'

Maria called from the kitchen, her hearing as sharp as a needle. 'No *chicha*! You have to work tomorrow!'

José grinned. 'Go and get a jug of *chicha*, brother. It will do us all good.'

Old Jorge said, '*Inglés*, what news did you hear?'

'Nothing else. We'll try and find out more tomorrow.'

'You be careful.'

'We will be.'

26

S oon Uncle Uberto came bustling back from his cottage, his dainty feet moving rapidly along the track, a glass jar of *chicha* clutched to his chest.

The secret of Uncle Uberto's *chicha* was in the filtering. A while back, some caring gringos had brought up a whole load of fine-meshed mosquito nets for the village. The people said thank you courteously, waved them goodbye and bundled up the mosquito nets again and took them back down to Santo Domingo to sell on market day for fishing nets or wedding veils. They even managed to sell one or two back to some gringo backpackers.

But Uncle Uberto had an unusually clever idea with his mosquito net. He unfurled it and held it up to the sky and examined its fine mesh and said,

'You know, this would make a perfect filter for my *chicha.*'

Uncle Uberto made the finest *chicha* for miles around. He used only the best *maiz blanco* which he ground in a stone mortar, and then soaked in *aguamiel*, honey-water, made from molasses. He allowed the sweet, soupy mixture to ferment in a small wooden barrel for a fortnight, and then boiled it down to a dough called *masato*, which he shaped with his soft, plump, doughy hands, and then placed in an even richer *aguamiel* to ferment for a further fortnight. Towards the end of this fortnight he added various secret ingredients, rumoured to include pepper, lime, bone dust, slivers of cow hide, pinches of rich black earth, and the parts of certain small animals. The end product was the very finest *chicha, chicha flor*, a liquor utterly different from the commoner *chicha de mitaca,* which any fool could make, and infinitely far above the weak maize beer, *runchera*, brewed by those without patience or craft.

Officially the making of homemade *chicha* had been banned by the government many years ago, but that law was made down in the capital, and had not yet had time to reach the Valley of San Antonio de las Flores.

Nicholas said he didn't really drink.

'But you must,' said José. 'It has been a long day, and my brother is the finest *chichero* in the valley.'

So they drank. And then Nicholas learned about the filtering process.

'You filtered it through ... mosquito nets?'

'A stroke, a stroke of *ge-ni-us*,' said Uncle Uberto happily.

'You know they're impregnated with permethrin?'

'Drink! Drink!'

He made himself take another sip. Perhaps he could learn to appreciate the distinctive chemical aftertang.

After a while they began to talk more loudly, and then they began to sing.

Then they saw Pedro Salazar Xom, the village elder or *atzj'ib*, standing silently in the outer darkness beyond the fire. Papa raised his hat and they said '*Adios.*'

'I want to speak to the girl,' he said abruptly. 'Where is the girl?'

Why on earth should he want to speak to Eulalia?

He saw her lying there asleep on the doorstep of the cottage, and stooped down stiffly, one hand on his knee, and shook her roughly awake. 'Is it true that you saw the soldiers this afternoon shoot a guardabarranca?'

How on earth could he know that? She felt foggy with sleep. 'It wasn't us,' she stammered, 'it was the soldiers.'

Pedro Xom stared at her so hard it was like he was looking right inside her.

'You saw them do this?' said Pedro Xom. 'You saw them

shoot it?'

'I, I ... Héctor picked it up. It was so pretty.' She could feel herself beginning to cry. 'It wasn't me, it was the soldiers. The colonel hit him. I –'

'Enough,' said José abruptly, draining his glass. 'Pedro Xom, leave her be. Go to bed, daughter. Father Pedro, what is this about?'

Pedro Xom ignored him, still looking down at Eulalia. 'Where was this?'

She was very tired and confused. Pedro's old hand was like a claw on her thin shoulder. It wasn't her fault. 'Back there. Just down the road, below the church. A soldier fired his gun and the birds all flew up from the forest and the colonel went and hit this soldier and then we found the guardabarranca dead in the grass.'

'Why did you not say?'

Guilt bore down on her like a black cloud. Her brain was full of humming, she didn't even understand the question.

'Speak, *señor*,' said José sharply. 'What is it?'

'I have misread the day,' said Pedro Xom. 'I have misunderstood.'

There was a long and anxious silence. Mama reappeared from inside and stood silently too. Something terrible had happened, or was about to happen.

'It is time you were in bed my children,' she said.

'Have you heard guns?' said Pedro Xom. 'In the forest?'

'I have,' said Jaime.

'Hunters,' said Papa.

Pedro Xom looked down at the ground before his feet. 'We must go,' he said softly. 'We must leave.'

'What do you mean?'

'All of us,' he said. 'We must go. We must leave. This valley is no longer safe. Death is coming.'

'We can't just go,' said another of the men. 'The maize is growing. The mountains are bitter at night. What do you mean?'

'Do not blame me for seeing,' said Pedro Xom. 'Blood will flow here.'

'That it will not,' snapped José. 'You heard the colonel. They mean us no harm. There was understanding. We are not to blame, we have done nothing wrong.'

'The birds of the forest are not to blame, the birds of the forest have done nothing wrong.'

'Then you go,' said José, and he was angry now and hot with *chicha*, and spoke disrespectfully. 'Off to the mountains with you, *viejo*, with your donkey and your pack. Some us have families and maizefields to think of.'

Pedro Xom said, 'A man cannot go alone. What is a man without his people? A dead tree.'

'Go where?' demanded Maria. 'Where? What is going on?'

'We are already earth, we are already dust,' said Pedro Xom, and their hearts froze inside them. Then he was turning away, gripping his stick very tightly and his purple lips hard and thin, making back to the heart of the village without another word.

They were stricken and silent. José rolled a cigarette and Uberto poured them all more *chicha*.

'The old fool,' muttered José.

A while later, Jaime picked Eulalia up and carried her inside. She was half asleep but she still knew it was Jaime. He rolled her under the blanket top-to-toe beside Héctor. Then he glanced back out of the door to see if the men were looking, but they weren't, so he bent down and scooped back her hair and kissed her on the forehead very quickly and she smiled in her half-sleep and then he went back outside to join the men.

But then she was awake again, her thoughts flooded with the events of the day. Pedro Xom had been angry with her, it was so unfair, and the priest had been taken away because he was a bad man. And he had taken her first communion only a few months ago.

She whimpered and Mama came and stroked her hair the way she loved.

'Hush, child.'

'But Pedro Xom was cross with me.'

'No he wasn't. He was cross with the world. You have done nothing wrong my pet. You are a good girl.'

'And they said the priest had been taken away because he was a *bad man*.'

'Hush. All men are bad men.'

'Even Papa?'

She smiled faintly. 'Even Papa. Though he is less bad than most men.' Her smile faded. 'All men are sinners. You know this. You have been taught this. It is why the Lord Jesus came. To save us from ourselves.'

It was very hard. Life was very difficult. Mama tucked her blanket in closer.

Héctor meanwhile slept as sound as a piglet the other way round under the blanket, his feet up behind Eulalia's back. There was a little gurgle in the back of his throat as he breathed. When he grew up that gurgle would grow bigger too, and he would snore like a great fat pig.

'Tell me a story.'

'Another night,' said Mama. 'You go to sleep now, *niña*.' And she sang,

> '*Dormite niñito, cabeza de ayote,*
> *Si no te dormis, te come el coyote,*
> *Arru, arruru ...*'

Sleep little one, pumpkin head,
If you don't sleep, the coyote will eat you,
Arru, arruru ...

Outside the men had fallen silent, and in the silence they could hear Maria singing over the child.

Eulalia dreamt of Héctor getting married to ugly Benedicta in a white dress, and of a humming bird and the bowl of the moon. Winter sunshine and cold nights, and in the morning the barefoot women in their lovely dresses going to fetch the water in clay jars. The dark wave of the mountains and the stars so near you could take them down and hold them in your hands like glow-worms. She rolled over … the warm blanket … Héctor's toes … the trees seeping honey … Babies flying through the air at night on tiny white wings, coming to the various homes in the village, spiralling down the chimney smoke and into the rooms and hearts of the sleeping family.

The men drank more *chicha*, but joylessly. Nicholas had seen enough joyless drinking to last a lifetime and, despite their pleading, went and untied his hammock and moved it further off and tied it again and climbed in.

He half slept and then awoke and could hear José singing on his own. Most of the men had left earlier, and then Uncle Uberto and Old Jorge, arm in arm for balance. José was very drunk. Nicholas leaned out of his hammock and saw him canted sideways on his upturned bucket, staring blearily into the dying fire. God he was drunk. Should he help him to bed?

He was singing that children's song.

Todos los negros toman café…

Nicholas slipped from his hammock and went over, but José was oblivious. Then in the doorway he saw Eulalia and Héctor.

'What are you two still doing up?' he whispered. '*Go to bed!*'

'But what about Papa?' said Eulalia anxiously.

He glanced back. José stood wavering and then went over to a tree and urinated, breathing stertorously, then came back clumsily zipping himself up.

'José?'

But he didn't react. Perhaps the *chicha* made you deaf as

well as blind. Or maybe it was the permethrin.

José stood swaying beside the watertrough. He gripped the edges very firmly as if afraid he might fall in. He gazed down at the reflection of the stars in the water, then he gazed up at the stars themselves, and began to sing again. Sometimes he stopped to burp.

'Dear oh dear,' said Héctor, peering out under Nicholas's arm and shaking his head. 'This isn't very good.'

Jose looked round and saw them and grinned. He raised his hand to them in salutation. 'My children!' he cried. 'My lovely lovely children! And Señor El Doctor Nicholas our most honoured guest from England. Have some *chicha*! I am accounted a wise man in this country round about.'

He cast his arm extravagantly wide and lurched and regained his balance and resumed.

'Then hear the wisdom of a wise man, to whom both past and future are as open books. Hear the wisdom of your father – *burp.*' He took a deep breath. 'He who is never foolish, is not so wise as he thinks.'

'Well I never,' said Héctor.

José staggered back and sat in the watertrough.

He muttered '*Puta*,' looking behind as if unsure what had happened. Then he looked back at them and beamed. 'All is well. For a moment I thought I had disgraced myself.'

Then Maria was beside Nicholas, arms folded, not saying anything. But they could hear exactly what she was thinking. Nicholas grinned apologetically. She ignored him.

José gazed lovingly at her. He sank a little lower in the trough.

'Ah, see, it is my beloved, the incomparable Maria de Los Flores! Is she not the most lovely, the most serene, the most soft-spoken and sweet-tempered –'

'José Silvestre Chacach,' she said.

Papa beamed.

'What example do you think you are setting your youngest children, by sitting there with your behind in the watertrough like a pig in the mud?'

'My beloved,' he said, and began to struggle weakly, slapping the surface of the water with the flat of his hands as if this would help him out again. 'My heart's desire, my angel, the loveliest flower in all the valley of San Antonio de las Flores – help me my angel, as did the Good Samaritan, and pull me up from the road where I so mournfully sit.'

'The man helped by the Good Samaritan was not drunk on *chicha*.'

'We are not told as much,' admitted José.

Maria had had enough. She marched briskly over, seized José under the armpits and hauled him to his feet. He stood there leaning against her at a slight angle, the seat of his trousers streaming with water.

His eyes swam with amorous intent. 'My beloved,' he murmured. 'My desired.'

'Dry yourself. Then go to bed.'

She marched back into the house. He sighed and looked ruefully at Nicholas and the children, his eyelids drooping, and then slopped after her into the house. They stood aside. He tried to lay his hands on his children's heads in benediction but missed, and then pretending he wasn't trying to anyway, raised one finger to his lips and said '*Ssshhh.*'

The children followed him inside. 'Why did he tell us to ssshhh?' whispered Eulalia indignantly. 'He was the one making all the noise.'

Nicholas went back to his hammock and stared at the dark and twinkling sky. A comic interlude indeed.

But what the hell were they going to do tomorrow?

27

Pedro Xom went up into the forest alone that night – that last night. His face still felt unclean from the hot blast of the colonel's angry breath, though he had washed in the stream. He went padding softly up through the pinewoods and the splashed moonlight with his woollen capixay over his shoulders. Sometimes he stopped and caught his breath and pushed back his straw hat on his head and looked up and felt the starlight on his face.

Then he padded on. He was going up to visit Pascal Abuaj deep in the forest, and say a prayer for the village, and burn copal incense, and throw a fresh handful of maize onto the sacred and perpetual fire.

Pedro Xom had heard priests say that reverence for Pascal Abuaj was a sin and a monstrosity, and even that the little black basalt idol of this supposed saint was nothing but the representation of a man's member. At which the women all bowed their heads in their bright pink headscarves, and crossed themselves, and nodded that it was indeed a sin and a monstrosity.

But then when the Day of Pascal Abuaj came around again, the women all went up there just the same, to where the little idol stood in his grove of ocote pines. They honoured him as before, throwing maize onto the perpetual fire that came out of a crack in the ground in front of him, putting a cigar in his mouth, garlanding him with orange blossom and hibiscus and *patas de gallo*. For they felt it was better to be safe than sorry. And as for him being no more than the representation of a man's member, well, they said amongst themselves later, hooting with laughter as they washed their clothes down by the river, it was a finer member than that of many a husband on a Saturday night.

When Pedro Xom arrived in the clearing, he laid some more branches on the perpetual fire, and took off his capixay and fanned the flames into life. They came up from Xib'alb'a, the underworld, full of strange power and comfort. On the branches of the trees all around the clearing hung fading bottle-gourd flowers, yellow for happiness, and purple bellflowers, the colour of heaven, and orchids red as blood, the colour of life.

He washed his face clean in the nearby stream, and his hands and feet, and he burned copal to the gods, for the Burning of Bad Moods, and to see what the sacred days would bring. The maize cracked and popped in the heat. He prayed by sunrise and sunset, by mountain and valley, by north and south and east and west, by the Blessed Virgin and the crucified Lord Jesus, the dying and rising god. He invoked all the ten thousand names of God, humming in a low tone.

> *'Heart of the earth, heart of the sky,*
> *Heart of the wind, heart of the rain,*
> *Heart of the mountain, heart of the valley,*
> *Heart of the frost and heart of the fire...'*

He prayed that God should watch over the valley and protect it in these darkening times. He bowed one last time to the little idol with the cigar in its mouth, decorated with flowers and surrounded by candles and tiny bottles of rum, and then he sat crosslegged beside the fire and pulled his capixay back over his head and drew it round him and bowed his head and slept.

28

The following morning Maria was up particularly early and made a lot of noise in the kitchen preparing breakfast. Nicholas got up and brushed his teeth with bottled water and splashed his face at the watertrough and dried it with his t shirt and brushed his hair. All he could think was, if Dr Hércules had really had a major cardiac, the clinic would be closed down and he would be certainly finished here.

Any morning might be his last morning. He would email his in-country co-ordinator and be posted to a main hospital, perhaps in the city. A medical elective was supposed to involve a hospital, for a greater range of patients and illnesses, injuries and treatments. It could not last here. It was never going to. What if he just stayed? What if he just dropped out? What if he took over the clinic himself and charged a small fee each time and became the village doctor? He walked restlessly about and found the deep sighs kept coming.

The children appeared sleepily one by one, and when Eulalia came trotting over and took his hand he pulled it gently away again because he could feel himself going.

José got up and sat quietly outside and drank coffee. He looked pale, and didn't go over the events of last night or shake his head and grin ruefully. It was not how he should have behaved. Not when troubles were coming. A man should keep his dignity. Drinking was cowardice, a great vice among his people.

He ate little, and then Maria said sharply that he should go to the city for that land licence. It would only take him two days. She would care for everything here, the children and the home and the fields. She said that Mekel the husband of Leticia and Luis the husband of Maria Alejandra Puac were both going. He should go down to Luis's house and ask. He nodded.

'I need to go down to Santo Domingo myself,' said Nicholas. 'To visit Dr Hércules Menendez in hospital, and to find out what we're supposed to do next.'

'Will they send another doctor?' asked Maria.

'I don't know,' he said, and he said it so sadly that she didn't ask him any more.

José's departure was like something very old, something medieval, the great departure from the village for the city with his satchel and his hat and his staff. Maria had made him a whole batch of tortillas, as if there would be no food worth eating beyond the valley. The children were very excited and begged him to bring them back presents. He shook his head. 'No presents. Your dear father's return will be your present!'

The children looked crestfallen. José smiled wryly.

It was all they could do to afford the licence. Nicholas had heard how much it was. But it was useless to try and offer them money, they would certainly refuse it.

In a box hidden in a hole in the back room was all their savings. Money in case one of the boys ever went to a university, a far-off dream, or one of them fell ill, much more likely, or for Abuelita's funeral, a certainty. Abuelita had said she wanted a lot of flowers. 'A *lot*. And damn the expense. I want the funeral of a Maya princess.'

José and Maria did not kiss or embrace or show any emotion but when he and Nicholas had gone, she went inside on her own for half an hour. She and José had hardly spent a night apart in eight years.

Nicholas walked with José in silence down to the village and then they parted company at Luis's door. He looked back and saw Luis appear and tip his hat to José and he could hear them saying *Ola* softly to each other. They both looked so small. Small backward country people. He hoped to God they would be all right in the city. He hoped it wasn't all coming to an end.

He went to find Lucy and Caitlin and then they waited for an hour at the aid station for Tumax to turn up.

Tumax looked even less pleased than usual to see them, shifty-eyed and irritable and with an added nervousness about him.

'Can you confirm that Dr Hércules is in the main hospital in Santo Domingo?' demanded Nicholas without greetings. 'And what was he taken in for?'

'I can tell you nothing.'

'What do you mean? You must know. This is the aid station for Christ's sake, it's your job to know.'

Caitlin held her arm out across him as if to stop him advancing and said to Tumax, 'Look, you are our direct source of information, can you really tell us nothing else? I mean, what are we supposed to do now? You must find out what the situation is.'

'I give you advice,' he said. 'You need to make contact yourself, you need to go into the town and use the email or the payphone there, ask your people, ask the co-ordinator. But I think they will say your time here is finished.' He nodded. 'It would be better to go back to England now, I think. Everything I have heard suggests it.'

'Have you talked to the soldiers, and that officer?'

Tumax shook his head and said nothing.

Nicholas felt a blind rage rising and stepped outside.

Nobody in this country knows anything.

It was all to be broken up. This sunlit dream. Nothing lasted, least of all something as gentle as this gentle village. So very unsuited to the stern realities of the twenty first century and the demands of the global economy.

The girls joined him outside. 'Come on,' said Caitlin. 'Let's go to town. I'll buy you a delicious sugary drink in a tin.'

29

José was already in a potato truck with Luis and Mekel. Mekel was an Indian name. When they got their land licences in the city he would write his name Miguel because they would not recognize Mekel as a name.

José leaned out of the back in case he vomited. That *chicha* was poison. Never again.

They got lifts in further potato trucks and pick-up trucks to save money, and then when they were stranded on the edge of some dusty town for two hours without getting a lift, they flagged down a bus and bought tickets from an unsmiling driver. Later they got a coach which would take them all the way to the city.

José drank a Coke and felt better and he also felt a mounting fear and excitement. *The City*. The coach was very cold though because of the air conditioning which they had turned up to maximum. What was the point of air conditioning if it just made you cold? He was glad Maria had made him pack his secondhand fleece jacket that she'd bought him on a market stall in the town and not an Indian capixay shawl because the *Ladinos* would have seen it and laughed at him for being primitive. The fleece said Budweiser on it. He had never had a Budweiser. He thought he would like one, but not now. Maybe later when he didn't feel so sick. Then he smiled sourly to himself. His life would probably be better if he didn't think his life would better if he had Budweiser to drink.

All coaches had a tv on board now set at maximum volume, and this one had a US news programme on it, and then the US president came on tv talking about their country! He was saying he wanted to bring Peace to Central America, and New Hope, and give the people a Road Map to

Democracy.

'Tell him we haven't even got any roads!' shouted someone at the back of the coach. People laughed grimly.

The President talked about a Task Force, and the man at the back shouted that the gringos only wanted our *puta* bananas anyhow. Why couldn't they just keep bombing the Mohammedans?

That man was going to get himself into trouble.

The driver switched channels and it was a film about a little boy who was poorly, but he began to get better again when he made friends with a mysterious talking bear.

José slept for a while.

The city was huge, horribly huge, and their excitement faded. They said Santa Cruz had five million people living in it now. Perhaps more. No one knew exactly. How was it that a great city made you feel small and dejected, but a great mountain made you feel small but exhilarated?

The city stretched for mile after mile of *favela* and *barrio* and tinroof shack, potholed roads, abandoned cars, broken bridges, garbage and rubble and countless dusty children staring at them from the roadside. Houses ruined and laid low by Huracán Mish fifteen or twenty years ago. In the mountains the hurricane had whipped the trees and flattened whole hillsides, but in the city and on the coast it had killed many thousands of people.

When the coach hissed to a halt in the bus station, a huge dirt yard, the three stood and shouldered their satchels and looked at each other and spontaneously shook hands. It was to say, let us stick together. Then we will be all right.

Mekel had written down the name and address of the building they must go to, the National Land Registry building, where they would be treated fairly and receive their just rights.

The bus station was very noisy and overwhelming and for a moment José wished he had listened to Old Jorge's cynicism and not bothered with the whole thing and stayed at home and just hoped they would be forgotten about. But he had rights, he was a man. He would go to the city and say to them, this is my land, here in my village of Chilitenango. This is my *milpa*. I wish to have a licence proving it is my land. It was the law. The law protected all men equally.

'Is that so?' Old Jorge had said.

'That is so,' said José. Old Jorge was an old lizard, with yellow eyes and a flickering tongue. 'We shall insist on it. If we insist on justice, this country will become a just country.'

Old Jorge had lived so long and seen so much, he believed in nothing any more. Life had hollowed all hope out of him, the way termites hollowed out an old tree.

The three men walked away from the bus station huddled close together, until a boy stood in front of them. Only a small boy, ten or eleven, with one eyelid down over his left eye and a scar above it like it had been cut by a knife and the muscles had not grown back. He was barefoot and filthy and wore jeans and a t shirt that said Hawaii on it and showed an island with a palm tree.

José had his money well hidden away in a plastic bag in a hidden pocket inside his jeans, but he had some coins in his back pocket and he gave the boy a coin.

'If you give money to every beggar you see, José,' said Mekel, 'you will have nothing left by the time we reach the National Land Registry.'

A taxi hooted at them and they stopped and stared. Then they realised it was offering them a lift. Meanwhile the taxi driver saw them more closely and drove off again.

'Bastards,' said Luis.

'Come on,' said José. 'We will not give our money to them. We will walk. City people say it is a long way, but it is probably nothing.'

They headed across the river and into the centre of the city and it was only about an hour and a half walking, nothing really. And there was the National Land Registry, a building as imposing as its name. There on the corner was the old Presidential palace. The new one was out on the edge of town with much more security. And nearby was the People's Parliament, with green lawns and fountains. It was splendid.

And there were queues. Immense queues of people snaking into the main entrance of the National Land Registry, shuffling forward with painful slowness.

'We will take turns,' said Mekel. 'One of us will hold the place in the queue, the others can go and sit in the shade if they want, or have a drink or something.'

'You want an American coffee!' José teased him.

Mekel grinned. 'I will bring you one back. We will not be long. There are lots of good coffee houses in the city.'

José stood perspiring in the queue and shuffled forward with the rest. He was very tired from last night, but that was his fault. No one made him drink so much *chicha*. The money in his inside pocket felt hot against his skin. But soon he would hold the licence. He would be a man of means. It would all be worth it.

Mekel and Luis came back and brought him his coffee in a styrofoam cup and it was so black and sweet and delicious. He inhaled it before he drank it. Then they said they were going to get some food. He said they could have one of his tortillas but they said they had seen a place that sold fried chicken, and they didn't come to the city very often. He said he was fine in the queue and they left him again, savouring his coffee.

He shuffled forwards.

There were many more people behind him now, which made him feel better. Close behind were two children staring at him and giggling and then they sang,

'A little Indio I saw,
Dancing down the street,
Laughing as he danced
On his two bare feet

147

Tell me Señor how you dance,
For I haven't got the art,
You do it just like I do,
Hand on your heart.'

The song was not an unkind song but it made him feel uncomfortable. And then the moment he felt uncomfortable, he realized to his dismay that he needed to pee. He looked around for Mekel and Luis but there was no sign of them. The queue shuffled forward. What could he do? Suddenly he needed to pee very much, and more because he knew he couldn't. He wondered about the man in front of him. He seemed a normal man, quite fat, placid, with a moustache.

He held on a few minutes longer, but it was torture and he could wait no more.

He said, 'Excuse me, *señor.*'

The man turned round.

'I need to leave the queue for a moment. Could you hold my place for me? I will only be a moment.'

'No problem.'

He went off into the parkland and found a way into a shrubbery and had a blissful pee and came back and found the man and tried to squeeze back in.

'Hey!' said the woman behind. 'Go to the back of the queue like everyone else.'

'But this is my place,' said José. 'I left it only a minute ago.'

The woman started shouting. He turned for help to the fat placid man in front. '*Señor*, please tell the lady. This was my place.'

The man glanced back and shrugged and said no more.

The woman closed up the gap and her friend with her. She folded her arms across her bosom.

'Please Madam, I only left my place for a minute. I have been waiting here for hours. It is wrong to keep me out now.'

'Then you should have thought of that shouldn't you?'

Everyone was staring at him now. He was covered in prickling sweat. He just wanted to melt away, to go home, back to the valley where he felt strong and respected. But that would be a failure. Indignantly he stepped forwards and tried to force his way into the queue. The women barged him out again, and someone just behind them said in a loud, hostile voice,

'See, they always cause trouble.'

'He's probably been for a shit in the gutter.'

Someone laughed.

Further off a man shouted 'Hey!'

José glanced up. It was a man in a black uniform like a policeman. José would be very polite.

'Stop causing trouble,' said the guard. 'What's your problem?'

José tried to explain but was drowned out by other voices, though he heard a girl saying that he should be allowed back in the queue. The security guard rested his hand on his holster and told him to go to the back of the queue. 'And don't cause any more trouble or I'll kick your ass.'

José's face flamed red as he walked back down the line, looking at the ground, his thoughts so disordered he could not think in words. He was angry, it was not good.

He came to back of the queue just as Luis and Mekel re-appeared. He told them what had happened.

'Bastards,' said Luis.

'It was not your fault,' said Mekel.

'Look,' said Luis, 'damn them, we will join the queue again. We will not be beaten. If we queue long enough, it will all be all right.'

José shook his head. 'No. I have had enough.'

They stared. 'What do you mean?'

'I am very angry. I will not obey them. I am going.' He started to wander off in a daze of shame and remorse.

'José, you are wrong!'

'I will not be humiliated.'

They pleaded and called to him, they said that the three of them must not be broken up, it was what they wanted. They must stay together. But he was deaf to them. He waved his hand once more, limply, hating himself for betraying them. That was the man he was today. He left them in the queue, staring after him. And then Mekel called after him, 'Go carefully, *compadre*.'

30

The four volunteers sat subdued on the bus into Santo Domingo, disappointed, anxious, irritable, close to relief all at once. They were leaving this country to its dark future. Bridge had never got to the coast and the turtles, he'd just counted and tagged a few iguanas, been eaten alive by mosquitoes, and come to rather hate the gloomy, sodden, relentlessly fecund forest. Caitlin never did find an orphanage to work at or get to practice child psychotherapy, just basic medical care at the clinic. And Lucy and Nicholas – what had they done really? Anything?

Dr Menendez had vanished, and Nicholas feared the worst. He had seen his first gunshot wound to a jaw. They had handed out some advice and worming medicine. They'd been to a baby's funeral they would never forget.

As soon as the bus came over the hill and down into Domingo, their mobile phones started beeping with incoming messages.

'Ah,' said Bridge. 'Oh. Shit.'

'What?' said Nicholas. 'I haven't got anything. *What*? C'mon.'

'Patience,' said Bridge.

Caitlin said, reading from her screen, 'Given the increasing uncertainty of the situation in your in-country following the death of the President-Elect...'

'*What*?' said Bridge.

'Has he been assassinated?' said Lucy, scanning her own screen.

'It doesn't say.'

'That's it,' said Bridge, 'I'm out of here.'

Caitlin went on. '... and following further advice from the

Foreign Office, it has been regretfully decided that you should blah blah blah.'

'What else? Just that?'

' … Flexible E-tickets can be collected at the airport on presentation of your passport and current return ticket … flight out to Houston, and connecting flight to London.'

'When? When do they want us to go?'

'As soon as. Tickets to be held for us, but … they want us to fly tomorrow.'

In Santo Domingo he headed for the internet cafe while the others wandered listlessly around the market. There they learned that the American Peace Corps volunteers had been pulled out only yesterday.

'Told you,' said Bridge. 'This is serious.'

'You gringos are all leaving, eh?' said the man who told them.

'Seems like it. Are things really that bad?'

'Here things are always that bad. But if the gringos leave it will get worse.'

'Was the President-Elect assassinated?'

The man hadn't even heard about that yet. When they told him, he just laughed and said he wished the whole government would be taken out.

They bought a few craft presents, miserably. A leather purse. A ball on a string that you caught in a brightly painted wooden eggcup. Bridge even bought an armadillo shell.

'Seriously?' said Caitlin.

He shrugged. 'Fuck it.'

The Indian women in their bright pink headscarves sat crosslegged on their rugs against the wall in the thin strip of shade and sold them their trinkets with a stony lack of expression. Faces from another geological epoch. Lines and wrinkles like petroglyphs. They would no more notice their going than the mountains.

Nicholas walked through the bead door of the Jesus Christ Is My Saviour Internet Café and said hello to the proprietor. The proprietor nodded and beamed. 'I bid you very nice day,' he said in English. 'Christ is coming.'

'Let's hope so,' said Nicholas.

He opened his email and messages flooded in. Mostly worthless. The same one as the others had had, summoning him home. And then one from his med school. He read it and read it again. The man at the counter was saying something more to him but he couldn't hear it.

He read,

'From the Director of Studies – Nicholas, would you please report immediately on your return to the admissions office, there appears to be some problem with your assessments which don't quite tally. I'm sure it can be sorted out, thanks, Sue.'

He sat back. The proprietor was talking. Offering a coffee. He shook his head.

He always knew it would come. A strange relief settled over him. Now he was here. He was fixed. A strange calm. He read the email once more and then got up and pushed his chair back and smiled at the proprietor and walked out into the street.

Finally, they went to the hospital. It was like something from the 1970s. They found what looked like the reception desk, though they couldn't be sure.

'Dr Menendez?' said the nurse.

'Dr Hércules Menendez. He was supposed to have been admitted yesterday. From Chilitenango. He sometimes worked up at the clinic there?'

She looked at her lists and shook her head. 'No. I know Dr Menendez a little, but I have not seen him. Was he sick?'

'Apparently.'

She shook her head. They walked out.

'He's probably been taken to the city,' said Lucy.

It was false comfort. She and Nicholas looked at each other. Perhaps the doctor was indestructible. But whatever had happened, they thought they would never see him again.

They went back to the village to their homestays and began to pack. There were more soldiers in the village, trucks, patrols. The volunteers would head for Santa Cruz tomorrow. There was one small consolation. A dance in the village that night.

31

José walked through the streets of the city guided by the slowly sinking sun, because the highlands and the village lay to west. But he didn't care, he wanted to be lost, and soon he was lost in an endless maze of dusty decrepit streets and single storey breezeblock houses painted half and half, covered in graffiti. Men stood around in gangs, youths, children played football. Cars went by with doors hanging off or with no windscreens, the drivers with handkerchiefs over their mouths and noses. There were flies. Vultures. Two dogs wrestling with a tattered hank of truck tyre.

He walked faster, his head thrumming, hot and desperately thirsty. But he would not buy a drink. Then in one narrow street, there was a black man in sunglasses and a tiny straw hat saying to him 'You want a piece a ass? I got the hottest for you my friend,' and then he saw black girls in doorways who were prostitutes. They were bigger than him! One put out her leg in front of him and it was very fat and shiny and her red shorts were very short and he could not help but look.

'Hey little man,' she said, 'I give you a ride if come with me.'

He walked out into the street to go round her leg and a battered truck tooted lazily and he walked on. But he felt his footsteps slowing despite himself.

Another *puta* up ahead was saying, 'Hey baby don't be shy, come inside with me, I'll be your *mamacita*.'

His head was humming. She had red ribbons in her frizzy hair. He stopped walking.

He went inside.

She enveloped him and put her hands around his back and clasped his bottom. Her breath smelt of marijuana and her breasts were immense. She kissed him and squeezed him like some plaything and said all sorts of obscenities and then she started to squeeze him there and unbuckle his belt. '*Qué papasote!*'

He pulled away from her and undressed himself and laid his jeans very neatly on the plastic chair, folded over twice so they made a square, and he felt the money in the hidden pocket safe and secure. Behind him he could hear the soft sounds of her undressing. When he turned round she was lying back on the bed naked apart from her bright red high heeled shoes, shining and naked, garish and triumphant.

He pulled his jeans back on hurriedly, his head bowed, his eyes on the floor. Circles and squares and stains of spilt beer. He felt he had no idea why he was sitting here. Was it really him? What had happened?

She teased him for being embarrassed. 'Why don't you love me? You want to get away from me? I am your honey. Stay and be my lover.'

He was the best she had ever had, he was a real man, she would love him as a girlfriend if he came again, she would do so many things, let him do so many things, they would do so many things *together…*

Even as he dressed he felt himself aroused again and how he despised himself. She hugged him and laughed and would not let him go, and for a terrible moment he thought she might actually be stronger than him, and keep him here imprisoned in a cage, raping him daily until he withered away completely.

He pulled away and said abruptly, 'Where's my hat?'

She put his hat back on his head and leaned under the brim and gave him a fat kiss.

He walked on for a while, tired and sated and thinking of a beer now, a *Budweiser,* then stopped and felt inside his jeans.

His money had gone.

Two hundred dollars.

God laughed at him, or the demon of the world. He felt in every pocket, and then every pocket again, not believing the money had gone. The bright sun sneered. He fell against the wall, fighting for breath, and the wall knocked his hat askew. What a stupid and ridiculous man, said the sun. Look at him and laugh at him. Look at him sweat, the small stupid man. Sweat and gasp for his stolen money.

He could not go back. Go back and demand his money! They would laugh at him or kill him. He had no money. He was a stupid peasant. He had no power and no money.

Two hundred dollars.

He went back.

The whore's door was locked. It was blue. He stood and stared at it dumbly. Pushed it again. It was locked. I AM LOCKED, the blue door said to him, but he was so stupid that it was as if he did not understand, with everything shouting in his head.

There was the negro with the little tiny straw hat. He was like a clown.

'I want my money back,' he said. 'Your *puta* stole my money.'

He shrugged. 'She's gone, man. She don't have your money.'

'I want my money back!' he yelled. 'Give me my money!'

The negro smiled and put his hands on his hips, drawing back his unbuttoned yellow shirt as he did so. Under his shirt he wore a white vest, and in his waistband was tucked a little gun.

'She don't have your money. We don't want any trouble and fighting now. This is a nice neighbourhood.' His voice was soft and purring and mocking. If a jaguar swallowed honey and spoke it would speak like that.

José was incoherent. 'I should be shot!' he screamed. 'Very well then, get your gun out, I should be shot! Give me my shitty money. I should be shot trying to get my money back. I should wrestle with you you thieving *tinto*, and I should be killed. That would be the right end of the story!'

The black man looked puzzled for moment, and then he stepped back and drew his gun and pointed it levelly at the screaming *Indio*, and pointed at him with his forefinger as well, strangely sighted along his gun arm.

'This is the just and rightful end of the story,' he said calmly. You walk away now. You don't call me anything more like a *tinto* or anything. You just walk away now. Go on. Walk.'

'Piss on you. Piss on you!' Yet he was already backing helplessly away.

'Go on now. There you go. And don't come back for a long time, little man.'

José walked away in an agony to be trapped inside himself.

Every morning his wife Maria, who had borne him five children, got up at sunrise and worked, and some mornings she got up even earlier and went into town and sold pots and eggs and potatoes and sometimes *huipiles*, cotton blouses which she had sewn herself with decorations of ribbons and lace. Sometimes the children had needed the eggs for breakfast but she had sold them for money so that if they were ill they could pay for good medicines.

And he had lost the money to a big black whore. He was more stupid than a dog, a pig. He was a pig, not a man. He was a grunting stinking pig in the stinking sweating bed of a big black whore. Grunting between her sweaty thighs like a rutting pig. His crotch smelt, his purse was empty, he had betrayed his family and all the people who loved him most. He was disgusting, he was filth, he was vermin, he deserved to be thrown off this broken-down bridge into the filthy brown river below, filth drowned in filth. He had taken the food out of his very children's mouths, his innocent children, his sweet children. It was better for a man to have a millstone tied around his neck and be drowned than cause harm to one of these.

He had wasted everything, all that precious time and labour of his beloved wife, all those days and months and years of hers that she had so laboriously turned into money, time that would never come to her again – he had thrown it all away for ten minutes of a black whore's papaya.

A man wanted to believe that he was good man, a wise man. And when he learned that he was not, it hurt more than anything else in the world.

He wandered slowly westwards. A wandering and forlorn outcast in his tattered canestraw hat, hoping to find the lost road to the west, the village hidden in the mountains and the sound of children's voices in the coming dark.

32

It was sundown and Nicholas was sitting outside the cottage on a log stump with his baseball cap in his hand like one of the humble. He had been here precisely two weeks now, and it was the last evening, the last time he would ever see the sun go down in the west over the mountains, leaving the Valley of San Antonio de las Flores to its long green shadows.

'I am sorry. It is the same for all of us. We are all being called home. They have booked our flights and everything.'

Maria didn't know what to say. The children didn't cry, they just stared. Eulalia stared most of all, from Nicholas to her mother back to Nicholas. Why was he going? Would he come back? When?

'If you are called back then you must go,' said Maria.

'It feels like running away.'

'Things will be all right here, I'm sure. I am sorry you cannot say goodbye to José.'

'Me too. More than I can say. But we are supposed to be gone tomorrow, if we can find flights. I'm just ... so sorry.'

Her heart went out to him. He had been almost at home here.

'Go to the dance,' she said. 'You go. It is like your farewell.'

He dressed in his clean jeans that she had washed for him. That she had beaten out by hand on the rocks by the river. No one would ever wash his jeans like that again, by hand, with such care. A buttoned shirt. He polished his boots as best he could with some dry grass. He was hollow. He could have stuffed his hollow skin with dry grass to stop it crumpling.

'You will come back soon?' demanded Eulalia.

'Yes.'

'When?'

'Soon.'

'*Very* soon.'

'Yes.'

'Will you come back with Papa?'

'Um. Maybe, yes. I hope so.'

'I miss Papa.'

'I know you do.'

She pulled his hand. 'In a few days.'

He didn't look at her. 'I expect so.'

'Promise.'

'I –'

'*Promise.*'

He looked at her. 'I promise,' he croaked.

When Maria reappeared from inside he said cheerfully, 'Come to the dance with me!'

He had misjudged. She looked genuinely shocked.

'Oh. Sorry. Is that not…?'

Jaime was laughing. His Mama go to a dance with the gringo!

Maria said, 'You would go to a dance with a married woman in your country?'

'Might do. If she was a friend.'

She shook her head. 'It is hard to understand. Here,' she said. 'Look. Your hair, at the back. Brush it.'

He patted it down.

'No!' she said. 'You will look so smart. Wait.'

And she went and got her brush and reached up and brushed it for him, quickly, firmly, motherly, so that afterwards his hair smelt of the flower oil that she wore. Jaime watched them.

'There,' she said. 'Now go on.'

He grinned and strode away.

Everything mattered on that last walk, that last evening. Everything. The whirr of insect wings and the smell of the cooling grass. The lizards' flicker. The smell of his hair that was also the smell of her hair.

The girls dressed up for it, Lucy in a blue dress, Caitlin in white, both distinctly shorter than the native style. They wore make up and flat shoes and each had an hibiscus in her hair. They looked pretty good. And Bridge got to wear his yellow corduroy suit.

Nicholas drank Coke. His life was in ruins and he would never be a doctor, *your assessments don't quite tally,* no they didn't. Maybe he could be a paramedic, or a pharmacist: last refuge of failed medical students.

At the dance there were the villagers and some of the soldiers and a captain who had a face like a fat little pig, eyes creased with inebriated bonhomie, chewing gum, dark moons of sweat beneath his arms. A band played local dances on guitars and shakers and a trumpet, every tune sounding exactly alike.

And then Colonel Maximo Inocencio himself, magnificent in his uniform and his medals, and somehow taking up as much space as three or four normal men. The village was honoured and the people received him with anxious courtesy. The soldiers were evidently determined to be at peace with the villagers, to quell any ill feeling, to help to pay for the drinks, to smile and be their friends. The villagers welcomed them warily. The soldiers danced with the young girls and the young men stood back and graciously allowed it. It was a good evening. There was no enmity.

Lucy and Caitlin danced with Bridge and Nicholas and then with the most handsome soldiers. They drank white rum and snapped away with their mobiles and dared each other to dance with the colonel.

'He is *so* handsome,' said Lucy.

Nicholas pulled a face.

'Jealousy jealousy!'

'No, I can see what you draws you to him. Check out those mirror shades.'

'I'm going to ask him for a dance.'

'Seriously?'

'Here I go. It's just made for Instagram.'

And so Lucy danced with the colonel.

Nicholas went out into the darkness and there were men smoking and he nodded to them. After a while he walked down the road and came to the locked clinic and crept round the back. It was very dark. After testing several places he crawled underneath and pushed at the boards above his head. They gave easily. He crawled up into the darkness and felt his way around by memory. He had already given his wind-up torch to the children, but eventually he found the kerosene lantern and the matches by touch alone and lit it with the thumbwheel turned down to its lowest. He crouched on the floor cradling it in his arms so the light wouldn't show through the window, and crept about the chair like some Boschian grotesque cradling a glowing egg.

On the right hand side of the chair was a broad dark bloodstain. Was that from the man who had been shot in the jaw?

He extinguished the lantern and replaced it along with the matches and felt in the medicine cupboard. Choosing only the packets, he held them up in the window one by one to what starlight there was, straining to read, and then pocketed one packet and replaced the rest. He slipped down through the hole in the floor and pulled the boards back after him and returned to the dance.

Now Caitlin was dancing with the colonel. And Bridge was dancing too, with furious enthusiasm. As he reeled from one side of the room to the other, fat clown in yellow corduroy flailing wildly, Nicholas wondered if he was going to get himself punched. But the villagers loved the loud careless gringo, he was quite without reserve, ridiculous, perspiring, like a fat child with his plump cheeks and curly hair. Some of the women wanted to take him home and feed him more.

Nicholas stood by with the stolen pills in his pocket, ready to spike the colonel's drink. But he could not. What did he know of him really? He could not betray himself by something so petty as giving a corrupt colonel the shits.

Without thinking much about it, he took a beer from the table. After that he had several more.

'Nick, you're drunk!' said Lucy at one point.

He felt himself grin stupidly.

'It suits you. You should drink a lot more.'

But he left the dance early.

He had spent half his life like this, walking home alone, wishing it were different and he could swim into the warm midstream and drown companionably with all the others. But once he got walking it began to get better. It was nice to be drunk for the first time in two years and walking home under the stars, feeling that anything was possible tomorrow. His thoughts were jumbled and verbose and he sometimes laughed out loud.

Maria sat alone on the bench by the cottage wall in her rose-patterned dress with a white shawl around her shoulders, but stood up as if embarrassed when he appeared. Why was she still awake? It was nearly eleven. Was she waiting up to make sure he came home safely?

He stood in front of her with his hands thrust into his jeans pockets and grinned.

'How much beer have you had?'

'None, I just drank Coke. Beer doesn't agree with me.' His grin felt goofy even to himself.

'You are such a liar. Why are all the men in my life drinkers?'

'Move up,' he said. 'Room for a little 'un.'

He sat down next to her on the bench and she immediately moved away to a respectable distance.

He moved up again. She moved along. Now she was at the end of the bench. He squeezed next to her.

'You are a drunken fool,' she scolded. 'I will go inside.'

'Please. Just sit. It is my last night. It is the last time I will sit here, on this bench, looking down this valley. The last time ever. Please sit with me a little.'

He was drunk and he sounded as if he was becoming melancholy and so she sat. They sat together in silence and then after a while he reached out and took her hand and she let him. They sat like that for a long time, watching the stars pass over. Eventually he said,

'Did you hear about the President-Elect? Apparently he's been killed.'

She hadn't heard. But she said, 'The situation in this country is very grave.' She said it so calmly. And then, 'When you go back to England, you will still be a student, yes? Not yet a doctor?'

'Not a doctor,' he said. 'Not yet.' His voice was muzzy.

'But it will be good to see your family and your friends.'

'Yes.'

'You have been very happy here.'

'Yes I have.'

'You should thank the Saviour that you have had a happy time here. You will always remember.' And then she pulled her hand free and stood. 'I am going to make you a coffee. Then I will go to sleep. You sleep out here.'

He nodded.

She looked back from the doorway and her lovely mouth was firm. 'I mean it. You stay here. In your hammock.'

'Yes of course.'

She went inside.

After a while he got up and went inside after her.

It was warm in the kitchen from the adobe oven and the water for the coffee was steaming. He went up behind her and put his arms around her waist. She gasped and put her hands on his arms and tried to push them down but he was too strong. She twisted and slapped him but he leant down and kissed her. She turned her mouth away. He let her go. She backed away glaring at him.

'You... you... How dare you!'

He went towards her again and put a hand on her neck beneath her hair and leaned down and kissed her. She pushed him away. She pointed at him as if he was the accused and she was the witness against him.

'Stop, now. You are being ridiculous. Hateful.'

He stared at her, mind in turmoil. He so wanted to stay here with her. With all of them. He didn't even understand what he was doing, and he felt ashamed at the same time as he so wanted to kiss her. Then she took two steps forward again, very deliberately, and struck him across the face as hard as she could. It was very hard.

He staggered backwards. There was a chair behind him and he slumped down into it, twisted at an awkward angle. The side of his face went from stunned to throbbing to very painful in a matter of seconds. His drunkenness left him and his mouth began to fill with blood.

'Get out,' she said quietly, holding her own hand in the other. 'My own children are asleep in this house. Go back to your hammock. You are leaving tomorrow.'

He went out and leaned across his hammock, everything spinning, feeling sick. His mouth was pouring with blood. He went over to the watertrough and sat on the edge and leaned and spat out blood on the ground again and again. He checked over his teeth with his tongue. The bloodflow began to ease. He pressed the back of his hand to his lip. It was fat and badly split.

He went back to his rucksack and groped inside for a dark coloured t shirt. He held it up to his mouth and pressed as hard as he could bear. After a while he went back to the trough and dipped the t shirt in and then tried to swab his mouth with it. Half his face throbbed. He pressed harder to make it hurt more. But worse was the thought of what he had done. What was he thinking? He didn't deserve to be a doctor. The assessments were right. He had the chemistry and biology but not the personality. He could be *volatile under pressure*. Well, he had once burned his own school down, though first he'd made sure no one was inside. Which was pretty considerate. And now for some reason he guessed his med school had run a criminal record check and found things in his past that made them nervous. Maybe that incident when he was in the young offenders, and was getting badly bullied for being middle class and had eventually over-reacted...

He was still sitting there when she came out and stood in front of him.

'Give that to me,' she said, and took the t shirt from him. 'You don't mind this getting bloodstained?'

He shook his head very slowly and carefully.

'Well, you know how blood stains well enough I suppose.' She wrung out the t shirt on the ground and then dipped it in the watertrough again. 'Lean your head back. Further.' Her voice was very neutral. She pressed the cold cotton to his mouth again. After a bit she said, with slightly more expression, 'I never knew I could hit like that.'

He felt so ashamed he couldn't speak. If she started being more light-hearted, or *forgiving,* he couldn't bear it. She should hate him.

She rinsed the t shirt one more time. 'Keep your head back,' she said, and swabbed his mouth again. He caught a glimpse of the back of her hand and two of her knuckles were grazed, and then he was overwhelmed.

She pressed the t shirt back in his hands. 'Here, wipe your eyes. Don't cry. Please don't. One day this will seem funny, maybe. Look at you. I hit you such a blow. The way you sat down suddenly –'

'Please don't think it's funny. It's not funny.'

'Ssh, not so loud. You'll wake the children. Look, tomorrow you are going. I am sorry for how you behaved. But we women know all about how men are. It does not surprise us.'

He almost wanted her to go away and leave him. But she went on.

'You have loved it very much here. I understand that. I don't know about your family in England but perhaps it is not so happy. I don't know, it is not my business. And you are drunk and confused. But you can't stay here. You understand that don't you?'

He sniffed a big ugly drunken sniff. He felt horribly young in front of her.

'So. Go back and sleep in your hammock now.'

He got up and went over to the hammock and she was already in the doorway of the cottage and she turned back and said quietly, 'Sleep well.'

33

In a daze José sat on a bus until they threw him off for having no money and they cursed him for a stupid *Indio*. He got a lift in a truck and then another one that was clearly dangerous. The driver babbled insanely about Jesus and a plot to kill him and how his car radio was listening to him and all the leaders of this country were Jews and devil-worshippers. But José didn't care. He sat blank faced and sunk in misery. Let the mad decide my course since God does not.

At last he was in the mountains, and somewhere near Graciosa, and it was near dark. He recognized the campanile of the church there and got out of the truck and walked away without another word. It was many miles back to Chilitenango over the mountains, and every step nearer home would only add to the pain of coming back to Maria and having her know what kind of man he was. If he lied it would not help him. 'I was mugged. Five strong robbers set about me. I could do nothing. I am sorry. They stole all my money.' It would not help. If he lied to her now, on top of everything else, he might despise himself so much it would kill him. Better have her despise him. He deserved it.

He would have to sleep out in the night but what did he care. He had no food and no water, not a drop, but what did he care. He was dirt. He walked and walked and eventually when it was too dark to walk and his vision was almost gone with the thunderous headache that made his brain feel it was on fire, he sat down crosslegged under a thorn tree in the darkness in the dust. He felt how it would feel when Maria embraced him upon his return, he felt her very arms around him, her beautiful dark hair against his stubble cheek, and he took off his hat and laid it in his lap and he bowed his head and wept.

The next day in a thirst and hunger dream he stepped into a clearing and there were men in the clearing loading barrels onto a truck. Miles from anywhere. A white truck with black lettering down the side that had been thinly covered over with white spray paint. They had a thickset dog with them. He removed his hat respectfully.

'*Adio'*.'

They nodded. There were several men, more than it needed. The barrels were heavy perhaps, like his own head. He was dizzy with hunger and thirst.

'Please, *señores*. I would appreciate some water.'

The dog regarded him but the men seemed to ignore him, to turn in upon themselves.

'I have not drunk water for too long. I am getting sick. I need water.'

His own voice sounded to him like the laboured whisper of a dying man dispensing his last wisdom.

'Please. Of your kindness, *señores*.' He limped towards them holding his canestraw hat towards them in supplication.

One of them turned. 'Come,' he said. 'Sit here on this barrel.'

He could have wept at their kindness. He was a fool. Hunger and thirst made a man's heart flutter at every breeze. He sat on the barrel and replaced his hat on his weary head. He realized his shoulders were slumped and he sat up straight.

Two other men continued loading barrels. One was entirely bald and wore a scuffed black leather waistcoat over his bare torso, and his thick fleshy arms were covered in tattoos, and he had a reddish drooping moustache. He saw José studying him and grinned and nodded. 'Out for a walk?'

'You could say.' He disliked being demanding, but he said softly again, 'Water?'

Another man he had not seen walked round behind him and there was no sign of a bottle of water for him, and then he felt with a certainty that it was as if he had wandered into the driest desert, a dangerous place, alone and far from home. The tall trees were bending over him, he felt their soft branches brushing his face, green leaves of forgiveness, Maria's beautiful dark hair forever against his unshaven stubble cheek he kept feeling, and behind him he heard a soft metallic click.

'Stand up,' said the man softly.

He stood.

'Turn around and walk away into the trees.'

He began to walk. For a moment he thought they were letting him go, and his heart leapt – but then he heard the man walking behind him, his jeans and his heavy boots scuffing through the speargrass.

'Please,' he said, 'please, my family... You do not have to.'

'Walk and do not speak. It is better that way.'

They entered the forest together, very close to each other, like old friends deep in quiet conversation, or as if in accordance to some unwritten but binding compact established long ago.

He could hear the thumps and scrapes as the other men carried on calmly loading barrels onto the truck.

'Kneel down,' said the man. 'Here. By this tree. And take your hat off.'

'Please,' said José. 'You do not have to. I have to go back to my wife and children.'

The man stepped near and flicked José's hat off and rapped his bare head sharply with the barrel of the gun.

'Don't fuck around. I said kneel.'

'I am no danger to you,' said José. 'I have no interest in you. I –'

Then simultaneously, it seemed, he heard his daughter's voice saying Papa, and the gun exploded in his ear, and he was running like crazy through the trees. Still not sure if he had

171

been shot or not, and *still annoyed that he had lost his hat*. He kept thinking about his hat as he ran, even after he could hear the other man crashing through the forest after him. He reached up and touched his head, half expecting to feel blood pouring from some terrible wound, but there wasn't anything. He didn't think he had been hit, but there wasn't time to make sure. Then the gun fired again and he heard a high-pitched whine and the whipping of leaves, and some birds squawked and flew off to his right.

At last, trembling with terror, he came skidding to the edge of ravine. One of these deep, dank, forbiddingly steep forest ravines crowded with strange ferns that could grow in its sunless depths, immense dripping fronds, overgrown and impenetrable. A natural dungeon, the sides nearly vertical and so sodden and crumbling you could never climb back out again. You could only follow it down and down, hoping for escape that way.

He turned to face his tormentor, gasping for breath, every limb shaking.

'Leave me alone!' he yelled. 'Just leave me alone!'

The man stopped only some ten yards from him and raised his gun and José could see his forefinger curl around the trigger and then there was a click. The gun had jammed or he was out of bullets.

'You little *shit*!' shouted the man, as if it was José's fault, and then he came running at him. José should have stepped aside but he froze and the man slowed and came up to him and planted his boot in the centre of José's chest and shoved angrily. José staggered back and fell over the edge of ravine and slithered down and down into its muddy depths. He lay there, blurrily aware that some forty or fifty feet above him, the man was still standing on the edge looking down at him. Then he realized the man was unhurriedly reloading his gun.

José tried to crawl but his arm and his leg hurt terribly. The man above took careful aim and fired his whole magazine down at José, and he felt at least two bullets go into him, thump thump. It was like being punched by very small hard fists.

He couldn't crawl so he rolled and a huge dripping fern covered him. He lay there in agony, panting like an animal in a trap. After a few moments he craned his head and peered out and there was no sign of the man. It was getting dark in the ravine and cold and he was slathered in mud and soaked through and sticky with his own blood. He rolled onto his front and groaned and dug his elbows into the soft mud of the ravine floor and began to drag himself forward. Along with the dense black smell of the earth beneath him and the sickly tang of his own blood he could also smell the pumpkin soup that Maria made. His right elbow struck a knotted tree root and hurt very much, so he waited a moment, and then he clamped his mouth closed and crawled onward.

34

Maria looked down at the ground and the children clustered around her and Eulalia and Héctor cried when he left in the morning. She felt very tired too. She had slept badly, dreaming that she was crawling through mud, being chased by some terrible beast, maybe a bull, maybe a monstrous dog. Something as black as a moonless night coming after her, and her crawling through mud up to her knees, up to her elbows, but so slowly, unable to escape.

'Is that why you've got a big bruise on your face?' Hector asked Nicholas. 'Because you're sad to be leaving?'

He couldn't speak, but ruffled the boy's hair briefly and Jaime called his kid brother a dummy. Eulalia hesitated, then ran and hugged him round his legs. 'Don't go too far away,' she said. 'You might need to come back again.'

Then he strode away without another word, half-choking with regret, and still stricken with shame almost beyond speech at how he had behaved last night.

Twenty minutes later he found the others by the side of the road waiting for the potato truck into Santo Domingo. He pulled the damp t shirt from his rucksack one last time and mopped his face and tried to calm himself.

Caitlin said, 'Blimey, what happened to you?'

He told some glib tale about tripping and falling in the road on his way home. 'And I've got *such* a red-eye hangover.'

She looked at him quizzically, and then he started asking about the dance last night. Lucy had actually snogged a younger soldier.

'He was called Romeo,' she said.

They got the bus and then the air con coach into the city and were at the tiny two-gate airport by early afternoon. It was all gone that quickly, vanished, unreal.

'Well,' said Bridge. 'That was all a waste of fucking time.'

They sat on orange plastic chairs in the filthy departure lounge and there were police with machine guns everywhere. The need to leave was obvious, the country was falling apart, but Nicholas blurted out to them suddenly in a kind of panic,

'They said in the village we mustn't leave.'

Bridge frowned. 'Hunh?'

'Like we were a kind of a guarantee of safety.'

'Bollocks,' snapped Bridge. 'And anyhow that's not why I came here. I'm a marine biologist, not some sort of ... I came here to study turtles, and then go home. You stay here. Maybe it's your kind of place.'

'He's right though,' said Caitlin. 'It's pointless us staying. We can't do anything.'

'Fuck it,' said Bridge. 'Take responsibility.'

Nicholas could almost have smiled, but his face would hurt too much.

'I'm going, and if you have any sense of responsibility, towards yourself, your family, everyone, you'll be going too. It's stupid to stay.'

But he couldn't leave. He didn't know how not to, but he couldn't leave. And then he was checking in his rucksack and couldn't find his passport. He had packed it that morning. It had been stolen from his rucksack on the bus or the coach. He thought he had never let it out of his sight but sometimes children got their hands into your bag under your very nose without you realizing it.

His world tipped.

He said nothing to the others about it. They would say he could get it back anyway. He could go straight to the British Consulate, or the Spanish Embassy. It would be no real problem.

He just told them abruptly, 'I'm not going.'

'What?' said Caitlin and Lucy together.

'I'm not going. Not yet.' He stood up and shouldered his bag. 'Have a good flight.'

'What do you mean?' said Caitlin. 'You've got to. It's not safe any more here. And there's nothing we can do here anyway.'

'Maybe not. But I'm staying here a bit longer.'

'You're nuts.'

'Nuts might be wise in a fruitcake. Now I'm going to buy a bottle of water. Back in a sec.'

'He's a twat is what he is,' said Bridge, looking after him. 'He's a show off. And he didn't get that bruising from falling over last night. Someone hit him. What was he up to?'

The girls were still laughing at the fruitcake maxim. Caitlin said, 'God, you still haven't got over him going for you that time he went for you in the bar, have you?'

'No I haven't actually. I think he was an arse. I couldn't care what happens to him. I hope I never see him again.'

'But you were so friendly towards him.'

'He's a psycho.'

'God,' said Caitlin.

The two girls prissily turned their backs on him. Bitches.

Bridge went off to the gents. Flying always made him want a dump. Especially after a night on the lash.

He hung his bag on the back of the door and sat and dumped voluminously. After using up the last of the lavatory roll, he fished a little maroon booklet out of his bag and studied Nicholas's passport photograph. Laughed to himself.

He had wanted to tear the passport to pieces page by page and wipe his arse with it, until there was nothing left but the cover and his arse was as clean as a choirboy's. But with a sigh he knew he couldn't do it, he was too kind a person.

Then he scrolled through the messages and photos on Nicholas's crappy old mobile phone which he'd cunningly purloined from his rucksack as well. God it was rubbish. Aw look, there was a photo of him with his little Indian family, all smiling like good obedient peasants. The lofty medical student looming over them with his sincere smile. Jesus.

Bridge put the passport in his back pocket, but tucked the mobile back in his bag. Did up his trousers and sauntered forth to greet the world with a cheeky grin and a hearty appetite for his airline dinner.

When Nicholas came back he casually held out the passport.

'Here,' he said. 'Found this in my bag. God knows why.'

Nicholas frowned. 'How did it get there?'

'You put it there, presumably.'

Nicholas looked at him hard. Bridge's eyes wandered.

Nicholas said, 'You keep it.'

'*What*?'

'A little memento of our friendship.'

'Nick,' said Caitlin, 'don't be weird. Have it back. You can't go wandering around without a passport.'

He gave Lucy a quick grin. 'Take care, gang.' Then he turned his back on all three of them and walked rapidly away. They called out but no one came running after him.

He hated long goodbyes and there was no point and they thought he was an idiot. Which doubtless he was. Let them go back to their country, worrying that they had not done enough, worrying that their lives were too comfortable. Sensible Caitlin. Bridge, just here for a laugh. Sweet-natured Lucy, not wanting to be here at all but feeling that she ought to be. To help the poor and less fortunate of the world.

He gulped down his water and binned the bottle and turned on his heel and walked out of the airport, alone and thin and free and faintly smiling to himself. Almost intoxicated with it.

He sat out on a step and ran through his possessions. A minimally light rucksack, no passport, no id, a roll of money in his right sock. Malaria pills, antifungal powder, nail clippers, clean underwear, a whole range of unhappy childhood memories, an erratic school career followed by a salutary period of time in an institution and then two years' experience at medical school. He had a toothbrush and toothpaste, razor blade and shaving oil, a pack of broad-spectrum antibiotics, a skeleton first aid kit, some facial bruising and several identifying scars and blemishes about his person.

And now he was stuck in a third world country whose President-Elect had just died in suspicious circumstances, on the brink of collapse, run entirely by crime lords and drugs money. He could go anywhere, do anything, and yet he had only one clear and burning desire in the whole world, which was a blissful thing to have. Which was why despite everything he smiled outright when he jumped aboard the packed and filthy yellow bus back into Santa Cruz. *Jehova es mi Pastor* on the sunstrip.

Standing in the gangway with his head bent down to shoulder height under the burning steelplate roof, rucksack round the front of him because of pickpockets, stared at woodenly by every other passenger. These people hadn't just come off planes. These were the airport cleaners, porters, hookers. The air of the bus was a trapped and reeking bubble in no way conditioned. Peering out through the occasional sliver of dustcoated window glimpsed through the sweating human biomass, clutching the sticky seatbar behind him for balance as the terrible bus belched and reeled from pothole to pothole, smiling happily to himself in the fetid crowded air. Let the adventure begin.

35

He got off at the central bus station and there was a boy asking him for money straight away in broken English.

'Hey mister. The Dallas Cowboys. LA Galaxy. Welcome to Alaska. Gimme money.'

The boy was about ten or eleven, but hard to tell. He had one eyelid half-down over his left eye, ptosis, and a scar above it like it had been cut by a knife and the nerves hadn't reconnected. He was barefoot and grimy with scabies and ringworm, and wore jeans and a t shirt that said Hawaii on it and showed an island with a palm tree.

'What's your name?' he asked him.

'Jennifer Lopez,' said the boy in English. 'I not know your.'

Nicholas grinned. The boy had a defensively aggressive way of jerking his jaw upward and narrowing his eyes when he answered. A man getting on a bus behind the boy took a last drag of a cigarette and tossed it in the dust. The boy swivelled round and crouched and scooped up the butt and stood up again and took a long, deep, satisfying drag. His eyes watered.

How had he seen that?

Nicholas thought for a moment, then said in Spanish, 'Come over there with me.'

'No. Where?'

'I'll give you money.'

'No. I'm not blowing you.'

'*What?*'

'I don't want your money. Go fuck yourself.'

179

'Look, I don't want you to … I don't want anything like that off you. I want you to give me some advice.'

'Advice?'

He nodded, already moving away round the side of the bus station and into the shaded street.

The boy walked after him, slowly, warily. 'How much money? What kind of advice you want from me? Business advice? Marriage advice? I'll give you marriage advice. Don't. Nothing but trouble there, man. Fucking nightmare.'

'Just follow me down here. Out of the way. And stop swearing.'

'And who hit you?'

'Oh, you mean – my bruising?'

'Yeah. This country beat you up, eh? It does that to everyone.'

'Come over here and I'll tell you.'

The boy stopped. 'I'm not walking one step further. Give me a dollar. Or twenty pesos.'

He meant it. Nicholas gave him twenty pesos. The boy nearly ran off.

'Hey! A hundred more for just a bit of advice. Look, here's the note. I've got it, here. This is yours.'

The boy eyed it greedily. A hundred pesos! Fucking gringos. Spraying money around like dogs pissing up a wall.

'What d'you want?'

Nicholas spoke very quietly. No one paid them any attention.

The boy stared at him. 'You come here and you sell us drugs? That's the wrong way round, man! You fuckin crazy!'

'That's what I'm offering. A whole aeroplane. I want money for it.'

'Man, there's drugs washing up in barrels all up and down the coast from here to Cortes. Fishermen down in Trujillo make more money fishing out barrels than fish. What makes you think this country needs more drugs?'

'Just take me to someone who might be interested.'

The boy laughed, a hoarse and croaking laugh full of dust and cigarettes. 'Man, they're bad men. They won't like you. Guys with tattoos. They kill people for fun. You sure you want to meet with them?'

The boy agreed to meet him at dusk on a certain street corner down near the bridge. He sat in a cafe until then, nursing a single coffee, to the owner's disgust. Feelings of bitter regret and exhilaration fighting for supremacy. But now, whatever else happened, *something was going to happen*. He was going to make it.

He wasn't at all sure the boy would show up again, but towards sunset there he was, coming down the street in his too-short jeans with his quick jerky stride. The boy beckoned and he followed him, weaving through the traffic and over the bridge and into the debatable zones beyond.

Later that evening he was in a room in a broken-down house, and knew that he had done a very risky thing. The boy had long since run away. Because he wasn't an idiot.

Nicholas was sitting in a chair and couldn't stand up because he was tied to it. He had been beaten, on top of the bruise from Maria, but he could still breathe and still see with both eyes and he could feel his own pulse rate in his neck and his throbbing left and it was about eighty, eighty five. His nose throbbed even worse.

It had been a long day, and he still had a hangover from last night. It had all happened so quickly it didn't seem quite real to him. He tried to hold on to that feeling. He closed his eyes and tried to imagine he was still sitting back there on that cottage bench in that highland valley, holding Maria's hand.

The leader of the gang in the broken-down house was called Julius. He wore a shiny black shirt and blew smoke in Nicholas's face. He had arrived in a fast sports car when the others rang for him on his mobile. The others had tattoos and wore white vests and red bandannas and expressions of tremendous stupidity. Several had automatics stuck down the backs of their jeans, and sometimes they took them out and waved them around for emphasis.

There were several rooms in the house that was some kind of gang headquarters, with the roof caved in here and there and the walls covered in graffiti and spattered with bulletholes. A boombox played next door. A couple of girls were dancing and another was sleeping in the corner. He didn't think they were very high up the ladder in the crime world, but it might be a start.

'Of course I'm not from the DEA,' he said thickly once more. 'Do I look like it? I'm not even American. I'm English. I'm a student.'

'What football team d'you support?'

'Chelsea.'

'Chelski!'

They talked about the Premier League for a bit. Mourinho. Blood dripped slowly and ticklishly from his nose onto his jeans. He didn't kid himself for a moment that he was bonding with them.

'You worship your footballers,' said Julius.

'Not personally.'

'You know we worship Santa Muerte here. Saint Death. The oldest and the greatest god of all. Here, smoke this.'

'No thanks.'

'No smoke, no deal.'

Perhaps it would take the edge off his throbbing nose. He inhaled deeply.

They clapped their hands together. 'All right!'

His lips were so bloody the cigarette got stuck, so they left it there, smouldering into his eyes. He managed to detach it and spit it out just before it started burning him.

Only a few moments later, another thin guy appeared with a needle.

'No, no. Please don't do that, you don't need to.'

The boombox was playing furious Caribbean *punta,* and

people standing around laughing, and there was a skinny girl who was naked apart from a thong and crop t shirt that stopped above her belly button which had a gold ring in it. She sat astride him and then she pretended to ride him.

'This girl she got SIDA!' someone was saying. 'AIDS, you know? Look at you.' They laughed. The girl bucked and rode him. Someone shouted, 'Hey, come and see Christina pretending to fuck this beat-up gringo! It's really funny!'

Someone else was patting his right arm. 'No. Please.' They had a strap between their teeth and someone else was squirting a hypodermic in front of his eyes. He guessed it hadn't come out of a sterile pack.

'Please, you don't need to.'

'We don't need to. No man, this is purely for fun!'

They had a teaspoon held over a candle, and some of the suspension arced out and fell across the front of the girl's t shirt. They tied up his right arm and found a vein and they pushed the needle in. The girl had her head on his shoulder, she was so drunk. They laughed. Then timed slowed and slurred and he sat a lot longer and there was no pain at all.

36

He came to on what might have been a derelict bomb site. Maybe just a vacant lot that was once a row of houses. He felt unbelievably sick. He must be so dehydrated. Water. *Water*. But he was still alive. They must have lost interest in him and thrown him out. Groggily he ran through a plodding checklist as he lay prone and aching. Breathing difficulties? No. Bleeding? No. Minor cuts and abrasions? Lots. Trembling, nausea, headache? Yes, all of those. Anxiety, restlessness, a terrible sense of impending doom? Well, that was just realism.

And this is only the start of it, he thought. Staring down at his own arm. Picturing the HIV virus already at work within, carefully and methodically replicating itself by the wonders of reverse transcription.

He clawed his way up a broken wall to a standing position and then his head throbbed so badly that he sank to his knees again. A small grubby face appeared the other side of the wall.

'Hey!' he hissed. 'Hey man! You OK?'

It was the boy.

'I'm just dandy,' he slurred in English.

'Speak Spanish.'

'I'm well thank you,' he said in Spanish. 'Jesus loves me. And how is your family?'

'You're full of drugs.'

'I think so, yes.'

The boy stared at him and then grinned wickedly.

'Did you sell me out?'

'Huh?'

'Did you get me into that trouble deliberately? They pay you?'

Instantly the small figure came racing round to him, and Nicholas actually thought he might get hit again, the boy looked so angry.

'How dare you say that!' he shouted. 'I practically risked my life to get you in there, this total stranger, they could easily have killed you! I fucking told you that, I told you it was a dumb idea, they're not nice people, and actually they just beat you up and kicked you out. You're fucking lucky to get out alive, and I hung around till now to see if you were OK, don't you fucking dare try to –'

'OK, I'm sorry.'

'Don't you ever accuse me of selling anyone out, I never betray anyone.'

'OK, I hear you. I'm sorry I said it.'

'Bastard.'

'I don't quite know what's what at the moment. It doesn't even seem real...' He gulped. He felt terrible. He never wanted to stand up again. After a bit he said, 'It all happened so quickly. Last night.'

'Lucky for you,' snapped the boy. They could have gone on much longer. Or just killed you. They'd like to kill a gringo. It's not my fault. I *told* you not to go.'

'I know it's not your fault. I mean, thank you for taking me there. Sort of.'

The boy shook his head at the idiocy of this blue-eyed gringo with the red and purple face. He looked like a fucking fruit salad.

'What am I full of?' said Nicholas.

'Eh?'

'What drugs did they give me?'

The boy shrugged. 'Why should I know? Bit of everything I guess. Your heart hammering like a drum, boom boom boom? Then they probably gave you coke mostly. But you all sleepy so must have been heroin too, or morphine or something like that.'

'You're a walking pharmacopeia,' he said in English.

'Talk Spanish, pissbrain. Come on anyhow, I'm risking my neck for this.'

'What?'

'Just come on. We need to get away from here.'

'Just a bit longer.' He curled up, arms folded tight across his chest, shivering. Trying to remember last night and sort out which bits might have been real. Hepatitis, septicaemia, HIV … The list was long.

'The worst thing is,' he heard himself slurring, 'I always suspected I was an idiot. Now I know I am. That's the worst thing. I have *no idea*.'

The boy was standing in front of him. 'Stop talking. It's making your lip bleed again.'

'Stop talking,' he repeated.

'And you need to do up your jeans. You all hanging out.'

He glanced fuzzily down. His jeans were still undone, halfway down his butt, and his cock was lolling shrunkenly – and was that … a *bite mark*? Dear God in Heaven, what had happened in there?

'Look I'm sorry man, I did warn you. I guess it didn't go too well.'

He did up his jeans very slowly. Even that much physical movement made him feel nauseous. And this was all effectively self-induced. He felt close to tears as he thought of the naivety, the colossal stupidity of what he had done. He was going to have to be more cunning.

He lay still again and croaked, 'Can you get me water, anything salty? Or some Coke?'

'You got money?'

'I doubt it. They've taken everything.'

The boy shook his head. 'They didn't take anything. Look. I took your bag.'

He heaved himself onto one elbow and stared.

'Is everything still in there?'

'I guess. I haven't opened it.'

He felt in his sock. Unbelievable. The roll of money was

still there, pesos and dollars. He pulled a note free. 'Here,' he said. 'Coke. Buy one for yourself. Buy me two or three.'

The boy vanished.

He groped in his bag and found some iodine solution for sluicing over the bright red gibbous moon on his cock that looked disturbingly dental in origin, and the two needlemarks on his right arm, and he very gingerly wiped the crusted blood from around his nose and mouth with another antiseptic wipe. One day perhaps he would tell this as an exciting traveller's tale.

The boy was soon back. He sank his Coke in about ten seconds, his thin belly visibly expanding. Burped cavernously. Nicholas drank his way steadily through three cans in half an hour. No germs could possibly survive in that dense phosphoric acid-and-sugar suspension, so it would act as an antiseptic sluice on his split lip as well. Phosphoric acid, H_3PO_4, was known to inactivate the foot-and-mouth virus, *aphthae epizooticae,* and could also be used to remove rust. In Africa, Coca-Cola was used a contraceptive. Women used it as a vaginal douche before and after intercourse. Some studies showed it had a 98% success rate, with Diet Coke being the most effective, although other studies were inconclusive.

'Shut *up*,' said the boy.

'What?'

'You're just babbling. Just *rubbish*. Why do I want to know about vaginal douches or whatever? Just *stop*.'

He hadn't even realized he was talking out loud. He lay back gasping, burping softly, and raised his can. 'This is some stuff.'

'Yeah all right,' said the boy. 'All I need now is a couple of cigs and I'm good to go.'

Nicholas still felt he could cry at any moment. Or laugh. All over the place.

'When did you start smoking?'

He shrugged. 'Can't remember. Always, I think.'

'Tell me your name.'

'Beyoncé. Barack Obama.'

'Really.'

'For twenty pesos.'

'No. For free.'

'I'm not telling.'

'Mine's Nicholas.'

The boy scraped a rock through the dust. He looked away. There was a vulture overhead and they could hear a distant police siren. There were three guys coming up the street.

'I think we should be moving,' he said. 'This isn't a very good neighbourhood. Come on, get up.'

He got to his feet, feeling terrible but at least able to walk.

'We need to go,' said the boy. 'As fast as you can.'

They walked away, round the back of the block and then down another steep alley towards the main street where there was more traffic and people and river beyond. The boy walked in front.

'My name's Pepito,' he said after a while, not looking back.

'Pepito. OK.'

They came down to the road and the river and he said, 'There's something I need to do.' And he climbed over the embankment wall and slowly down a rusting ladder set into the concrete, clotted and barnacled with its own outgrowths of rust, and then dropped down onto the muddy foreshore. Still half-dazed and unreal. The boy followed him.

He knelt and rummaged towards the bottom of his rucksack and brought out the package wrapped in black plastic that had lain there ever since he found the crashed plane in the forest with the children. He had been going to flush it down the pan at the airport before flying, and then he might have sold it, and he changed his mind about it again now.

He set down his rucksack in the mud and walked to the edge of the river.

'Hey,' said the boy, 'what is that?'

'*Cincuenta mil dolares*,' he said. '*Cincuenta mil dolores*. Does that make sense? Fifty thousand sorrows.'

And he reached back to pitch it high into the humid grey air over the river. But the boy was suddenly hanging onto his arm, tugging like a dog on a leash.

'Don't be such a *puta* gringo! Give it to me!' They struggled together in the shallows. The boy was made of wire. 'What the fuck are you doing? Why don't you give it to me?' Then he did some nasty street-fight thing of turning and jabbing his hard little heel directly down into Nicholas's kneecap. Nicholas gasped and sank down and hobbled back to the shoreline and sat.

'You little *bastard*. Kicking me now, when I've been beaten around all night. You little shit.'

'Only because you're stupid. Give it to me.'

His kneecap really hurt. That was some trick. 'You're not having it.'

'Then we're finished. And you're a fucking idiot. I know what's in that package and you're an idiot to think you can just throw it away.'

Nicholas rubbed his kneecap, looking around. Why was everyone *hitting* him nowadays?

At last he sighed and dropped the package back in his rucksack.

'Where do I go for a good doctor?' he said.

A doctor at the International Clinic got him cleaned up as best she could. She shook her head in disbelief at his carefully modified version of the story, and said 'This city.' She gave him a tetanus booster and a month of anti-retrovirals for eighty dollars, and they discussed interactions with other drugs. She said they should assume he had been given cocaine, which metabolized fast, so he should start the anti-retrovirals now. No sex whatsoever or other drugs. And he should get an HIV test back home in a month's time, and another three months after that.

'And any other blood tests you can think of, to be honest. When do you go back to England?'

He hesitated.

'You should go home,' she said. 'You look in a terrible state. It's obviously not good for you here.'

When he came out of the clinic Pepito was still there, sitting on a wall in the sunshine, swinging his legs.

'Look at you. A new man. So what now?'

'I'm going to go back to my village. Where I was working before.'

'What's the point of that?'

'I'll see.'

'So you're leaving?'

'Yes.'

The boy stood very suddenly and started walking away. 'See you then.'

Nicholas stood watching him go for a long time. 'Thank you!' he called after him. 'Pepito!'

37

It was an odd and sad day after that. Papa had gone to the city and still not come back, and then just like that, Doctor Nicholas had vanished too. Eulalia was furious with him. He was supposed to be her friend. The whole family was quiet that day. All down the valley was a coming and going of trucks, and down in the square there was a huge bulldozer that the boys stared at as if it was the most interesting thing in the world.

Then Uncle Uberto came puffing by.

'Pedro Xom has gone into the church,' he said. He stood bent forwards to get his breath back, hands on his plump thighs. A big drop of sweat rolled off the end of his nose. 'He's trying to toll the bell, and the men are trying to hold him back. They think he's gone mad, or he's been bewitched.' Uncle Uberto stood, his face glistening with sweat and fear. 'My sister,' he said softly, 'What shall we do?'

But Mama seemed distracted and cross, as if it was Uncle Uberto's fault. 'Nothing. It will all be fine. Everyone is going crazy.'

Including even Old Jorge, it seemed, who had seen everything and believed nothing. Old Jorge came back from the ridge, telling everyone he passed that he had heard shooting in the next valley, and that there was smoke and fire. He started loading up his last two mules. He said they were burning the villages.

Everyone in the village was bewildered by the rumours which spread like a feverish plague. Hadn't the dance only last night been a great success? All was well then. But others talked about how a civil patrol over at San Jerónimo had been accused of firing on an army jeep in a panic. Rumour had it that the jeep was left a burned out wreck after it exploded in a mighty fireball, like in the movies, and the soldiers had been killed, and that two of the men from the foolish patrol had been summarily executed, their headless bodies left by the roadside as a stern warning to all...

At these feverish rumours, some of the villagers of Chilitenango rushed frantically about trying to find their children, already weeping. Some drove their pigs and goats into their cottages and then barred their doors with broomsticks. One simple man sat under a cart and softly sang his chorus, cradling a kitten. It really was like everyone had gone mad, and nobody knew the truth, and it was very frightening.

Then the whole village fell silent, cowering in the valley like a dog waiting to be whipped. Nobody spoke. Even the birds were silent.

'Mama,' said Eulalia, 'can I go up to the pool?'

She nodded. 'But don't be long, *niña*. Everyone around here is going crazy.'

It was all so stupid. And she herself was stupid. A stupid woman. She longed for her José like never before.

Eulalia climbed up through the forest to the hot springs and the pool there, with El Pipón gambolling along behind her with his tongue out. As she left the cottage she could still hear Héctor going 'Pxiw! Pxiw!' with his imaginary gun.

She pulled her dress off over her head and laid it on a rock and slipped in bare. El Pipón sat and stared at her and wagged his tail. She told him not to come in. He leaned down and started to drink the water. He didn't like the taste, she could tell from how puzzled he looked. It was warm and full of salts, Papa said. So he looked at her like it was her fault, and then he drank some more. Puppies were mad like that. They often ate and drank things they didn't even like.

She lay back and gasped and then relaxed and wiggled her

toes. There was a girl who swam in the river bare on Good Friday. Her Mama told her not to, but she was a bad girl. And when she tried to get out of the water she couldn't, she was all covered in fish scales, and there was a flipper where her feet had been. Then she gave a great cry and sank back into the water and was never seen again.

But today wasn't Good Friday, so that was all right.

Poor old Pedro Xom. He was a mad old stick. Papa had nearly shouted at him the other night! But it was frightening. When would Papa come back? Then they would be safe.

She scooped back her black hair with its two pigtails and rested her head on the side of the hot pool where it had been worn away to a smooth curve by generations of girls and women lying there just like her.

If only the trucks would go away, and Papa come back. Everyone was mad today. As if they would ever leave this valley! This was the best valley in the world, with hot springs up here in the forest gushing out mysteriously from deep crevices in the rocks and sending steam rising up into the canopy of the dripping trees, making the monkeys leap about and squawk, making clouds. Here the women sat in the afternoon still wearing their dresses, half-submerged and gossiping and laughing about men.

She held her nose and sank back down under the water, and wondered if dying would be like this.

Suddenly the trucks were driving all over the village and making their engines roar and officers in gold braid were shouting orders. It was chaos, it was frightening, and most of all because some of the soldiers themselves looked frightened as well, stricken and jabbering, afraid of losing control, not sure what was going on, ready to strike out at anything they thought was a threat. But they kept telling the people they had come to protect them. Then they said something that made the people's hearts die within them.

They said everybody must leave the village.

Underwater, Eulalia's eyes flared wide open with terror. The water above her trembled. It was an earthquake.

She shot upright, gasping, choking, forgetting to hold her nose. She shook her head and her ears opened and the air was filled with noise, but it was not an earthquake.

She scrambled out of the pool when she heard all the trucks down below and the shouting, and pulled on her dress while it was still wet and her red plastic sandals and looked about for El Pipón.

'Pipo! Pipo! Where are you?'

She thought she heard him yapping and ran after him. Up into the forest, away from the village.

It was not safe. They wanted to take everyone down to the town where they would be well looked after. The soldiers said they needed to clean out this valley like a woman would clean out her house and beat her rugs and her blankets on a dry and windy day.

Mama was close to tears, which was very frightening. She hardly ever cried. The boys were all very worried and huddled together. Lala was still up at the spring.

Several other villages were being *depopulated,* they said. All down this valley and others. It was the only way to defeat the *narcotraficantes* and the guerrillas.

'We do not deserve punishment!' cried a woman with a baby.

'You are not being punished, you are being protected,' said an officer. 'Please, step aboard the truck. You do not need to take any possessions, everything will be provided. It is only for a few days.'

It was chaos. It made no sense to anyone.

And there was another cry, which was Mama saying she would not leave without her daughter or her husband or aged mother.

'Have no anxiety, *señora,*' said the soldier. 'Everything is here on this manifest. Look. All the names. They will all be accounted for, have no fear. Please. You are just being taken down into the town. They will be in another truck. Come along there. You, leave that bag behind. You do not need anything. It is only for a few days. Don't make a nuisance of yourselves. Step up now, hurry along. That's it. Hurry along.'

Mama held on to a rung of the metal ladder and refused to be moved, wailing like a wild woman.

'I will not go! I will not leave without my daughter!'

The boys were very embarrassed. Eventually a soldier told Alejandro that he must take care of his mother there, and Alejandro understood that he had been appointed head of the family while Papa was away. Alejandro forced his mother to let go of the rungs and he helped her up into the truck, weeping beyond measure. Up in the truck, Alejandro looked anxiously out over the crowds of people. Suddenly they had changed their minds and everyone was shoving now for a place on the trucks. It broke his heart to think that among them was his little sister. But she could not be far away and someone would recognize her and hold on to her. It would be all right. They would be re-united once they got into Santo Domingo.

The little girl in the forest ran and ran, terrified and crying, and knew she was utterly lost.

The trucks came down into Santo Domingo and did not stop. They headed out on to the main road out of the highlands.

'What is happening? Hey! Stop! This is not what was promised! What are they doing? Where are we going? What will become of us? My daughter, my daughter!'

Some of the men tried to get down even as the trucks were rolling but their wives forbade them. The soldiers who guarded each truck shouted orders more harshly now.

Some of the men began drinking in their grief. Some were already very drunk, lolling over the sides of the trucks as if their bones had turned to water.

'It is not safe in the department,' said a soldier. He stood at the front of the truck near the cab with his rifle held across his chest. 'You are to be taken down to the coast.'

'The coast?'

'We are being taken prisoner,' said one man quietly.

'No, no. This will be resolved. Let us sit quietly.'

'This cannot go on.'

'There is a great injustice being done here.'

'We will never come home again.'

'Yes, yes. Of course we will.'

'No, no. Never. My heart is heavy. We will never see our Valley of the Flowers again.'

And Maria was speechless with bitterness, her tears ceaseless and silent, thinking how swiftly the punishment of God had come upon them, for reasons that they could not understand.

38

She saw a bright valley down below her, and though it was not her valley and she recognized nothing, and she was in anguish because El Pipón was lost, still, he had been lost before and had come home again sooner or later. She prayed that he would again. She began to climb down the steep slope between the trees and then she stopped and shook with terror.

The day was deafened with gunfire, the trees thrashed, the air howled. The guns went on and on, like the barking of mad dogs, no one could stop them. Bullets splintered the branches of the trees, they whipped the leaves to shreds. People screamed.

She was under a bush with her hands over her ears but she could not close her eyes. Staring out at nothing. Still sounds came to her ears, the barking of the guns, bangs and howls, screams and cries, shouts and commands. More gunfire, more and more. Then angry explosions, bombs, her ears banging, her whole frame trembling with them. A bittersweet smell on the air. Smoke going up from the village, the roar of flames, thatched houses shimmering through the heat haze. One scream rose above the rest, a woman's scream, and it went on and on and on. Then there was more gunfire and the screaming stopped. Eulalia shook and shook and there was more gunfire and it went on and on.

Stomping boots and slamming doors. The roar of the engines as the trucks drove away. The shouting dying away down the valley. Furious silence.

An hour passed. She was in another village, another valley.

197

She had lost her village, Mama, her family, her puppy. Everything was gone.

High above the smouldering ruins of the village, the vultures were already circling. She would wait here and drive them away when they came down. She must go down. It was safe now. But she could not move. She could only crouch and tremble.

After a long time she stood painfully upright and came down out of the forest.

Small fires still burned. The little stream was clouded with red. Further down, the stream had begun to brim and burst its banks above the dam of heaped bodies.

They had even burned the church down. A cottage was just two low blackened walls, the adobe oven a black cowl. Two dogs were shot dead by a water trough. Blood spiralled red in the water.

What odd shapes the bodies of people made. Others looked just asleep. Another here, a burned black head, very small, with no ears, and two dainty ashen feet poking out from beneath a sunken petticoat of ash.

On the front step of a cottage, two bare legs, burned off at the knees.

She knelt by a dead dog and laid her hand on its furry side. Still warm. She stroked its silky ear. It flopped up and down There was a screaming noise in the air, piercing, unchanging, but when she turned to look there was nothing there and the screaming stopped. It was inside her head. She started to tremble again very violently and stayed kneeling beside the dead dog for safety, holding on to it.

The sun went higher up the sky, and the shadows of all the dead people lying around got smaller and smaller. That was their souls shrinking away. She wished she could shrink away with them. But she didn't think she could move. She would stay here. It was very quiet here.

When she looked up again the vultures were down on the ground and squabbling among the bodies. Scraggy heads and necks and lizard eyes. A dog sloped about there too.

If she stayed very still here and didn't move and didn't look up or look at anyone dead and just kept stroking the old dog then it would all be all right. Nothing else would happen if she did nothing here. Time passed. It was very quiet now, and it would all be all right.

It began to get dark and cold and she was very afraid.

She was too scared to walk about the village to see if anybody was still alive. She was filled with horror at the thought that she might hear a groaning sound, and find someone not dead but dying. But she hadn't heard a sound since she came down from the forest, and she thought everyone was dead. She didn't want to look anywhere. She didn't want to find anyone. It wasn't her village. She was lost.

When it was very cold and her shivering was almost uncontrollable, she stood up and very carefully retraced her path back into the forest by the light of the moon, treading exactly where she had trodden before so she wouldn't encounter anything that she hadn't already. The forest might be full of survivors. But they were only dead people pretending.

Away up the path lay the sorrowful and ominous forest, now half hidden in cloud as the daytime temperature dropped. Droplets of water condensed in the darkness among the clusters of glossy leaves and dripped continually. The wide staring eyes of creatures hidden among the fern-grown branches and the hanging mosses, peering out into the timeless gloom, and everywhere, the lost souls of the village walking silently between the trees, their white robes stained with blood.

She crawled into a patch of undergrowth and pulled branches and leaves around her and didn't know how she would live another day and she sobbed and shivered the whole night through.

Towards the evening of that day, one of the soldiers, or at least one of the men dressed as a soldier, went into the forest to have a piss. And as he stood there relieving himself, arching his back pleasurably, he saw an old woman wandering towards him through the forest. Like the *haruca* herself. The Old Woman of the Woods who sucked up men's souls. Who bound their wrists with babies' birthcords and suffocated them with babies' cauls. A hellish midwife who delivered men unto death. He tried to stop and buttoned up hurriedly, wetting his trousers in blotches of darker green, and shouted out angrily,

'What are you doing here? This is prohibited land!'

'What am I doing here?' said the old woman in an unnervingly amiable tone, stopping in front of him. 'I was born here.'

They put her under arrest and talked about it. They were supposed to have cleared out every last one of them. It was their responsibility. The boss would be furious with them if they'd managed to leave anyone behind. They looked across at the old woman with her two front teeth.

'I'm glad I was left behind really,' she said to them chattily. She was crazy and clear-headed all at once, the way old women are. They were afraid of her a little.

'Yes, I'm glad,' she said. 'I was nothing but a burden really to my daughter, and the children, well, I had told them all the wisdom I have. I don't wish to leave the valley, really I don't. I was born here, you see. You should not worry.' And as she said this she was actually looking across at them, and looking down at their guns, and then looking back at them and beaming. Crazy old bat.

So they walked her deeper into the forest, but really quite politely, and one of them actually took her skinny old arm to help her over a fallen treetrunk, and she thanked him for it. It was unreal. Finally they came to enough thick cover to dull the sound of the shot, and she said,

'Really you mustn't worry yourselves now, boys. What will be will be, and it is all in God's hands after all, not yours.

200

It is probably better this way. No matter how bad things get, just remember they can always get a lot worse!' She laughed. And then she said to them,

'People are children. All their lives. Playing among the gravestones like children. And then running crying to the heavenly Father with their bloody hands.'

She was tiny and it didn't need much of a trench to bury her, and she weighed next to nothing when they swung her in. As they walked back, they wished she had fought and screamed and they had been able to kill her as an enemy, as someone who hated them. But she had gone gently, almost as a friend.

39

Towards dawn Eulalia must have slept because she awoke to the chatter of a monkey and the sun was already coming up. That was the first of many mornings when she awoke from dreaming, and then the horror all came back to her afresh.

She thought she heard some hooves on the road and she came down out of the forest shivering.

There was nothing there. Only a soft wind and a bad smell and the vultures warming their wings in the morning sun.

She crouched by one of the dogs beside the water trough and touched it. It was cold now.

The hooves sounded again. She looked up, and there riding through the burnt village and on up the valley was an old woman on a dusty donkey. Thin strands of grey hair hung down either side of her face under her headscarf and straw hat. Her eyes were milky and watery and she had an unlit cheroot in the corner of her mouth.

She seemed to be oblivious to the dead all around. Hadn't she heard the gunfire? Wasn't she afraid? She must be deaf and blind. She must be a witch. Her bare withered feet almost touched the ground as she rode.

Then the old woman stopped and turned her head very slowly and stared back at her. Eulalia started shaking again. She held onto the cold dog. The old woman was a spirit. A *nahual*. Instead of fingernails she would have claws, red with blood. Eulalia looked down. There were ants around the dog. Flies around the hole in the dog's side.

When she was little she would have put her hands over her eyes so the witch on the donkey couldn't see her. But she was too old to do that now. Shaking all over, she kept her face bowed as if that would make her invisible. That was what all her people did. Keep looking at the ground. Then only the ground will see you.

One of the vultures rose up nearby, flapping its huge wings, its bald bloody throat thrown back squawking. The old witch never turned to look at it. She regarded the child squatting among the corpses steadily.

'You there. Leave the dog alone. Get up here.'

She didn't move.

'I see you, child.'

The screaming was there in her ears again. Her eyes swam and her limbs were too weak to move. The flies buzzed. She tried to stand and needles shot through her legs where she had been squatting and she gasped and froze. Then she felt very ill and bent forwards and was sick on the ground.

She stood upright. She still felt sick. She wiped her mouth with the hem of her dress and looked back at the witch so she didn't have to look at anything else nearby. The old witch waited with her bleary eyes.

'Get up behind, child. Quickly now.'

She went over and took the old witch's skinny bare arm. The skin was dry and cracked and slid down loose over her bones as she pulled on it and she jumped and hauled herself across the donkey's rump on her stomach. Then she turned carefully and sat side on.

'Do not look back,' said the old witch.

The donkey's dainty hooves clopped in the dust.

'Be like the wife of Lot, look away from the village, do not look back. Do you hear me? I am almost blind, which is a good thing sometimes in the world that is. Your eyes are young and bright. But be blind now.'

After a while the road gave out to a mere rocky path and became much steeper, the old path up to the peaks.

'Hold on,' said the witch.

But Eulalia didn't want to touch her. She laid her hands flat on the donkey's back to steady herself. Bony old spine rippling under the bristly dusty coat.

The path grew steeper. It was very hot. Her head pounded. The donkey's rear leg shot out over a loose rock and she jolted violently. She put her arm round the old witch's waist and held on.

A few moments later the old witch twisted where she sat and stretched out her arm. Eulalia tried to duck but the evil woman had already clenched her skinny old arm around Eulalia's neck and forced her face savagely down into her smelly old clothes. Eulalia struggled and cried out in terror. She felt the donkey trotting on faster, she bounced and screamed, her neck hurt. The old woman's arm was like steel around her neck, like a noose. She clutched the woman's arm with her fingers and tried to squeeze, but it made no difference. If only she could bite her.

She couldn't move, couldn't see, could hardly breathe, her head clamped beneath the old woman's arm, her face buried. The smell of onions and woodsmoke and damp and old woman's sweat. She was a witch, taking her to cook in her black iron pot. She would break her neck, snap it like a twig.

The donkey slowed and the old woman gradually relaxed her grip on the girl. Eulalia pulled herself free and gasped for breath. She hated her. She began to slide off the donkey.

'Stay where you are,' rasped the old witch.

Eulalia struggled between fear and fear, but she stayed on.

She glanced back. They had just passed by a deep ravine to the right of the track, under the trees.

'Don't look at it, girl,' snapped the witch.

Eulalia carried on looking back over her shoulder but she couldn't see anything. Just where the deep ravine was under the shadow of the trees. The buzz of numberless flies.

'What was in there?'

The old witch didn't say anything.

'Are they all dead?' she whispered. 'Is everyone dead except me?'

After another minute or two, round a corner, the old witch tugged the donkey's rope and it halted. Ahead the path grew still narrower and steeper, winding between thorn scrub. They would have to get off and walk the animal soon.

She urged the donkey a bit further onward, round the corner from the ravine. And then it was better they walked. It would give the little one something else to think about, the steep rocky path to the peaks, dodging the wicked thorns.

She told her to get down. Then she leaned back and raised her leg up over the donkey's head and got down herself. She straightened her back again slowly, clenching her jaw at the pain in her bones, and took the donkey's halter.

The child stood with head bowed.

She clacked her tongue. 'Walk on.'

The child would have to follow.

A sniff and then a terrible sob came from behind. She started walking.

After a while she passed the child a scrap of cloth.

Later they were walking through sparse pines and the air was fresh and sweet. She suddenly said over her shoulder,

'Never speak about this. Lock up your heart, still your tongue. Never speak about what you have seen. Do you understand me?'

Eulalia walked numbly on, desperately tired and hungry.

'Do you understand me, *niña*?'

She nodded. Then remembering the old woman couldn't see much, she whispered, 'Yes.'

'What did you see?'

It was wrong to lie. 'Nothing,' she said.

'What do you say?'

'Nothing.'

The old woman stopped and looked back at her blearily.

'Nothing. *Nada de nada*. And if they ask you, and threaten to beat you, pretend to be deaf and dumb. You understand? Pretend you are an idiot child. Make the signs with your hands. Act dumb. This way you will live. Do you understand me, child?'

She nodded. And for practice she made the sign, swiping the tips of her fingers across her mouth to signify that she couldn't speak. God had wiped away her words.

The old woman nodded very slowly, peering at her with her bleary eyes as if she might change her mind and say more. But Eulalia kept her heart locked.

A bit further on they remounted and turned right along a ridge at the edge of the forest, and a dark narrow path silent with pine needles. The donkey flicked its ears.

'What's the donkey's name?' she asked.

'It doesn't have a name.'

'He must have a name.' After a while she added, 'My puppy is called El Pipón.'

After a while the old woman said in a voice not so harsh as before, 'His name is Pedro.'

Pedro. She leaned out to one side and watched. 'Pedro,' she said.

Pedro twitched his right ear.

They rode on.

After a long time they dropped down into another steep valley, down and down, below the pines and back into thicker forest again.

The old woman lived in a tumbledown cabin of banana-leaf thatch supported on four cornerposts that looked like it had been built a hundred years ago. She had five chickens and a tiny donkeycart and a black iron cooking pot just like Eulalia had guessed. She also had a fat black cat who stared at her with wide green eyes and look disgusted to see her. There were no dead bodies lying about.

The old woman warmed up two tortillas on her hearthstone and gave them to her to eat. Immediately she had eaten, Eulalia felt so tired she could barely stand, and she had a headache. The old woman made her drink some water as well and then found her a blanket.

'Sleep in the donkey cart,' she said. 'Under this.'

'But it's hot now.'

'Sleep under it anyway. I will wake you later.'

'And it's daytime. I have to find my family.'

The old woman laid cool narrow leaves across her forehead for the headache.

'Everything is crooked today,' she said.

40

She awoke some hours later towards the end of the day. The shadows were long, the birds sang, the insects hummed under the trees. She lay in the donkey cart with her feet over the edge, too hot under the blanket, staring into the sky. Everything came back with a rush again, and her guilt was overwhelming. Why was she the one turned out alone? She must have done something terrible.

Her heart was so heavy she felt she would never stand up again. She could not live the rest of her life alone, or she would die of loneliness. She would never eat again, her heart was too big and heavy, there was no more room inside her for anything else. Tears ran down her cheeks, tickled past the corners of her mouth as she lay there silently. She would die bit by bit, where her mother had not kissed her on her cheeks, where her father had not kissed her on the top of her head, where Héctor had not put his hand in hers for them to walk down the road to the stream. She ached all over with loneliness.

The old woman was standing at the foot of the cart.

'Ay,' she sighed. 'Dry your eyes, child. Come and eat.'

The old woman stirred the pot, looking blindly across it into the darkening forest. She had lit an ocote pine torch and also an ancient kerosene lamp and in the lamplight her wrinkles were blackened by years of woodsmoke. In her pot were beans, corngrains, tomatoes and a whole plantain still in its skin. She was a bad cook.

Eulalia sat on a tree stump wrapped in the blanket. It was very smelly and made her want to sneeze. The old woman stirred the pot. The plantain oozed through its split skin and frothed. Eventually she ladled some out into a tin bowl and handed it to her.

Eulalia shook her head.

The old woman could see that much. 'You must eat.'

But she didn't want to. Partly because she was too sad to be hungry, and partly because the old woman was such a bad cook. The plantain skin floated like thick green slime on the bubbling surface of the nameless stew. It made her feel sick to look at it.

'Eat,' said the old woman more harshly. 'Or sleep in the forest with the snakes.'

She lifted the foul black spoon to her mouth and slurped. It tasted odd, but not so bad. She was glad the old woman hadn't tried to feed her meat. It could have been anything.

After she had finished what was in the bowl, the old woman poured some white milky stuff into a plastic beaker and filled it up with water.

'Here. Drink this.'

'What is it?'

'Drink it.'

It tasted a bit musty but then it was warm in her throat and stomach.

'You'll sleep again.'

'I want my family.'

'In time, *niña*.'

'My family weren't there. We live in another valley.'

The old woman stared at her and her white eyes were very eerie in the firelight. 'Are you telling the truth?'

She nodded.

'What were you doing there?'

'I got lost. I was in the wrong valley. I was looking for my puppy.'

'And this is the truth?'

She nodded. 'Where's my mama? Do you know my village?'

The old woman crossed herself first at this sudden blessing, and then wondered what she was supposed to do.

209

Aside from shootings there had been villages that had been cleared out and many people driven away. All was chaos and nobody knew what was happening, but everyone knew they had been killed, like every time before.

'Which is your village?'

Eulalia pointed. 'Over there.'

'I mean, what is it called?'

'Chilitenango.'

'I have heard of it. It is in the Valley of San Antonio.' The old woman poured herself a drink as well. She needed it. Eulalia felt warm and tired and thought if she went to sleep again she wouldn't wake up for days.

'We have had a blessing, child. For all the horrors. Have hope in God. It will be made right.'

'Do you promise?'

Dear God, a child's eyes. A child's hope. It was the cruellest weapon, a knife to an old woman's heart.

She said, 'We must do all we can. Perhaps it can be made right. Sleep now.'

'What's your cat called?'

The old woman looked vaguely in his direction. 'Bernardo,' she said after a moment.

'Why is he so fat?'

'He is a very great hunter. You wouldn't think it to look at him.'

Bernardo licked his paw and looked haughty and unamused.

'But in truth he hunts like a jaguar in the night. Nothing escapes him. I feed him nothing, and yet look at him. As fat as the President himself.'

'Is the President fat?'

The old woman cackled, the first time she had seen her face crack wide with laughter. All moles and toothless gums and shaking grey locks. '*Is the President fat!*'

They sat in silence a while and then Eulalia blurted out, 'If I have lost my family can I stay here with you?'

The old woman stared at her and then raised her bumpy hands to her face and covered it for a while. When she lowered it again, her milky blind eyes were teary.

'O child, you will break my heart, you will sunder my soul. I am sick, and very old. I will not live much longer. And then you will have nothing here but' - she waved her hand about – 'this old *cabaña*, and an old black cooking pot, and a donkey nearly as old as I am. This is no place for you, *niña*. I swear before God I will protect you. But your place is not here.'

Eulalia looked away.

'We will go tomorrow. Trust me. We will find them.'

At dawn the old woman sat her on the donkey and the dusty fur tickled her bare legs, and the old woman walked alongside very slowly, the donkey solemnly nodding his head in time to her small steps. They went over the high pass among the rocks where there were birds with ragged wings sailing high in the sky, and down into another valley among the pines, and then thicker and thicker forest.

They could hear the sound of heavy machines rumbling and a lot of crashing, and finally they looked down on the valley that had been hers.

'My village is down there,' she said, excited and fearful.

'Stay.'

'But it is!'

'Stay. You cannot go down. They have occupied it.'

'Who are they?'

'Who indeed? They are the World.'

Huge machines were dragging away trees, and in the forest you could hear chainsaws going in a clamorous chorus. You could tell which tree was going to come down next because the top started to shudder and then it fell very slowly and vanished below with a giant crash. Big yellow bulldozers were tearing up the ground and beyond that there were trucks and gangs of men and a lot of shouting.

'What other family do you have? In town?'

Eulalia was still staring down at the valley. She didn't understand. She said,

'My Uncle Uberto lives in the village too. He doesn't have any children. Then there's my Uncle Miguel, but he drank and went to the bad. My mother has some sisters, they live in another village. But they are very poor, and my Auntie Elisa is sick. And there's my Auntie Rosario. She lives in the city.'

'The big city?'

'Yes.'

'Do you know where?'

'In the *barrio*.'

'The *barrio*. Ay.'

The sun sat on the rim of the mountains just for a moment, and then slid down behind.

'That would be where your family have escaped to, perhaps.'

Eulalia looked at her, but all she saw was all the dead people. The old woman, near-blind though she was, shifted under that childish stare.

'What else do you remember of your Auntie Rosario?'

'She was very kind. She bought me chocolates.'

'I mean, what did she do? Did she work?'

'She sold shoes.'

'In the marketplace, or -?'

'In a shoe shop, Mama said, to rich ladies. Shoes with high heels.'

'Let's ride back.'

'But this is my valley!'

'We go back. Your valley has gone.'

She boiled water and made coffee and wondered if everyone had been killed. There was no way of knowing. Perhaps the girl was probably an orphan. Then what to do? What became of an orphan girl in this country? Nothing good.

She said, 'Now listen. There is chaos in this department and many people will have been moved on. Your family have been moved on too. We will find them, but it will take time. You will not find them here with me. We will find you a bus to the city.' The little girl had started crying again, but she hardened her heart and kept talking. 'It goes along the top road there tomorrow, sometime in the late morning. If it is still going in these days. We must hope it is. The man will not charge you, he never charges his own sister. I will put you on the bus and find someone to look out for you on the journey. It is best. These valleys and villages here now are not.... War has come to them now. War is terrible, nothing is worse. It is a civil war, do you understand? Brother fights brother, one village fights another. And the army fights everybody. It will be very terrible.'

'I hate them!' She clenched her fists. 'I hate them!'

'Calm yourself, still your heart, lock up your tongue. You must go to the city. You must find your Auntie Rosario. She is your family now. And for the poor of the world like us, family is all we have. The rich have gold and cars and aeroplanes, but the poor have family.'

She led her back to the donkey cart and put the blanket over her again. Against the mosquitoes as much as the cold. She didn't kiss her goodnight like Mama.

As she turned away, Eulalia said angrily, 'What has happened?'

The old woman looked at her briefly and then looked away, her white eyes wandering around, as if she was looking for her own eyes that had fallen out and rolled away into the grass. Her voice sounded heavy and tired, and she just said, 'Ours to wonder, not to understand.

41

Maria stood throughout the eight hour truck journey, aching and cold with fear all the way. She held the boys' hands. They trembled, but it was Jaime, clever sly Jaime, the teaser, who wept most. The village had been wrenched in pieces, not the buildings but the people. A village was its people, its families, its children.

She prayed and prayed and prayed. *Bring her back ... keep her safe ... let me find her ... keep her safe...* This was not her punishment, that was absurd. But she had failed as a parent, as a mother. She would have died to save Eulalia's life, but she had lost her. She only had to picture her child for the tears to start coming again. The huge eyes, the gap teeth, the pigtails. The right-hand one usually soggy where she chewed it, deep in thought. Even now Maria kept thinking she might throw herself from the truck and run back. But then the boys would be alone too. She was torn in two. She prayed and prayed. God must stay with them. Let Him not leave them.

For nobody cared for anyone on the dreadful journey, nobody had the spirit to comfort their neighbour. They were all stunned into solitude and misery, crammed into that truck like livestock. Then in a town, out of the mountains, they were herded onto a bus and given a biscuit each as their reward.

The coast was hot and flat and dull to the eye, mile after mile of dark green plantations. At last they came to some huge gates and drove in and were herded off the bus again and a man all in white addressed them. The people were so dazed with tiredness that they barely listened or understood. They just wanted to sleep. But Maria was still too cold to sleep.

Eulalia was gone, José was gone, Abuelita was gone. She felt close to hysteria all the time. She had been for hours. But she would not break. She would find them. She was already planning to go back there, come what may.

There was a clinic and a doctor here full time. A camp doctor. 'You will be well cared for,' the man was saying. 'The medical care you receive will be deducted from your wages. You will of course be paid a fair wage. Soon, we hope that each family will be assigned its own private cabin. That is the whole philosophy of a plantation such as this. It is founded upon the highest principles of fair trade and worker welfare, with generous foreign investment.'

Then they were shown to their quarters. The men and women slept separately in large dormitories, but the man said that as soon as the new buildings were finished, families would be reunited. It would only be for a week or so. They must not be anxious. Maria's bed was in the middle, a row of about twenty, with twenty more opposite. She sat on the bed. It was very clean and comfortable. There was a grey blanket on it. She was very cold. It had been so hot on the bus as they came down across the flat coastal plain and the humid air hit them that she had broken out in perspiration, and yet still she had felt cold. Now she slipped her hands under the blanket to warm them. Outside the door a woman sat on a chair like a security guard outside a shop.

The men went to their dormitory uncomplaining. The people were so humiliated and bewildered that they did not even complain when the man in white began to lead their children away from them again, to be divided and assigned to more dormitories. But Maria complained. She was instantly furious.

'Boys, you stay here!'

The three stopped and looked back.

The man in white frowned. 'The children sleep in their own dormitories.'

Maria went towards him. The man held his hands in front

of him.

'My children stay with me. At all times. They do not leave my sight.'

Héctor immediately trotted back and took her hand. Alejandro and Jaime looked a little uncertain. They didn't want to look as if they needed their Mama, not at their age. The man in white began to argue, but then the other women gathered round him in a belligerent group, and some made mention of the fact that her girl had gone missing, and she would need her boys near her until the girl was found again. Some crossed themselves.

Finally the man in white relented. Maria was given a space in the far corner of the dormitory with three beds for Alejandro, Jaime and Hector.

There would be schooling in the morning. Proper schooling. It would be deducted from the parents' wages. There were showers which were free, and meals were provided in a refectory. It was all organized. They would be very well cared for. There was even a chapel, a beautiful chapel with a clean white interior, and a priest who heard confession once a week.

But none of it meant anything until she found her daughter again.

The *finca* seemed to stretch for miles, and all around it was a great perimeter fence topped with barbed wire to keep out the thieves and deer and peccaries. They grew every kind of fruit there, pineapples, guavas, bananas, mangoes, some of it for home consumption and much of it for export that would earn much-needed foreign currency. There were beautiful green lawns watered with sprinklers, and flowers in pots. Across the green lawn was a big showerblock. It was astonishing. There was a feeling of calm and order here that the villagers could not help but like. It was unbearably hot and humid but apart from that it did not seem so bad.

The men wanted to know what rent they would pay for the

cabins. Maria despised them for even asking such a question when she had lost her daughter. The overseer told them it would be deducted from their wages so they would hardly notice it. When they calculated what would be left over, well - it was far, far more than they had earned in the village, or selling their eggs and squashes in the marketplace of Santo Domingo, sitting from dawn till dusk. Compared to that, it was really a very fair wage.

Maria's mind raced all that night. The very idea of sleeping was ludicrous. How dare she sleep? Where was Eulalia sleeping? Was someone caring for her? In her racing thoughts she tried to imagine that perhaps even José had found her, perhaps they had become reunited somewhere outside of the village as he came home. Oh my beloved. Oh God please, take care of her. Our heavenly father, who lost your own son, who saw him die. Oh please dear God, let her be safe, let her not cry, let her come back to me. For if you do not, then there is no God the father and we are all lost children.

She remembered and lived over and over again every detail of the chaos that had come to the village, that dreadful truck journey. Should she not have let Lala go off and bathe on her own in the hot springs? Should she have gone with her? Should she have refused to get on the truck until Eulalia was found?

She cried and prayed, and every few minutes she raised herself up on her elbow and looked around to see her three boys sleeping.

At first light she went straight to the overseer. If he could not tell her when she and her daughter were to be reunited, could not prove it to her that Lala had been found and was safe, Maria was determined to leave at once, putting the boys in the strict care of the other women. The very thought frightened her, but she would have to do it. Her aged mother and her husband would find their own way, but her child...

217

The overseer was already at work on his computer. He was a very busy man.

She said, 'I want to talk with you.'

After a moment he looked up. 'Yes?'

'I want to go out and find my daughter.'

The man looked puzzled. 'How?'

'I will go back to the village.'

'But the village has been cleared out.'

The man was an unspeakable fool. *She had lost her daughter*. She had vowed not to lose her temper, but she did so almost immediately, burning with exhausted anger. She even thumped his desk.

'Then *where is she*? You moved us all out of our village like … like *animals,* like *pests,* and did not even care that my daughter got left behind. You –'

'Madam, we took every care,' he said firmly. 'But you have to understand that there was great danger. In fact,' he said, moving his hand back and forth across his chin, 'I can tell you now that I have been on the phone this morning. There has been shooting around the village.'

'Shooting! And my daughter still there!'

'Do not be anxious. The area has been secured. She will be safe, I assure you. But it was because of this fighting around your village that we had to move you to safety.'

His hand stopped moving, his fingertips resting on his lips.

'What was the name of our village?' she demanded.

He frowned and then glanced back at his screen. 'Chilitenango.'

Her anger ebbed a little, but not her determination.

'Listen to me,' he said. 'I understand how you feel –'

'You do not understand! How can you understand? Have you children of your own? Have you ever lost one of them?'

'That is not relevant.'

'How can I possibly not worry about her, how can I not do something -'

'Really,' he said, 'you must trust that all is being done. The

218

whole department has been secured now, and everyone is safe. We are concerned for the people's welfare, and we have far greater resources for finding your daughter than you could have on your own. You must be patient. I understand it is a terrible thing to be worried about where your child is, I truly do. But we will find her. Of course we will. In fact she has probably already been found and is being held safely somewhere. Made a great fuss of. Think about it: we went to all the trouble of moving you out of the villages, of securing a very troubled department, all for your own safety. Would we have done all that that if we did not care for you?'

She was very tired. He was calm and confident and there was some sense in his argument.

'But how can I just sit back and wait patiently? What mother could do that?'

'Listen,' he said. 'Go back and be a good mother to your other children. You have others?'

She nodded.

'Today, this morning, I will make more phone calls. I will find out all I can about what happened in, in this Chilitenango. I am just as concerned as you are. We want all our workers to be happy. And as soon as I have learnt anything I will come and tell you in person. I will make sure that everything is being done. You must trust us to do the right thing.

'Now – do you have any knowledge of where she might be? How she became lost?'

She explained to him as best she could.

'Do you have a photograph?'

She shook her head. 'There was a gringo who stayed with us, one of those volunteers they send us. He had a photograph on his telephone but,' she said bitterly, 'even he has abandoned us.'

The man looked her over and thought for a while and then he said, 'In fact, I want you to come back and see me this evening, after you have finished work. Come and see me here at seven o'clock. We will talk some more.'

She said sharply, 'And after that I will make a decision. If you can tell me nothing definite this evening, then I will leave to find my daughter myself. What are you going to do to stop me? Shoot me?'

The man held his hands wide. 'Please.'

She cut across him. 'I will go back to the village, I will find lawyers, there are human rights organizations -'

He harrumphed. 'What has this to do with human rights organizations? Please. Your daughter has only been missing for a day or two.'

'Only? *Only*? How long do you think a six year old girl should be separated from her own parents, left behind in a valley where you say yourself there has even been shooting and fighting, and the parents not worry themselves sick about it? You ... you *dolt*!'

The man sighed. 'This will not help. Come back to me sooner - at six. Please trust me.'

'And if you have nothing to tell me, I am packing my bag and going. With my boys. Make sure they open the gates to me or there will be trouble. There will be a revolt.'

She could hardly eat that day and it didn't help that Héctor kept asking when Lala and Papa and El Pipón would come back. Some time before six she went back to the office.

The overseer wanted to walk with her privately over the thick green lawns, and then away from watchful eyes, round the back of the immense steel barns where the crates of fruit were stored.

He stopped and looked very troubled. 'I am so sorry,' he said. 'It is for pity that I have not told you before.'

She stopped dead. 'Told me what?'

'You have to believe me.'

'Told me *what*?'

He put his right hand on her shoulder. 'My dear, I do not know how else to say this. The rest of your family are dead.'

'What do you mean? They... What do you mean?'

'I learned on the phone this afternoon. They were among those murdered by insurgents. Their names were on the lists.'

'What lists? Show me.' She was shaking, everything was dissolving around her. 'This is not true. I do not believe you. My daughter only went up into the forest. My husband was in the city, getting a land licence. Where are the bodies?'

'I am so sorry,' he said.

'You *lie*! My husband was in the city. My daughter ... my daughter...'

'Madam, it is wrong to accuse me of such a thing. What man or monster would lie about such a thing?'

She looked at him, and she realized that no human being would lie about such a thing. And so it must be true.

The woman howled, she broke down in the dust.

After a time, the man raised her up again and held her in his arms.

'Much goodwill has gone into these *fincas*,' the overseer told them the next day in his morning address. 'Much foreign aid has been given to establish this place and the others like it along the coast. For fair trade and for fair pay. We should all be very grateful.'

Afterwards, Maria went out and walked a little away from the cabins on her own for a while. She had still not told the boys and did not know how to. She felt many miles away from everyone else around here, as if living in a different world where every sound was muffled.

At the end of the immense row of thick glossy mango trees she looked back. All along the rows she could see her people in clothes that were now cleaned in huge drums once a week, peacefully tending mangoes under the tropical coastal sun. Their children and hers were in school, but her mother and husband and one of her children was dead. Her only daughter.

The overseer had showed her later on the computer, though she could not read and her eyes were full of tears. He had called up documents and shown how the government was pursuing every avenue for peace and for those responsible to be brought to justice. He talked about *narcotraficantes*. The man said that there had been great violence in the valleys and in the city and alas, her relatives were among the lists of the dead. She could not believe anything but that her daughter was gone, that José would not return, that she would never see her mother alive again.

She wanted to kill those responsible. She did not even know where Lala lay. Mangoes were better cared for. Mangoes were fed and watered better! She had no coffin, no grave. Mangoes were gently wrapped in crates and flown abroad. Over seas, over forests and deserts.

Last birthday she had had a new t shirt with coloured beads on the front. Her gap-toothed delighted smile then when she first wore that pink t shirt. Let it all be closed down. Her mind was wandering. Her heart hurt but she was also numb throughout. At last she sat down at the end of the row and turned her back on her people tending mangoes and bowed her head and closed her eyes and shook with pain and uncontrollable tears.

42

Eulalia awoke in the morning to hear the old woman coughing a lot.

They were just eating their tortillas, there was only enough cornflour for one each, when the old woman stopped chewing and held out her hand. Then she said,

'Quickly, back in the donkey cart.'

'What is it?'

She didn't say any more, just pulled her over to the cart and made her lie down in it, and threw a blanket over her. Then she brought over some branches and laid them on top of her.

'What is it?' Eulalia was suddenly very frightened. Her heart hurt. 'Is it the soldiers again?'

'Sssh,' said the old woman. 'Not a sound now.'

Then she heard voices. Men's voices. She held her breath.

There were eight of them in green combat uniform. They lined up in front of the *cabaña*, grinning and jostling, resting the butts of their guns on the ground. Cold muzzles good in their palms.

'Hey pretty lady, spare us a tortilla?'

'I have no flour left.'

'Sure you have. You want us to search?'

'There is nothing here. There are some orange trees further on.'

'Eh, but soldiers like us, we need tortillas. Or a steak. You got any steak, you pretty thing?'

'I reckon there's only some tough old stewing steak, from what I can see,' said one of them.

They all laughed.

The old woman sat still on her stool and gazed steadily ahead as if they weren't there.

The leader of the soldiers suddenly got angry and frowned.

'You should show some respect, old woman. You seen any guerrillas or *communistas* hereabouts? Or you heard about a plane crash in the forest?'

She shook her head. 'I heard some guns. I believe there's people been killed round about. Just people in the villages, so they say. Done nothing wrong. Which is a puzzle to me. But then what would a crazy old woman like me understand of such things?'

'You seen anything else you want to tell us about?'

The old woman just rocked gently on her stool and sang in a quavery old voice,

'*A storm blew up in the night time*
And took my children from me,
But the sun came up in the morning
And the storm fled away to sea...'

'She's no *communista*,' said another soldier, 'she's a crazy fucking bat is what she is. Hey, crazy *abuela*, we'll get you singing a true song yet! You seen any guerrillas? Sure you have, Señora Loca, that's why you got no cornflour left! You gone and fed the entire rebel army with your dirty tortillas!'

'You think you can trick us by singing a couple of crazy songs so we think you're just a harmless old granny? You think we're that dumb?'

'God strike you all blind,' said the old woman. Her blood was vinegar.

There was no more spoken, just an ugly shoving and grunting, and Eulalia couldn't stand it any more. She came slithering out from the under the branches and the blanket and saw the soldiers had shoved the old woman to the ground and were kicking her. She came running with her fists bunched.

224

'Leave her alone! Leave her alone!'

There was a whirl of green camouflage and a thump on the side of her head and some shouting and laughing in the far distance. The next thing she knew, she was lying beside the old woman on the ground with the soldiers laughing all around them, and she had a cold ache in her head. She sat up slowly.

'You little fool,' hissed the old woman. 'You *fool*.'

The soldiers jeered.

'Hey little Indian girl, what you doing with your granny here? Your Mama run off to town in a red dress to work on the streets, eh?'

'We'll look out for her. What's her name?'

The old woman was up and on her feet very quickly, leaning on her stick and staring round at the soldiers with her unblinking milky eyes.

'You leave us be. We're no communists, we're not your rebels. And if you do the innocent any harm, you will pay a terrible price. It is certain.'

Now the soldiers were roused and smiling sardonically. They milled about, pushing their bayonets lazily through the banana thatch, kicking at one of the cornerposts until it came loose and the whole roof sagged, knocking over the cooking pot and treading in the spilt stew.

'You threatening us, old crone? I don't see you've any M16s around the place.'

'What you going to do to us, Señora Loca, you going to come at us with your stick maybe? Your little granddaughter, she going to beat us to a pulp with her fists, strangle us with her little pigtails?'

'Or maybe your communist friends come out of the forest and come running to your rescue? Is that what you mean, old mother?'

'No, that is not what I mean. Not at all.'

The old woman's voice was suddenly crisp though quiet in the clearing of the forest. The soldiers stopped their search and fell still. There was something creepy about *La Ciega*.

She smiled toothlessly. 'How scared you boys are of women! It is why you violate them all the time.'

'You shitty *puta*.'

Her eyes held them. One soldier twirled his bayonet in his hand and then fumbled and dropped it. It stuck in the ground close to his foot. Overhead there was rustling in the trees. The clearing was gloomy and even at midday got little sun. The soldiers shifted from one foot to another. More rustling overhead. Guerrillas moving like cats through the high canopy, wearing green face paint and necklaces of severed ears. Guns training down...

But maybe it was just an iguana looking for birds' eggs.

They didn't know what to do, but to walk away was weak. Maybe they should just kill them anyway and have done. The forest heat was oppressive and there was no light here, no breeze. There was a howler monkey further off. Strange birds hooted and screamed. You heard stuff about what still lived in these forests.

The old woman looked around at the soldiers and their uneasy sweaty faces. 'Ah,' she said, 'but you have already understood what I mean. Evil is real and is always punished. That is why you look afraid.'

'We ain't afraid of you!' yelled one soldier, stepping towards her, ready to strike her again.

She didn't move, didn't turn a hair. She said, 'You are afraid. For what you have just heard and felt in the air and in the trees, and what will come to you if you lay another hand on me or on the innocent here. You have seen it with your own eyes. It is the Spirit of God moving among the trees. The Spirit of God knows all and sees all, and you know it. You think you are tough soldiers, but you know this is true, and you can never not know it.'

She was an evil old one.

They began to move their feet. Turn around.

'Old *puta*,' they muttered. 'There's nothing here.'

'Back to the jeep, boys. We're wasting time.'

'Fuckin' Indian witch.'

'Move on, boys. There's work to be done.'

'That old witch has got disease coming out of her eyes, man.'

'Ay. *Vámonos*.'

'Fuck it. Boring.'

There was the tramp of black boots along the forest path and the sound of vines being desultorily hacked with bayonets in passing and they were gone.

To calm the shaking girl, the old woman sat her on a rock and unplaited her pigtails and washed her hair. Then she took off her dress and wrapped her in the smelly old blanket again. She went off to the stream in the forest to wash it, a stick in her other hand to find the path.

The girl made a sharp animal whimpering.

'Peace, child. I'll not be gone long.'

Yet her noises were of sheer terror.

'Or come with me then.'

Eulalia needed no further encouragement. She trotted after the old woman barefoot, only her face peeping out of the big old donkey blanket.

When the dress had dried out on a bush in the sun, she put it back on her and combed her hair.

'And my pigtails,' said Eulalia.

The old woman shook her head.

'Why not?'

'Tch.' She carried on brushing her glossy black hair. 'I'd pick the embroideries out of your dress if my eyes could see to do it.'

'No you won't. My Mama made it. Why would you?'

'Too Indian.'

'But I am Indian.'

'Ay. And there it is.'

'Except Papa says we're not Indian, we're Maya. Indians

is what the others call us.'

'For now you're just a girl, remember? My granddaughter, and nothing more.' She stood back. Her back creaked like an old tree in a high wind. Christ's blood how it hurt. 'It's time to ride up to the road for the bus.'

'Will the bus take me back to my family?'

'In time it will.'

The little girl knew that it wouldn't and her face slowly crumpled, and then she threw her arms around her bony waist. 'Please don't! Please let me stay here with you! Please don't send me away! They'll come and find me here!'

For a moment the old woman pictured it. Why shouldn't she? How sweet to live out the last of her life with the child in this glade. Her childish chatter, brushing her hair daily, laying the blanket over her each night. She herself would live longer for it. But no, it was not possible. It was not safe. It would only be selfish. The soldiers would be back. The guns would be heard again. These valleys were not safe for anyone now.

'Listen. I promise you, I will not put you on a bus unless you will be absolutely safe. Unless I find another to look after you. Do you trust me?'

Eulalia continued to sob and hug her.

The old woman sighed.

They rode up out of the valley again and turned eastwards towards the high road.

The moment they emerged onto the road they saw a roadblock only a quarter of a mile away. The soldiers whistled and summoned them towards them.

'Which village you from?'

'From just down below,' said the old woman. 'From the valley.'

The soldiers frowned. 'Where you travelling?'

'We are leaving here now. It is best not to live here longer. We are going to my daughter in the city. We are waiting for the bus.'

'The bus?' The soldiers grinned.

'The bus is running?'

'Maybe. Maybe not.'

They tethered Pedro the donkey and waited in the shade of a dried-out pine tree and the old woman prayed. The girl fidgeted and cried. The crickets sang. At last the ancient yellow bus came grinding along the road. The soldiers narrowed their eyes at it and waved it through. The bus stopped and chugged beside them.

The old woman called up to the driver. 'Let us on. But only the child is travelling. We have no money.'

The driver said nothing.

She clambered up, holding on to the handles, her stick tucked under her arm. Eulalia climbed up behind her.

The old woman stood in the gangway and looked down the bus. 'Listen to me,' she said. 'I ask one of you to care for my granddaughter. She is going to the city. You understand why. She cannot stay here, not now. Her auntie is there. And she still has family, but they have become separated. Who will look after her? Who among you knows the city?'

People shifted and stared sullenly or looked away. One fat woman in a yellow headscarf clamped her arms around the basket on her lap and glared at Eulalia as if she thought she'd try and steal it from her. As if it was all her fault. She had never felt more wretched. She wanted to crawl under the nearest seat and stay there asleep forever.

'You know the times,' said the old woman. 'She needs looking after. For the love of Christ.'

'Sit her here,' said a woman's voice. 'I know the city. She will be safe.'

The two women sitting behind the woman who had spoken, plump peasant women with baskets of potatoes and eggs in their laps, tutted scornfully. One muttered loudly, 'From one witch to another.'

'*Vamos, vamos,*' the driver called back.

229

'In time!' cried the old woman. 'I will not be hurried!' She peered at the voice.

The woman who had spoken had long hair, chestnut red from some bottle of dye, and cheap jewellery dangling from her like fruit on a tree. She was young-ish and she smiled.

'Well,' said the old woman. 'God himself knows.'

'That he does,' said the *puta*.

'But if you fail her or abandon her, or worse...'

'I know,' said the *puta*. 'I know it.'

The old woman turned around and laid her bumpy old hand on Eulalia's head. 'Now, child. You sit with the lady here. You will be safe with her.'

Eulalia wanted to cling to her like her own mother, but she couldn't in front of the busload of people all staring at her with expressionless faces, as indifferent as the world itself. She bowed her head to hide her tears.

'Why aren't you coming too?'

The old woman answered so that the child would understand. 'I have to care for the donkey,' she said. 'He cannot live in the city, he would be too sad. He can only live here. Who would care for him if not me? He is my oldest friend.'

The child sniffed loudly.

'Go,' said the old woman. 'Sit with her.'

Eulalia pushed past her and sat next to the red-haired woman without looking at her, swinging her feet furiously, staring down at her fingers twirling around each other in her lap.

'Jesus Christ love you,' said the old woman. 'The Mother of God love you.'

One or two people on the bus looked away, shamed by the names.

'All will go right with you. All will be well for you.'

Then she turned and shuffled back up the gangway and stepped carefully down to the road. She didn't turn again or look back, knowing the child would never look at her again or forgive her or wish her farewell. But that was permitted. That was to be forgiven. She was only a child.

She untethered the donkey and climbed slowly onto a tree stump and remounted him and pulled him around and headed back down to the valley.

'You're not going too, old mother?' called a soldier.

'No,' she said. 'I am too old.' She looked back at them with her milky eyes. 'You know where to find me.'

43

'I like your dress,' said the lady. 'It's very pretty.'

Eulalia sniffed and said nothing.

'What do you think of mine? It's one of my favourite dresses, but still not as pretty as yours.' She sighed and shook out her hair. It smelt nice. 'Ay. I'm as hungry as a wolf. And all I've got is some *habas fritas*. You want some?'

Eulalia shook her head.

'Well.' The woman took out a plastic bag and ate some of the salted beans. 'Here,' she said. 'Hold out your hands.'

Eulalia shook her head and then did as she was told. The woman poured some *habas* into her hands.

'In case you change your mind,' she said. 'Or I'll eat them all myself. So.' She munched and swallowed. 'You ever been beyond Domingo?'

She shook her head miserably.

'I'm going to La Concordia. But you're going to the city?'

'I don't know.' Her own voice sounded very quiet in the noisy bus. 'I don't know where I'm going.' She could feel herself beginning to cry again. The lady put her arm around her.'

'Do not be afraid. But your grandma's too old to go to the city, I suppose?'

'She's not my grandma. But I'm supposed to pretend she is. And there's the donkey to care for.'

'Ah.' The woman was raising the bag of *habas* to her mouth again but she stopped.

'She said my family would be in the city with my auntie. She said they would have escaped from all the shooting.'

The woman said, 'Sssh now. Not too loudly.'

'But are we going to find my family?'

'No doubt about it.'

'Really?'

'I bet they'd have made it there.'

'There was all the shooting -'

'Shshsh ... I know. But many escaped.'

'My family live in another valley. Will I find them again?'

'With the love of God. You must have faith.'

'I saw lots of dead people, and a dog.'

The red-haired lady looked at her sharply. 'You mean you saw this yourself?'

'They burned it, I saw the fire. But I don't know what became of my Mama and Papa or my brothers and El Pipón because I was in the hot pool. And then I got lost.'

The woman turned away and stared at the cracks in the smeary window. She swallowed. After a while she said, 'Never fear. We will go together to find your auntie in the city.'

'But you said you were going to La Concordia.'

'Ah no. I meant, I am travelling *through* La Concordia. That's where my house is. But I must go on to the city myself tomorrow. To buy ... some new shoes.'

'My auntie works in a shoe shop!'

'Truly? Well let's go and find her! I can buy my new shoes off her. Some fine red shoes. You think?'

Eulalia nodded.

'And then she will know where your family is. Let us pray.'

She gave the little girl a hug, and after a while the little girl raised her hand to her mouth and ate some beans.

'What's your name?'

'My name is Juliana. And you?'

'Eulalia.'

'Eulalia. A most beautiful name.'

She stared around at the bus and the people and studied

everything. She had only been on a bus a very few times before, the village bus, the Little Virgin of Suyapa, who was always tired and breaking down. This bus was called La India Virgen. She leaned out and looked down the gangway. The windscreen was very cracked in front of the driver, so he leaned a bit to one side too, so he could see out. The driver played his radio with lots of loud music and some wires running up to a speaker behind the mirror for combing his hair in. He also had a long red cord to pull on and sound his horn. He stopped to pick up a lady with two small children.

'That's his sister,' said the lady Juliana beside her. 'She doesn't pay.'

The driver's sister and the two children stood at the front crammed up against the windscreen so they could chat to him on the journey and keep him company so he wouldn't get lonely. Another little boy, about six, got on as well, and went up and down the aisle selling sweets and antibiotics in foil wrappers, speaking very fast and high-pitched and saying that they would cure eye troubles, piles, melancholia, cancer, itching, palsy and sexual malfunction.

They went through Indian villages called Jicalapa, and Cojutepeque, and Guarizama, where the bus slowed right down to drive around a dog asleep in the middle of the road. Then Azacualpa, and Yarauca, where the driver stopped altogether so he could chat to a friend of his by the side of the road for about ten minutes. It wasn't a fast bus.

Two filthy children played in front of a tin shack by the roadside, and on a crate there was a shot dead spider monkey with his arms wrapped around an empty rum bottle, his head tilted back as if drunk, his tiny pink mouth agape.

There was a grove of firs, bark chopped away above the roots, turpentine weeping. An idiot boy on a stone emitting animal noises and whoops, little piglet squeals, fist crammed in his scabby mouth. A man making a net bag, a woman breastfeeding a dirty little baby. A lazy man in a chair, moving it round to catch the shade, a human hour hand. A little boy like a tiny Chinaman.

She leaned into the aisle again.

'What does that notice say? At the front of the bus. Why isn't it in Spanish?'

The woman looked where she was pointing and read,

'"The Bluebird Bus Company. Your children's SAFETY is our Business. Fort Valley, Georgia." This is an old North American school bus, and that's English.'

'You can read English?'

'Read it and speak it. I've got a lot of customers, so it helps to speak a lot of languages. I'm an entertainer. I entertain people.'

One of the women sitting behind made a rude noise.

'In a circus?'

'In a circus, yes! How did you guess?'

'With baboons and hippopompuses?'

'Oh yes. And monkeys, lions, all sorts of animals.' She leaned close to the little girl, her big black-lined eyes shining and her huge gold earrings dancing. 'In fact, I was born in a circus!'

Eulalia's mouth opened wider. The woman touched her under the chin and shut it again. 'If you are good, I will tell you all about it. My life in the circus – riding on the backs of lions - and sailing on the high seas with the pirates – and, and, many other things.'

Eulalia swallowed the last of her beans in one gulp and nearly choked and the lady had to bang her on the back to save her life. Then she settled her hands in her lap and stopped swinging her legs.

'Well, said Juliana. 'Some thirty-five –' She stopped. 'Some thirty, in fact *twenty-nine* years ago, my mother bore me in a circus, the greatest and finest circus in all of Central America…'

It was after dark and windy when they pulled into La Concordia and they all climbed off the bus. The square was

235

poorly lit and there were lean dogs sloping about in the shadows, furtive and mean-eyed from regular whippings. Loose tin roofs lifted and banged in the dusty wind, and there were some men sitting under the trees, swigging from bottles and staring at them.

Juliana took her hand. 'Don't be afraid, *niña*. You know what I always carry in my handbag? A Bible – and a carving knife! I am ready for anything.' The woman pulled her along. 'Let's get home and I will cook you supper. Besides, I know everyone in this town. More to the point, they know me!'

'*Hola* darling,' called one of the men under the tree, standing up. 'You two make a nice…'

He didn't get any further before Juliana turned on him and unleashed such an astonishing barrage of curses that the man shrank back as if slapped. She even called him the son of a pig!

'Christ, I was only saying …' he muttered.

Flame-haired Juliana strode on down the street, the little girl trotting at her side.

Her house was painted pale blue and on the end of a line of houses all stuck together in a cobbled street. Inside it smelt of perfume and flowers. She made her some chili and rice and a boiled egg, and there was *iguaxte* sauce for the tortillas made from roasted pumpkin seeds and tomato and spices.

'Very good for you,' she said.

Eulalia tried to eat but couldn't eat much because the food made her think of her mother and her longing for her was too great.

On the walls were animal skulls and drums and some tails and those toy skeletons that were sold by street seller children for the Day of the Dead, when old women strewed golden flowers in the road, *flores del muerto*, so that dead might find their way home.

Juliana saw her looking and nodding towards the things on the wall, she said proudly,

'I am both kinds of Indian. Both Gypsy and Maya. What a combination that is!' Fire flashed from her eyes.

'Don't you have children?'

She shook her head. 'My way of life is not that of a mother.'

Eulalia looked down at her bowl. She couldn't eat any more.

Juliana clasped her cheeks between her nice smelling hands and kissed her.

The next day they went to get the bus for the city. Eulalia asked when she would see her family again, but the lady said she would find her aunt. Eulalia wept and wept.

'Peace, child. Look at me. Look at me, and stop your crying.' Juliana took out her own hanky and wiped Eulalia's nose. 'Listen to me. I will not abandon you. Not ever. You understand?' She knelt before her and held her tightly by her arms. 'I will go with you through the streets of the city, until we find your auntie or your family. There are government departments, there will be lists of people who have been moved away in the disorder, catalogues of where they have gone. We will find the names of your family in the lists, we will see where they have been transported to. People to help us. I swear it on my own mother's grave. What do you think I will do, turn you out in the heart of the city and then gaily wave you goodbye? To fend for yourself there? Eh? Surely you don't think that even I am such a wicked woman?'

Eulalia shook her head.

'Well,' she said. 'I am a wicked woman sometimes, but that is because of the way of the world. But sometimes I must do good deeds to balance out my wickedness, must I not? Or I will live out eternity in hell, with all the other interesting but wicked, wicked people.'

And she stood again and crossed herself with the sign of the cross at the same time.

'Well then. *Vámonos*. Upon this next great adventure!'

The bus to the city was another big yellow bus covered in bright paintings and sayings and was called El Nazareno. It was also covered in bumps and scars and scratches, and appeared to have suffered a fire on one side. The windows all had huge cracks in them, along with the occasional bullet-hole, and there was no door on the back. The bumper hung off the front nearly touching the ground, clanking when the bus came into the station over a bump and braked, and across the top of the windscreen was a green strip to keep the sun out of the driver's eyes.

'Here we are,' said Juliana. 'The luxury coach to the city, complete with air conditioning.'

She got up and paid the driver. He jerked his head at Eulalia.

'She doesn't pay,' said Juliana.

'Everyone pays,' he said.

'I tell you, she doesn't pay. She has paid enough already, understand?'

The driver glared a little more. Then he muttered a badword and stared ahead.

'Now mend your manners,' Juliana scolded him. 'And drive carefully.'

Eulalia thought the driver would get angry at the way she talked to him, but he just shrugged.

They went and sat down.

It was a long and winding journey through the country to the city, the bus going over hills and down into valleys, swinging round hairpin bends and leaning out over precipices with the brakes squealing and the chickens all clucking in alarm. Somewhere near the back of the bus was a goat not enjoying it very much either, and people held onto their baskets and their babies very tightly, praying with fervour.

Juliana told her all about the Gypsies on the way. The Gypsies were from India but not Indian, while the Maya were called Indian but not from India. It was important to be clear on such things.

The Gypsies came over with the conquistadors from the Heart of Old Spain, from Castile with its many castles, and Andalusia where the ladies wore black mantillas and the long red dresses. They clicked castanets in their hands as they walked along the streets of Seville at midnight, swaying beneath the orange trees with little glow-worms shining in their raven hair.

They lived in caves outside Seville, and they stole aboard the mighty sailing ships of the Conquistadors, hiding in the bottom of the ships along with the rats and the biscuits.

'We learned about the Conquistadors at school,' said Eulalia. 'Cortés and Don Pedro Avocado, who had a red beard and red hair, not red like yours but horrid red. And our priest was sent back to town because of neo-Imperialism and saying the government was corrupt and full of self-serving badwords.'

'Badwords, eh?'

'You hear a lot of badwords.'

'You do,' said Juliana. She was always laughing and then sad again suddenly. 'Well anyway. The Conquistadors were led by the great and terrible Cortés, and Pedro Avocado, who had pale red hair and icy blue eyes, as you so rightly say. The same as the cruel and fearsome English pirate Francisco Draco, which means Francis the Dragon, who sailed in a ship that was shaped like a dragon and breathed fire from its mouth.'

'And he killed Tecúman, the Indian chief.'

'I believe he may have done.'

Eulalia looked up at her. 'I'm going to school again one day.'

'Most certainly you are.'

'But first I must find my Mama and my Papa and family.'

'Yes you must. And we will.'

Eulalia stared out of the blurry window and crinkled up her eyes from the sun. One day she would be an educated person.

And come home to the village covered in wreaths and wearing fine coloured robes to show she was educated, and her Mama would weep and hug her, her heart bursting with pride in her clever and beautiful daughter, and all the people of the village would bow down before her as she stepped between them like a great lady, yet gazing down upon their prostrate forms with a kindly smile nevertheless, and taking care not to tread upon their hands.

Then she thought of the village, and the vision vanished.

Juliana pulled her face down into the folds of her red skirt and laid her hands on her thin shaking shoulders.

'Ay *niña*. Cry on me.'

44

Finally towards dusk they emerged out onto the wide plain leading to the city. An unsettling wind was blowing up strongly ahead of a storm, and the little bus was buffeted left and right, slaloming along the potholed road. Curtains of thin dust raced away across the fields stretched darkly away but the little shacks along the road twinkled with occasional lights, bare bulbs hanging from loose strung cables. People huddled around braziers or crouched in doorways. Sometimes Eulalia saw their faces as they glanced up at the passing bus, and they looked afraid.

They were still some way from the city, and they would arrive long after dark.

She reached out and took Juliana's hand.

And then they saw a roadblock up ahead. There were oildrums burning at the sides of the road and they gave off an oppressive orange glare in the black night.

Juliana said a badword, but quietly. She said to Eulalia, 'Excuse me.'

'That's all right,' said Eulalia.

People craned against the windows to see.

'What's happening?'

'Who knows? Nobody knows what's happening in this country any more.'

The bus came to a halt, chugging and juddering, and a soldier came by with a machine gun under his arm.

'Be calm,' said Juliana, holding her hand very tightly. 'Say nothing about anything you have seen.'

The soldier stood at the door and jerked his head.

241

'Everyone off the bus.'

There was a frightened stillness, and then another soldier came over and kicked the side of the bus and they both started shouting. Suddenly everyone was on their feet, chickens clucking, goat bleating, sleepy children wailing, pushing and shoving their way down to the front to get off the bus as the soldiers had ordered.

'Say nothing now,' said Juliana. 'Be very brave.'

There were jeeps and trucks parked along the side of the road, and several other cars and trucks had been stopped. Eulalia saw a man pulled roughly out of a very dirty saggy car and marched away to one of the huts nearby.

Other groups of soldiers squatted round a fire and smoked in the darkness. Another rode round and round in circles on a motorbike grinning, while a man in a white shirt stood nearby and looked on helplessly. It was his motorbike but the soldier had stolen it.

The first soldier with the machine gun under his arm ordered their chickens and the goat on a rope to be taken away, and then he made the people all line up beside the bus and walked up and down in front of them like the colonel had in the village. He was short and dark and wore his cap pushed far back on his head and he had bad skin. The pitted scars flecked little shadows over his firelit face. He narrowed his eyes and jerked his chin a lot as if he were a great man or practising to be a dictator.

'You,' he said, pointing at one of the women. 'Show me what's in the basket.'

She showed him. It was eggs and some spoons and some clay pots.

He took one of the pots out of the basket and threw it to the ground. Then he took one of the eggs and smashed that too.

'Be careful,' muttered Juliana. 'It might be a bomb.'

He told the woman to take the rest of the eggs over to the soldiers by the fire and leave them there. Then she could get back on the bus.

'With my sister?'

The soldier ignored her. She went with her sister.

Another soldier had the driver up against the bus at the front and was poking and prodding him to see if he was carrying a gun, and then he demanded his papers and scowled at them.

'I don't have any papers,' whispered Eulalia, terrified.

'You're with me,' said Juliana.

Another soldier, a fat man with a gold braid flap on each shoulder, came over and looked straight at Juliana.

'You.' He pointed at the ground in front of him.

She stepped out, holding tightly on to Eulalia.

'Leave the young one behind. Just you.'

'She goes everywhere with me.'

The fat man smiled very broadly. 'I said,' he repeated softly, 'leave the little one behind.'

'I will not.'

The fat man turned and called to the soldier with the machine gun.

'Remove this one and search her.'

'No!' wailed Eulalia, clinging to Juliana for life.

Juliana covered her with her shawl, but the soldiers enjoyed a challenge like this. One of them came up and butted Juliana on the shoulder with his gun, and she reeled and staggered. Eulalia lost hold of her hand. She darted forward to her as Juliana fell to the ground, but then another soldier simply swept the little girl up under his arm and carried her away. She kicked and screamed, until suddenly she felt something very cold and steely digging into her cheek. She stopped and froze, and was dropped to the ground in the dust. She felt something cold and steely dig into her cheek again.

'For shame,' she heard one of the women say.

The soldier stood over the little girl for a moment longer, the muzzle of his rifle digging into her face. Then he raised it up again. Eulalia lay and trembled.

'For shame,' said the woman more vehemently, crossing herself.

'So it is,' drawled the fat soldier with the gold braid. 'All the country is shamed by the actions of the rebels and the guerrillas. They are fighting even now to the west of the capital. There are trees down, roads and bridges destroyed, villages laid waste. In this war, *señora*, no one is innocent. You hear me? Everyone is suspect. Even this little one. Who knows what treason is plotted in villages like hers?' He stared down at Eulalia with his fat piggy eyes. 'On your feet,' he ordered.

Two other soldiers were pulling Juliana up. She shook her head and began to scream. They held her by the arms.

'She stays with me! Let me go, she is mine! Leave her be!'

The fat soldier went over and slapped Juliana across the face and then when her head sagged he gripped her chin in his hand.

'Listen to me, *puta*,' he said. 'We give the orders around here. So shut your dirty mouth.'

Juliana spat in his face and kicked at him and cursed him. She was like a wildcat being taken off to the circus. She said that God would curse them, that she would never rest until he was dead and she was reunited with the little one. The fat soldier nodded and another soldier stepped up and knocked Juliana on the back of her head. Her head fell forwards and her hair fell down over her face, and over her chin there ran a trickle of blood.

'Take her to the hut.'

The two soldiers grinned.

'*Si, teniente.*'

'And you,' said the fat man, turning back on Eulalia with sudden ferocity. 'Not another word out of you, you understand? Now get back on the bus, and be grateful we've saved you from the clutches of that *puta*.'

'She was very good to me.'

The fat man face went very blank, and he leaned down a

little. 'Did you hear what I said? I said, not another word. Are you stupid, *Indita*, as well as bad?'

Eulalia's eyes were blurry as she stared back at him. But she didn't move, didn't cry, didn't shift her gaze. Be calm, Juliana had said. Be very brave.

The fat soldier stood upright again. 'Back on the bus,' he said, and then turned away as if bored.

They were dragging Juliana away across the dusty yard. She watched her go. One of her shoes came off as she was dragged. Eulalia wanted to run after her and pick it up. She would keep it for her until they found each other again. But the soldiers would stop her. She watched. They kicked open the door of the hut and dragged Juliana inside and kicked the door shut again. The red shoe lay on its own in the dust.

After another hour, perhaps two, the bus slowly drove away into the darkness. Eulalia huddled in the corner of a seat sobbing, but nobody took any notice. Many other people were sobbing too. Several had been parted from a husband or wife, brother or sister. In all, eight passengers had been taken away to the huts for interrogation. One woman who had answered back too much, for instance, and a man who wore glasses and was carrying a book.

No one else cared for her. No one dared. Because the world had come to an end.

45

Nicholas got back as far as Santo Domingo before he ran into a roadblock. The truck driver who had run him this far took his twenty dollars and turned around in the road and called after him,

'You should be leaving with me. This place is no good now. You're a fucking idiot, sir!'

He said to the soldier boy on the barrier that he was a doctor, a colleague of Dr Hércules Menendez. He needed to return to the Valley of San Antonio. The soldier boy, younger than he was, shook his head.

'Show me your ID.'

'It's up at the clinic. Please let me pass.'

The soldier didn't even reply, he just walked away and started talking to another.

Nicholas walked around the barrier and approached them. Immediately they unshouldered their guns and butted him back, shouting. 'Get back you idiot, what do think this is? This is an army checkpoint!'

'What's happening in the valley?'

'None of your business. Get back to the city. You're running a risk travelling without ID. You should keep quiet.'

'Where have all the villagers gone?'

'The army is restoring order. We don't have to talk to you. You work for an NGO? You really need to get lost, amigo.'

'I need to see Colonel Inocencio.'

They stopped barracking him, looked at him hard. One said, 'You know Colonel Inocencio?'

'He wanted me to report here. As a doctor.'

'You're lying. You just know the name.'

'I'm not lying. Colonel Inocencio and I met at a social

function. In the capital. He asked me back here, he said I would be a great help. He told me to report to him as soon as I arrived from the city.' He started improvising his most grandiloquent Spanish. 'He said that my advanced medical and psycho-pathological competence would be invaluable for the project.' *Mi competencia avanzada médico y psico-patalógico...* He was rather proud of his invention, whilst noting that even as he was eaten up with anxiety, he could still find room for personal vanity.

The soldier boys looked flummoxed. They fell back and talked among themselves. After a while they just looked bored and one even wandered away. Hell.

'Come on,' he said. 'I need to get on.'

One wandered back and let him through without another word, jerking his thumb up the road.

The valley was in turmoil, a roaring, clanking invasion of heavy trucks and diggers and rolling red dust. And no locals to be seen anywhere.

He flagged down a truck and peremptorily demanded a lift up to the village. Swaggering now. 'On business,' he said. He was only a boy, but he was a gringo. Maybe he really was someone. The driver took him without argument.

And there in the aid station sat Tumax. Amidst all the chaos. As if he hadn't noticed a thing. As if the aid station inhabited a parallel universe, with only fitful and discretionary relation to the one around it, being on a higher level, devoted only to the highest principles of philanthropy.

Tumax stood and gawped at him. 'What are you doing back here?'

'I could ask you the same.'

'And what's all the bruising on your face?'

'Something didn't go quite according to plan. Tell me what is going on here.'

'It is not safe for you here. You are crazy. You need to leave.'

'And more important, where are the villagers? Where have they gone?'

'I don't know. My conscience is clear. I am leaving soon myself. Stop accusing me.' Tumax looked away out of the dusty window. 'There has been a very ugly massacre in the next valley. It is the drug gangs.'

'Why on earth are they fighting here?'

'For land. They killed twenty or thirty people. They're animals. I bet they're El Salvadoreans come across the border. They're savages.'

'How do you know all this?'

'Do not question me. I am telling you this out of politeness.'

'Have you money in the bank, Tumax? Have you done well out of it?'

Tumax stared at him sullenly. 'I don't understand what it is all about.'

'You must be stupid. I do, and I'm not even a local.'

'Just leave here,' muttered Tumax, sitting down again.

'I came here to help, as you well know. Why do you stand in my way? I can give you money.'

'I don't want your money.'

'And if it works out, maybe Colonel Inocencio will give you more.'

Tumax said, 'Colonel Inocencio?'

Finally Tumax showed him 'the manifest'. 'It is here on the manifest,' he kept saying. He was proud of the word. 'Look.'

'So where is the family of José Silvestre Chacach?'

They scanned it together until Nicholas saw the names of Maria Chacach along with Alejandro, Jaime and Héctor. No Abuelita, no José, and no Eulalia.

'They will have gone too,' said Tumax. 'Perhaps separately.'

'How do you know?'

'Because everyone has gone. They were in danger here.'

'To the coast, you say? To work on the plantations?'

'So I believe. They are government-owned plantations. Bananas, pineapples, mangoes. It is a very good place to work. A safe place.'

'But there is no record of who has gone where? Which plantations?'

Tumax just shrugged. 'Do not blame me. I do not have the records. Someone will have them.' He saw the look on the English boy's face. He was a curious, insolent, domineering person and Tumax longed never to see him again. But the expression on his face was fierce and sad. Tumax said, 'Do not be anxious for them. They will be well treated. The people in charge mean them no harm.'

'If you were me, if you wanted to find them, what would you do?'

Tumax looked thoughtful, then said, 'I would try to cure myself of wanting to find them.'

He paced around the small cabin, mind racing. Then he knelt down suddenly on his right knee and flipped open his rucksack and loosened the drawstring and delved into the inner mesh pocket. He had a photo of the family on his mobile. Now he remembered. But his mobile was gone. He unpacked the entire bag. Tumax watched him patiently. It was gone. Though they'd left him all his money, and a kilogram of uncut cocaine. It was like this country itself was hanging on to him, whether he wanted it or not.

He hung over his scattered belongings, on his knees. He could feel his face sagging with gravity. He could stay still like this. He could lie down among his stuff and just stay still and sleep forever like a tired child. An immense effort.

He began to pack up again slowly. 'I need to go back to the village.'

'That is impossible.'

'I just want to go back to the house of José Chacach. It is vital. I do not need to stay long.'

'Quite impossible. It is expressly forbidden.'

He stuffed in the last of his clothes and his book and tightened the drawstring and the straps. Stood and shouldered it. 'I'm going. Don't worry, Tumax,' he said gently. 'It'll be all right. I'll get hold of a new phone. And give me your mobile number. Just in case.'

'Just in case what?'

'Just in case you decide to do a good deed, and find out for me where the family of José Silvestre Chacach have gone.'

Tumax wrote his number very slowly on a scrap of paper and gave it to the boy doctor. The boy tucked it into his shirt pocket and walked out of the door and Tumax watched him go. He was a very extraordinary person.

He was annoying as hell, a very demanding character, and no doubt more than a little mad.

He took that long half an hour walk up through the straggling village along the red dust road to the upper reaches of that wide sunlit valley with the rocky stream away to his left and the trucks parked up along the road. Men lounging and smoking and staring at him as he passed by. Away in the forest to the right he could hear chainsaws and bulldozers and the tops of the trees were trembling and swaying in that machine wind.

On a rock by the roadside with his stick sat Pedro Xom. Unchanged. Watching, waiting, a spirit turning to stone. And then nodding and greeting him as if everything was quite usual and not a dream.

'It does not surprise me you have come back,' said the old man. 'Though you know there is nothing here now. Your friends have flown, passage birds wiser than you. You have bruising to your face.'

'Yes I *know*.' This was getting tiresome. 'And my knee still hurts. But ... how are you still here?'

Pedro Xom did not explain himself. Perhaps he had been

hiding out in the forest. Was he not afraid? On other matters though he was positively garrulous.

'The Valley is being peopled anew, though not by my own people. They are making the valley into a plantation, for the people, for the country to become wealthy. To become more like the *Estados Unidos*, so that we will be richer and happier. You see. These diggers here will make us happier.'

'What will you do? Are you leaving? People must fight against this.'

Pedro Xom ignored him. 'I have heard that within some plantations, in only the next valley from here, at certain choice sites among the virtuous plants there are others planted too. Coca plants. And who is to say if such a thing will not be done here too, and that this cottage before us laid low will not really grow *cocas*? It is not in our culture. We never took *coca*. It is South America. But the need for it is very great, we understand, in countries besides our own. Am I right? And also I have heard that there are laboratories making other drugs. And the young women and the girls are separated and sent to Mexico to work in the whorehouses, with their will or without it. Others are sent still further, to the *Estados Unidos* or to Japan or Russia, wherever the need is great. This need will never die.

'Men love war not only because it is glorious, but also because it is ruinous. Men have always longed for the end of the world, and nothing has ever been taught by man to man.'

Nicholas tried to think of something to say to this, but Pedro Xom was unstoppable today.

'But who am I to judge? An old fool. Live long and see much. The sun shines on us all, rain chills us all. It is all one. This is an old man talking, is it not? Is it because I am wise or I am weary? You are young. You still see good and evil as sharply as night and day. I see only dusk. Are you young and foolish, or are your eyes better than my old eyes? I know nothing because I am old, and everything I have known is ended.'

Nicholas felt absurdly awkward, now Pedro Xom had fallen silent and evidently had no wish to talk or listen any further. The whole thing was unreal: that Pedro Xom was here, that *he* was here. He tugged at the peak of his baseball cap and said, '*Adios, senor*,' and then walked on. He wanted to look back but never did, afraid that Pedro Xom would have died upon his rock.

46

It was strange to find the cottage still standing but deserted, even the chickens gone. The soldiers would have taken them to eat of course. The cottage was oppressive in its dead silence. The bulldozers had not yet come up this far.

How quickly they had fled. Maria used to smear the table legs with sticky pine resin to trap the ants, but still they had found a way up and now streamed across the tabletop to devour the remains of a single tortilla that lay there. In the back room the dividing curtain was snatched back to show José's and Maria's mattress on the floor, which someone had pointlessly ripped open with a bayonet. He drew the curtain closed. That was where José and Maria had lain together in gentleness and privacy.

But there it still was, what he sought. In the niche in the kitchen wall. With the jar of flowers browned and hanging, breeding tiny hopping flies, and the whisky miniature he'd brought them, and the picture of the blue-eyed Virgin, rose-cheeked maiden with her plump pink babe – the photograph he'd printed out from his mobile. The family, all of them. With him there too, looming at the back.

He took it and rolled it, and as an afterthought he took down the picture of the Virgin. Then he set in back again in a chill of indecision. What if she was the Spirit of the House? If he took it away, they would never return. But then if he found them – when he found them again – and José and Eulalia and Abuelita too, down on the plantation – he could present them with this picture and they would make a new home around her, the blue-eyed mother goddess.

He left her there in her niche with the whisky and went outside and stood staring at nothing.

He sat on the edge of the watertrough and he remembered the night José fell in, the night he tried to kiss Maria and she hit him. Remembered everything.

When he looked up there was an old woman on a donkey on the path up behind the cottage. She was looking past him.

He turned away, swiped his face dry of tears with the cuff of his shirt.

'*Adios,*' she said.

He waved tiredly.

'It is dangerous here,' she said. 'What are you doing?'

It was a good question. He didn't know what he was doing. He waved the photograph at her, shook his head.

She looked at him a long time until it annoyed him.

'What?' he said. 'What do you want? Ride on.'

'The soldiers will arrest you. What have you in your hand?'

'It's nothing to do with you. I am just sad that the people have gone from here. I should go too. I am from England.'

'I didn't take you for an Indian.'

He looked at her sourly.

'It is a sorrowful matter about the villages around,' said the old woman.

'You could say. Do you know where the people from these villages have gone?'

'They say, to a plantation on the coast,' she said. 'But I am not foolish. In another village the people were killed. I am near blind but I can smell dead bodies well enough. In a ditch up this very path they lie. The vultures come by day, the foxes by night. Their spirits have flown.'

Now he was cold. They could not simply be dead. Things were not that bad.

'Who do you say killed them?' he croaked.

'Evildoers.'

'But was it the army, or drug gangs, or leftist rebels or what?'

'Is there a difference?'

He shook his head again. 'They cannot be dead.'

He looked so broken. Through the white cloud in which she saw everything move now, human figures like wraiths in a perpetual evening mist, she saw him sitting there, the foreign boy. His voice was young, but he sat there in the mist crookbacked like an old man leaning on his stick.

'Come here,' she said.

'Why?' It made no difference whether he did or not. But he should probably just keep going now. It was easier than stopping. He stood and went over to her.

'Show me.'

He showed her the photograph and she held it almost to her nose and looked it over inch by inch. Then she prodded it with a forefinger. 'Well of course,' she muttered. 'She's gone to no plantation. She's gone to the city to find her Auntie Rosario.'

He reached out and held onto the edge of the photograph. 'What?'

'In a shoe shop. The little girl. I found her in another valley.'

Nicholas was breathless. 'Lala? On her own? In the city?'

'Not alone. She went with a woman on the bus. She was separated from her family.'

'Where did the others go?'

'I do not know. There was confusion. Some say to the coast, to the plantations. I say they were killed. I found the child in another valley from here, where people were certainly killed and there was a lot of fighting. She was very lost.'

'You could have cared for her.'

'It was not safe. It is still not. Believe me.'

'Who did she go with?'

'A woman.'

'Who?'

'I knew I could trust her from her face.'

And she nearly blind.

'But her family have gone to the plantation,' he said.

'So I have heard.'

'Do you know which one?'

She just grimaced.

'But they will go and look for her,' he said. 'Her family. They will not just forget her about her.'

'No they will not forget about her. But they will not go to look for her.'

He felt a rising anger with this decrepit prophetess. 'Why not?'

'Do not shout at me. If you shout at me I will ride on.'

'I will not shout. But, but … how could they not look for her?'

'They are highland people. Gentle people. They will be utterly bewildered, there on the coast. If they have become separated from their children, they will cry, they will pray, and hope. But they may believe she is already dead. They will not go around the country demanding to find her, let alone go to the city.' She sniffed. 'I am sorry but that is how it is.'

'Then no one will be looking for her. I don't believe you.'

The woman shook her head. 'But I pray she will be looked after. It is a dangerous country,' she said. 'It grows more dangerous by the day. But some people still have kind hearts. I pray for the little girl daily.'

In the distance there was the sound of a jeep engine. It was coming up the road. The soldiers were coming now.

'How can I find the little girl?' he asked again urgently.

'You cannot.'

'Don't be stupid, I *must*.' He said, 'There is no choice.'

The woman stared at him. 'She is in the city, among millions of people. You cannot find her. But I believe she will be cared for. I am no old fool.'

The jeep was coming nearer.

'This is a dangerous place,' said the old woman. 'We are both crazy to be here. I am riding on up the track. You are not from here, you must go back to your country.'

'I can't. It isn't mine.'

'And people think *I'm* crazy!' She was already riding away up the track beyond the cottage. 'I can hear the jeep coming. You should be gone. They will not like you here. You should be going home.'

The jeep appeared and came to halt. The woman turned her back and rode slowly away up the track on her doddering donkey but they were not interested in her. The soldiers looked across at him.

'I'm coming,' he said.

47

Eulalia was asleep and dreaming when the bus stopped and the engine was turned off. She opened her eyes and the world erupted around her.

They were in the city, in a bus station. It was still night time but terrifyingly noisy and she was hungry and thirsty but above all she was alone and afraid.

'C'mon, everyone off the bus!' shouted the driver.

She crept to the front of the bus and whispered to the man, 'I haven't anywhere to go.'

'Well I have, and that's home to my bed. Now off the bus.'

She crept down from the bus and stared around.

It was dark but there were harsh white lights blazing down from above and fires burning in braziers and oil drums. One man was beating the side of an oil drum with sticks and grinning foolishly. Groups of shabby people crouched around another cooking chili and beans in car hubcaps. There was a man slicing up a huge grey truck tarpaulin into smaller pieces with a knife. There was a woman lying down right by the door of the station ticket office shaking all over. There were young men roaming around and dogs sloping about and a broken down taxi and a dead bus on its side with a man standing on a chair trying to wrench off one of the wheels. There were no trees and the world had come to an end and she didn't know anybody. She must find somewhere to hide and just stay there.

She crawled under a bench and went to sleep. Or tried to, but she couldn't. She was too scared and lonely and hungry and exhausted with sadness. She cried and cried and imagined that somehow her mother would appear and lift her to her feet and hug her and she prayed. Near to her lay the shaking woman. The woman lay on her side and stared out from under the bench, her eyes open but hollow and far away.

Some time later, the woman near her stopped shaking and lay still.

It was early morning and the sun was up and the air was hot but that wasn't from the sun, it was from the hot breath of the buses. There were twenty or thirty of them in the huge dusty bus yard, all crowded together and inching past each other, yellow and brightly painted and hooting loudly from the huge silver horns on top of their roofs. The air was gritty on her tongue, the noise was deafening, and everyone was shouting at the tops of their voices.

She crawled out and stood in bewilderment in the heart of the bus yard, hollow with hunger and sadness. She had never seen so many people in her life.

There was a boy scooting past on a narrow board with wheels. He hadn't any legs and he pushed himself along with his fists, thickly bandaged with old rags to save his knuckles.

'Out of my way!' he cried as he whizzed past her, head down, 'Out of my way! I'm on government business!'

There was an old woman wearing a hat made out of newspaper and sitting beside a wooden wheelbarrow full of pineapples. There was a blind man, bare to the waist and very skinny. There was a man selling cheeping yellow birds in a cage. Through the barbed wire fence in the next yard, there were young people, students, in new jeans and t shirts waiting to get onto a gleaming new coach. They had brightly coloured rucksacks and shiny hair and all of them were laughing and happy because they were going to school, and they all had mobile phones in their hands. There was a security guard with a shotgun standing near them.

Beggars came by on crutches, showing official documents and even photographs of how and where they had lost parts of themselves along the way. There was another yellow chicken bus up on blocks and men lying underneath it mending it and shouting to each other and then peering out with oily faces. The air was cloudy with exhaust fumes and people were pushing and shouting everywhere, and other men and some small boys were selling tickets to them. There were security guards in sandy uniforms with guns over their shoulders, checking people's tickets and looking in their bags, but they weren't hitting anyone with their guns like the soldiers last night. There was a very pregnant lady carrying a huge watermelon under each arm, rolling from side to side as she walked, and there were two little girls with pigtails, younger than her, sitting crosslegged under a cart, picking the nits out of each other's hair. Eulalia wondered if she could make friends with them.

She was parched with thirst. She must drink some water.

An old woman had some water bottles on a stall, but when she asked for a bottle the woman said she'd have to pay and she didn't have any money and the woman looked away.

The small boys selling the tickets looked very serious and tired, and there was a three-legged dog. He ought to belong to the no-legged boy, the one whizzing by on his wooden board. He ought to be his dog, they could race along together. But the three-legged dog was nobody's dog and on its own and people kicked it away.

There was a sizzling stall selling *tamales* and *refrescos*, but everything cost money here and she didn't have any. There was nothing like mangoes or oranges just falling off the trees or the clear stream running down from the mountains that you could drink out of. There was nothing you could get without money here, and she would certainly die and they would all be sorry. Where was her mama? How could she find her here? She was too tired.

There was a soldier in a green uniform, green trousers and green shirt and green cap and big black boots. Just like the soldiers last night, and in the village. There was no escape from them. She had come here to the city and they were here too. They were everywhere. The dead burned bodies.

She was going to faint.

A bus hooted its huge horn at her.

'Get out of the badword way, sister, that bus'll go straight over you!'

She turned around and there was a very dirty boy with a funny eye in a blue t shirt shouting across to her. She didn't move, she couldn't think straight, she couldn't even speak.

'Jesus,' he muttered, 'get out of the badword way.' And he came across the yard and pushed her sideways out of the way of the bus and then let her go again and glared at her. 'Malediction,' he said. 'You high?'

'No,' she said.

'Tch,' he said.

'I'm going to faint,' she said.

'You done too much glue. At your age. Go and faint over there by the wall.'

Her head throbbed and she didn't move.

He pulled her by the arm again and let her go by the wall. Stared at her. She waited but she didn't faint, though her face felt white and sweaty.

'I'm dying for a smoke,' he said, looking around.

'How old are you?'

'Twenty two.'

'You're not twenty two.'

He patted the pockets of his filthy jeans. 'I look good for my age,' he said. 'All the smokes and the women. Keep me looking young.'

He was a rude and a liar and dirty and his teeth were bad and he said badwords and he smoked.

'I need a drink of water,' she said. Her voice sounded very faint.

'A drink of water,' he mimicked, waggling his head. Then he examined her. 'Well.' He pointed at the old woman by the water bottle stall. 'Go talk to her.'

'I already did.'

'Go talk to her again.'

'She'll shout at me.'

'Trust me.'

Hesitantly she went over. The old woman turned on her this time and shouted at her to go back to the rubbish tip.

She ran away, and there was no boy to be found. She was going to die here. Her head throbbed, her throat burned, her heart ached. She was going to die.

She heard a whistle. There was the boy, standing just round the corner by a long-distance coach, leaning against the end of the wall, one dirty trainer up behind him.

She went over.

'Here,' he said, bringing his hand out from behind his back. He held a bottle of water, like the ones on the stall.

'Where did that come from?'

'From the Blessed Virgin herself. She appeared to me in a vision.'

He had stolen it from the stall when the old woman was shouting at her.

'Look, do you want a drink or do you want to die of hypothermia?'

'Of what?'

'Or whatever. Just drink.' And he shoved the bottle into her hand.

She carefully unscrewed the cap and drank a bit. As it was stolen she expected it to taste horrible, or to scald her throat. But it tasted just like any other water. She felt a bit better.

They both sat down in the dust with their backs against the wall.

'Drink some more,' he said. 'Keep drinking it. Sip sip sip.'

She did as he told her.

'So what's your name? Saint Theresa?'

'Eulalia.'

'Eulalia.' He laughed. He examined her some more with growing interest, up and down, side to side,

'You're too young to be here on the street. You just arrived? You ain't got no one have you?'

'My Auntie Rosario. I'm going to visit her. She lives in the city. In the *barrio*.'

'Yeah? Which *barrio*?'

She stared at him. She felt her lips begin to tremble and bit down hard.

'You don't know do you? You don't know nothing but she's called Rosario and she's your auntie. Sister, you know how many people live in this city?'

She turned her head as far away from him as possible until it hurt.

'Well,' he said, 'neither does anyone else, to tell the truth. But it's a lot. Five million or something, and growing all the time. It's going to take you a while to find your auntie. She got money? I'll take you.'

'She works in a shoe shop.'

'Yeah?' He tilted his head. 'You a country girl, eh? *Indita*. Little Indian girl.'

Only a few days back, an Indian guy off the bus had given him a coin when he held his hands out, though the Indian didn't look like he had that many coins to give away himself. They probably weren't so bad, the Indians.

But Eulalia thought he was mocking her. He had no idea what she had seen or where she had come from.

'People were all killed!' she shouted at him furiously, getting to her feet. 'The soldiers came and killed us all! Everybody got burned, and last night they took away Juliana too!'

The boy was staring at her aghast, and then looking rapidly around. Her furious high voice carried, and over by one of the buses, one of the guardsmen scowled over in their direction. She was still mouthing off, about soldiers and killing and stuff. He leapt to his feet and his grimy hand shot out and clamped over her mouth and her head knocked back against the wall.

'Shut the badword up.'

He took the bottle off her and screwed the cap back on one-handed and stuck it in his back pocket, looking about him all the time.

Then round the corner of the silver long distance coach came a soldier. His left hand rested lightly on his machine gun slung under his right arm. He turned his head and stared straight at them.

'Hey, you kids,' he called. 'Come here.'

'*A toda madre*,' said the boy softly. 'Now you done it.'

She mumbled behind his hand.

'Slowly, real slowly,' said the boy. 'Smile a bit, like a dog going to be whipped.'

Something was very wrong and dangerous. The soldier was still staring straight at them. Over by another bus, the security guard too had stopped checking the people's tickets for now and was looking over. Then he told the people there to wait and walked across to join the soldier.

The boy dropped his hand down and spoke very softly out of the side of his mouth, without moving his lips. 'When I say run, run like hell,' he said. 'Out the main exit and into the market. Follow me, don't lose me. They won't shoot and they're too old to run. But run like hell anyhow. You understand?'

She said nothing. She was terrified. She didn't know if her legs would even work.

'Little girl,' said the soldier, walking towards them.

'Run!'

Everything whizzed by and she ran and ran, the boy ahead of her running so fast it looked like his legs were whirring. But she was good at running and she had had some water and soon they were into a dark narrow alley full of hundreds of people under saggy awnings and lots of little stalls. The stalls whizzed past them as they ran - chickens and coconuts and pineapples and machetes and tortillas and watches and lightbulbs and newspapers and shoes and bananas and bicycle tyres and songbirds and ladies' underwear, and no bullets ever came after them. They had to slow down and dodge in between people, weaving in and out and sometimes bumping into them and getting called rude names. At one point the boy jumped right over a dog, and then he ducked down and scooped up a cigarette butt off the ground and then carried on running.

At last he shot down an even narrower alley to the left and leaned into a doorway and stood there gasping for breath.

She stopped in front of him panting.

'Jeez,' he gasped, sticking the dirty cigarette butt in his mouth. 'You're just one long excitement.' He found a few matches in his jeans pocket and struck one against the wall and lit the cigarette butt and sucked on it hard.

It was no wonder he got all out of breath.

'So you don't smoke, I guess.'

'Of course I don't. Papa does.'

'And you don't do glue either.' He laughed to himself.

He was a silly boy. 'Do what with glue?'

'Resistol,' he said. 'Shoe glue. But you no *Resistolero*.'

Gradually he got his breath back. He stared at her. 'OK. I heard what you said back there. I won't ask no more. This country's fu-. In a bad way, you understand? People on the move, people running away, people hiding. Big fights in the mountains, the army, the police, the revolutionaries, the drug lords. Everyone's at it. And now there's you. *Niña del campo*, little country girl, all on her own in the big city.'

He pulled the cigarette butt out of his mouth and stared at it. It had already burned out.

'Tch.' He threw it on the ground, and then hoiked the water bottle out of his back pocket and handed it to her. 'Here,' he said. 'Stay pure.'

She drank a bit more. She was very hungry now.

'You going to find your auntie, yes? But you can't sleep at the bus yard after dark. You were OK last night?'

She shook her head.

'Well then you can't sleep there every night, on your own. There's bad men. Bad stuff. You understand?'

'All men are bad, my mama says.'

'Your mama's not wrong there. OK. Let's get back to headquarters.'

'What's headquarters?'

He just walked off. She followed him, trying not to think about her family and the village as much as possible. It only made her feel sick.

She saw his hand shoot out now and again as they walked along, but nobody else did. He was like a monkey. By the time they emerged out of the other end of the market, he had three chocolate bars and a bag of crisps stuffed up his t shirt.

He handed a chocolate bar to her.

'It's stolen.'

'Yeah, and you're hungry.'

She still looked doubtful.

'Look sister, everyone steals in this country, and the biggest thief of all is the President. Now eat.'

She had never tasted chocolate, though Papa said the Maya invented it. But now all the chocolate was bought by the rich and the Maya never saw it any more. The chocolate bar had writing written on it and when she peeled back the wrapper it gleamed silver on the inside and when she bit into the chocolate it tasted so beautiful she wasn't surprised the rich took it all for themselves.

'*Chicas*,' said the boy, waving his arm as if addressing the whole world. 'They all love chocolate.'

She finished the whole bar and still felt sick, but in a nice way. She pointed at his t shirt.

'Where's that?'

He looked down. 'Hawaii?'

'Have you been there?'

'Been there? Sister, I own it.'

'You liar.'

'The whole island. I'll take you there one day.'

'You are such a liar.'

266

'Lying's the only thing that keeps me true to myself.'

'That doesn't mean anything.'

'Does to me. Come on. We should keep moving.'

They came down a steep cobbled street and there at the bottom across a busy road was a sludgy brown river and a concrete bridge with lots of slogans written on it. Upriver was another bridge that had fallen into the water.

'The hurricane,' he said. 'The rains made a landslide and it brought the whole side of that mountain down. Killed thousands. They still digging the bodies out today.' He was talking like her brothers did, all hard and manly and knowing and trying to frighten her. 'And the old bridge, they still not got round to mending it yet. The *Yanquis* sent loads of dollars for a new bridge. But you know what? It never got built. I reckon,' he leant close and whispered in her ear, 'I reckon the President ran off with the money and spent it all on chocolate bars.'

She nodded. 'He's as fat as a pig, I was told.'

He laughed and slapped his thigh. 'So you follow politics too, eh?'

She nodded solemnly. 'I follow neo-Imperialism.'

'Is that the case? Well ain't you just full of surprises?' Then suddenly he put his arm round her shoulders, which you weren't supposed to do unless you were family, not in the village. But they were in the city now, and the city was very different, and it was nice having his arm around her shoulders like Jaime or Alejandro used to that she nearly cried.

'Sister,' he said. 'I think we gonna get along.'

'But I'm not staying with you,' she said, pulling away. 'I'm going to find my family.'

'No you're not.'

'Yes I am. You can't tell me what to do.'

'Yes I can. You haven't got a hope on your own.'

'Leave me alone!'

He had a tight hold on her arm. 'If you go off on your own

267

in this city, you'll end up like the rubbish dump kids. Or even worse the Adopted Evangelical American Kids, aaarrggghhh! Want to see the rubbish dump kids? How they live?'

'No. I'm going now.'

'No you're not. And if you run off the police will get you anyway. And then you'll see the Black Van.'

She didn't like the way he said that. 'What's the Black Van?'

'You see, you don't even know. Every street kid knows when they see the Black Van. And then they run like hell. Now how would you survive without me? Eh?'

'But I *have to find my family!*'

'Ssshhh! OK. Look, it'll be all right. Jesus. *Chicas.* Always so *emotional.*' He put his arm round her again. A passer-by was looking at them. 'Look. We'll find your family, I promise. But you have to stay with us. For now. We know how to survive here. You don't. Honestly.'

She sniffed. She hated him but it was true. She didn't really know where her auntie was or anything.

'Come on,' he said. 'Walk this way.'

'Where are we going?'

'Come on. I'll show you.'

They went up a steep main road full of noisy filthy cars and blaring bellowing trucks, and she could see the great circle of dark volcanic mountains that ringed the city, half lost in smog. Looking over the wall on their left they could see the river down below the steep embankment, very low with the dry season. Splintered timber and huge lumps of clotted plastic bags and a dead cow and two smashed up cars and a refrigerator. Further along was a wide loop of stony shoreline and a lot of very dirty children foraging.

'You could be one of them,' said Pepito. 'If you wanted.'

She shook her head.

'Then stay close and keep moving.'

Near the top of the hill they crossed the road and clambered up onto another crumbling wall, carefully avoiding the broken glass bottles embedded in the cement on top, and looked down. There was the rubbish dump.

It was surrounded by little houses that were the *barrios* where her aunty lived. Now she saw why she had sounded foolish and she was ashamed. There were thousands and millions of them. Mile after mile of square whitewashed shacks topped with tin roofs, spilling down the steep mountainsides like handfuls of white dice or a giant's teeth.

The boy waved his hand. 'Welcome to the *barrios*. You could see even more of 'em if it wasn't for the smog.'

The dump was a vast mound of rubbish that stretched away across the mountainside. It would take half an hour to walk from one side to the other. Bulldozers nibbled away at the edges, but it was like they didn't really know what to do. They made no difference. Vultures circled above and came down to scavenge here and there, and everywhere there were little half-naked children with grey teeth and burned faces, picking over the stinking mounds, sometimes yelling out and holding up a metal bar or a coil of wire and running over to the huts at the side. A man in overalls came out and stared at their offerings and shook his head, or sometimes he took it and gave them a coin or two.

'Here we go,' said the boy. 'Here come the trucks from Zones 9 and 10, where the rich live. The best pickings. The kids go crazy for them.'

Two trucks backed up through the gates beeping and tipped out their loads while hissing and groaning like great animals. The children skipped out of the way and then came swarming back to pick over this fresh opportunity. One little girl pulled out a black plastic bag and it was full of clothes thrown out by some rich lady. She shrieked with glee, then the others crowded around her and they all started fighting.

Further off, the vultures watched the squabbling children with heavy-lidded eyes.

'Sometimes you see this sudden flash of white light through all the dust,' said Pepito, 'and that's some tourist up there taking photos of all the kids. The sun's in the sky but the air's so dark with dust that their cameras flash anyhow like it's night. Gringos are weird, eh?'

She thought of Doctor Nicholas. He had taken photographs. He left them just before everything went wrong.

There was a boy coughing behind the Zone 10 rubbish truck, doubled up and spitting. And the vultures rising in a slow tornado above him, lifted on the hot foul air of the dump, a spiral staircase of black wings. Their necks stretched out, their cold eyes on the scavenging children below, and the coughing boy.

'I don't like it,' said Eulalia.

'Well I don't suppose they like it either,' said the boy. 'But business is business. My point is, sister, if you don't stick with us, you'll end up down there with him. These kids, they're here because they ain't got no one, no family, no gang, *nada*. If you stick with us, you'll be OK. But if you slip away or lose us, you'll end up working with those kids down below. They the lowest of the low, and they ain't got no one. That's why I'm showing you this place. I'm sorry about everything else and your village and stuff. But stick close to us and you'll be OK. And make sure you show respect to Marcello.'

'Who's Marcello?'

He grinned like a little fox. 'You'll meet him soon enough. Marcello's someone you *really* have to get along with. Or else.'

270

48

As they bumped back down to the centre of the village in the army jeep, Nicholas knew that the only thing that mattered was what the old woman had told him. Eulalia wasn't dead. Misguidedly or not, she had been put on a bus and sent to the city. The rest of them – he didn't want to think about it too much. He believed Tumax. He chose to believe him. They were on a coastal plantation. José would find his way there too. And Eulalia was still alive, but in the city. It was as if that was all he knew: the only fact in his head now.

It was too painful even to imagine Lala's terror, though he could imagine it all too easily. Day by day, second by second, she would be afraid, unless perhaps she was asleep. But day terrors invade the night too. And then when she awoke again she would be flooded anew with the old terror.

Where was she? Where would she be? A six year old innocent village girl separated from her family by two hundred miles and with no idea where they had gone. Would she try somehow to get back to her valley? How? She would only survive if someone else looked after her. There were many people who would not look after her. It was a question of who got to her first.

He must find her. She was everything. He had been made for this, it was why he was here.

The army headquarters was an old school building a little off the main road among dense trees.

'Well,' he said, 'things have changed since the army and the villagers all danced together the other night.'

'Yes they have,' said the man with three stripes. 'Wait here.'

He sat on a plastic chair in the school entrance hall and waited. There were still children's drawings on the wall. He stood and walked over and read them. Down in the corner was one in orange pencil, a little faded, showing a mountain with a fire coming out of the top of it, and up in the sky a boat with some fishermen in it for some reason. Below this it read,

My country is very beautiful full of lakes and volcanoes and flowers
We have the most dangerous volcano in the world which is called the Santa Maria volcano after the Blessed Virgin
I would like to be a doctor and make people better
I like sweets and cake a lot

It was signed Eulalia Chacach, aged 6¾.

'You are a doctor?' said the sergeant.

'No, I'm a medical student. I'm not fully trained yet. I'm a volunteer.'

'You were all recalled to your home countries. Why are you still here?'

'For one thing, I mislaid my passport. And for another, I care very much what has become of my family.'

'Your family?'

'My homestay. The family I lived with, here in the village.'

'What is it to you?'

'I should like to know where they have gone. I should like at least to say goodbye to them before I return to England.'

'They've gone. Relocated. For now you are being seconded to the military clinic. There have been some casualties the last day, with fighting in the hills.'

'I can't possibly treat military casualties. I...'

'You treated a man with gunshot wounds at the clinic. With Dr Menendez. We heard about this.'

He was startled. 'And the man almost certainly died.'

'Nevertheless, there are no other doctors here now. You come with us.'

'So what happened to Dr Menendez?'

'Please. Come with me.'

The clinic was an aged shed of dusty splintered wooden planks, a stiff cold water tap over a tin sink, a table and chair and a light and a crate full of medical supplies. Suddenly he was very afraid. Low-level anxiety had been his companion for a long time, but now he felt afraid. He foresaw soldiers being carried in screaming, missing arms, legs, bowels hanging loose ... and he would be expected to heal them. He was descending into a nightmare. He recalled the golden rule about medical electives abroad. *Students should not work beyond their level of competence.* He tried to see the blackly funny side to steady himself and failed.

He had just found some handgel and was rubbing it in when the door behind him slammed. He looked round to see ... Colonel Inocencio. His handsome face was pained and shiny with sweat.

'I'm your first,' he said, and came stiffly over to the table. 'What happened to your face? Anyhow, get to work.'

He stayed calm. 'What's the problem?'

The colonel didn't answer. He climbed slowly onto the table and very slowly lay down on his stomach. The entire right buttock of his army fatigues was drenched in blood. Nicolas drew breath.

'This isn't a bullet wound. Was it shrapnel or something?'

'Just get on with it,' said the colonel, face down, forehead on his arms. 'There's nothing to dig out.'

Jesus.

He started to delve into the crate of medical supplies, hands shaking, but could find nothing he wanted. It was hopeless. Eventually he picked it up and tipped the entire contents out on the floor. Most hygienic. And there was a pair of stainless steel scissors. *Never cut a tube unless you can see where it's going*. That was one useful shred of surgical advice he knew. And *always make sure you can see the tip of your scissors*. There were shots of ketamine and lidocaine, and a pair of single-use surgical gloves, though they could always be washed and re-used in extremes. But no iodine, no antiseptics, no surgical dressings. A bottle of what looked like worming medicine.

He retrieved the handgel from the sink and rubbed the blades of the scissors and began to snip away at the seat of the colonel's trousers, dropping the sodden strips to the floor because there was nowhere else to put them.

'I really need an assistant,' he said after a while.

'No assistant. Just you.'

'And more handgel. A lot more handgel, and hot water.'

'You will manage.'

His hands were still shaking, and if the tip of the scissors jabbed the wound the colonel would jump in agony.

'I need to give you a shot of anaesthetic. Though obviously I'm not a trained anaesthetist and have no fucking *idea* what I'm doing.'

'Doctors shouldn't swear. And no anaesthetic.'

'I have to. Otherwise you'll be jumping all over the place.'

The colonel grunted. 'Do it then. But if you make me lose consciousness you will pay in blood.'

He examined a pack of lidocaine. He wished his top lip would stop sweating. What evolutionary purpose did *that* ever serve? The lidocaine was foreign medic-aid and actually had instructions in English, though they still left him hazy.

'Administer by local infiltration, peripheral nerve block, paracervical block, sympathetic nerve block, central neural block (e.g., epidural block), caudal block, or subarachnoid (spinal) block... For IV regional anesthesia, use 50-mL single-dose vials containing lidocaine hydrochloride ... For epidural or spinal block, avoid using preparations containing antimicrobial preservatives (e.g., methylparaben), since safety of intrathecal administration using these preparations not established...'

And he particularly liked the instruction, 'For spinal block, inject slowly.'

He decided on 50-mL local. 'In my country,' he said by way of calming conversation, 'people take anaesthetics like ketamine in nightclubs.'

'Because they're in so much pain?'

He laughed nervously. 'Yeah, right,' he muttered in English.

After allowing a few minutes he began to relax a little. When he had finally cut away the material and saw the state of the wound, he said, 'You're going to have to remove everything from the waist down.'

'*Hijo de puta.*'

'Please. I need to wash it down. And that tap water's not drinking water is it?'

'Would you drink it?

'No. So, look, I'm going to need bottled water. To wash out the wound. Several litres.'

The colonel sighed. 'Ok. Go to the door and shout.'

A few minutes later a soldier was knocking at the door with six litres. Nicholas told him to bring any clean towels he could find, freshly washed, never used, and another small table, and alcohol.

'Not beer. Anything stronger. Spirits.'

'Cane spirit?'

'Fine. Plenty of it.'

The colonel was lying on the table naked from the waist down now. Holed and darkened trousers thrown over the nearby chairback. Muscular legs and thighs, blackhaired, trickled with blood. And a ragged crimson crater in his right buttock, still oozing blood, an atrocious mess. The sight of the blood, and even more the smell if it, suddenly made Nicholas feel, for all his attempts at cold medical rationality, like he had stumbled into something monstrous.

'This was a dog bite, wasn't it?' he said as calmly as he could.

'Just do your work.'

'And a bad one. Must have hurt like hell.'

The colonel said nothing. Nicholas had to admit, his patient did pain pretty well, unless he'd already taken a load of analgesics before coming in. He didn't think so.

'OK,' he said, holding up a litre bottle of water. 'This may still hurt.'

'It hurts anyway. Pain is real.'

He uncapped the bottle and poured it out in a stream over the wound. Rosewater foaming away over the table and onto the floor where the dusty floorboards drank it in and turned glossy and dark. The colonel bucked violently but made no sound. The lidocaine must be doing something, but not much.

'I trust you shot the dog. For being an insurgent.'

He didn't know why he was trying to be jovial, there was nothing funny here. It was nerves.

The colonel said, 'I have heard all the jokes, my English friend. Soldiers are great jokers, living as they do in the presence of death. The Greatest Joker of All. Now get stitching.'

'I have to clean a bit first.'

Debridement, it was called in medispeak. It meant scraping out and severing the dead and damaged meat. Never did the human frame seem more like an assemblage of raw meat and nothing else than when you were engaged in debridement.

'But I must tell you again, I have learned no surgery, especially not trauma surgery. I am only part-trained to deal with everyday ailments and diseases. Not wounds like this.'

'You'll deal with it. You know stuff. There is no one else.'

'What about Dr Menendez?'

'Just do it.'

'If you're sure –'

'I'm sure. Stop talking and do your work.'

'I'm nervous. Believe me, talking helps calm me. You should allow it.'

'Then can't you at least talk in English so I don't understand your babbling?'

Despite everything, he was warming to this man.

He poured on another litre of water and then looked at what was revealed and felt the closest he had ever felt to nausea. 'Look, I'm not joking, but you have lost a lot of tissue here, as well as blood.'

'Tissue?'

How to put it plain and soldierly? He said, 'The dog must have run off with a whole hank of your arse in its mouth.' *Una loncha de su culo*, he said, quite proud of his phrasing. 'It's an open wound and pretty messy. There's no skin to draw together and sew up. You understand? The best I can do is get you started on some general antibiotics, because I'm afraid a dog's mouth and saliva are absolutely filthy, generally. And I'll pad it with clean towels and maybe some raw alcohol and bind it, and then you must go to a proper hospital. You may even need a skin graft.'

'I don't have time.'

'I think you're being proud. I think you're ashamed of people knowing that a dog bit your arse. I think-'

Without notice the colonel rose up from the table and turned on him, his face so black with anger that Nicholas backed away until he came up against the wall beside the door, his arms spread out wide against it. The colonel was bellowing at him spittle-flecked, coming towards him, naked from the waist down except for his socks, but there was nothing comical in the sight, nothing at all. Nicholas was too afraid to understand what he was shouting at first. He had seen men angry before - on the verge of madness with pain and anger and above all perhaps, humiliation - and it was never funny.

'Wipe my arse! Wipe my bloody dog's arse bitch! Do I look like a man you fuck with? Eh? Fucking gringo son of a whore fucking motherfucker?' He slapped him across his already bruised face. 'Do I? I will fuck you in the arse, in the mouth, I will fuck your eyeballs out, I will rip you in two and fuck your guts. Do you understand me? I will shove a snake up into your brain, I will tie you to a chair and make you cry for your mama and she will never come, you hear me shitface? I will make your whole life midnight for you.'

The colonel's wound had started to gout blood again when he stood and strode across the room and he swiped it with his right hand so that it came up bloody and he bunched it into a bloody fist and with his mighty left hand he clamped Nicholas to the wall by the throat and with his right fist he made a dumbshow punch at Nicholas' face. Nicholas tried to twist away but he was clamped tight and the colonel's fresh blood speckled his cheek.

The colonel stood there before him bunched muscle and rage, black hairy thighs and cock half roused and tight bull balls and shirt stretched taut and massive black haired fist and fevered black eyes and pale bloodless face half insane. His nostrils were flared and full of black bristles, his lips drawn back from white teeth, his chin jutting forward like another fist. He was indeed alpha male all over, and he would indeed fuck him in the arse and shove a snake up into his brain – had he *really* said that? what did it *mean*? - to prove his primate primacy. The colonel was born to fuck the whole world and it was not an act of love and nothing less would satisfy him.

Nicholas knew the type. Paralysed with fear, pinned against this shuddering wooden wall clamped by the throat, carotid artery throbbing, as in a dream Nicholas saw the colonel briefly as another man. Another mansized bully boy who wished to be an alpha male but could not, and so ruined children instead because he had not the strength or power to ruin the adult world.

He knew him. The blood, the tuberous cock, the look, the snarl, the borderline madness – a man to follow, this Colonel Inocencio, magnificent in his way, in his brutish murdering alpha primate way. That other was a sick and weak old man who lived in his dressing gown, and not a man to follow at all.

He felt the first signs of oxygen deprivation, the colonel still addressing him at furious volume yet with nose-to-nose intimacy. Absurdly, all he could think of was the NHS sign in A&E. 'Staff have a right to work here free from physical and personal abuse, and disruptive patients may be refused treatment.'

Then the colonel suddenly released his grip, reached behind him and grabbed Nicholas' buttocks so hard in his powerful hands that it hurt. It seemed to be in order to make some point that remained obscure to him.

The colonel was shouting that he, the gringo *puta* doctor, was in no position to make bargains or demands. Nicholas didn't know he had. The colonel said that he was here to follow orders and he did not give a shit about anything else.

'Lie down,' said Nicholas. His voice so faint and desperate. Dysphonia. Sometimes a side effect of steroidal asthma inhalers. May be relieved by gargling. 'Lie down. Let me go. Lie down. I'm doing what you want. Just lie down. Please. Please.'

There was a scared knock at the door and without releasing his right buttock, the colonel reached out and flung the door open. A quaking boy soldier stood there with a stack of towels, a bottle of spirits and a plastic chair. The colonel roared incoherently and seized the towels and flung them into the room, followed by the chair, and then seized the bottle and violently kicked the door shut again with his shoeless foot, appearing to feel no pain. He pulled the cork from the bottle with his teeth and spat it at the wall where it rebounded with a thock, and upended it and poured the cane spirit out over Nicholas' head, shouting,

'I baptize you in the name of *fuck*!' Veins stood out on his neck and forehead. 'I baptize you in the name of Jesus, Mary and *fuck*!'

Nicholas kept his eyes closed tight but still some of the

spirit ran in and stung atrociously.

His closed eyes only enraged the colonel more, and he began to throttle him again with bloody hands. 'Is this funny?' he shouted. 'Should we be laughing?'

'I don't understand,' he choked.

'Is this funny? *Tell me what you believe*!'

'I, I … I don't know…'

'Yes?'

He was sucking air through his throttled gullet like sucking it through a straw. '… This is crazy …' he choked, beginning to black out. And he couldn't do that, because he had to find Eulalia.

'That's it!' cried the colonel triumphantly, releasing him and stepping back three or four paces, holding his arms wide like the Rio Christ, only half-naked. 'That's it exactly. We can only live by deceiving ourselves, eh! Life is a horror show! Yes?'

Nicholas clamped his own throat, gently rubbing it. It hurt very much. Throats bruised easily. You saw it in domestics frequently, in A&E. Women's throats the colour of ripe plums.

'The only way we can survive is through self-delusion!' cried the colonel. 'You think all this has a purpose?' He pointed out of the dusty window over the valley. 'My little empire? Of course not. It is all self-delusion! It is all for nothing. It is to make the time pass.'

Colonel Inocencio was happy again. His anger had passed like an April shower.

He was turning back to the table, psychopathic genitals detumescing visibly, the excitement over. Taking a huge gulp from the remaining half-bottle of spirits, then lying down again with the bottle standing on the floor below him. Nicholas was expected to unpeel himself from the traumatized wall and return to doctoring the man's hideous bubbling wound as if nothing had happened. His previously shaking hands somehow firmer and more confident now, after his vivacious patient had nearly strangled him in a bid to *make some philosophical point.*

Should we be laughing? All the way to the giggling grave?

Nicholas stood the chair upright again, retrieved the towels from the floor and looked around for the best clean surface – the chair itself was filthy, stained with spilt coffee, possibly worse. He mopped the spirit from his eyes with the top towel. They felt like they were burning red, but at least the spirit might kill off any bacteria introduced by the colonel's venomous spittle. Could you get rabies of the eye? Probably. You could get herpes. He laid the innocent white towels on top of the first. You could even get *herpes of the brain...*

It was just as well that most people knew so little about disease and pathology, had such a weak grasp of scientific reality. It would only make them unhappy.

'I like you, English boy,' said the colonel as Nicholas craned over him again, eyes still blurred and watering, blinking rapidly to try and clear them. Some of his alcoholic tears fell onto colonel's bare arse, even in his wound. Tears were sterile though, like urine. No harm done.

'I know you have intelligence,' said the colonel. 'My men are all so bestially stupid. *Mestizo* idiots with their wide faces and passive stares. But it is good to talk to you.'

Yes indeed, the conversation was delightful. Later, perhaps they would discuss the future of the troubled Bolshoi ballet, or the novels of V.S. Naipaul.

'I was all ready to shove my bloody fist in your mouth, but what you said interested me. '"We live only by deceiving ourselves." These are perceptive words. Only a strong man can see that either there is no God, or if there is, he despises us anyway.'

With the typical unpredictability of involuntary reflexes, Nicholas had stopped shaking. But he remained so afraid that it was only with great effort he could move freely and think clearly. Hysterical laughter was close at hand, like an old companion. In the spillage from the crate he at last found one inadequate surgical pad, and began taping it over his troubled patient's wound in silence. It was with relief that he found his hands beginning to shake again, the backs of his hands feeling weirdly chilled, his throat sand dry.

When he was finally done he stood back. The colonel crouched up, dropped off the table, pulled on his trousers, ordered Nicholas to kneel and lace his boots up for him. Which he did without argument: disgraced half-doctor, shaking sawdust supplicant, still blinking away the spirit tears...

Colonel Maximo Inocencio turned and left the room without another word.

49

He was given the corner of a classroom to sleep in, on an army mat, along with half a dozen other soldiers who mistrusted him and ignored him. That had its uses. The first time he was left alone in the classroom, he rolled off his bed, crouched down, tested the floorboards. He found a looser one and prised it up using the leg of a metal chair. And underneath the boards he hid the black plastic package that he'd taken from the plane.

There was one young soldier called Joachim who was more friendly, and lent him his Bible in Spanish. It was all Nicholas had to read, having got through the last of the books he'd brought with him.

'Do you read the Bible, Joachim?'

The boy soldier nodded shyly. 'Sometimes. It reminds me of going to church. When I was a kid.'

'Are you from the highlands?'

He nodded. 'I shouldn't be talking to you.'

'Because it's all supposed to be kept secret?'

Joachim shrugged. He was heading for the door when he turned back and said, 'I am sorry you have got stuck here.'

Nicholas said, 'I'm sorry you've got stuck here too.'

Joachim gave a quick smile and was gone.

He lay on his back on the hot damp sheet. The grating calls of cicadas crowded in at the open window. The small Spanish Bible hovered over him like a bat as he held it, his arm aching.

Hubo un hombre en la tierra de Uz llamado Job. Aquel hombre fue intachable, recto, temeroso de Dios y apartado de mal...

He had nightmares that night and the following. A gape-jawed garish behemoth issuing threats and repulsive commands, lurid dumbshows of innocence and ravishment and tortuous revenge, which left him sweatsoaked and shaking and longing to be free of it all. But that he could not do, and so willpower and endurance were everything.

He lay in bed in the morning, having nothing to do that day, planning how he could escape and find them. He imagined saying to the colonel,

'What I injected you with. It wasn't antibiotics. It was a toxic solution. You need an antidote within twenty four hours. I can give you this – if you let me go.' And the colonel just laughing at him, telling him he was a terrible liar...

The colonel was older and wiser and stronger than him in every way. He saw himself interrogated, tied to a wooden chair. A soldier standing over him, grave of mien, cattleprod in hand, and the burnt horsehair smell of his own singed pubic hair in his nostrils.

He found the sergeant, and tried to tell him they were keeping a foreign national against his will. A foreign national of a powerful country. The sergeant just shrugged.

'We are at war now,' he said.

And so he lay uselessly on his bed, his insides in knots, thinking about them, thinking about the family.

50

The boy led her back to the new concrete bridge and then suddenly scrambled over the wall and started to climb down. It was a long way down but there were handholds and footholds where there were holes in the wall and sometimes there were pipes or bits of twisted iron sticking out.

He looked up. 'Come on.'

She climbed over carefully. She was a good climber though she had mostly climbed trees before. The wall was very hot in the sun and her hands were sweaty. The boy went ahead of her along the shoreline and in under the bridge. She ran after him.

It was very wide and traffic rumbled overhead, and in the wall there was the entrance to a huge tunnel that snaked back in underneath the city. He spread his arms out wide like Jesus in the mouth of the tunnel, though it would take four or five boys to reach from side to side.

'Storm drain for the rainy season,' he said. 'But as it's the dry season, we're good in here.'

'What happens when the rains come?'

'We move on.' He turned his back on her and hollered into the tunnel. 'Anyone at home?'

Silence.

He glanced back over his shoulder.

'Come on then. I'll show you to your suite.'

They went thirty yards or more up the tunnel, and the circle of daylight behind them got smaller and smaller. Then in the concrete dusk there was a grubby pink mattress with big lumpy buttons on it, but apart from that she didn't notice anything else before she fell asleep on it.

'Tch,' said the boy, standing over her. 'You tired, little country girl.'

She woke up feeling cold beside a smoky woodfire, and for a confused and happy moment she thought she was back in the village and that was Jaime or Alejandro sitting opposite her. But then it all came back in an anguished rush.

'Here,' he said. 'Have a banana.'

She didn't want to eat but she was very hungry. After a bit she started to peel it.

In the twilight there were other children. A little girl, and an older boy holding a plastic bag up to his face and sniffing.

'Hey, not now, eh? Not with our new guest. She comes from the country and fresh air and badword.'

The other boy was older, he was called Osmin, but he was a sad boy. They told her later that he had the mark on him. The mark that meant he wouldn't make it.

Now Osmin put the bag down again and glared and then dropped his head back against the wall of the tunnel and snorted up his nose and closed his eyes.

'What's her name?' he said in a slow slurry voice.

'Eulália,' said the boy.

'What's yours?' she asked him.

'He's La Triqui,' slurred Osmin. 'Fagbutt. For obvious reasons.'

'The younger boy ignored him. 'Pepe,' he said. 'Pepito if you have to. Though I'm too old for that baby name.'

She finished her banana.

The light at the end of the tunnel was fading and turning pink. She would easily go to sleep again tonight. She could sleep for a week. The smaller children who had been foraging along the riverbank were creeping into the mouth of the tunnel now, she could see their small silhouettes, and curling up like puppies there.

'They sleep down there sometimes,' said Pepito, 'when

they're not at the dump. Us up here. Even here there's rich and poor.'

Eulalia felt sorry for the smaller children. They were only her age. But she was glad she wasn't sleeping down there with them. Why had she been taken into the gang and not them?

'They're OK,' said Pepito. 'The police leave them alone. It's us they come after.'

'What have we done?'

'Well, you not done nothing yet. But – hey Ana, get us some more wood.'

He meant the other little girl. She emerged from the darkness and trotted down the tunnel and out into the evening. She came back with some thin sticks and a wooden fruit crate.

'This is a good place,' said Pepito proudly, slapping the walls of the tunnel. 'Warm and dry, the cops never find us, and right by the street market. End of the day we get bananas and oranges and all that healthy badword that keeps us such healthy little badwords. And we get all the smashed up fruit crates for the fire too. Plenty of wood, and plenty more coming downriver. We do OK, eh?'

Ana put the sticks and the fruit crate on top of the fire and it burned up nicely and she sat down on the edge of Eulalia's mattress in the orange glow and said,

'Hello.'

'Hello.'

'I'm Ana Maria.'

'Aw,' said Pepito. 'Sweet.' He dug a cigarette butt out of his pocket and lay down on his stomach and lit it from the fire.

Ana used to walk with her father about the streets selling kerosene from a horse-drawn cart, and holding the horse when her father went into a shop to deliver the cans. But then her father got sick and died very soon after, and she was alone with nothing but a cart and an old horse and some cans of kerosene.

'What did you do?' asked Eulalia wide-eyed.

'A man said I could stay with him if I gave him the horse

and cart, and I said yes, and he led the horse and cart away and said he'd come back for me, and I never saw him again. Then I came here.'

'*All men are bad*,' said Pepito in a singsong voice.

'What did you do?' asked Ana.

'I came from our village,' said Eulalia, and then stopped.

'Hey, Ana,' said Pepito softly. She looked up. He shook his head.

The others found her a blanket. The distant whisper of the choked-up river. The vultures, the sunset, the lice. Falling asleep.

She learned lots of new words over the next few days. *Cipote* meant a boy and *cipota* a girl, *chequé* meant something was good or cool, a *chorreado* was a slum-dweller in a *barrio*.

'Isn't that like us?' said Eulalia.

'No it is not!' said Pepito indignantly. 'We tunnel people are way superior to your *chorreados*.'

A *sapo* was a snitch or a grass, *borracho* and *bolo* and *mamado* all meant drunk, and a *chunte* was a policeman.

'I don't think I ever met a proper policeman,' she said.

'Lucky you.'

Pisto meant money, and was much the most important word in the language. *Chamba* meant work, and was to be avoided at all costs.

'You can work in a backstreet *maquila*,' said Pepito, 'making clothes for gringo chainstores. And go blind. Or you can work like the kids at the dump. They work ten hours a day, they got lungs like eighty year olds, and they still not got enough *pisto* to buy a new pair of pants from a backstreet *maquila*. Work it out.'

'Also,' said Osmin, 'if ever the cops stop you and start asking questions, where you live, who your people are, just play dumb. Never answer questions.'

'Oh,' said Pepito, 'and if you see the Black Van, run like hell.'

'What's the Black Van?'

The boys looked at each other and laughed, but Ana didn't.

'*Negro como la boca del lobo*,' said Osmin. 'Black as the mouth of the wolf.'

'The Black Van,' said Pepito, 'is driven by the Devil himself. And it takes kids like us straight down to hell.'

Sometimes they heard gunfire from the hills around the city, and that was the fighting going on between the government and the rebels. But everyone said it wouldn't change anything and the city went on just the same, people going to work and stopping to chat and buying bananas.

She met lots of new people up on the street and around the marketplace and the cathedral square. More people than she'd met in her whole life before. Apart from the other children in the tunnel, up above there was another girl she didn't like very much called Catalina who hung around sometimes and didn't sleep in the tunnel. She came down and told Pepito or Osmin that there was a job to do or an errand to run and she was friends with Marcello. She was about thirteen and wore tight t shirts with no shame, sometimes with silver lettering on them saying *Amor* or *Cariña*. She wore jeans shorts that were far too short and sparkly sandals, and she never smiled and she chewed gum all the time and had quite short hair and hard eyes.

The first time Pepito pointed to her and said, 'Meet the new girl, she's Eulalia,' Catalina just stared straight at her hard and unblinking, chewing her gum, and didn't say a word. She looked as if she wouldn't be impressed even if you took off and flew through air in front of her. She often had bruises on her face and arms. She never wore earrings because Pepito said someone always ripped them out sooner or later.

Eulalia held her hands up and cupped her own ears at the thought.

'Yeah.' Pepito laughed. 'We better think of selling yours pretty soon too.'

Then there was Crazy Pastora and her impassioned sermons, haranguing the cars at the crossroads. Eulalia and Ana loved listening to her, sitting on the wall nearby swinging their legs.

'What if the earth was the sky and the ocean was a desert?' she cried. 'What if lead floated and cork sank?' She stared wildly around and held her hands out wide, fingers splayed. 'For the last shall be first and the first shall be last, said the Lord, and the poor shall be feasted and the rich shall be turned empty away.'

'She's going to get herself arrested,' said a grumpy man at a stall nearby, dropping lemons into a paper bag.

A car hooted at Crazy Pastora. She rounded on it in fury, smacking its bonnet, her long grey hair flying wildly.

'The jaguar will howl like a wolf beneath the moon, and the horses will roar in the desert! And both of them will flee from the white lamb with its mouth full of blood! The generals will be beggars, and the beggars be clowns! And the Lord Archbishop will be stripped of his robes and put out to sweep the steps of the Cathedral like an old woman.'

'She is *done for*,' said the grumpy man.

'And the old women will tear his robes in strips for headscarves! They will dance in the Cathedral like young girls! The poor do not speak, but they see! How they see!'

Crazy Pastora fell silent. The cars roared past oblivious, the trucks spewed their fumes against her. Eulalia and Ana Maria both clapped politely.

There was One Handed Hassan, who she first saw gnawing an avocado by a market stall. She watched him eat the skin and everything, and she wondered if he'd swallow the stone as well, a huge lump in his throat sliding slowly down, like a snake swallowing a bird. But he didn't, he just saved the stone at the end and polished it carefully on his shirt and then put it in his pocket like it was very precious.

'He's *loco*,' said Pepito. 'But harmless.'

Others called him *El Trunco,* The Stump, and mocked his

missing hand, asking him how he clapped when he went to the grand opera house.

He was long-haired and wild-eyed and a bit smelly, and sometimes he started shouting about how he'd lost his hand. Sometimes it was in fighting against the Americans, or the Spanish, or the Russians, or that accursed country next door whose inhabitants were all sons of badwords and whose very name would not pollute his lips. Or his mother had cut his hand off when he was only a Baby, saying that he would be without sin, and thrown it into a volcano.

He said he had no money and no shoes and no hope, but along with all that, it was true, he had no sin. And so he praised Christ his Saviour ever more.

He was very *loco*. Sometimes he gave her one of his polished avocado stones and sometimes tortillas with his one hand while she tried not to look at his stump which she found so fascinating. He called her *Indita*, but in a kindly way, and he prophesied that the Kingdoms of the Maya would one day rise from the jungles again, and the rest of the world would be drowned.

She thought he should get married to Crazy Pastora.

'Hassan get married?' He frowned. 'To Crazy Pastora? With his tremendous visions, and his pockets as empty as the Great Void, and his one sad hand that prays by itself all alone? Why so, little sister?'

'Because she's mad too,' she told him. 'Then you could both be mad together.'

'Ah,' said Hassan. 'What a vision. What a vision.'

There was Broken Down Evangelina, who sat all day beside the cathedral door, and at night slept on the steps, or limped away and slept on one of the benches or under a market cart. Mostly she just sat beside the cathedral door though, as the poor of the city came and went, leaving coins or sometimes a note in her upturned hat. Broken-Down Evangelina sat with her old hands over her face quite motionless and never said a word, as if she had been sitting for many years mummified there, and no one ever tried to move her on, neither policeman nor priest, out of respect for her mysterious sorrow.

But then sometimes she would set off walking, to nowhere in particular. You could hear her broken down old shoes slipslapping against the cobblestones as she came along, with her knobbly old stick and her knobbly old hand that looked just like a part of the stick. There were lots of them like that. They were all hungry or maimed or broken down but they all kept on going.

Broken Down Evangelina made Eulalia think of the old woman with her donkey, and everything made her think of her lost family and the village. But Pepito was her friend, though he said badwords, and she and Ana Maria were friends too. They often sat together under the banana cart laughing at the passers by, and at night they combed each other's hair with their fingers and picked out the lice.

There was Ernesto the manic shoeshine boy, who walked very fast through the crowds swinging his thin brown arms. He lived with his family on the edge of the *barrio*, Pepito said. Eulalia asked him if he knew her Auntie Rosario but he shook his head.

He carried his shoeshine box on his back, moving through the forest of legs, his eyes downcast, barely noticing what people looked like above the knees, his whole world no more than a river of shoes that needed shining, all day long.

Then a soft tap on the arm. '*Señor -*'

'Don't bother me.'

But sometimes someone would nod and he would take them aside and set down his box and whip out the cloths and brushes and polish. The man would put his foot up on the box and Ernesto would crouch and go to work so lightning fast you could hardly see his hands. Eulalia loved to watch him work. Sometimes she tried to talk to him, but he was always too busy. He was very serious and hardworking.

At night in the tunnel she asked Pepito, 'What does Ernesto do with all the money he makes?'

'All the thousands and thousands of dollars, you mean? He got family. Got a sick mother. Kid sisters and stuff. He got to work hard just so they don't starve.'

'Is his Papa dead?'

'I don't know, sister.'

'When will my family come to find me?'

'I don't *know*.'

He sounded annoyed.

She twisted her fingers in her dress and stared into the fire. 'Is your Papa dead?'

He was looking away, then lay down on his mattress. 'My Mama's dead,' he said flatly. 'My father. Who cares? Aunts, uncles.' He shrugged. 'I got an Auntie Rosario too somewhere, just like you. But she don't wanna know.'

'Is it sad?'

'I can live with it.' He rolled over. 'Just give me a cigarette and a song and a pretty *chica* and badword the rest.'

'You swear a lot.'

'Yeah,' said Pepito. 'I'm a bad badword and I'm going straight to hell.'

'Not if you believe in Jesus.'

'Not if Jesus don't believe in me.'

He turned away and picked at another cigarette butt. He wasn't really against Jesus, he was just sad.

Then he said, 'One day I stole a chicken leg and came down under the bridge to eat it and this little mutt came over and stared at me. I kicked it away but it just came back and stared again, licking its chops all hungry and eyes fixed, trembling, one paw up, cocked ear, you know.'

She nodded. 'I had a dog too,' she said softly.

'Huh. Well I knew it wouldn't bite me, it wasn't that kind of dog, it was just hoping. It was just this sad old bag of skin and bone, it didn't mean no harm, and it eyed the same chicken bone I was eating. And I thought, then,' Pepito laughed, 'I thought, hey, we're brothers!

'He was a dog and I was a human, well as best I can manage, but we both eyed the same chicken bone just the same, both licked our lips, both had bellies rumbling and eyes staring. And I suddenly thought now I'm the rich badword, the rich man, you know, and the little dog is like an orphan, and now I'm doing just what the rich have always done. I got my chicken bone and you got none, well badword you, loser, I'm all right. And I thought, but I always hated the rich for that, so now who's to blame?

'So when I got near the end of the chicken bone I threw the skin to the little dog and it chewed it up and swallowed it like it hadn't eaten since last year. So now the dog sleeps at my feet at night, and every day we walk the city and people know us and sometimes that's a pain because some badword *sapo* only has to say to the police, it was the kid with the little dog and they know who that is. This little dog who loves me has become a danger to me. But then sometimes it's cool because people know who I am and say, hey, Triqui! And I get a cast off or two and we dine like royalty off some fine old steak some fat guy left behind up at the steakhouse.

'Well I get caught one day stealing and the police haul me down to central jail and beat the badword out of me and when I get back all broken up and bleeding the dog is gone. I don't know how, but as I was getting beaten he was whimpering with his tail tucked up and cowering, they said. The other kids told me. And then he could stand no more and he ran away. I called out for him for hours and days, I walked everywhere and asked everyone and no one knew. My voice was so hoarse from calling out for him, and eventually I went dumb and couldn't speak for three days. And I never saw him again.'

After a bit Eulalia said, 'I'm sorry about your dog.'

'Yeah. Well.' He looked away. 'Me too. But – he ran away from me so I wouldn't get recognized again. Wouldn't get beaten again.' He nodded. 'That's how I think it was. I shoulda called him Jesus.'

Later that night she woke up when there was a lot of gunfire that sounded nearby and she saw he was sitting up again smoking. He had a tiny photograph in his other hand and was looking at it and then he pressed it to his forehead and his heart and then leaned to one side and slipped it back in his jeans pocket. She shouldn't be watching him. Then he blew out the smoke and tossed the cigarette butt away and laid his arms across his knees and laid his forehead on his arms and stayed still for a long time. She didn't see the photograph but she didn't need to, and she didn't say anything the next day or he would be angry with her. But after that she knew he was not the same boy as he pretended to be. And every morning and every evening she prayed that he would come back to his family, and she would come back to hers.

51

Twice a day, morning and evening, Nicholas gave the colonel his antiobiotic and re-dressed his wound. Since there were no more pads he used wads of freshly boiled towel. So far, miraculously, there was no infection, and the slight temperature that the colonel had had was already passed. No doubt he had the immune system of a shark, or some cold-eyed pachyderm that had waddled imperviously through the steaming jungles of the Triassic beside the shallow Panthalassian Sea. Bite wounds from atrocious, lumbering saurian encounters healing over eerily in just hours.

He could have walked from here to England then. Under the equatorial sun, across the red desert continent of Pangaea, where Ghost Ranch dinosaurs hunted in packs of thousands.

If they wouldn't let him go he would have to escape, and try not to get shot. He must find her. She was everything. He must find her before the dinosaurs did.

And what of José, and Abuelita? The only names on the manifest were Maria and the boys. He must be sure what had happened before he could leave this country that had its claws into him. He must find them and be sure. Nothing else mattered.

In those cold and curious years of his youth, when his sister had gone and his parents did not speak to each other or to him for weeks and months on end, he would retreat to his remote bedroom full of old dark furniture and family photographs from three or four generations back, and he would lose himself in books. He read *The Selfish Gene*, *Case Studies in*

Psychopathology, Guns Germs and Steel, The World Without Us, Global Catastrophes, A Brief History of Infinity, Your Inner Fish, One Hundred and Twenty Diseases, The Quantum Universe, A Mathematician Reads the Newspapers, The Atlas of the Prehistoric World, The Coming Collapse.

He read some other stuff too - a bit of history, a bit of fiction - but it was the science that he devoured. He loved the sense of order that it gave him in those years, and he loved its clear-eyed and comfortless vision of life as well. It was like someone very bleak and calm and clever was talking to him. He began to see for certain that everything was about to go wrong, that humanity's advanced and omnivorous civilization could not last another century. The reason why we had failed to make contact with any extraterrestrial civilizations was because such civilizations only existed for a brief, bright moment before they destroyed themselves. As would we. He found strange consolation in this. And he began to wonder whether a useful preparation for the coming catastrophe might be to train as a doctor.

And now here he was, lying staring ceilingwards with the *Book of Job* hovering batlike above him, a half-trained doctor, but with a psychometric assessment which his medical school had finally twigged made him almost comically unsuited. At least in their view.

Though the time might yet come when the whole world would look like this sweet, sick little country, and people would be glad of any doctor or half-doctor they could find. Ash falling like rain on the desolated landscape, the great cities lost, never to come again. People lying like dogs under the hot trees, tornadoes howling out in the dark desert air. The sunset out west like a furnace.

And even then the silos still appearing, missiles still purring out of forgotten hills. And the people coming to him, bringing their sores and their sorrows, running to him, to him who never expected any other future but this...

The next night he tried to escape. It was absurd. He retrieved his package under the floorboards and then just walked out of the building. Then he tripped over a sleeping sow in the darkness and she erupted from the earth like an indignant fungoid blob and nearly bit him. Moments later he had a riflebarrel coldly pressed to his temple and he was marched back to the school building and into the dormitory again. That was it. They didn't even deign to punish him. And they still didn't search his bag.

Joaquim whispered to him, 'I heard the squealing. Was that the pig?'

'No, that was me.'

Joaquim laughed. Then he said, 'You shouldn't try to escape. Believe me. They will not be patient for very long.'

52

In the morning, Colonel Inocencio summoned him and demanded to know what he was planning. Where on earth was he going to go anyway? Really? How was that going to work?

He said nothing.

The colonel was peppery and irritated this morning rather than psychotic, which was a relief. Striding about the room with a smouldering half-cigar, gesticulating with brimming energy.

'You like to think you are a mystery, you like to think that I do not understand you. But I understand you very well. You are one of those gringos who comes visiting a poor country, and you like the poverty, and the danger too, so you can brag of it. Your heart is filled with excitement and compassion. You would adopt my country, *my* country, like an orphan child, or protect it as you would a child being bullied in the schoolyard. You see my country being bullied by the *Estados Unidos*, you see the UN telling us how to run our elections, the WHO overseeing our hospitals, our factories being run by Mexico, our dams being built and our politicians bribed by China – and like a true romantic and man of great heart, like Bolivar or Che, you want to fly to my country's side and protect her. To die with her if necessary. To die ... *ideally*.'

He said nothing.

'Look at you. Like Christ before Pilate, you see yourself. I see a troublemaker and a fool. Though I still like you and all that pride and willpower in you, even while you sit there cloaked in your saintly and mysterious silence. I don't trust you, but you do interest me.'

He lugged luxuriantly on his cigar.

'One must be proud. There is a find old Spanish proverb. *Soberbia es hermosura*. Pride is beauty. Most of you stoop-shouldered Europeans don't get this at all nowadays, always shuffling around the world mumbling apologies.'

He couldn't help smiling.

'You have read Darwin?' snapped the charming and erudite psychopath.

'Quite a bit, yes.'

'Most things are doomed to extinction,' observed the philosophical and buttock-torn nutjob.

'Actually, *everything* is doomed to extinction, give it enough time.'

'Yes of course, you are right. This is a brutal reality is it not?'

'Kind of.'

'Don't be so diffident. I know you have strong convictions. Willpower. Few others would have tried to escape from me - even if you did trip over the pig. You know the great thing about the will: once you begin to exercise it, strongly, you discover most other people really have none at all. None. They are desperate to surrender to you, desperate to be told what to do, what to think, what to believe. Exercising power over people is as easy as breathing. Make bold assertions, never provide facts, never apologize or show humility. Sway their emotions. Promise them freedom from doubt and from death, promise them heaven on earth. And you are King.'

He smiled and held his arms wide. 'And here we sit, like old friends!'

Nicholas smiled too. 'Absolutely.'

The colonel sat companionably close. 'Now in the native here there is too much admixture of the passive Indian and the Negro.'

'I'm sorry?'

'There you go again. Only the strong survive. The strongest used to be the Europeans. Cortés. You British. They were a proud people, they didn't shuffle about the world apologizing. It is natural for whites to lord it over the world, man over woman. The whites are superior to other races. I call the great heresy today *Egalismo*. Equalism. A great lie. It can't last. Lies never do. The truth endures. The average IQ in this country is 81. This is very low. You are intelligent as well as proud. You know what this means. Yet it is also pleasant for you and me to be surrounded by the stupid, because we feel our superiority more sharply.

'The feeling of one's own power is the sweetest thing in life. Watch wild animals, they feel it all the time. A hawk loves being a hawk. A pleasure that never palls. I look at you and I see you feel this too. You are homosexual?'

'No.'

Dear God what was coming next?

If about to get buggered, medically speaking, the most important thing was to *relax the sphincter*. Less chance of anal fissure and subsequent infection.

The colonel nodded. He suddenly stood. 'I need a woman,' he said. 'But it is good to have an educated man to talk to.' And he was gone.

Perhaps it was meaningless to call him a psychopath or a sociopath. He was what he was. A hawk loves being a hawk.

A few moments later Nicholas got up and went to the door. There was a soldier outside without a gun who stared at him.

'Can I go now?'

The soldier shook his head.

'Can I have a drink?'

Long silence.

'Clean water, an unopened bottle.'

Eventually the soldier said, 'You wait in there.' And slouched off.

The soldier came ten minutes later – along with the colonel. Practically zipping up his flies.

As he came through the door, he was already saying, 'The African Negro has an IQ more like 70. No wonder African history and politics look the way they do. They are never more than young teenagers. But it would be wrong to criticize them for it, wrong to expect otherwise. The white West is very cruel to keep telling blacks that they can compete, that they can be equal, that soon Africa will look like New York or Singapore. Or that they can come to the West and ascend to living like white people. A cruel lie, far crueller than the old Imperialism, where the natural hierarchy was acknowledged by all.'

'Interesting,' said Nicholas.

'Ha! That is a very weak thing to say. Very *cautious*. You are still afraid of me.'

'Isn't that wise?'

'Well, I suppose I *might* have you killed. You hover right on the cusp of being interesting and being a damn nuisance.'

'I'll try to be interesting then.'

'Do you have any questions?'

'Yes, two. Do you have any iodine tablets? I don't trust this water. And do you feel guilty when you kill someone?'

'I'll get you some iodine. And no, I feel no guilt, sometimes pleasure. I do not think it is sexual. It is the triumph of myself over another. You have not killed?'

'No. I've hurt people I hated.'

'Did you feel guilt afterwards?'

He looked uncomfortable. 'Not as much as I thought I would.'

'There you are. You have the germ of a superior man in you, because of your honesty. If you join me as my personal physician you could have anything. *Anything*. Beyond the common law. What would you have?'

He was silent.

'Gold, power, naked slave-girls by the dozen! You are so imprisoned! Look at you! I have read about these young Mohammedans. It amuses me. Here we have very few Mohammedans except for some Lebanese traders, who love

302

money more than Allah, Christ be thanked. But in Europe all these young men are fleeing to join the Jihadists in the Middle East and it is a great puzzle to you, a great despair. Because you are Equalists and Benevolents and believe in Progress and Utopia! It is very funny – apart from the fact that you are doomed. I'm sad about that, because I admired old Europe. I follow international politics keenly, because in two years' time I will be this country's President, and take my seat in the hallowed assembly of the UN.'

Nicholas raised his eyebrows politely.

'Of course! There is no one like me. I will make my fortune and then buy my way to power. I am half-way there already. Already I am loved in the army, more than any other officer of my age. You will read about me in the papers soon.'

The name Inocencio had such a pleasing irony at first, but the irony had waned. He really was an innocent. He had no conscience, so everything he did was innocent.

'But your Jihadists now,' said the colonel. 'In the West, in London or in Paris, a young Mohammedan lives in some slum or runs a shop or answers the telephone and is despised and is dying inside of boredom. And the West is puzzled when he runs off to join the Jihadists where he is a hero, fighting alongside his brothers in arms, killing his enemies, taking their women for himself, as many as he wants - a young man's dream! How can life in the West compete with such a dream?

'It is too funny. A saying of Ghengis Khan's, though from my researches I think it is false but nevertheless, it was a saying attributed to him, "The sweetest thing in life is to kill your enemy, rape his women and steal his gold!"

'This is a great truth. If the West does not understand this, it is finished. Then it will be others' turn. The Believers.'

53

He said bluntly to the colonel as he changed his dressing again that evening,

'Listen, I know what is happening here. You have told me everything. To be honest, I don't care. Get up and throttle me again if you like. You see I am past caring. I only care for one thing: for the family I lived with here, and for the little girl who is not on the manifest. I think she is lost.'

'Why should you care?'

He eased the bloody pad off the wound and found that it was indeed, scabbily and messily, healing over. It would leave a scar the size of his palm. But the crust should now be more than enough of a barrier to any skin-borne bacteria. He looked closely. It was made of countless little segments, like scales, as all skin was. Tessellated like the skin of a rhinoceros or that triassic pachyderm. Dozing in the shade of the giant bromeliads or tree ferns, murderous and contented ruler of the earth.

'Speak to me, gringo.'

'She is very young, only six years old. She has already been lost a week or so now. I think she is in the city and I want to reunite the girl with her family.'

'Ah, the heroic gringo! I see through you like glass.'

'I want you let me go, and then I can tell you where there is a crashed plane in the jungle.'

'Why should I care about that?'

'You will want its cargo. It is under thick canopy. You will never find it otherwise.'

The colonel turned on his side and cuffed his hands away and propped himself on one elbow and stared at him. 'How do you know?'

'I like walking the forest trails.'

'You are crazy. What is in this magical plane?'

'There's a dead man in the cockpit and another thrown out of it – what's left of him. In the cargo bay there are black sacks full of white powder.'

The colonel stared at him. 'How you do interest me, Englishman.' He even waggled his forefinger. 'Your people from Europe are all soft because life in your country is soft. In England. Heh? But you are not so soft. What is your history?'

'I was born on a mountain top and raised by eagles.'

'Ah, you are tedious now. Fuck yourself.'

Nicholas smiled, what he hoped was a charming and evasive smile, not a contorted grimace. He said, 'I will take you to the plane, and you give me five hundred dollars. Then you let me go.'

The colonel lay down on his belly again, chin on the backs of his hands. 'I love your optimism, gringo. Why don't we just march you into the jungle and shoot you in the back of the head?'

Despite himself, Nicholas thought he could trust this man. The colonel liked to think he was a man of honour.

'Is it a deal?'

'Finish the dressing. I'm thinking.'

He spent another day thinking about the family, wondering if someone might be looking after Eulalia, perhaps missionaries or something. Planning his escape, and treating soldiers for crabs and clap. Then that night, he was half-awakened by shouting, and then fully awake and sitting upright and afraid when a soldier kicked his door open.

'English! Come!'

He was led into his clinic, as it was called, and a grey man lay on the floor, a groaning man on the table. There were several soldiers in there, blocking the light. They gesticulated at the grey man, interrupting each other.

'How did it happen? How did he die? Feel his pulse.'

He said, 'I don't need to feel his pulse. He's –'

One of the soldiers shoved him hard in the chest. 'Do as I say!'

'Then stop fucking hitting me.' He knelt. A musty earthy smell, a cellar door opening, a gust of something unclean. He was still only just waking up. 'No pulse.'

'How did he die?'

'I can't say. I'm not a coroner. Even if you make me cut him open, I still wouldn't be able to tell any more than you. You should take him away now.'

'He's been dead some days?'

'Yes.'

'There's a bullethole in his back, look.' They rolled him on his side. 'But it hasn't come out anywhere so it must still be in him, no?'

Smart thinking, sergeant. He nodded. 'You should take him away.'

They carried out the grey corpse. As they bumped him through the doorway the sergeant called after them,

'Dig that bullet out of his back! For evidence. Then bury him above the water.'

He went over to the table. The groaning soldier was Joachim, who had lent him his Bible. He was filthy with earth and sweat, as if a buried bomb had gone off in his face. But it was his leg wound which would kill him. Nicholas carefully drew off the sodden bandages and the improvised splint and it was a terrible mess. He wanted a surgical mask just to filter the smell of putrescence and blood. He tried to think of Dr Menendez standing just behind him, sprinkling sardonic wisdom and cigarette ash.

The last of the improvised dressings – strips of torn up t-shirt – were stuck to the wound. He loosened them with warm water and eased them off. Joachim shuddered. There was a hole the size of an orange and he could see right down to the slick shining shinbone. Anterolateral. And there was brown rotting tissue with no evidence of healing.

'Please,' murmured the boy soldier. 'For the pain.'

He gave him 200ml of lidocaine and the boy's head fell back and he relaxed.

He needed a hospital. Although what he really needed, at this juncture in his country's chequered history, was not to have been wounded in the first place. That would be his best bet.

'Are they coating the bullets?' asked the sergeant, leaning over him, scowling.

'What?'

'With poison? To engender this…'

'No. Well, I don't think so.'

'So why does it rot like this?'

'The bullet has carried in other material. Threads from his trousers which would have been muddy. Specks of soil. Bacteria already on the skin.'

'There are germs on the skin?'

'Yes.'

'In this country?'

'Every country.'

The sergeant backed away in disgust.

And sweet-natured Joachim was dying. Whom he had talked with just yesterday. For some reason the boy soldier suddenly felt a bolt of pain through the lidocaine and sat up with a high-pitched wail, and then lay back just as suddenly, breathless and exhausted. Sweat ran from his forehead, cleaning trails across his earthen temples.

'He must go to a proper hospital,' said Nicholas.

'Cut his leg off then,' said the sergeant.

'Don't be ridiculous. I'm not a surgeon, I don't even have a saw. He needs a proper operation.'

'You refuse?'

'Of course I refuse. If you want your soldier to survive. You must take him to proper hospital.'

'Very well. Go back to your bed and rest.'

'What are you going to do? Let me take him to a hospital. I will go with him. He will get better, he is young. Please –'

The sergeant jerked his head and he was propelled from the room.

He lay there wondering if he might be a news item back in England, to take his mind off the dying Joachim. Now he felt faint and seasick. Imagine imagine. Take the mind off the hook. Endure until escape. He pictured his hunted-looking passport photo on the TV screen. Later he half-slept, and pictured Eulalia beside a huge city rubbish dump and there was firelight and a great white bird of prey spread-eagled in the sky above her.

Towards dawn one of the soldiers came and crouched beside him and said Joachim was dead. He said that the sergeant had had them rub down a woodsaw with boiled water, and then sawed Joachim's leg off himself.

The soldier crossed himself.

'Did they give him any more lidocaine? Painkillers?'

The soldier shook his head. 'He was very brave.'

Nicholas rolled over, sickened and exhausted, haunted by images of the boy soldier Joachim.

54

Days and days went by, and Eulalia kept nagging Pepito to find her auntie and then her family.

'How we going to find your auntie?' he said.

'She works in a shoe shop.'

Eventually he said maybe she worked in one of the rich shops along the Boulevard Morazán. 'Trouble is, the Boulevard Morazán isn't exactly our part of town. The cops see us, they just think we're thieves.'

'But we are thieves.'

'You may be a thief, sister. I'm an entrepreneur.'

'A what?'

He pondered. 'OK. Let's go swank up and down the Boulevard Morazán. Maybe we go for a cocktail after at the Hotel Hilton, eh? Sit by the pool.'

She nodded eagerly.

He slapped her on the back. 'You have ambition for a little Indian girl. But if we see any cops, or even anyone watching us and reaching for the phone – we run like dogs. You hear me?'

There was no sign of Osmin, and Ana Maria didn't want to come as she felt sick. Last night she'd eaten half a burger that someone had left behind on the wall. So they left her to sleep in the tunnel, and set off east for the new town.

It took more than half an hour to walk up through the steep cobbled streets of the old city and past the cathedral square and the huge statue of Francisco Morazán on a horse, and then past the museum, and once magnificent opera house, now dilapidated and roofless and full of screeching parakeets. At nights they lit bonfires in there, and men crouched round swigging rum and betting on cockfights.

They emerged out onto the wide Boulevard Concordia, with shiny low-slung limousines and huge sinister jeeps with blacked-out windows, and you wouldn't think there was a war on at all. Maybe there wasn't here. It was all in the hills. It was the first time Eulalia realized how big the city was, and she would have been frightened if she wasn't with Pepito. But he strode along like he was a millionaire and owned half the city.

They passed beneath the shadow of the huge new football stadium which only went half the way round and then stopped because they had run out of money to build it, and looking back they could now see the huge statue of Jesus on the mountain of El Picacho, stretching out his hands in blessing over the city. Then they walked up another narrow street and out onto the enormous Boulevard Morazán, which led all the way up to the Presidential Palace at the other end like a white wedding cake in the distance.

'Is that really where the President lives?'

'Really. He's probably sitting out on the balcony right now, stuffing his face with chocolate and watching us through binoculars.'

'*Aie!*'

'Come on.'

It was frightening and exhilarating all at once to see so many cars and shops and huge hotels and a vast shopping mall called the Mall MultiPlaza. Here rich people got out of their limousines and jeeps and a man in a smart long coat helped them up the steps into the Mall. Many of the rich women wore trousers, tight trousers, which was a shame and a disgrace. There were enormous hotels and hissing water sprinklers everywhere to keep the lawns of the hotels green, and Pepito said the grass wasn't even grown to feed sheep or goats, just to lie there looking nice and green!

There weren't many people walking though which made

them cautious. They kept to the shade under the trees along the Boulevard and Pepito's eyes darted about constantly, always on the look out for policemen and remembering the last likely looking escape route they had passed. Or they could try just jumping on a bus, even though they didn't have any money. It might get them far enough away to be safe.

The shops had huge glass windows full of plastic ladies wearing pretty dresses and big hats and looking very haughty, and handsome men in suits, and jewellery shops and cake shops and even one huge window with a real whole car in it, which made her laugh and laugh.

There were coffee shops and restaurants and people sitting outside wearing dark glasses and smoking and eating thick oozing steaks that made their mouths water just to look at.

'On the way back,' said Pepito, expertly scanning one pavement restaurant, 'we could do a bit of waiting at tables. The restaurants here are a bit classier than round our patch, eh?'

She nodded.

'Girl, you gotta wise up. You gotta learn a bit more.' He stared at her, scowled a bit, then shook his head. 'But then if you wised up, you wouldn't be you any more, eh? You wouldn't be a little *Indita* from the mountains any more. You'd be just like the rest of us.'

They walked on, she trotting to keep up with his quick jerky pace down the wide pavement under the jacaranda trees.

In the window of another shop were more than a dozen televisions, some of them with screens bigger than her mattress, all showing different channels.

'You seen TV before?'

'Of course I have,' she said scornfully. 'In the grocery store.'

On the nearest screen there was a picture of the White House which was the Presidential Palace of the gringos, and

311

then a picture of some blue and white helicopters flying over the jungle carrying big crates hanging from cables beneath them. There was a newsreader with a round face and moustache, saying that the counter-insurgency against the rebel forces was intensifying and looking very placid about it. There were ranks of soldiers with their faces painted green and black, eyes gleaming from the mask, and dogs panting on leashes.

'Is that this country?' she asked.

'Looks like it.'

The man in the shop was moving along behind the screens and watching them.

'C'mon, let's keep going.'

And then they found a shoe shop! Rows and rows of the most beautiful shoes, red and white and green and skyblue and silver and gold, ranged out on white racks and gleaming glass shelves, and there was soft lighting, and they could even hear a little background music, as if the shop was a restaurant and rich ladies went in to sit and devour the shoes with fine bone-handled knives and forks. Afterwards they would burp and their breath would smell of leather, but very expensive leather.

'What do you want?' called one lady, instantly indignant at the sight of this barefoot urchin peering in at her doorway like some begrimed goblin popped up from the underworld via a storm drain.

Eulalia backed out.

Pepito said, 'That's no good. Ask her if she knows your auntie Rosario.'

'She doesn't like me.'

'Not half as much as I don't like her.'

'And I'm *so hungry*. I can't concentrate. And it's so cold in there.'

'Air con. Go in and ask her.'

'Come with me then.'

'I'm coming with you.'

'Please *señora*. My auntie –'

The woman rounded on her, almost spinning on one her high heels. 'What do you want?' Her shoes were slim-fitting and bottle green, and her legs were very taut and slim and white.

Eulalia didn't dare look any higher than her legs. 'My auntie says she works here.'

'What do you mean, girl? Speak up.'

She could hardly hear her own voice. 'My auntie Rosario,' she whispered.

'Is there anyone called Rosario working here?' put in Pepito behind her.

'Out of my shop now! Only one of your lot in here at a time, I know what you're like!'

'I'm not in your shop, I'm just outside it. Anyhow I don't want your shoes. They wouldn't suit my style.'

'Or do you want me to call the police?'

'Rather you didn't.'

'Right, that's it.'

'No, wait,' said Pepito, 'just tell us, is there anyone called Rosario working here?'

'No there isn't. Just me. Now go away.'

'Or at the other shoe shops?'

'I have no idea. Now *go away*.'

They went away downhearted.

'She must be lonely to work on her own all day,' said Eulalia.

'She deserves to have one of her shoes shoved up her badword,' said Pepito.

It was just the same story at the other two shops. The third shop had a man in it but he wasn't any nicer. They asked him if there were any more shoe shops he could think of but he just shrugged.

'You could try the Mall.' He looked at them, resting his

313

chin lazily in the palm of his hand, his eyes heavy-lidded. 'If they let you in.'

There was a big black sack lying half in, half out of the gutter.

They walked nearer.

It wasn't a big sack.

'Badword,' muttered Pepito, veering around it. 'Keep walking.'

'You shouldn't say so many badwords,' said Eulalia. 'Say, Goodness gracious.'

He held his hand up to his mouth. The smell was sickening.

Eulalia walked very close to him, keeping him between her and the thing in the gutter. She wanted to look back but didn't. She remembered the village, the dead dog.

'Just *lying there*,' muttered Pepito furiously, not looking back either. Looking straight ahead and walking very fast. 'Just lying there. And nobody doing a thing about it. Like it's *normal*.'

They arrived back at the enormous Mall MultiPlaza and there were cars pulling up and disgorging people and others collecting people with their shopping bags and driving off, and two security guards with pump-action shotguns at the glass entrance doors.

'Just keep walking,' said Pepito.

They marched up the steps, Eulalia swinging her arms very hard and determined like a soldier, her bare feet cold on the fine marble.

'A moment,' said one of the guards.

They stopped.

'Let's see your credit cards. Who are you with, Visa? Amex?'

The other guard laughed.

'We don't have credit cards,' said Pepito. 'We consider them injurious to the morals. We prefer to use cash.'

'Is that a fact? And how much cash are you carrying today,

314

sir? If you don't mind my asking?'

'Because it could be a security risk,' said the other guard. 'You might need protection if you're carrying that much.'

'OK,' said Pepito, 'so we don't have any money. We just want to go in quickly so we can –'

'Steal a few things and then be on your way. Trouble is, our job is to keep thieves and vagrants like you out of here, not let you –'

Eulalia suddenly shouted at them, 'I'm not a thief and a vagrant, you rotten men! My auntie works in there and I just want to get in to see her because I'm tired of sleeping in a tunnel!'

She felt Pepito's hand on her arm. 'Easy, sister.'

The guards looked annoyed. 'Beat it,' they said. 'Or else.'

As they moved away, Pepito said, 'Is that opening times?

She looked. There was a big sign with times of day on it. She nodded.

'What time does this place shut up then?'

'Ten o'clock at night.

'Ay.' They walked slowly away. 'Your Auntie Rosario. Would she know ... about your village?'

'She wrote a letter to Mama sometimes, and Pedro Xom the *ajtz'ib* would come and read it to her. I could have read it to her too but I was a bit slow. But she didn't write back, Mama, she never went to school.'

'Your Auntie Rosario got kids?'

'She couldn't have, she was all dried up inside. Her husband left her for that. Mama was very angry.'

'That why she came to work in the city?'

'I don't know. Some of the women in the village were unkind to her for not having babies.'

'Come on,' said Pepito. 'Time to wait at tables.'

They went back to the restaurant where they had seen people eating those juicy steaks, but a waiter spotted them loitering with hungry expressions on their faces, and shooed them away. He shooed away some pigeons on the tables at the same time, waving his big white napkin.

At the second restaurant they struck lucky. A family of four were just getting up from a table still covered in food. The mother had only eaten a little, the daughter even less.

'Rich women aren't allowed to eat much,' said Pepito, crouching behind the neat hedge. 'Else they get too fat and their husbands dump 'em and they end up becoming *putas*. Price you pay for being rich.'

Eulalia was bewildered. Surely the whole point of being rich was that you could eat as much as you liked? You could eat chocolate all day long, breakfast, lunch and supper, stuffing it in your mouth while sitting happily in the sunshine like the President on his balcony.

'Nope,' said Pepito. 'If you're a rich chick, you actually have to eat *less*. But that means ... all the more for us!'

He moved like lightning, slipping up to the table and seizing almost everything on it in the blink of an eye. An angry waiter bore down on him, and for a terrible moment Eulalia thought the man would seize him by the scruff of the neck and lift him up and bear him off to the kitchen to be chopped into mincemeat for his next customers. A Pepito-burger! You wouldn't make many out of him though.

But Pepito ducked right under the table and out the other side and kicked a chair over and swivelled away, clutching a big napkin bulging with food.

Eulalia stared open-mouthed.

'Run!'

They only stopped running when they were deep in the alleyways of the old market. They crouched down behind a crumbling cinderblock wall, out of breath, and Pepito reverently laid down the napkin and drew back the corners.

'The rich man eats when he's hungry, the poor man eats

when he can,' he said solemnly. 'Check that out.'

Eulalia gasped. There were two and a half soft white rolls, the half bit with butter already on, and two pieces of steak and some green beans and some bread sticks and some fried potatoes and a soggy grilled tomato that had gone splat all over the napkin and a slice of chocolate cheesecake.

'And,' said Pepito proudly, and pulled from his back pocket nearly a whole bottle of Coca-Cola.

'She probably ordered Diet Coke and this came by mistake, and she didn't want to drink it or she'd get fat, and then, you know ... the whole *puta* thing. You ever had Coke?'

She shook her head.

'Here,' he said. 'You have it.'

'Half each?'

'Well,' he said. 'Have what you want and then I'll finish it.'

She took the bottle and raised it to her lips.

It was sugary and brown and fizzy and just delicious. She burped.

'So. What first?'

They both reckoned it had to be the chocolate cheesecake. So they ate that first, squidging it very carefully into two identical halves with their fingers. Then they ate the fried potatoes, then a bread roll, then they ate one of the steaks, then they ate the other bread roll, then they ate the green beans which had gone cold now but still had butter on. Then they stopped and sighed.

'What about the tomato?'

She burped again and shook her head. So he slid the red goo off the napkin and then wrapped up the breadsticks, saying they'd keep, and the other steak and the buttered half bit of bread roll.

'For Ana.'

She nodded.

'Wow. I am so full.'

'I can't stand up.'

'Nor me. I could still eat more chocolate cheesecake though. Lying down.'

They laughed.

'I like waiting at tables.'

'I think we're pretty good at it. It's so important to take a pride in your work.'

Pepito said they ought to think about moving on for a bit. They shouldn't stay too long in the same place. Because of the Black Van.

She began to see the Black Van in her dreams and nightmares. It was like a monstrous bull with glaring yellow eyes set wide apart as it bore down on you. It roared and stamped and poured out dust from behind its tyres as it bellowed angrily through the streets of the city, and she and the other children and Héctor too, they ran and hid under piles of rubbish or in bins. Then peeping out from under their piles of rubbish they saw the Black Van charge past, and it had a row of tiny windows down each side, blacked out and heavily barred, and at each window as it went by, they caught a glimpse of a pale child's face, staring out like a frightened ghost.

And after they climbed out of the bins they found nothing but a desolate plain covered in dead bodies, and flies, and shot dead dogs, and vultures circling overhead.

55

One evening, after she and Ana had been sitting all day under a market cart watching the people come and go and eating bananas dropped from the crates, they were walking back towards the bridge, and it was now already dark and they had stayed out too late and the streets were strangely quiet and they held each other's hands.

'Let's go down the backstreet,' said Ana.

They didn't know why but it would be better tonight.

The main road along the embankment was very quiet, just a few blacked-out jeeps and of course no pedestrians, not this late. A dog barked from a nearby hillside, occasional fires burned. They crept down the dark cobbled alley that would bring them out just above the road by the bridge. And as they came round the corner, there, parked right by the wall where they dropped down to their tunnel, was the Black Van.

The girls froze and then shrank back into the shadows. They peered out again.

There were two men walking round the back of the Van, and they came to the wall and leaned on it and looked over the river below. One spat.

The girls prayed that nobody was in the tunnel, or if they were, that they would keep very still, and they hoped nobody had lit a fire tonight.

The men had guns at their sides and one still wore his dark glasses even though it was night time.

There was a sound like a gunshot from a nearby hillside *barrio* and the dog started barking furiously again. Then other dogs started.

The men leaned on the wall and smoked. The girls waited

in agony. Where was Pepito, where was Osmin? Was Catalina around?

Eulalia could have cried. This city was an evil place, though sometimes it seemed fun. They would always be hungry here, and often sick, and people would always want to get rid of them. They would never be safe.

Even when the men tossed their cigarettes over the wall and walked slowly back to the Van and got in and drove away, she felt no relief. They would come back. They would kill them all.

'What are we going to do?' whispered Ana.

But she didn't know. They sat huddled on the low step at the bottom of the alley and shivered.

Half an hour later, they heard a noise behind them.

'Psst.'

It was Pepito! Eulalia could have hugged him.

'We saw the Black Van.'

'We all saw the Black Van,' said Pepito.

As he came nearer, out of the shadows, she saw that he was all messed up. He had only one shoe on, and his sweatshirt was torn at the seam at the top of his right sleeve, and he been punched hard in the mouth and the nose and had dried blood there, and his eyes were all red and bloodshot.

'What happened?'

But he just said in a funny voice, not like him at all, 'They hit you. You live sad.'

The two girls stared at him.

'C'mon,' he said. 'We belong in the Cemetery.'

They crept down dark back alleyways and dashed over the broad empty boulevards like feral cats, briefly splashed yellow from the few sodium streetlights that stood there. Flitting out of the shadows and briefly shining and vanishing again like night time mirages.

They walked for half the night, Pepito going barefoot,

carrying his one shoe, until in the northern part of the city they came to a broad flat road and no lights at all but for the thin moon and the tropical stars overhead, and westwards a single bus in the night, its headlights sweeping back and forth as it ascended the winding switchback road into the mountains.

All along the side of the road over a low white wall stretched the huge Cemetery of La Recoleta. The Secluded. They were very tired and here at last they slept.

In the daytime, people came to lay fruit and flowers on the graves, and set paper flowers of coloured tissue in tin cans and plastic bottles. And the three came out like ghost children even as the mourners turned their backs on the dead, and longed to eat the fruit but never did.

Along the far side of La Recoleta were the common graves, all marked *non nato*, not born. And in the middle was a small whitewashed chapel, its floor always strewn with aromatic pine needles and fresh green grass. On the forlorn altar, on the worn pink altarcloth, people left gifts of money, cigars and rum, lone petals, herbs, candles, and the hearts of immense and gaudy flowers. They laid them there for luck and protection, and they prayed for their loved ones who had disappeared or died, their parents, their children who had gone before them, whom they buried in small white coffins of unplaned boards.

When they turned to go, some mourners thought they glimpsed a child darting behind the gravestones and vanishing, and they crossed themselves and went away wondering as well as grieving. The gifts they left in the chapel were never stolen.

La Recoleta was like a great garden all to themselves, full of flowers and trees and butterflies and birds singing and lizards darting over the gravestones. But they were very hungry there. They begged from the food shack at the side of the road, and in the evening the man there gave them his last stale tortillas.

321

But they were very hungry all night and slept badly and got bitten by lots of bugs. Pepito said they'd get their revenge by eating the bugs for breakfast.

Eventually Eulalia gave up her earrings which she'd kept hold of all this time, and the man gave them three *tamales* for them.

'When can we go back to the tunnel?' asked Ana.

'Not yet,' said Pepito. 'We're like bandits. We gotta hide out awhile.'

They begged from those visiting the graves, and made a few coppers that way, and bought some more tortillas and some delicious *tamales*. But hunger always stayed with them, their hollow-eyed faithful companion.

On the third night a hot blustery wind got up and the stars in the sky shimmered and shook like leaves.

'Maybe the rains are coming,' said Pepito.

The plastic bottles and rusting tin cans on the graves were bowled over and rolled about and bounced off the gravestones with musical little tocs and rings. In the morning the paper flowers had been torn apart and lay strewn across the cemetery like so much litter.

Eulalia slept late in the warm hazy sunshine on her favourite grave, a soft grassy mound with small yellow flowers at her head. Sleepily she heard voices. She opened her eyes.

It wasn't Pepito and Ana. Pepito and Ana had gone.

Her stomach felt cold. Where had they gone? Why had they left her? She would be terrified to be alone. Perhaps the Black Van had taken them away. But why hadn't it taken her? It would be terrible to be taken away in the Black Van. But it would be even worse to be left behind, all alone. She would die here in the cemetery, and nobody would ever even know.

She stood up carefully behind the low gravestone and peered out, still hidden from view, trying to not be too frightened. The gravestone belonged to Alicia Izabel García,

Nuestra Querida, 2011-2015, *Con Dios*.

There were gringos walking round the cemetery with a local guide, talking in Spanish and taking photographs.

'Just awful,' one of the gringos was saying. A tall slim pretty lady with long fair hair held back with a brightly-coloured bandanna, and sunglasses pushed up on top of her head, and lots of bangles on her slim brown wrists, and a black vest t shirt, and those baggy trousers with enormous side pockets that all gringos wore to keep all their many possessions in, and interesting bouncy rubber shoes.

She carried a huge black camera and looked around and shook her head. 'A place of like this,' she said quietly, 'and look at it – just covered in garbage.'

Her husband wore a broad-brimmed brown leather hat and beads around his neck like a girl and looked rather grubby for a rich man.

'It was the storm,' said their guide.

'A civil society in meltdown,' said the white lady. She squatted down and took some photographs of the strewn cans and flowers.

The local guide lit a cigarette and looked in the other direction, back towards the city. Then the white lady saw her. She froze in fear.

'Hey, come here sweetheart. I'd like to take your photograph.'

Immediately, without thinking about it, Eulalia ran away and hid. She heard them calling but she stayed hidden, thinking furiously.

A lot of travellers and gringos and *blancos* wanted to take photographs of her people. Some of her people, like Pedro Xom the *atzj'ib* and some of the elders, were very against it. But Eulalia had had her photograph taken before, in the village, and it didn't hurt.

They were very nice people, the couple who took photographs in the village. They came from Europe, like

Doctor Nicholas had done. They smiled and gave out sweets and asked if they could take photographs. Which was respectful as the gringos in Santo Domingo on market day usually just snapped away which was very impolite. They said they would pay for the privilege and Papa thought for a while and spoke quietly to Mama and then said it would be all right, they didn't want any money.

Now there were more gringos wanting to photograph her, in a cemetery! They were very strange people.

She came forth. 'Give me some money,' she said boldly, like Pepito would.

The two gringos looked at each other. They didn't look very pleased. Then the lady unzipped the pouch that she wore round her waist and pulled out a note and said to her husband, 'Dependency culture.'

Then she said to Eulalia, 'OK, here you go. Now honey, if you could just sit there like that –'

So Eulalia sat neatly cross-legged like she used to at school on the grave of Alicia Izabel García, taking care not to squash her yellow flowers, and tried to smile nicely, and not to worry about Pepito and Ana. The fair-haired lady peered through her camera at her and then lowered it again and looked uncertain.

'Honey – could I ask you, y'know, not to smile? Could you look kind of sad? You've got a lovely smile, but could I ask you to do that for me? And I tell you what, could you sit differently too? If you uncross your legs and sit –' she tilted her head thoughtfully to one side, '– tell you what, if you kind of half lie down, OK? Like you're tired, say?'

So Eulalia awkwardly half lay down across the grave and thought sad thoughts, which wasn't too difficult, and the lady took a photograph, and then another, and another. She must have taken about twenty. And then she said thank you very much to her and they all went away very happy.

Eulalia looked down at the note in her hand and then flattened it out. She could hardly believe it! It had a picture of a very thin faced stately gringo on it with a ridiculous beard just on the edge of his chin, and on the back there was a fine building with lots of columns, and it said Five US Dollars.

Just wait till she found Pepito and Ana and told them!

At that moment she heard Pepito calling to her from the road.

It was if the sun had come out from behind a thundercloud and she ran to him. He and Ana had just been up a bit earlier to see if there were any tortillas to spare at the supermarket down the road, and they had two to share between three. Eulalia was so happy that she told them without pausing for a single breath. And then she showed them her Five US Dollars.

'Goodness gracious,' said Pepito, staring at it.

'That's better,' said Eulalia.

56

Eulalia wanted to change her five dollars into *quetzales* at one of the little glass booths on the Boulevard Morazán, because they looked so important, but Pepito said that was crazy. So they found a stall in the old market where they got a deal which Pepito approved of, after much hard bargaining. She couldn't believe the roll of notes they ended up with. It was bigger than her fist, so Pepito carried them in his front jeans pocket.

'Think of me as your banker,' he grinned. 'As honest as any of 'em, I am.'

Then they went to a burger restaurant and the lady there told them to leave and Eulalia grandly ordered her personal banker to show her the roll of money.

The lady said, 'And where d'you get that from? Street kids like you?'

Eulalia said a white lady gave it to her for looking sad in a photograph, and the lady said 'Yeah, and I'm Eva Perón,' which wasn't true as her name badge said Juana, and then grudgingly she put them on a table well away from the window so as not to distress the other customers.

Eulalia read the menu out loud to Pepito and Ana, very slowly and carefully, every single item on it, and it took about ten minutes to read it all. By the end they could hardly think straight. Then after a long discussion they ordered two burgers and chips and some extra chips and two fried chicken pieces in crispy chili coating and one ice cream and one Coca Cola and still had just enough to order one orange cheesecake after that, and by the end they had eaten so much they felt slightly sick.

'I need to lie down,' said Eulalia.

'Back to the tunnel,' said Pepito.

Osmin was sitting in the mouth of the tunnel with another boy, Teodoro, who had a bad leg.

'They been,' he said. He waved them in.

Some horrible men had come. They hadn't been able to do much damage as there wasn't much there anyway. But they had set fire to the mattress and burned it down to a few blackened springs, and kicked everything about and smeared woodash everywhere. Pepito said to be careful as they would have done *caca* here too, probably.

'Will the men come back?' said Ana.

He shrugged. 'I dunno. We'll be OK though. They won't be back in a while.'

'Are you sure?'

He looked away. 'Sure.'

The loss of the mattress was the worst thing.

'We'll have to keep a look out for another,' said Pepito, 'or some cushions, an old armchair or something.'

Meanwhile they had only big pieces of cardboard to sleep on, which weren't very comfy. Ana curled up on the single sofa cushion. Pepito and Eulalia shared the cardboard.

'Sleep end to end,' said Eulalia.

'Huh?'

'You know. Head to toe.'

'Why?'

She didn't say.

'You're weird. That how you slept in the village, you Indians?'

She glared at him with such ferocity that he held his hands up to ward off the evil eye.

'OK, OK. Lie down there. And I'll sleep upside down next to you if it makes you happy. OK?'

She didn't say anything. She felt him lie down.

'Well,' he said. 'This is a new one on me. You OK now?'

She was. But she wasn't going to tell him.

The fire went out and it was very dark and quite cold and she whimpered through dreams of bad men and Mama and Héctor and El Pipón.

Up above on the volcanoes' sleeping sides, the deep darkness was studded with scattered fires. Where the few street lights of the old city surrendered to the great sprawl of the *barrios*, spreading out across the mountains all around the unlovely city. Huts and hovels and half-built or broken houses tumbling down the slopes; barking dogs, snoring pigs, goats, chickens, cries, dirt roads and drinking shacks randomly illuminated by single glaring lightbulbs and woodfires in dustbins. There was her Auntie Rosario somewhere out there, and in another few hours she would be busy at her oven, making her tortillas and her morning coffee, waiting for her. And then Mama.

It was because of the cardboard and not sleeping that Eulalia and Pepito were awake in the heart of the night and saw the candles coming down the river.

'What are they?'

Pepito stared. 'I think it's like, some ceremony up in the *barrios*.

'Is it February now?' said Eulalia. 'Is it *La Candelaria*?'

There were hundreds, thousands, of small wooden crosses stuck with blossoms and single white candles, floating downriver, turning and turning in the lethargic eddies. Some stuck against the reefs of rubbish, some capsized, but most went on right past them where they sat in the mouth of the tunnel, floating under the bridge and away downstream. The children stared after the squadrons of tiny cruciform boats, clustering and separating, each cross a memory of one of the disappeared, from somewhere now silent upstream.

57

A few mornings later Catalina came whistling over the wall.

'Hey, *Indita*, there's a photo of you in a shop window on the Plaza San Carlos!'

'What you talking about?' said Pepito.

'Go and see.'

So Eulalia and Pepito went up together to the Plaza San Carlos, a neat and tidy little square the other side of the cathedral where there were some shops and cafes for the rich. They walked all round it under the colonnade looking in the windows, and then they both stopped and stared, open-mouthed.

'*Madre de Dios*,' said Pepito softly.

There in the window, on a wooden easel, was a huge photographic print, about half the size of Eulalia in real life. And there she was, lying across a grave and looking up at you with her huge dark eyes, very mysterious and pretty. At the bottom right hand of the print was a discreet handwritten sticker that said $350.

'Three hundred and fifty dollars, that says, yeah?' said Pepito.

She nodded.

'Badword.'

They pressed their noses to the window again and when they stood back they left smeary marks. A tall woman with glasses on a string resting on her bosom suddenly appeared behind the prints in the window and made shooing away motions.

'But that's her!' cried Pepito, pointing.

The woman scowled and made a telephone sign with her thumb and little finger.

They backed away

The woman reached into the window and straightened the big print though it didn't need straightening and then glanced out at the little girl in the street and back at the print and then straightened it again and then turned away into her grand and silent shop.

The woman had a dreadful day after that. Every time she looked up, there'd be another filthy little urchin pressing its nose to her window. It would need a thorough wash tomorrow.

It was quite appalling. All the street children and lunatics in the city seemed to be foregathering in the Plaza today. There was a man with only one hand, for heaven's sake, and a crazed looking woman mumbling incessantly to herself, and several more barefoot urchins, riddled with lice no doubt. All come to stare at the marvellously moody piece called *Death and the Maiden* by de Haan and de Haan.

Eventually she went to the door and yelled out that if they didn't move on, she'd call the police. The Plaza San Carlos was no place for their sort. And like some bedraggled miniature army they slowly departed.

They'd only grow up into thieves and muggers and worse, soon enough. Something would have to be done.

'So,' said Pepito, back among the market carts. 'A toast!' He raised an invisible glass of champagne. 'Lala the supermodel!'

'You are very pretty,' said Ana quietly.

Eulalia felt frozen with a sudden sadness and homesickness and the other children just didn't understand, which upset her even more. And now she felt embarrassed and flushed with pleasure all on top of that. She looked down.

'She's too pretty,' said One-handed Hassan.

'She sure is,' grinned Pepito.

'No, I really mean it. She's too pretty. Understand?'

Pepito's smile faded. 'You think?'

One-handed Hassan nodded gravely.

'He's right,' said Teodoro with the limp. 'Trouble, man.'

'Yeah,' said Osmin lazily, sitting back against the wall, his eyes almost closed. 'There's all kinds of photos you could be in, pretty *niña* like you. There's a place down the road –'

'Leave her alone,' said Pepito.

Osmin's voice sounded funny, and his eyes opened properly now and wouldn't leave her alone. Eulalia didn't think she liked him very much. She felt her own eyes hot up and prickle.

'Just shut up,' said Pepito.

'All men will be brothers,' said One-handed Hassan.

'The police close it down sometimes,' said Osmin, 'but then it opens up again soon enough, because other police run it really anyhow. They run all the *casas*.'

'I said, Shut up!'

Pepito leapt on him and Osmin held him off for a while, still laughing lazily, rolling across the dusty pavement. Then Osmin rolled over a sharp bit of concrete and shouted 'Ow!' and dropped his guard, and Pepito's small hard fist shot out and caught him on the side of the face, and Osmin, four or five years older, had had enough.

'Badword, man,' he said, leaping up and cradling his ear. 'Badword you.'

'You shouldn't talk like that in front of her.'

'I'll talk how I badword want, you little runt.'

'Go away. Leave us alone.'

'The Peace of Christ,' said One-handed Hassan.

'I'll go away when I feel like it, you dirty runt.' Osmin stood there a while longer, still cradling his throbbing ear. And then as no one else would talk or even look at him, he went away anyway, cursing them feebly.

Pepito thought for a moment and then said, 'Hey sister, how d'you like us to cut your hair?'

'No!'

'Kinda, really neat and short. Because, if you keep your hair long and pretty like that, rich women will see it and send their husbands round to kidnap you.'

'You never said that before,' said Eulalia.

'No man, but that's right!' said Teodoro. 'They'll take you back to their big house out of town and keep you locked up in some cellar, and rats and stuff'll come and suck blood from your legs every night when you're sleeping!'

Pepito said, 'Easy man.'

'The Peace of Christ,' said One-handed Hassan.

'OK, no, not rats, but it'll be bad anyhow,' jabbered Teodoro, 'and they keep you in this cellar and you grow your hair, and they come every week and cut if off for the rich lady of the house, she glues it on her head, she's as bald as a mango, all rich women are, but they steal the hair of the poor, you know?'

One-handed Hassan crossed himself. 'For the sorrowful tresses of the Poor,' he murmured.

'So we got to protect you,' said Pepito, 'we got to cut off your hair to save you. Your hair will grow again though.'

'Ay,' said One-handed Hassan. 'When it's safe. When the Lord Jesus comes down to earth in his golden glory, and restores at last the sorrowful hair of the Poor.'

So they went down to the tunnel, and Teodoro produced a small knife from his pocket, and they sawed off much of her hair. Then they carried it down to the river and it floated slowly away after the candles on the crosses from last night, and Hassan said that it would finally float out to sea at Trujillo, and be picked up by the pelicans to build their nests out in the golden Bay of Amatique.

And then they heard a rocket exploding in the streets behind them.

They sat deeper up the tunnel, very excited. 'This is our

bomb-proof shelter,' said Pepito. 'We're safer than the President here.'

Teodoro said, 'This city is going to burn.'

'What are they fighting about?' asked Eulalia.

Pepito shrugged. 'Everything really. People like fighting, I reckon.'

They went out wandering later to see if they could find where the rocket had fallen, and found it had exploded on the ruined opera house, which Pepito said was a waste of a good rocket. Policemen and soldiers milled about in great numbers, uncertain how to tidy up a ruined opera house. For good measure, they pushed passers by around and shouted a lot to show they were in command.

A plume of smoke went up from a nearby mountainside, and a second or two later they heard another dull crump.

'But why are they blowing up the *barrios*?' asked Eulalia.

'To set the people free!' cried Pepito.

58

The cardboard bed was so uncomfy and hard and cold, and her short hair made her feel even colder, that she woke up before dawn with a headache and a sour taste in her mouth.

She stared down towards the mouth of the tunnel and there was a man standing there.

She took in a gulp of musty air to suppress her scream of terror and kept very still. The man was standing in the mouth of the tunnel silhouetted against the night sky, turning dark grey with dawn. He held something in his hand and seemed to be looking straight at her, sniffing the air like a beast of prey. He took one step into the tunnel and stopped again. He filled the whole mouth of the tunnel.

Her throat clenched to stop herself from screaming, she leaned over and jabbed Pepito in the ribs. An instant later she thought to clamp her small hand over his mouth, because he came up out of sleep protesting loudly. He mumbled and glared at her in the dark and saw her put her finger to her lips. Then he saw the man coming up from the mouth of the tunnel.

The man stopped again and called back,

'Hey Luis, bring that badword torch over will ya?'

Pepito moved amazingly fast, scuttling over on all fours like a monkey to where Ana lay curled up on her cushion and shaking her awake. Then as silently as they could, they bent low and began to creep away into the blacker and blacker darkness ahead of them.

'Here you go,' said Luis behind.

'Something up there,' said the first man. His voice was horrible. 'And if those are rats running about, they're the biggest badword rats I ever heard.'

There was a click and a powerful beam penetrated the tunnel. The children swerved back and forth across it, terrified.

'Badword brats!' shouted the man, his voice roaring up the tunnel like a foul wind. 'Look at 'em go! Little vermin!'

The terrified children scrabbled to left and to right up the sloping sides of the tunnel, desperately seeking for a hiding place from the torch's beam.

There was another, louder click from down the tunnel.

'Run!' cried Pepito desperately.

Eulalia glanced back. Though half-blinded by the torch's beam, she thought she saw the man raising something to his shoulder. The children ran screaming. The man had a gun.

And then suddenly they were scrabbling against a steep slope and being pushed round to the left. The tunnel had turned a corner, and they were in pitch darkness again. They collapsed together against the side of the tunnel, trying to make their painful gasps for breath as quiet as possible, straining to hear.

The circle of torchlight played on the wall of the tunnel only ten yards away, but it couldn't go round the corner.

They heard the men's voices, deep and echoey. They were still a long way away. One of them laughed, a low, malignant chuckle.

'Go on then,' he said. 'Try a ricochet.'

There was a moment of agonizing silence, and then a bang so loud filled the tunnel that the children thought their ears would burst. Above the bang came a falling whine like some monstrous insect, and instinctively they dropped their chins into their chests and clasped their arms over their heads.

There was more silence, the circle of torchlight still bobbing inquisitively on the wall nearby.

The men laughed. 'Well,' said one. 'That'll teach them.' He raised his voice. 'We'll be back! No place for you here!'

The torchlight went off and the sound of their footsteps

335

retreated. Near the mouth of the tunnel they made some kicking and scuffling noises and then they were gone. But Pepito wouldn't let them move for what felt like an hour.

'What'll it teach us?' whispered Eulalia eventually.

'To hurry up and die,' said Pepito.

The men had stomped all over their pieces of cardboard, and crushed Eulalia's flower bottles, and taken Ana's cushion away with them, but hadn't been able to do any more damage than that as there wasn't anything else there.

The children crept to the mouth of the tunnel and looked warily out into the dawn. There were no men about. The river was running low again, a shallow slick down below, barely moving around the sills and reefs of rubbish and splintered timber and dead cows and car tyres and clotted plastic bags.

'We got to find somewhere else,' said Pepito. For once he sounded really anxious. 'We're not going to make it here.' He glanced sideways at Eulalia and she was crying. He put his arm round her. 'Don't cry sis,' he said. 'It'll be OK.'

She said, 'I don't remember what my Mama looked like any more.'

A while later, Osmin came by again with Catalina, trying to impress her with his knife-throwing skills. She chewed gum and looked unimpressed.

'Hey, Triqui. Marcello wants to see you.'

'What's he want?'

'I dunno. He wants to see you soon though.'

Pepito stared down at his scuffed up trainers.

'Who's Marcello?' whispered Eulalia.

Ana whispered back, 'A bad man. He kills people.'

'Oh, and,' said Osmin. 'He said to take one of the girls with you.'

'Cati?'

Catalina looked scornful.

'No,' said Agustin, 'one of the *niñas*.'

'Badword. Why?'

Agustin ran the blade of his knife over his tongue. 'Just get your ass over there or we all in trouble.'

Pepito started to move off, signalling to Eulalia.

'Not now,' said Osmin. 'After dark. You know Marcello's a vampire bat.'

'And how we supposed to walk through Zone 4 after dark?'

'How should I know? Take a badword limousine.'

Catalina laughed. Then she stopped laughing and looked hard at Eulalia and smiled as if at something secret.

59

They spent the day anxiously in the market place and the cathedral square. Pepito said it would be OK in the tunnel until dusk, as the men would only come back after dark, but Eulalia and Ana were too scared. Teodoro was carrying a clear plastic bag and sitting by a wall sniffing out of it. He grinned stupidly, the skin round his nose all red, and held it out to Eulalia and Ana.

'Happiness in a bag,' he said. 'Try some.'

Pepito smacked the bag down, then they walked away from him.

'Does it really make you happy?' asked Eulalia.

'Nah. It just makes you forget you're unhappy. Then it makes you sick.'

They sat and squinted out into the dusty square.

'What are you thinking about?' said Eulalia.

'Ssh. I need to think. Very hard.'

'Please can we not go and see Marcello?'

'Ssh.'

Marcello lived over the bridge in Zone 4, west of the river, an even more dangerous area than the old city. Tourists never went there, though in the old days one or two of the more stupid ones would ask locals in the market for directions. They had heard it was very colourful and authentic, and wanted to experience it for themselves.

'My friends,' they would tell the tourists, 'if you go over there you will not come back. They will take you down a dark alley, put a gun to your head, and strip the clothes off your back.'

'But aren't there any policemen over there?' the tourists would ask indignantly.

'My friends,' they would grin. 'It will be the police themselves who are doing this to you.'

'Keep your eyes down, don't ask any questions, don't stare,' said Pepito. 'And walk fast. We'll be OK. We'll be fine once we get to Marcello's.'

'Do we have to go?'

'Yes we do.'

'Why?'

'We just do. It's not safe in the tunnel any more. And we do what Marcello says. He's the chief, the *Tatascán*. Y'know? The Man. Believe me, it's better we do what he says.'

They went after dark. Eulalia was tired and wanted to go to bed, but there was nowhere safe to go to bed any more. They would have to go and sleep out in the cemetery again, but that was half a night's walk away. And someone said that the rebel army had taken the hillside overlooking the north of the town now anyway and was already firing rockets there. Why would they do that? Why would they try to kill people sleeping in the cemetery who they were already dead? She imagined the gravestone of Alicia Izabel García standing half-shattered by a rocket. Why was that?

They left Ana sleeping under a bench in the Cathedral Square near to where Broken Down Evangelina sat like someone mummified. Ana said she would be all right there, if she knew they were coming back in the morning.

At the corner of the square, Pepito looked back and took a last drag on his cigarette butt.

'Will she be all right?' said Eulalia.

He threw his butt down and ground it out angrily. 'I don't *know*. I don't know everything. Come on.'

339

Marcello lived down a narrow alley full of litter with a smouldering heap of something and a kitten eating a dead rat twice its size. They rang a buzzer beside a yellow painted door, and a voice came out of a box. Pepito said his name. There was a long pause, and then a panel in the door shot back and two narrow eyes stared out.

'Jump up and down you midget, I can't see you.'

Pepito jumped up and down.

'Stop.'

There was the sound of unlocking and shooting bolts and then the door opened. A couple of metres inside it was another door made of steel bars like in a prison, swung back against the wall of the narrow corridor.

'*Que tal* Fernando.'

The older boy ignored him and they filed in and he re-bolted the outer door and then locked the steel bar door and put the big key in his baggy jeans pocket. Above his wide leather belt protruded the handle of a gun. He pushed past them and they followed him up some very narrow stairs which were studded with broken glass fixed in cement so they had to go very slowly and carefully. Fernando was naked to the waist and had a huge tattoo on his muscly back that rippled as he climbed the stairs. It was of a big cross with a red rose dripping blood, and at the foot of the cross were two crossed daggers.

Upstairs was a big, almost empty room but quite clean and newly painted. The curtains were drawn and all the lights were on.

Marcello stood up and greeted them. He had a desk like a businessman, and wore jeans and a very thin white shirt. When he flexed his arms, Eulalia could see the dark blue shadows of tattoos all over his biceps, and another big tattoo on his chest.

He smiled.

'Hey Triqui,' he said. 'My disciple.'

Pepito grinned.

Marcello sat down again and steepled his fingertips together. The two children stayed standing up, aware that Fernando was just behind them. Marcello and Pepito talked but Eulalia hardly understood a word they said. She was so terrified her legs were wobbly, and she was furious that Pepito had brought them here. They should never have come.

Pepito was saying, 'I do this for you, I want *pisto*.'

'Badword you you cheeky runt,' said Marcello.

'I'm just saying....'

Fernando moved suddenly behind them and grabbed Pepito by the scruff of his sweatshirt with one hand, twisting his ear hard with the other.

'You looking for a beating, little brother,' said Marcello.

'I'm honestly not,' said Pepito, his voice exactly the same as before even though Fernando was twisting his ear half off.

'Or to lose an ear, maybe.'

'But we could still do the journey for you,' said Pepito. 'If you pay us for it.'

Marcello sighed. This little runt was such a stubborn one. He jerked his head and Fernando let him go. Pepito's ear looked like a piece of red coral.

'Don't you know there's a war on?' said Marcello.

'So?'

'You should be grateful for anything that comes your way. Pay towards your passage out of the country when it all comes down. What all the rich folks are doing.'

'We're not going nowhere.'

'No you're not. And you,' said Marcello, smiling at Eulalia. She shrank further inside herself, like she was tiny. There was something horrible about his smile. She longed to be back in the tunnel. But Marcello knew they lived there.

He looked back at Pepito. 'This your new *Indita* friend, eh?'

He was a big bully, like at school. She remembered what her Papa had taught her about bullies, and clenched herself all over and said, though her voice was a tiny hoarse whisper,

'I'm not a little Indian girl. I'm a little Maya girl.'

Marcello's eyes narrowed. 'What you say?'

The silence was horrible, the air was in a cold sweat.

She looked straight at him. 'My name is Eulalia,' she said. 'And I am not a little Indian girl. I am a little Maya girl. Indian is what other people call us, but they're wrong. Because we don't live in India.'

She was an entertainment. Marcello said, 'And who taught you that?'

'My Papa.'

'My Papa,' he mimicked. He and Fernando laughed at each other. 'And what's become of your Papa now eh?'

Her eyes were filled with tears but she held on tight, not letting a single one drop from the dark bowls of her eyes.

'I think he is probably dead,' she said softly. 'But what he said is still true.'

A siren sounded somewhere in the night. The man and the girl kept their eyes on one another.

At last Marcello looked away and cracked his knuckles. 'Well,' he said. He rested his elbow on the table and jabbed a forefinger at her. 'Whatever. Now listen to me. We don't want to argue with you, cos we your friends really. Yes? And your best friend is Ana, isn't it?'

'Ana Maria. And Pepito.'

'And Pepito here. Now listen very hard. We going to give you a package.'

'No,' said Pepito. 'Not her.'

'Did I ask for your badword advice?'

'Don't, don't involve her.'

'Listen, runt, you are really beginning to really bug the badword out of me tonight. One word more out of you and we strip you naked, put a blade up your ass and throw you out on the street. Then your beloved little girlfriend here can find her own way back through Zone 4 in the dark. So if you don't want her to end up in pieces in the Rio San Juan, then shut the badword up.'

Pepito made some kind of very quiet hissing noise, but said no more, standing and fidgeting in furious silence.

Marcello turned back to Eulalia and smiled. It was a smile like someone who secretly had toothache.

'So: a package. The thing is, and this is very unfair but what can we do? The thing is, it is our package, it belongs to us, but if we take it, other people, policemen, soldiers, will search us. You know how they search you when you get on the long-distance bus?'

'On the bus!' laughed Fernando. 'We don't even have to run a car for this, we use public transport!'

Marcello grinned. 'Yeah. And kids her age travel half price.'

'Man, you are an *operator*.'

'I think of everything. Including keeping our overheads low.'

'Tch.' Fernando slapped the wall.

'Anyhow,' Marcello said to Eulalia again, 'it's for some of our friends, in San Pedro. We like our friends very much. They are very nice friends.'

He thought she was so stupid, the way he talked to her, he must think she was about *four*.

'But we drive, they search us. We go on the bus, they search us. You know what they're like, checking for guns and stuff. And if they find our packages, they take them off us and get very *very* angry, hit us and lock us up and all sorts. You understand? It's better if we don't take the packages ourselves.'

'They would be *nasty* to us,' put in Fernando.

'Yeah,' said Marcello grinning, looking at him and looking back at her. 'You understand that? They would be nasty to us.' He twirled his fists in his eyes. 'Boo hoo. But you, you see – you, they wouldn't mind about. They wouldn't even check your bag.'

They were stupid men. They were all sly and cheating and

they treated her like she was *four*. But she wasn't stupid, and she was nearly seven. So she decided to stop being difficult with them and nodded and looked all wide-eyed like she did when she wanted something out of her Mama or Papa, and looked as if she believed every word they said and trusted them and thought they were terribly clever men really. And they were so stupid and vain they were pleased by her looking wide-eyed.

'Excellent,' said Marcello. '*Chequé*. You are our new delivery girl.'

'What happened to the old one?' asked Pepito.

'Pepito, you'll go with her. Like brother and sister. Now this is very important, so listen carefully. When you get to San Pedro, it's a big city like this one, you go to this address here we write down, and you just hand in the bag. OK? It's that easy. Then you come back here and tell us you done it and we give you a big present. Whatever you want. Got it?'

She nodded dumbly.

'You'll wear this nice pink Mickey Mouse backpack, see?' Marcello lifted it up from behind his desk. 'How you like that?'

'Man, where you get that?' laughed Fernando. 'You are an operator.'

'Here you are, baby. This lovely backpack with Mickey Mouse on it. Now the biggest thing of all is, you never ever look inside it, you understand?'

'Yes.'

'Never ever. Not once. We know how kids can't keep stuff secret, how they want to look, but you never ever do. OK? Otherwise you will get into very - serious - trouble. Get me?'

She nodded.

'You hand it in at the door in San Pedro, come back, and that's it. Job done. Now turn around.'

She turned around and he took her arms one by one and shoved them into the straps and tightened it up on her back. She couldn't believe how heavy it was.

'You can take it off on the bus,' said Marcello. 'But don't leave it there.'

He went back and sat down again and then leaned forwards across the desk, his eyes without any light in them at all. 'Now you know we mean what we say. We got to be very strict sometimes. So. It's like this. If you don't come back, if you lose the package, if you open it, if you run away, if you talk to the police, if you fail to deliver it, any of that, thinking you'll be safe from us and we'll never find you ... we will find you and we will cut off your head.'

The room rang with silence. Even Pepito beside her suddenly stopped fidgeting and went very still. Her heart was drumming under her dress and the skin on her face felt very tight and cold. She thought she might faint. She scrunched up her hands and feet hard to stop herself.

'Did you hear me?'

She nodded.

'We will cut your head off, and do it real slow, and it will really hurt. And it will all be your fault, for being a bad little girl, and for betraying us. You left us no choice. You believe us, don't you?' he said softly.

She believed him.

'So.' He sat back and relaxed and smiled and held his hands up in openness. 'But relax anyhow. It's easy. It's not a problem. You just do what we ask and all will be well.'

She wanted to kick him so much, but she just said quietly, like a good little girl, a good little dumb *Indita*, 'Yes.'

'When do we go?' asked Pepito impatiently, like he just wanted to get out of here. So did she.

'You go tomorrow.' He looked at his big silver watch. 'Today, actually. Like, now. The first bus leaves from Central six a.m.'

60

They kept to the foreshore of the lazy river, out of sight of any night cops. The sun was already starting to come up over the silhouettes of the jagged mountains, but the city all around felt calm and still.

'It's so heavy,' said Eulalia, trudging along.

'I can't carry it,' said Pepito, following on behind her. 'Got to do exactly as the man says.'

'And it smells.'

'Well tough.'

'Like old cheese.'

She walked on until she was aware Pepito had stopped following her, because she couldn't hear his footfalls on the pebbles any more. She stopped and looked back.

He was staring at the bag on her back with a funny expression.

'What?'

He still said nothing, didn't move.

'*What?*'

There was a long pause and then he said, 'I thought it was just money or medicine.'

The expression on his face frightened her. 'What is it?'

'How could they do that?' he murmured. 'How could they make us do that?'

The sun rose up over the mountains. The river glittered like a bronze road.

'Lala,' he said. 'I think you should take the bag off.'

'No! They'll kill me! They'll kill both of us!'

'Look.' He began walking slowly towards her, gently. 'Look Lala, honestly, I've just realized something. I think there's been like, a mistake. It's more complicated than I realized. But we'll be OK.'

'But they *said!*'

'You trust them more than me? Have I ever let you down?'

She looked so frightened and small.

Fuck them, he thought. Fuck Marcello. God's curses on them, truly.

'Please Lala, just take it off. Here look, down here.'

'No!'

They moved down to the edge of the water. 'OK,' he said, 'let's just take it off and put it on the ground here.'

He lifted if off her. It did weigh heavy too. They had made her carry this. How could they? The deadweight of that sack on her tiny girl shoulders, the pull of the straps leaving marks on her skin.

Her shoulders ached so much.

'What are we going to do now?' said Eulalia. 'We have to run away.'

What *were* they going to do? Pepito always knew what to do, didn't he? Or else he had to pretend.

He lifted the bag. His nostrils filled with it. He went a little distance away. 'Stay there.'

'It's my bag. They gave it to *me*.'

'Honestly, stay there. I'm not joking, sister. Don't come over here. Just stop there.'

He squatted down and carefully unzipped the bag and glanced inside and then he zipped it up again. He stood up and walked away leaving the bag on its own for a while. He felt sick. When he turned around again he looked lost.

'Stay there,' he said again.

'All right, all right, I'm not deaf.'

He knelt down and picked up some rocks and bits of rubble.

'What are you *doing*?'

He unzipped the bag again and without looking inside he started to drop the rocks inside it. Two, then four, then six, until the bag was bulging and must have weighed a ton. Then he picked up the bag and turned towards the river.

'What are you *doing?*'

He didn't say anything. For one horrible moment she thought he was going to drown himself. There was a lady in the village who was sunk in grief Mama said and filled her dress with stones and drowned herself in the river. Pepito waded right out until he was up to his waist in the river and then he took the bag and twisted back and hurled it out over the water as far as he could where it sank with hardly a splash.

He came back with his jeans dripping and dark blue again like new ones.

'What are we going to do now?' she whispered. 'Marcello will come after us.'

'I'm sorry sister. I didn't know what else to do.'

His voice was so sad she felt cold.

'What was in the bag?'

He shook his head.

'Tell me. It was my bag.'

'I'm sorry. Come on.'

She hated him not telling her and not knowing what to do now. He *always* knew what to do.

They sat in the entrance to the tunnel in silence and then he suddenly got up again in his wet jeans and said harshly to her, '*Stay there,*' and marched off.

He went back along the foreshore. There was where they had stopped. He waded in desperately now, noisily, stooping down here and there with his face screwed up against the filth of the splashing water, his hands searching about blindly in the muddy depths. A rising panic. How could he be so stupid? *He* could have taken the fucking bag. He. Not her. That would have been something. Marcello might never even have known. How could he have done this?

He couldn't find it. His foot caught in an underwater reef of concrete rubble and he staggered and went under, and it was then he thought that God had turned against him and he would never find the bag. More determined than ever he searched and searched, set against God, but never found it. He came out sodden and exhausted and sat on the shore of the river which was sullen and still again. A huge sullen serpent that would not give up what it had swallowed. The river ate stuff like that all the time. It liked it. That river made by God. He crossed his arms over his knees and bowed his head and cursed God.

He went back and into the rear of the tunnel where she couldn't see him undress. Screwed his clothes as dry as he could and returned wearing them damp and wrinkled. Told her what they must do.

'Because they might come back and kill us?' she said.

'Just anyway,' he said.

'Are you coming too?'

'Come on.'

'Don't leave me Pepito, please!'

'I won't leave you. Don't scream sis, and don't cry. I won't leave you. Come on. It'll be all right, I promise. It's all going to be all right.'

They walked across the market square in the morning sun and past the white cathedral and up some cobbled streets and had one last look at the huge photo of her in the window in the shop in the Plaza San Carlos. Unreal! Then out of the old town towards the richer and richer zones. Every step they took was a risk now. The cops wouldn't like them here. Nobody walked here, especially two ragged kids from the tunnels and the dumps. Everybody went in 4x4s with blacked out windows.

There were glossy darkleaved orange trees and lemon trees planted all along the streets and guards in cubicles with shotguns at the head of every street, and sometimes there was another man with a shotgun outside the house. You couldn't see much more of the houses than that because they were hidden behind tall hedges and razorwire security fences and solid-panel gates with big silhouette stickers of fierce dogs on them.

'We shouldn't be here,' said Eulalia. 'The dogs won't like us.'

'It'll be OK,' said Pepito. 'Keep moving.'

Finally they came to a single storey white house on the corner that was less guarded than the others though there was a still a metal gate and a security camera, high hedges and white walls topped with barbed wire and broken glass. At least it didn't have a photograph of a snarling dog, with the words 'I live here'.

Towering over the wall was a wide billboard which said, 'Suffer the little children to come unto me', and 'For the Love of Jesus Christ', and another the other side which said, 'Little Angels Adoption Agency'.

'This is where they're going to take care of us,' said Pepito.

'Both of us?'

'Yep.'

'Promise?'

He was reading the sign. He nodded. 'C'mon. Stand there. In front of the camera. OK.' He took a deep breath and buzzed.

Nothing.

A dragonfly went down the road.

After a while he buzzed again.

Then there was an electronic fuzz and woman's voice said sharply, 'No callers.'

'Please, we –'

The electronic fuzz snapped off.

Eulalia looked hard at Pepito. 'Well that wasn't a very good plan, was it?'

61

Inside in her office, Felicia Veracruz was having a difficult day. The aircon was playing up again, she had a headache, and her inbox was absolutely inundated with emails from the States asking about the situation in-country. Were there many orphans from the war? How were things looking? What could America do to help? There was even talk of a TV documentary being made about the work of Little Angels.

And a church in South Carolina was offering to send money – just like that! By Western Union! Without any apparent need to know where the money would go, whose pocket it would end up in. God love 'em, they were so trusting. They knew nothing about how this country worked. It must be nice to live in a place like South Carolina. But it wasn't her country. This was.

There were more specific enquiries too relating to the Little Angels website. 'Click here to see our Foreign Treasures!' Yes it sounded tasteless, she knew that, and needed to be re-written. So much to do.

The buzzer went again. She pressed the unlock button and there they were again. In the eight years of Little Angels' existence, this had never, ever happened.

They had had visits from the police, sometimes friendly, sometimes indefinably threatening. A clever, unshaven lawyer came once, representing a powerful international human rights group, talking about the USA as a 'child-stealer' and a 'vampire'. Felicia Veracruz had soon seen him off. It wasn't American vampirism that was the problem, it was American innocence.

Once, at the airport, she had taken a last photograph of one of her boys, Enrique, going off with a couple from Iowa.

When she uploaded the photograph later, she saw that the Americans looked like children, Enrique looked like an old, old man.

But never once in all this time had they actually had children at the door. Not surprising really. Street kids stayed on the street, with the people they knew. She had often wondered what she would do if this happened, and she didn't know.

She didn't know now.

'What is it?' she said.

'Please listen to us,' said the boy in a Hawaii t shirt. 'Please listen to us. Don't cut us off.'

The girl with him was much younger. Pretty. Cropped hair. Graze on her cheek. Staring up at the blank eye of the security camera. They were both so thin.

'I'm listening. But be quick.'

'I'm telling the truth. Our lives are in danger.'

'Honey, I'm – This isn't the right place for –'

'Then where is the right place?' he snapped. 'In this country? And don't say the police.'

'Listen we –'

'What are we supposed to do?' demanded the boy 'There are people after us. What are *you* supposed to do?'

What a question.

Felicia Veracruz was uncharacteristically tongue-tied. This she hadn't expected. Finally she asked, 'Have you really got no one?'

'We did have,' said the boy. 'People we worked for. But they're now the problem. They're the danger to us. They were all we had.'

Her finger hovered over the entry button.

'So here we are,' said the boy.

The little girl was staring up at her still. Just standing, staring up. That huge-eyed stare could melt gates of steel.

There was always a way. God always found a way.

A blaring buzz and the gates swung open.

Eulalia stepped in cautiously. The first thing she saw was a butterfly on some flowers and a neat path up to the door of a white house with lots of windows and a round front. It looked like a ship on the sea. The gate was closing behind them again. She looked round and realized with horror that Pepito hadn't had time to get in.

'Pepito! Hurry!'

She turned back to the house and gesticulated wildly. Someone in there had to press a buzzer or something for Pepito. And then the gate clanged shut and she was alone in the garden.

'Pepito!' she cried.

Felicia Veracruz heard her even from inside the house.

Eulalia howled against the closed gate, hammering it with her small fists. 'Pepito!'

She knew he was just on the other side of the gate, just standing there. In his damp jeans and damp Hawaii t shirt all creased. Head down, listening to her. Not saying anything, hands flat against the cold gate, crying just like her.

'Pepito, come in! Come in Pepito! Don't go away! Pepito!'

He was standing there crying and saying nothing. He was still there. The metal gate between them.

The door of the house was flung open and the woman came hurrying.

'Open the gate!' screamed the little girl. 'Quickly, open the gate! Pepito is still outside!'

Felicia Veracruz pressed another button built into the stone gatepost and slowly and heavily the gate began to swing open again. She held onto the little girl as she was pulled forcibly forwards, the little girl trying to run. They stood out on the pavement a moment. The little girl stopped trying to run.

There was no one.

'Pepito!'

Her piping cry was agony to hear. It clawed at her heart. She held her and held her. 'Was he your brother?'

But it was no good. All the little girl could cry was

'Pepito!', trying to run after him again as Felicia held her, tears streaming down her face, the little girl's hands reaching out to the empty air.

Eulalia lay in a small bed quite silent and numb. She had not said another word since she cried out 'Pepito!'

She lay in a bed in a room with two other girls' beds. There was a white cover with big red flowers on it and the sheets were white but still she felt nothing. She could think of nothing to say. Not a word. For a lot of the time she kept her eyes closed even when she wasn't asleep. Earlier she had had a bath and the lady here by her bedside had shampooed her hair and brushed and combed it very carefully and given her a big t shirt to wear in bed. It was all very comfortable and clean and she felt nothing.

Felicia Veracruz would sit by her bedside until she drifted off to sleep, which might be a while as she hadn't eaten. She couldn't eat. But Felicia had made her drink some water. Later the two other girls would creep into their beds too. In time she would talk, but not yet. Not yet.

There were American toys and Coca-Cola and Bible readings and games and television and walks round the garden and multivitamin pills and lots of other children. Mostly they were very well behaved and quiet and some were as silent as she was and some cried quietly at night under their sheets.

Then on the third night a big blonde lady arrived at the house and she was like a giantess walking in. She walked in as if she had no fear of any danger anywhere and she had a big blonde mane that she tossed about. Eulalia couldn't take her eyes off her. None of the children could. The boys dreamt about her. She was an American. Her name was Shelley Ann and you could tell Señora Felicia Veracruz was very happy to see her there.

And then Shelley Ann and Felicia Veracruz came and sat by her bedside when she went to bed! Hers! The other two girls hadn't even come to bed yet. They had come to see just her.

'How you doing honey?' said Shelley Ann, tilting her head on one side so her blonde hair fell down in a radiant curtain, and laying a beautiful fair arm along the headboard of Eulalia's bed. The headboard had a sticker of a kitten on it. Eulalia had tried to peel if off last night when she was awake and thinking so angrily about Pepito, but she couldn't get it off.

'You doing OK?' She spoke Spanish with an American accent.

Eulalia had been quite prepared never to speak again or even nod or shake her head again or look at anyone as there just didn't seem to be any point and she wanted to stay locked away and mostly with her eyes closed. But now she looked up at Shelley Ann, though she still didn't say anything.

'Tell her what happened to you last week,' said Felicia Veracruz.

'Oh no,' said Shelley Ann smiling.

'Go on,' said Felicia. She nodded at Eulalia. 'You want to hear don't you?'

Eulalia wanted to hear very much and she nearly felt herself nodding, but she managed to stop herself.

'We-ell,' said Shelley Ann.

'I want to hear it again,' said Felicia laughing. 'I really do.'

'Well,' said Shelley Ann. 'This was just last week … and I was in the city, at a gas station. It was getting late at night and maybe I shouldn't have been out but – I needed the gas, you know? So there I am and this guy comes up to me out of the shadows and knocks on my window and I roll it down and he pokes a gun in my face! Now what do you think of that?'

Eulalia goggled.

'So I said to him, "Sir, I come from Texas and I know what a gun looks like. And if you don't take that thing out my face I am gonna scream until this place falls down around your ears. Now how'd you like that?"'

Felicia Veracruz was already starting to laugh as if she couldn't help herself, with her hand held up to her mouth. Eulalia looked from one to the other of them and pressed her lips together. The story shouldn't be funny really with a gun in it but somehow it was, because of Shelley Ann.

She went on, 'So then this guy looks totally nonplussed and confused like he doesn't know what to do, and there's this *other* guy there with him now, and *he's* got a gun too, a rifle would you believe! And they're basically holding up every car that comes into the gas station and robbing them. So then I really lose it I gotta say, and before I know it I've got out of the car and I'm facing up to these two guys. I mean, *really* angry!'

Felicia was laughing so much now she had to push her chair back to make more room for it.

'And these guys are totally *nonplussed,* like it just hadn't occurred to them that there would be any problem. And one of them says to the other, "Move her out of the way." Just like that, like I'm a sack of corn. As if they're going to shove me aside and get in my car and drive off and just leave me there.

'And at that I'm so – pardon my language but I am so damn angry that I just shove him back and I shout, "How *dare* you! How *dare* you, mister! How dare you push a woman around like that!"

'And I just don't think they'd ever been spoken to like that before or knew how to handle it because they both froze up. So I said, "Now, lay your guns down on the floor. Do as I say!"

'And you know what? *They did!* Meek as lambs. Just knelt and laid 'em down there on the ground at my feet and backed away. And then I say - like I *hear* myself saying it, like I don't know where it's coming from – but I hear myself yelling at them, "Now I don't want to get all Old Testament about this but if you come one step closer to me I'll whap you, by … *golly* I will!"

'I was yelling at them and telling them what I thought of

them, they were worthless pieces of dogdirt and they ought to be ashamed of themselves, and they just stood there with their heads down like a couple of schoolkids in front of the headteacher! My it felt good, I got to tell you. I mean really *good*. Then I turned on my heel and got straight back into my car and drove off to find another gas station. I was still half expecting a bullet to come flying through the window or something, but – nothing. Last thing I could see in my rearview mirror was them still just standing like there like I'd left them, not daring to move one inch. Now how d'you like that?'

Felicia was laughing so much it made Eulalia smile. When Felicia had mopped her eyes she said, 'Now that's what I call fighting for women's rights. Hey?'

Shelley Ann got up and moved her chair back to the wall.

'But you see,' said Felicia Veracruz, 'you're pretty safe here now with someone like Shelley Ann around.'

She was still exhausted and heartbroken and full of longing for people she had known, but she did feel safe here. She'd had a gun pointed at her and pressed to her face too, by the soldier when they took the lady Juliana away off the bus. But she couldn't help thinking of Pepito and it made her so confused. She was guilty at sleeping in a proper bed like this while he was still sleeping on cardboard, and he had lied to her and left her and gone away and she slept under flowery covers. Her dreams at night were all of fear and longing, and in one dream she got up and it was morning and she looked out of the window and the garden was full of hundreds of puppies all exactly like El Pipón.

Pepito trudged through the dusty streets of the city past fallen breeze block walls and dodging trucks, hooted at by drivers and ignored by roadblocks and moving always moving. Because he was the little dog who loved her and to save her he had to run away.

Coughing, searching for fagbutts and smokes for salvation. Looking down all the time like that he even despised his own dirty feet. But there was only one thing left to him now and he wandered in a wide circuitous loop so as to leave it as late as possible that day, and even looked askance at the smoky city sun and hoped for it not to sink.

But as ever it sank, and he came across the river under a pale cloudless uneventful sunset, wondering why people didn't try to stop him, didn't try to save him. But he must go back to Marcello. Because it was all his fault, he had taken Lala to Marcello in the first place, showing off like an idiot about how he was in with the chief, the *Tatascán*, and hey look at me. And now he had to pay. You always got to pay in the end. So he must go back to Marcello and tell him what had happened, and that the girl had gone now and that she could not be reached any more. Marcello was weird like that and he pursued people to the ends of the earth like a great crusade if they had wronged him. How could a girl that age wrong him? Jesus he was a turd.

But someone was looking out for him that wretched day because when he came to the door and asked to see Marcello, the shavenheaded *compadre* on the door grunted and said,

'He's not here. Gone away.'

'Where's he gone?'

'What's it to you, midget? On business. Up country, in the highlands. Now beat it.'

'When will he be back?'

'I said beat it.' And the *compadre* started unlocking the steel door to come out after him and give him a thump.

So he beat it. Running and tripping sometimes over the broken paving stones and past the sizzling all-night food stands where men stood around chewing slowly and staring at him dashing past and him not caring, because Marcello was gone and he was all right for now and it was going to be OK. He missed Lala very much and it was agony to do what he did but it was the right thing and she was going to be OK.

He sneaked on a bus for the airport. There was always money at the airport. And then he was going to buy a whole pack of new cigarettes and have a decent smoke.

62

'Well Don Nicholas,' said the colonel, grinning broadly. 'I have made up my mind. It is not safe for you here and you have done enough. You will be escorted back to the airport.'

He held out his hand to shake. Nicholas ignored it.

'You're not letting me go? Like we agreed?'

'Don't be stupid. I never said such a thing. And the idea that you should wander around this country now, looking for some displaced Indian family is ridiculous. The stuff of fairy tales. Don't be a fool. Shake my hand.'

'What about the plane I found? In the jungle. Don't you want me to –'

'You are such a boy.' The colonel's voice was harsher and he dropped his hand. 'We've found it already. How can you be so stupid? We *don't need you.*'

They had found it already. He let the disappointment sink in. It had seemed like his one chance of – seizing some power back. But now he had none again.

'So why are you letting me go at all?'

'Strange to say, Don Nicholas, I like you. You are … I like your spirit. I know you have been shitting yourself every night here, but you have never shown it. Courage is only a mask over a terrified face, but you wear it well. Hope is for the slaves, courage is for the masters. Still, do not come back to this country ever again. Ever. Or you will surely drown.'

He went back to his room to get his bag, eyes darting – and the room was empty. He hurriedly took up the creaking floorboard one last time and stowed the black package at the bottom. It was as if it would never leave him.

A few minutes later he climbed into the back of an army jeep with his bag and they drove away and he never once looked back.

As he rode down to Santa Cruz in the army jeep in the gathering dusk, he marvelled that as well as the kilo of coke, even after all this time, and all his exciting adventures, he still had six hundred dollars rolled up in his right sock. Nestled into the concave proximal articular surface behind the navicular bone (connected to the tibia posterior muscle and the last of the foot bones to begin ossification.)

It wasn't thrift: there just hadn't been that many shopping opportunities.

It was the fatfaced sergeant with the stammer who accompanied him. He would find him a seat on the first plane to Mexico or the US, any that were still flying, probably with a bunch of defeated NGOs. Nicholas still entertained fantasies of a thrilling escape, even though it was all over now and everything was lost. He would snatch the sergeant's pistol from his holster and club him senseless and then vault from the back of the speeding jeep....

He was such a boy. How could he be so stupid?

As they neared the city towards dusk, they became spectators of the garish nightmare circus of a Third World country collapsing in on itself: a slow-motion collapse that went on for ever and had no end. Roadblocks of steel barrels, a randomly burning truck, a woman with long grey hair skipping among the ruins and apparently preaching. 'The generals will be beggars and the beggars will be clowns!'

What traveller's tales he would have to tell. Perhaps he could write a piece for a magazine. How he worked in a clinic in a country threatened by war. How he was captured by a narco-colonel. Perhaps if he wrote about it, it would be better. And now there was this.

Prostrate bodies. An outpost of UN peacekeepers in blue helmets who looked like they might be Malaysian or maybe Indonesian. Various tatterdemalion militiamen cavorting in the headlights of parked up lorries and jeeps, accoutred in random fashion items. One in a looted fur jacket in the hot tropical night, wraparound shades and mirror shades ubiquitous, a truck stereo playing, the selfmade soldiers danced to a joyful party pop song from America. Flames glowing brightly on the barrels of the Kalashnikovs, and a boy soldier with some kind of bazooka or rocket launcher, mercifully without the rocket. Perhaps he had fired them all off earlier in his festive glee.

The sergeant waved at them. 'They are loyalists.'

'They look like they're celebrating.'

'So they are. Freedom.'

After the chaos of the city, the country's only international airport was eerily quiet and orderly. The sergeant whistled a policeman who came slowly over, clutching a can of soft drink.

'Keep this one under your guard. I am going through to the departure desks.'

'Tell me what is going on.'

The sergeant prodded Nicholas. 'He is flying out of here. Today. I just need to find him a seat. He has no passport but I will vouch for him.'

The policeman regarded the tall, clean-featured gringo boy sceptically. 'He's a criminal? He looks like a schoolkid.'

'Neither,' said Nicholas.

'Well,' said the sergeant. 'Do not move from here. Do not take your eyes off him. He must leave today.'

The cop and Nicholas sat side by side on the plastic bench. The cop put his can down on the ground at his feet so he could light a cigarette. From the sound it made, Nicholas could tell it was still half full. After a moment Nicholas leant down to retie his shoelaces, moving his hand over the mouth of the can as he did so. Then he sat back and waited. He might have given himself up to prayer, except the only divinity he could picture, given the evidence, was not the sort to lend a helping hand.

So he decided just to wait.

Sodium phosphate is a saline laxative that can take up to six hours to work, but often, especially with higher doses, may work in as little as thirty minutes. It is recommended that those using it should remain close to a toilet at all times.

Why Dr Hércules should have had some in his clinic was a mystery, but still Nicholas was glad he had stolen it on the night of the dance in the village. Surely there was some justice to it. He looked continually towards the departure desk, and the minutes went painfully by. Then he saw the fat-faced sergeant coming back.... But no, it wasn't him. It was another in military fatigues. Come *on*.

Beside him the policeman's guts suddenly gave a huge uneasy rumble. He shifted onto his right buttock and exhaled cigarette smoke unhappily and then sat straight again. Another giant rumble and then a moment's respite.

Suddenly the policeman stood. 'Come over here with me.' He marched towards the public lavatories, unshackling his handcuffs from his belt as he went.

The policeman handcuffed him hurriedly to the wheel of a huge fire hose, leaving him facing the wall, and then hurried through the lavatory door without another word.

'Hey mister,' said an airport beggarchild behind him.

'Fuck off,' he said quietly in his sour anger, and felt immediately ashamed. Why not give some urchin his six hundred dollars? For all the difference it would make. 'Here,' he said, twisting around as best he could, 'reach into my...'

It was the boy. The urchin with the fallen eyelid he had met at the bus station, and then the earlier of his two attempts to become a major narco-dealer.

The boy recognized him instantly and danced around him

with glee.

'Why you in handcuffs? It's very funny!'

'It's hilarious,' he said. 'I can hardly contain myself.'

'I love it!' said the boy. Pepito. 'You're always in such fucking trouble. Worse than me.'

'And you're always swearing.'

'And the first thing you said to me just then was Fuck Off! Anyhow I like swearing. It helps me channel my anger.' He stopped dancing and stood merely jittering, surveying the defeated gringo. 'You got any smokes?'

'I don't smoke.'

'Why you sad to be leaving? I'd be glad to be leaving this shithole and going back to the USA.'

'Not the USA. England.'

'There. Yeah. Anyhow.' He swiped his nose. 'Why you handcuffed like that? You caught picking pockets?'

'I'm being escorted onto a plane by the cops. They want to make sure I leave.'

'And you don't?'

'No. I have more I want to do here.'

The boy twirled his forefinger against his temple. 'Lo-co! Hey. Rich gringos adopt kids all the time. You could adopt me.' He said it with a bitter sarcasm.

He looked towards the check-in desks for the returning sergeant. 'I haven't got a wife.'

'We could get you one. You're not bad looking. On a dark night.'

'Thank you.'

'To a blind chick.'

'Thank you.'

'Who hasn't had a guy for like, years, and is really desperate. Christ, you could buy one here for about five dollars. Anyone you wanted, pretty much. Rich gringos do, you know. They buy 'em on the net. Come out here, pick her up and off they fly. Sixty year old guys with twenty year old girlfriends. They just buy 'em up. That's what I'm gonna do one day. Keeps you young.'

'Is that right?'

'That is right. Wrong but right.' He swiped his nose again. 'So anyway. Where's your cop gone?'

'He's in there.'

'What – the toilet?'

'Uh huh.'

'Pissing?'

'Um...' What a bewildering child. 'No, more than that I suspect.'

'Having a shit?'

'I believe so.'

'And you want to get away?'

'Well no, I—'

'Stay there,' said the boy. 'Like you got a choice!' And he headed on into the toilets.

A couple of minutes later the urchin came trotting back. He quickly went behind Nicholas and started fiddling with his handcuffs.

'What are you doing?'

Pepito didn't say anything. The next moment Nicholas felt the cuffs open.

'How did you –'

'*Move* you idiot.'

And the boy was moving very fast out of the airport without actually looking like he was running. Or fleeing the scene of a crime, say. Nicholas went after him.

63

Outside he was about to flag down a taxi when the boy punched his arm. 'Don't be dumb. You got a banknote?'

He pulled a five dollar note from his pocket.

'One dollar's plenty. Gringos. This way.'

The boy led him to a huge dusty sunbaked truckpark and they stood at the gate and flagged down a truck that was just pulling out. He waved the banknote. The truck lurched to a halt and they scrambled in. The truckdriver was obese, apparently basted in lard, and wore nothing but y-fronts originally of a light blue shade when fresh from the packet. He took the note and stuck it under the waistband of his underpants. They lurched forwards again and headed down into the city.

'Why couldn't we take a taxi?' said Nicholas.

Pepito looked up at him. 'Because if the cops were looking for a gringo who just fled from the airport, they'd go round asking all the taxi drivers. Because *gringos take taxis*.'

The boy wasn't stupid.

'And what happened back in there?'

Pepito turned on the truck driver. 'You don't listen.'

Their bright and glistening chauffeur shrugged his plump shoulders.

'So?' said Nicholas.

'So, the cop won't be coming after us for now.'

'What do you mean? What did you do?' He kept looking in the truck's huge side mirrors, expecting to see the cop running after them with revolver drawn, trousers still round his ankles.

'I fixed him,' said Pepito complacently.

'What do you mean, you fixed him?'

'No one's safe with their pants are down.'

'Is that another of your colourful national proverbs?'

'Nope. One of mine.'

'What have you done?'

'I snuck in the next door cubicle and climbed up on the seat and lifted up the cistern lid and leaned over the wall and dropped it on his head. Man he was making a stink.'

'Good God. Is he all right?'

'And all as silent as a panther.'

'Hey, is he all right?'

'Well he was slumped half off the can with his head one side. So no, he didn't look particularly all right. You should be thanking me. I just risked my life for you. And that cistern lid thing weighed a ton. I think I pulled a muscle in my shoulder.'

'But what about his head, you little idiot. How was his head?'

'Well, it was bleeding a bit.'

'You might have killed him.'

'I don't think so. Cops have thick skulls.'

Nicholas was in an agony of Hippocratic indecision. How to balance the fact that he was in very serious danger, and needed to get away, and needed to try and find Eulalia, against the urge to go back and tend to a cop slumped in the toilet with probable cranial fractures, heavy bleeding, as well as an acute bout of iatrogenic diarrhoea? Medispeak for doctor-induced squits.

'If I got caught for that they would kill me,' said Pepito, sullen now, sliding down in the seat. 'You know that?'

Nicholas glanced across at the driver. He was impassive, except when the truck passed by any female walking at the side of the road. Then he tooted the enormous airhorn on the cab roof, but irritably, as if it was a tiresome obligation rather than an expression of desire.

'You and me,' said the boy. 'We're both in deep shit.'
Nicholas didn't disagree. They drove on.

The trucker dropped them on the busy road that ran alongside
the river with the broken down bridge.
'What now?' asked the boy. He had perked up again
already.
'Why are you asking?'
'You're fun to be around. Funny stuff happens.'
'Are you serious?'
'As fuck, man. I never dropped a cistern lid on a cop's head
before.'

They started walking. Back streets and alleys. Cloaca of the
city.
'So why you here and why you staying here?'
He could have talked about Dr Menendez disappearing.
About the fact that he had got into medical school without
telling the whole truth about his own past, and possibly ruined
his own career. He could have explained that he once had a
sister, called Elizabeth, Lizzie, who had run away from home
when she was fifteen – because home life wasn't always
happy. And how she had never been seen since.
'Are you gonna answer me?' said Pepito, squinting up at
him.
'D'you want the long answer or the short answer?'
'Short. *Really* short.'
'I – I was working as a doctor, and lost a family here, you
could say. I loved them very much.'
'Well there's a thing. I lost a family too. My own, in fact.'
The boy spat a huge gob of smoker's phlegm, opaque mustard
splat in the dust. 'Fuck knows what I did with 'em.'
So hard, so wry.
'I stayed with a family and they got separated, especially a
little girl, and I don't think anyone is looking for her. And you
know this country isn't a good place for a little girl.'

The boy gave a croaky laugh and changed the subject abruptly, saying, 'You stand out everywhere we go, this tall white guy. If the cops are looking for you it won't be difficult.'

So Nicholas bought a new white baseball cap from a street vendor and wore it pulled down low.

'Yeah,' said Pepito, 'like that'll work. You're pretty dumb for a doctor. So what do we do now?'

'We?'

The boy nodded.

And it was true, he did need the urchin. He had had no plan before, when still believing the colonel would release him, but to try officialdom, government departments, sheer dogged persistence, an unsmiling masquerade of rich gringo arrogance. But that was impossible now. At the airport, like everywhere, the beggarboy had been invisible. It was he himself who had assaulted the cop, he himself who had escaped his chains. He was the criminal.

Nicholas thought for a moment, turned to the wall, imagining every passing car was looking for him. It wasn't that he didn't have much time left in this country. He didn't have *any* time. But he needed to do one thing. He needed to find Eulalia.

Pepito said, 'They're going to be looking for you. An injured cop and everything.'

'I know.'

'You can't stay here. You can't just wander round the streets. You're like this weird white zombie come back to life.'

'We need to go to a hotel,' he said.

A darker look, instant suspicion. 'You and me both? Why me?'

'You don't have to. But I do. A cheap nasty hotel where they don't ask for anything but cash.'

He stopped briefly at a pharmacy and then they went to a hotel that cost five dollars a room and was mainly a by-the-hour brothel. The man looked at the two of them and said not a word. They were given a room with a concrete balcony that had mostly fallen away but retained a last jagged corner supported by air. Pepito immediately went out and stood on it.

'Get inside, you idiot.'

The boy stood up on the bed with his filthy bare feet. 'This is cool. I'm sleeping in the bed tonight. You're on the floor.' He started bouncing. The bed emitted foul odours beneath him. 'So you're looking for a girl huh? You could get one here. I get you one. For five dollars.'

'She's a little girl from the highlands,' said Nicholas glaring at him.

They boy stopped bouncing.

'I was told she was brought to the city. This old woman. It's a total ... I can't see how she'd last a day on her own and I, I just...'

He sat on the side of the bed and held his hands together and looked out of the window. Suddenly he looked really sad, like he was about to cry, which would have been a fucking embarrassment, so the boy jumped off the bed and leaned against the wall.

'What she look like anyway? Describe her.'

'Well – she's small for her age. She's a country girl. An Indian, you'd say. From the highlands.'

Pepito bounced back and forth off the wall. 'Indian?'

'Well, Lenca.'

He stopped bouncing. After a time he said more quietly, 'How old is she?'

'She's seven now. She could be six though, to look at.'

'You're kidding.'

'What?' Nicholas turned round.

'Nothing.'

'What?'

'Just, shit. You know, a little *Indita* like that, in the big city.' He was staring far-off out of the window.

Nicholas turned back and bowed his head. 'Makes me cold just to think about her.'

'She'll be all right.'

'I'm glad you think so.'

'Someone might have picked her up.'

'Yeah, exactly.'

'How come her family aren't looking for her?'

'I think they think she's dead. Here, I've got a photo of them.'

He waved his hand. 'Nah, I don't wanna to see it. Dirty *Indios*.'

Nicholas looked at him sourly and said he was going to face the ordeal of the bathroom.

The instant he was in there, Pepito raced across the room and knelt and rummaged in the gringo's pathetically small bag and found a kind of notebook and in it was the photo.

Village family, *Indios* from the hills and the highlands, straw hats and sunburnt and barefoot, in their old other world up there in the mountains. Tall gawky gringo among them. And there she was, Lala, no doubt about it.

Oh God what had he done.

The gringo wasn't as dumb as he looked and glanced back out of the door before he flushed.

'Hey, get your hands out of my bag!'

'Just looking. Might be a bomb.'

'And if you tried to steal off me again you're back on the street.'

'Jesus.'

Nicholas washed his hands and tried the shower and amazingly it worked, and with lukewarm water as well. Clearly a very superior class of brothel.

By the time he came out again, Pepito was lying flat on his back on the bed staring up at the ceiling looking dazed.

'What's wrong with you?' Then he saw there were three

371

miniature bottles by his side. One Mexican tequila, one Chinese vodka and one Chinese whisky. The hotel actually had a kind of mini-bar. And the urchin had drunk it dry in twenty seconds.

God it was like having a demented chimp in the bedroom.

'You just drank all these?'

The boy's head rolled towards him and he gurgled.

'You are going to be so ill.' He read a label. 'Finest Scotsh whiskey. Made in London.'

'I feel so funky,' said the boy.

'You're an idiot. Now,' he produced the bottle that he'd bought in the chemist, 'get your clothes off and get in the shower and rub this all over you.'

The boy stared at him a moment, and then rolled across the bed towards him by way of attack, screaming that if he laid one filthy hand on him he'd bite his cock off and spit it in his face. 'You can beat me to a pulp all you like sick fuck I will still –'

Nicholas fended him off without difficulty. The boy looked like he might vomit at any moment. 'I won't touch you you little idiot. It's medicine. Now get in the –'

'What the fuck's in there?'

'DDT. Weedkiller.'

'Eh?'

'Permethrin soap. Go in the bathroom and soap up all over, Clothes off obviously.'

The boy attacked him all over again. It would have been comical if Nicholas hadn't guessed precisely the pains that lay behind it.

'You're sick sick sick sick all of you fucking sick it's not my fault I'm not painting myself baby oil sick fucker you sick fuck fuck –'

Lavaflow of anger welling from the core. How well he knew it. The boy struggled furiously and drunkenly and kicked out at him but he was barefoot and then he went limp. He knew just knew this gringo, this Anglo whatever he was wasn't after him. Not like that. In a way it was worse, more confusing that this Anglo meant well or at least meant him no harm. He was so used to hating men that now there was one not to hate it was hard to handle.

Eventually Nicholas let him go and set him back down on the edge of the bed and held his arms straight a moment longer to make sure the boy didn't slither to the carpet senseless.

'You OK?'

The boy struggled for breath and nodded, looking down, still dizzy. Nicholas found the bogroll in his bag and gave it to him and the boy blew his nose and wiped his eyes and glared at him.

'You are such an idiot,' said Nicholas.

Pepito said, 'You're the idiot. You've got a turd for a brain.'

'Seriously I'm embarrassed just walking down the street with you. It's like walking down the street with a … clown next to you.'

'You're not even a gringo, you're a … grongo. You're just like this big turd alongside me. I don't even know where you came from.'

'You really are a drivelling idiot. With a face like a bag of piss on a bad night.'

The boy burped sourly. 'You festering … turd.'

'You've said turd already.'

'It's the only right word,' said Pepito. 'You're just this big turd … only shaped like a human being. Like someone has sculpted you … out of pure turd.'

'Now why would someone do that?'

'Because they're fucking stupid, just like you.'

Suddenly they both grinned. Male bonding through mutual insult.

'Now get in the shower. Except first drink this bottle of water, all of it. You are going to have such a headache.'

'I can take my liquor.'

'Few can drink Chinese whisky and live.'

'You're fucking nuts,' said Pepito. 'Here,' and he held out his hand. Drained the water bottle dry, belched mightily. 'Happy now?'

'Ecstatic. Shower.'

'And you better not come in.'

'Kid … Pepito … How can I put this so as not to hurt your feelings? The truth is, even with your clothes off, I really wouldn't fancy you. OK?'

The boy looked sickly at him and vanished into the brown and malarial bathroom. Drunk in a hotel with a weird gringo about to paint himself all over with weedkiller. And some people thought life made sense.

Night was falling and it had been a crazy long day. Only that morning he had taken Lala to the House of Jumping Jesus and then had scooted to the airport and then dropped a cistern lid on a cop's head and then met this crazy gringo and then come here and now this and he was supposed to know what to do? How the fuck was that going to work?

The gringo, Doctor Nicholas, had his shower and then went out after dark to buy some food even though Pepito told him not to. No one went out after dark in this part of the city, especially a gringo, but of course he went anyway the nut.

He lay in the dark, mind racing, sick with whisky and guilt and dread. For a few mad minutes he even entertained the idea that this gringo was working for Marcello too, and was hunting for her amid all his lies. When he found her he would kill her in punishment for … the severed head thing. But then he remembered he was drunk and calmed down again. The gringo wasn't like that. He was a nut but not a childkiller.

But still he couldn't tell the gringo the truth. How he would despise him. Pepito had abandoned her. He had taken her to the Jesus House and abandoned her, Lala, without a friend in the world. He who had been like a brother to her, little lost girl. And she would now be transported to America like a sack of premium coffee. Was that right? And now this gringo had come looking for her, Nicholas, with his photo of Lala and her family, there they were, all alive. And this gringo was desperate for them and wanted to know and Pepito was keeping it from him for fear and guilt. Jesus Jesus Jesus what to do.

The gringo came back with some orange juice and biscuits and some peanuts and they ate and as soon as Pepito had eaten on top of the liquor he fell asleep.

Nicholas lay awake. The urchin snored.

64

That same night in the valley empty of people, Pedro Xom went walking. A halting man in search of his people. Already dead, already dreaming, already gone from here.

He had heard the priest in the Catholic Church say that the breath of man goes forth and he returns to dust and on that day all his thoughts perish. But the Lord shall feed the hungry and open the eyes of the blind and free the prisoner from his chains and raise up those who are humbled and protect the widow and the orphan child. He was Lord of the Poor. Look, it was written in the Bible of the Church. No wonder the landowners and the army hated the church and sought to do it evil. Pedro Xom had even heard of priests shot and strangled in the city. And what hope could there be for a country that despised and killed its own priests for preaching mercy and justice? The sun itself looked away in shame at the evil that men did on earth. There was no future that could heal a past so ill.

A year ago when his friend Santos Jolomocox was leaving them, he said that he began to hear the voice of God more and more.

'All my life He has been silent,' said Santos, 'silent as the forest on a cloudy night. However I pleaded, whatever I suffered. He never answered one prayer in my life. And now He will hardly stop talking as I lie dying.'

Yet the dead would come again. Only a fool thought the world stopped at the horizon.

Death might be birth but our life is a sea of sorrow. At least we all drown together in that sea, hand in hand, our one consolation. Brothers in arms at last when we are dying. Pedro

Xom is too old to care now. He knows nothing. Old age both a curse and a blessing. The old man detaches himself from the crowd of the world to dance alone with death.

The People have gone to the coast to grow pineapples and sugar cane, and anyway they no longer listened to the words of Pedro Xom nor marked the sacred days. The idea of the village wise man made them laugh. They said he was drunk. The young find the answers to their questions on the computer in the internet cafe. They go to the city. They live in a land quite apart from Pedro Xom and his wheezy old words, wheezy and slow as an old mule.

Look down. These cheap sandals made from old car tyres that carry me over the mountains, even my shoes cause the youth to laugh at me now. Their white teeth flashing, white trainers made in Asia. Pedro Xom is in exile from his People now and forever and old and tired beyond caring. Soon now and now they are gone, the sacred days slow to nothing and time stops, for when there is only one man left, nothing happens, and so there is no time. Only the still silent valley emptied of people, a dark bowl emptied of bright water. The children gone. The whole village uprooted and moved like a squash plant. How damaged the roots in moving.

He flatters himself, old fool Pedro Xom. They do not even laugh at him now, they do not think of him, he is invisible, a shadow in the forest. Look at his old gnarled hands, stretched out blindly before him. Fragile and fading, turning into leaves.

The heart is withered too small even to care that the young go to the city to be eaten. You dine well in the city and after dinner you pay with your soul. They devour it in front of you, jaws dripping, grunting like hogs. They toss the bones of your soul into the street for the vultures to pick over.

Lord the world cannot go on like this. Lord let the rain come down as it did in the days of Noah, the fire and rain. Or is this only an old man's vanity? I am ending, so let the world end too? Insult me not with the world's going on without me, barely noticing my muttered farewell, the world in its springtime endlessly reborn.

Here it comes again, such pain in my chest. Lie down here old fool and take your rest, here against the buttress of the unmoved ceiba, roots in the earth, heights to blue heaven, laughing and vanishing infinite. Glimpse through the leaves the vanishing blue. How I have loved her, the village of Chilitenango and the valley of the flowers!

Man comes from the mud, he walks out of the fire, he is born from the dark womb of the years. Who knows where a man comes from or where he goes? Nobody knows. Pain stops the breath. None will know or mark it. All a man's loves and thoughts die with his death.

Weep not little bird, tribelonely, nestless, words on your lips that hold the people's histories more rare than gold. God has willed it, dry your eyes. The world turns. A people dies.

After a time, Pedro Xom took off the bright silver crucifix that he wore around his neck, and he laid it down on the ground beside him. He looked down at it for a long time.

And then leaving it there, still beneath the ceiba, Pedro Xom rose up and walked on. And he was never seen in that valley nor any other again.

65

The papers had been finalized and the money had come through by electronic bank transfer so it was all settled.

'You sure we should tell her?' said Shelley Ann. 'She won't sleep a wink.'

'I always do,' said Felicia Veracruz. 'I reckon they sleep on it and dream about it and it helps.'

So Shelley Ann went up and sat by Eulalia's bed and woke her very gently and told her, 'Honey, your new mommy and daddy are going to be flying in from Denver and then Houston Texas. They'll be in the day after tomorrow, and they are *really* excited to meet you. So we need to go to the airport nice and early day after tomorrow. OK? Now you sleep well, and tomorrow we're going to have a goodbye party for you. It's all gonna be fine honey. They're good God-fearing people. They will be your new mommy and daddy and they will love you so much. I promise you.'

Eulalia said nothing.

Well, she would need a lot of love. Some of these kids, the things they had seen... But that was OK, the parents would do that. She had been to their homes, and this couple radiated love. They would love her like their own. Many of them weren't even wealthy and they would spend tens of thousands of dollars to help just one child from Russia or India or Guatemala. She had seen it with her own eyes. Love and stability was what the kids needed, and then they blossomed. One little girl adopted in the early days was now going to UCLA. It happened.

Eulalia lay in her comfy bed with the flowery coverlet and felt her mind spinning. *They were taking her to America*. Nothing made sense any more. It was so confusing, she couldn't even decide how she was supposed to feel about it.

Was she being sent to America because she had been naughty? But they told her as if it was a treat, and there would be a farewell party. Were her family in America now? But they had said she was going to a new family. Was that a good thing?

She missed Pepito. She missed her Mama and Papa, and Héctor and the boys, and El Pipón, who must be much bigger now, almost the size of a wolf. But if she found him again he would still love her and follow her around.

She missed everyone really.

When she slept she had tumultuous thoughts and dreams. She was back in the tunnel. Héctor was there too, and her older brother Jaime, and he was talking about poisonous snakes. He said in Amazonas there were snakes a hundred metres long which swallowed cows whole and then slept for a year. Spiders as big as houses. And then he told her of a tidal wave that would come up from the sea as big as the mountains, bigger, much bigger, darkening the whole sky. And as he described it, it actually happened. In her dream she was looking out of the tunnel mouth and up at the mountains, and then realized with terror that one of the mountains was really a wave of water, rushing down on the whole city.

She could hear it coming too, roaring like the wind. The ground was shaking, the palm fronds and banana leaves tossing, and the monstrous wave came cresting the mountains, extinguishing the volcanoes in a gigantic hiss, a shining obsidian wall a hundred miles high crested with snow white snarling horses, sweeping away mountains and forests, villages and towns and people.

66

Before dawn the kid woke him up.

'Listen, about the girl you're looking for,' he said abruptly.

Nicholas stirred and stared up at him from the floor. 'Eh? What?'

'The Indian girl you're looking for. You should quit, go home. She's gonna be all right.'

He sat up. 'Why are you telling me this now you arse? It's … five in the morning. This carpet smells of sick. And you snore.'

Pepito looked away when he spoke. Telling the truth made him awkward, he'd been lying so long. 'The little girl,' he said casually. 'I know her.'

'Don't talk bollocks.'

'I never lie.'

'You lie all the time.'

'Suit yourself,' and he lay down again.

Now it was Nicholas who was bouncing on the bed. Shaking him.

'I've got a headache,' said Pepito.

'What are you talking about? What little girl? Are you still drunk?'

'The little girl. *Indita*. I said I know her.'

'How can you know her?'

'She got off at the bus station. Where I hang out. There or the airport. International traveller me.'

'There was supposed to be a woman looking after her.'

'Nope. She was all on her own.'

'And then what? Where did she go?'

'She hung out with us for a bit. She wasn't going to last five minutes in the city, this little country girl.'

'Are you serious? I swear to God, you better not be lying. This is not a joking matter for me.'

'Chill man. I'm cool.'

Nicholas felt everything ticking, pricking, trembling. Epidermal horripilation, in medical techno-speak. 'So where is she? Are you saying she's still alive?'

'Course she's still alive!' said the boy with a touch of anger. 'I was looking out for her.'

'You need to get up, now.' He was already dressing. 'So where is she?'

'You sure you're not weird about her?'

'*What*?'

'You sure you're not – you know. About Lala.'

'Lala?'

'Eulalia.'

His heart sang at the name. He was nearly dressed already, socks inside out. He hauled the boy out of bed.

'No. No I am not. So where is she? Now?'

'She's got people to look after her, save her soul.' He put his hands together in prayer.

'Tell me. I promise I'll pay you.'

The boy looked contemptuous. Hardly once in his eleven years had an adult made a promise to him and kept it. 'I'll show you. But I need a Coke. It's the *yanqui* evangelicals and their orphanage, up in Zone 2.'

'But she's not an orphan.'

'I don't think they're fussy. It's *muchos dolares* exporting kids, you make more than coffee.'

'*Muchos dolores habrá para el impío.*'

'You a fuckin' priest now? Jesus.'

'Move your scrawny arse.'

'Arse yourself. Arse-face. Dog's-arse face.'

They clattered down the scuzz-brothel stairs.

'Arse-brain. Pickled arse-brain urchin.'

'Ballbag arseface dogshit gringo.'

Out into the grey dawn.

'You sozzled knobhead.'

'You toxic binbag of gringo dog's fart.'

'Hey, that was quite good,' said Nicholas. 'So where is this place?'

They sat on a low concrete wall facing away from the street, in case any cop cars went past. Pepito slurped down his Coke and belched cavernously. Whisky and caramel breath.

'Come *on*,' said Nicholas.

'OK, OK. I can't hurry Coke, it gives me indigestion. And I need a cigarette. Buy me some cigarettes.'

Nicholas stood up. 'Right, I'm going.'

Pepito sighed. 'OK Jesus.'

'Why are you calling me Jesus?'

'Cos it's funny.'

They hurried through the streets of the city that was gradually waking up. Pigeons cooed on the ledges of the bespattered west front of the cathedral, the saints in their niches baptized with trickling dung. Street sweepers moved slowly over the pavements as if still asleep, one trailing his broom behind him. From narrow and shady alleyways came the sounds of people opening their grocery stores, metal shutters being hauled up, barred gates clanging back, ready to receive the day's delivery of fruit crates from the rumbling vans.

But much of the capital was still dozing under the ochre smog, and in the hushed plazas there was still an air of a ghost city. The strengthening sun brought out all the odours of the old streets, odours of pulpy tropical fruit and close-packed people, fresh baked tortillas and exhausted drains.

A single stray dog looked pointedly at Nicholas, as if longing to speak. He felt that something extraordinary had happened, or was about to happen, even by the standards of this extraordinary country.

Eventually they found a cab running and took it out to the glaring suburban sprawl of Zone 2, with its white walls and big houses and hard light and its perpetual background music of lawn sprinklers. When they came to the street of the Little Angels Adoption Agency and stepped out of the cab, their eyes almost closed at the burning glare.

Squinting at the entry panel on the gate, Nicholas rang the bell. After a few moments woman answered.

'A little girl called Eulalia,' he said urgently, leaning forward. 'Where is she?'

'Who is this?'

'A friend of the family. A little Indian girl called Eulalia. You've got her. Let us in.'

There was a shocked pause. Then, 'I'm sorry, we can't just let anyone in. Please tell me who's speaking?'

'I'm a friend of the family. In this country. They became separated.'

'So why haven't her family come to look for her?'

'I ... I don't think they know she's still alive. Please.'

'I'm sorry, but –'

'*Look...*' In impatience and frustration, feeling intensely now that Eulalia was just inside these barbed wire walls, Nicholas banged his fist on the gates. They clanged far more loudly than he'd expected.

'Hey, don't be an idiot,' hissed Pepito. He glanced around. Down on the corner of the street, one of the armed guards who kept Zone 2 safe was already craning forward out of his shaded sentry box and staring at them.

'Look,' said Nicholas, leaning close to the box. 'Please. I'm an English doctor, and I know Eulalia and want to take -'

'You're a qualified doctor?'

Sweat trickled down his back. 'Well – no. I'm still in training. Look – can you please just let us *in*. Then we can talk.'

'I'm sorry, we have been told that the little girl is in danger from some quarters. We were told this when she first arrived.

I can't let just anyone in.'

'You think I'm a *danger* to her?'

He was shouting now, yelling into this obtuse box on the gate.

'For God's sake...' hissed Pepito. Then glancing round he saw the guard in the sentry box already on his feet and strolling towards them, shotgun over his shoulder. The sight of armed and uniformed men approaching always made him panic. In a flash he was running away in the other direction.

Nicholas stared after him, back at the guard, back at the box. So close, and yet so far. He hadn't planned for this. He had no plan.

'Look,' he tried to explain more calmly. 'I'm sorry I was shouting. If you will just let me see her. Tell her I'm here. Nicholas.'

'Are you her legal guardian?'

'No. She's not even an orphan, for Christ's sake.'

There was a slight pause, enough to communicate disapproval. 'So where are her parents?' said the woman's voice. 'Can you get them to come here in person and pick her up?'

'I...' He felt himself losing his way. And there was a guard with a shotgun standing just a few feet away, staring at him blankly in his mirror shades. 'I don't know where they are.'

'Then I'm sorry, but I don't see what I can do. Have you got ID at least?'

No... He hadn't. He'd given his passport to Bridge. Why had he *done* that? What an idiot. He stared down at his feet, feeling like he was staring down at nothing. This couldn't be happening. Not now.

'Hello?' said the woman's voice.

Tongue-tied, he slapped his hand against the gate again. Oven hot metal.

'Hey,' said the guard.

He was perspiring, dry-mouthed. He couldn't believe Pepito had led him this far, and knew all about her, only for –

The guard said, 'Please sir, step away from the gates.'

He stepped back slowly.

'Please walk away now. You are not going to be admitted.'

His mind worked furiously but he could think of nothing sensible to do. *Nothing*. It was so ridiculous. He took a deep breath and walked away down the street. There was a green patch of parkland at the bottom with palmtrees and a bench. He needed to think.

He hadn't been sitting long when he heard a whistle. Pepito, ducking out from behind a palm tree.

'You are such a fucking idiot,' he said, creeping over to him like he was crossing a battlefield under heavy fire.

'I don't need you to tell me that.'

'So what now?'

His mind was grating through the gears. Chin in his hands. A few cars went by. 'It's crazy. I mean, you say she's actually in there – like a *prison*.'

'Well, as far as I know. That's where I left her. It wasn't safe for her on the streets.' He wondered briefly whether to try to explain to the gringo about Marcello and everything, but decided not. 'So, yeah, like a prison. But at least we haven't lost her. And I reckon once it's dark…'

The boy tailed off.

'What?'

'I can get in. Some of the wall is only spiked with broken glass. They set it in cement. All you need is a thick blanket or that plastic stuff with bubbles.'

'Are you serious?'

Pepito grinned and nodded. After a moment or two, Nicholas smiled faintly too.

'But then what are we going to do?' said Pepito.

'Don't worry,' he lied. 'I have an idea.'

They sat in cafes and walked and watched the river and the people. Nicholas bought an ethnic rug woven by ladies of an

386

indigenous co-operative, and stowed it in a roll under his rucksack straps. Pepito was scornful.

'Such a waste of money,' he said. 'You could just use plastic, cardboard, any old thing. Fucking gringos.'

Nicholas kept an anxious eye out for cop cars, and watched the TV in the cafe for over an hour, half-expecting an image of himself to appear on screen. Have you seen this man? Wanted for assaulting a police officer at the airport with a toilet part. Believed to be extremely dangerous. Do not approach.

But there was nothing.

Pepito said, 'So you still haven't made it, huh?'

'What?'

'As a TV celebrity?'

'Very funny.'

Pepito thought for a moment, sucking on his straw. Then he wiped his sticky orange mouth with the back of his hand and snorted thickly and said, 'I really need a cigarette. The truth is, we're all in trouble.'

'What, like, philosophically? You mean the whole human race?'

'Don't be a dumbass. I mean *us*. Us three. You, me and Lala. I mean, Lala's stuck in there. I'm *always* in trouble. And the cops are after you for escaping from a cop, even when you were handcuffed and everything. And they were actually chucking you out of the country too. Why aren't they looking for you?'

Nicholas stared uneasily. 'I don't know. Because they're sort of useless in this country?'

'They're not *that* useless. And they usually kill anyone who assaults a cop. Down a dark alley, bullet to the back of a head, pow.'

'Great.'

'Well I'm just saying. I mean, you really ought to leave this country soon. Like, now. It's a shithole anyway. You could get over a land border, probably. You still got dollars?'

He nodded.

'Then give someone a little handout, cross into El Salvador or something. Then fly away home.'

'But I'm not leaving Eulalia. I told you. She's got family. We've got to her out.'

'But then what do we do? Just, like, walk around with her? Where? And you don't know where her parents are do you?'

'Well … no. Not yet.'

'So then what? And also, she and I got into a bit of trouble with this guy.'

'What guy?'

'This *guy*. Marcello.'

'And?'

Pepito sucked his straw a bit more. 'Well he's not a very good guy. And we were supposed to do this job for him, but it didn't work out. That was why I took her to that adoption place to start with. Cos it would be safer there.'

'What sort of job? You and Eulalia? How come she was suddenly working for someone called Marcello?'

'Look, don't get angry with me. I was looking out for her. Where were you? We were going to make some money. You know where we were living? In a *tunnel*. She didn't have a fucking hope. And then, OK, we shouldn't have worked for Marcello but you don't have much choice like that. You want to know what we were supposed to do? What your friend Lala was supposed to do, to deliver for him? A fucking *head*. A *severed head*.'

The woman behind the counter turned away from the TV and stared at them. Nicholas waved and forced a smile. 'It's OK,' he said. 'Just something he heard about.'

The woman turned back.

After a time Nicholas said quietly, 'Jesus. I'm sorry.'

Pepito wouldn't look at him, glaring out of the window. 'You have no idea,' he muttered. 'No fucking idea.'

'I'm sorry. What … what happened?'

'I threw it in the river. But it was kind of valuable to

Marcello. He won't be happy.'

Nicholas turned the image over in his mind. He had no idea, no. No idea what this boy of just ten or eleven – no point asking him, he wouldn't know – what this boy had seen and gone through in his short life. And how he had protected Eulalia as best he could - better than any adult, better than anyone else had done in this city.

He saw him standing at the swollen river's edge, hurling a severed head into the air. The clotted head turning and falling, the heavy splash. The boy up to his knees in tidewater. Lala hidden away, protected....

'Look,' he said, 'let's just get her out somehow. Then go somewhere low key. And then – I don't know. We'll manage something. Could we *all* get away overland?'

'What, all the way through Mexico and over the Rio Grande?' The boy's lip was curled in a sneer.

'We'll manage something.'

'Yeah? We haven't managed anything so far. Not a damn thing.'

67

After dark they came back to Zone 2, just round the corner from the Agency and out of sight of the guard. But after dark, the guards in their sentry boxes were even more on the alert. And they would shoot freely. So Pepito picked a broken brick out of a pothole and handed it to Nicholas, gesturing at a nearby parked car.

'Just enough to set the alarm off,' he said. Then he crouched down at the corner and peered round to watch the guard box.

Nicholas brought the brick down hard on the windscreen, which shivered and frosted over but didn't break. No alarm went off.

Pepito looked back at him and shook his head. Checked around the corner again.

'Hang on,' he said.

He sidled down the street in the shadows. Even in this prosperous neighbourhood, streetlights were thinly scattered. Backed up under a big acacia tree he was virtually invisible in the darkness. Then he gestured to Nicholas.

'Lazy bastard's asleep,' he whispered.

The only security camera they could see was on the gate of the Little Angels house. They stood at the foot of the wall further down, as far from the nearest street light as they could get, and Nicholas unfurled the ethnic rug, clutching it by the top corners. He jumped up, trying to throw it over the wall. It fell back.

'Take your time,' said Pepito sarcastically, still crouched down and looking around. 'No pressure.'

He tried again and failed again. The sound of a car going

past the end of the street made them both sweaty with anxiety. Then Pepito was up on his back like a monkey, snatching the rug from his grasp. He stood wobbling on Nicholas's shoulders, and managed to get it partially over the wall. He placed his hands on the top, hoping the rug would be enough to soften those shards of jagged glass, and hopped up. He crouched and looked back.

'Do it very quickly,' he hissed. 'Don't put any weight down.'

Nicholas found a thin ledge in the stonework and stepped up but couldn't get any further. Pepito disappeared over the wall, landing softly. Then he called back,

'Pull yourself up on the rug itself. I'm holding it!'

He did so, and despite the difference in weight, the rug held, snagged on the shards of glass. He got his feet on top, and jumped down the other side, landing in a crouch. The hot tarmac smell of the dry dusty street was gone, the air instead cool and damp and full of the odours of well-watered lawns and night jasmine. And Pepito was grinning like a little fox.

Then he stood and grasped the rug by the corners and flicked it hard, as if shaking the dust out, and tugged it down after them.

'In case the guard sees it,' he said. 'Dead giveaway.'

He rolled it into a bundle and stuffed it down in the shadows of the wall.

Nicholas was glad he was here, the urchin.

The garden was not well lit and there was no moon yet. They crept around the house, ready to run if a dog appeared. The house was single storey, and three of the windows had their curtains drawn already. It was just before 10 p.m. Another room with glass doors out into the garden was brightly lit. Standing well back in the darkness, they could see in: a TV, a blonde woman, and a girl in her teens maybe, lying asleep on a sofa. Toys and games scattered across the floor. No Eulalia.

One pair of drawn curtains was still slightly apart, so they crept closer and tried to peer through. But the room was in pitch darkness and it was impossible to see anything inside. Nicholas and Pepito looked at each other. Then Pepito tapped on the window with a single fingernail, and he and Nicholas fled back into the shadows below the wall.

Nothing happened.

'Is this really our best idea?' whispered Nicholas.

'It'll work, just you see,' said Pepito. 'They'll come to the window. They always do.'

After a time, Pepito crept back and did it again, a little harder. Back into the shadows. They repeated the process at a different window, until there was a stirring and the curtains were pulled apart and a small, dim face peered out.

It wasn't her.

When the face had vanished again and few more minutes had passed, they tried again at another window.

Very soon the curtains were lit up from within as a bedside light came on. And then nothing.

They sidled closer. 'Come *on*,' hissed Pepito.

He took one step nearer and was just about to reach up and tap again when the curtain was pulled back at one corner at out peeped a face. The pigtails were gone, a strange raggedy haircut. Pink pyjamas. And then the incomparable gap-toothed smile – for the light from the bedroom fell on Pepito's anxious upturned face, illuminating him like a star of the silver screen. And though the window was still shut, Eulalia's scream of delight seemed to sound all across the garden.

'Pepito!'

And all through the house....

Then she was fiddling to open the window, her face glowing with excitement.

And from within the house came the sound of doors banging, of hurrying footsteps. A woman's voice calling –

Nicholas came racing forward.

'And Doctor Nicholas!' screamed Eulalia.

The window swung open and she was even starting to

climb out....

The footsteps were very near now, another door slammed open and the woman was running, calling out. They would never get away in time and back over the wall without the guard being alerted.

'Lala, Lala,' said Nicholas, pushing her gently back in. 'Get back into bed, quickly. You had a bad dream. You didn't see us. A bad dream – OK?'

'No!' cried Eulalia.

Pepito was pushing the window shut again from the outside. 'Just stay in bed,' he said urgently, 'just a few more minutes.'

'You didn't see us!'

And then Nicholas and Pepito were melting back into the shadows, waiting, hearts hurting and drumming.

They saw a woman – the tall blonde woman from the TV room – come striding in and over to the window at once. Lala stood back behind her looking crestfallen. But they could see she was saying something. The woman looked out for a while, then ducked back in and shut the window and snatched the curtains closed.

'Shit,' muttered Pepito. 'Has she locked it? Have we blown it?'

'I don't think so. Just wait.'

'What if they move her to another room? Or the woman sleeps in there with her?'

'Give it a chance.'

The moments passed, and then at last the bedroom light went out.

They crept forward crouched low.

She was smart. The moment Shelley Ann was out of the room and away down the corridor, Lala was back out of bed and opening the window again, the bedroom still in darkness. Nicholas sprinted forward.

Behind her, he saw that the woman had left the bedroom door wide open.

'Lala, Lala!' he whispered urgently, 'not a sound now! Quiet as you can, come on – quick and quiet as you can. There you go....'

She half-clambered, half-fell into his arms, quivering with excitement. She looked like she might burst.

'But, but –' she said. 'You went away.'

'Well I came back.' He set her down on the ground. 'Quickly now.'

'This is amazing!' she said. 'Have you got El Pipón with you?'

'Er ... not right now. But I'll explain later.'

'Ohhh!' she said. Why did adults always want to do everything *later*?

The three of them trotted away over the lush lawn, Nicholas clutching her hand. Lala barefoot in her pink pyjamas.

'And won't they be cross with me?' she whispered.

'No, not really,' said Nicholas. 'Don't worry about it. They made a mistake.'

'Is my Mama with you?'

'Soon.'

Pepito climbed back up again using a shrub for support. He found a narrow stretch of the wall where there was only one shard of glass upright, and laid the rug flat and doubled-over. They managed to push and pull her up to him.

'Stay just there,' said Pepito. 'There's bits of glass. Don't move your feet.'

He dropped down the other side into the still-deserted street. Lala hesitated on the top. Nicholas scrambled up beside her using the shrub, and then jumped down the other side, bending deeply at the knees to take the force. He turned back and said,

'Jump! Jump! I've got you!'

She was very anxious, it was such a high jump.

'Quickly, Lala! Or they'll catch us!'

She took a deep breath and closed her eyes and imagined

she was jumping into the water and then jumped, and Nicholas caught her cleanly and set her down.

Pepito was crouching.

'What are you *doing*?' hissed Nicholas.

He didn't answer. Swiftly unlaced his battered trainers, grabbed Lala by each ankle in turn and laced her tiny feet into them as tightly as he could.

'Ew!' she squealed. 'They're all hot and sweaty.'

'You OK barefoot?' said Nicholas as they hurried down the street.

'You got a spare pair of shoes in your bag?' said Pepito.

'No.'

'Well then.'

'This is so exciting!' said Eulalia.

If only they could get a cab. But it was too risky. And how could they stay in a hotel? White man, two native children, one still in her pyjamas, one a barefoot streetkid … Like that wouldn't raise any suspicions.

They hurried on.

When a car passed by the end of the street, they shrank back into a gateway.

'What are we doing?' said Eulalia. 'Can't we go home now?'

'Nearly there, darling. Um....'

'*And* I had a goodbye party,' said Eulalia.

'What?'

'They made me a special cake and sang a hymn and everything. It was amazing.'

'They... Why were they saying goodbye?'

'Because I was going to America. But they were good god-fearing people. Aren't I going to America now?'

'Um...'

Nicholas was desperate and joyous at once. *They had found her!* She had her hand in his, and she was unhurt. It was, as Lala said, amazing. But –

'We're going to sleep in a car tonight,' said Pepito.

'A car! I've never slept in a car before!' She trotted along. They came to a main road, which wasn't a good idea. They cut down a side road again. Up ahead was a lit-up bar. A man sitting on the edge of the pavement with his feet in the gutter, a bottle by his side. A child lying asleep beside him. They turned back.

'What are we doing? Don't you know where we're going?'

'Of course we do,' said Nicholas.

'And will I see my Mama tomorrow? It's been *ages*.'

'We'll see what happens tomorrow.'

'But *what* happens? Tell me!'

'It' a secret.'

'Ohhh!'

The area got worse, the buildings looked broken down and semi-deserted but for the occasional bar or corner shop where the cashier crouched behind a security grille.

'I'm *tired*,' said Eulalia.

Nicholas carried her for a bit. But she had to walk again when they scrambled down a steep embankment, otherwise he was afraid he would slip and drop her. And then they came to their overnight accommodation.

'Goodness gracious!' said Eulalia, staring around open-mouthed. 'Look at all these dead cars!'

It was a breaker's yard surrounded by a high wire fence. But Pepito knew a way in, through a small, low hole in the wire just near the embankment. He had slept here before.

It wasn't a bad idea, considering their situation. They turned it into a game. Lala could choose which car they slept in.

She immediately chose a bright red Nissan teetering on top of a stack of four other wrecks. So they gently dissuaded her, and Nicholas guided her towards a big old 4x4, a Mitsubishi, with one door hanging off.

'Look!' he said. 'Leather seats!'

'Yeah,' said Pepito, 'and air con, power assisted steering, the works.'

Eulalia was scrambling into the back seat. 'Can we drive it? Does it go?'

'Well, maybe tomorrow.'

'Tomorrow, tomorrow,' she grumbled. She pulled off Pepito's shoes and handed them back to him. 'Thank you very much.'

There was broken glass on the driver's seat, so Nicholas sat upright in the passenger seat, mind racing, hoping the mosquitoes wouldn't torment them. They loved breeding in old car tyres.

The children were to sleep in the back, Lala across the middle seat of mouldering cream leather, Pepito in the back. But too excited to sleep, Eulalia said,

'So are you two friends? You never told me.'

'Nah,' said Pepito. 'We keep bumping into each other, but we can't stand the sight of each other really.'

She giggled. After a time she said, 'They were nice to me there though really. Will they be looking for me?'

'I'll write them a letter explaining,' said Nicholas. 'That it was all a mix up. Don't you worry. You go to sleep now.'

After some time he heard the children's regular breathing. They needed it. The sun would be up again and burning in only five or six hours. And then what?

There was no British Embassy in the country but there was a Consulate. Surely they would help? Or a charity, an NGO? But they were all busy at the moment, with the chaos upcountry, and he had a horror of some brisk bureaucratic decision saying that Eulalia would have to go back to the adoption agency. In the current situation, it would be the safest place for her.

Meanwhile he was under grave suspicion of having committed a serious crime in the country. The Consulate could not protect him from that, only plead for lighter sentencing. And he didn't want to spend time in San Pedro jail, where prisoners regularly set each other on fire.

It was a mess. But she was here. *She was here.* It was a joyous but immense responsibility, and he was very tired and anxious. He checked his roll of dollars once more. Still $520 to go. And that dreaded package. He checked it every morning, always humbled that Pepito had not stolen it in the night and fled with it. But he never did.

Otherwise all he had to go on were the words of the old woman in the mountains, outside the ruined cottage. That people from the village had gone to a plantation, to the coast. But the old woman had thought grimly that most of them were dead. In which case, the Little Angels adoption agency it was.

Surely life could not be so cruel? After all this? Oh but it could, it could. These things happened all the time, and everyone's an orphan in the end.

Behind him, Lala stirred and whimpered. What childish nightmares did she endure? He leaned back and gently stroked her forehead and her hair, as he had seen Maria do so many times before. She started and her eyes opened and she stared at him, but perhaps she didn't really see him. After a time her eyelids dropped and her eyes closed and she didn't whimper again.

Sometime before dawn he awoke, his back aching, and he could hear the two children breathing. The tropical moon rose up straight over the yard and was a starburst of white light on the splintered windscreen.

Nicholas arched and turned his head and out of the side window he saw a lean dog sloping past, the moon backlighting her bristly spine. A bitch with low-hanging dugs, a rat in her jaws still gently squirming. Then he realised it wasn't a rat, it was a puppy, one of her puppies, and she was carrying it to some new sanctuary among the broken cars.

68

He jerked awake to a violent rapping on the car roof. A fat man was glaring in at them. Oh shit.

'What the hell are you doing?' he shouted.

Nicholas reached for the handle and forced open the creaking car door. The man stepped back.

'It's OK, it's OK,' he said. 'We're – we've got some trouble. Let me explain.'

The man's eyes narrowed. He looked prepared to fight. He was fat and very strong, both belly and biceps bulging. He was naked to the waist, wearing baggy jeans and heavy boots. His big meaty fists were ingrained with motor oil, his head was as round as a football and his nose a pugnacious blob. 'You foreign?'

'English.'

'So what the fuck you doing with those kids in the car? Hotel wouldn't take you in, huh? I swear to God you bastard, if you've been mistreating those kids I will beat you to death right where you stand. Slowly.'

'OK, but don't talk like that in front of them. They've been through enough.' He glanced back. Both children were awake already, watching anxiously through the grimy glass. Then Pepito came scrambling over the back seat, over Lala and out of the door because he couldn't open the boot from inside.

The man was now growling in Nicholas's face. 'Don't you tell me what I can and can't do in my own yard, you *fuck*. Or I will bury you alive right under that fucking car.'

'Hey, mister,' said Pepito. 'This guy is cool. And don't speak like that ... the girl,' and he jerked his head back at Eulalia.

Still glaring ferociously, the man said, 'So tell me what's going on. And fast.'

Nicholas took a deep breath and thought about the bitch he had seen last night with her puppy and took in the man's round football head and his burning indignation and decided to tell him everything, as simply as he could. Because they needed help.

'A *cistern lid?*' said the man at one point.

Pepito nodded.

'Well I'll be damned.'

When he had finished, the man looked them over. 'I reckon I believe you. You look too dumb to make all that stuff up.'

Nicholas smiled faintly.

Then he said, 'You are in a whole heap of trouble, friend.'

'I believe we are, yes.'

'And I thought *my* life was difficult, what with eleven kids and all.'

'Eleven?'

'C'mon. Follow me. You need some fucking assistance.'

'Language,' said Pepito, following him as he stumped away across the filthy yard.

Nicholas had to carry Eulalia because she refused to wear Pepito's shoes again and there was broken glass and rusting metal everywhere.

'He's scary,' she whispered into his ear.

'Yeah,' said Nicholas. 'But I think he might be all right really.'

They came to a tatty shed, the man's office, and he led them inside. There was one chair, a desk and some papers all covered in oily fingerprints.

'You got money?' said the man.

'I've got dollars.'

'Give me thirty. I ain't Carlos Slim.'

He snatched the dollars and was gone with amazing

abruptness, slamming the door behind him.

'How do we know we can trust him?' said Pepito.

Nicholas sat Eulalia down on the chair, his arms aching. 'Just a hunch.'

'He smells,' said Eulalia.

He was back in a matter of minutes with two bags. He set three styrofoam coffee cups down on the desk and some bananas. From the other bag he took two big bottles of water, some more food – bags of dried pineapple, fried beans, some biscuits – and some clothes. He stooped down in front of Eulalia and slipped a new pair of flipflops on her feet.

When he stood up again, fists in the small of his broad hairy back, he caught a slight smirk on Nicholas's face.

'What's so funny?' he growled.

'Nothing.'

'Then why you laughing? I don't see anything funny. You think it's funny I buy some pink flipflops?'

'With flowers on. No, I … no.'

In response the man made a kind of bearlike growling noise. His personal setting was stuck on Maximum Aggression – but Nicholas thought they needed someone like this, or they weren't going to last another day.

'And don't just look at it,' he said, punching the air above the food. 'Eat!'

They ate.

'So,' he said, raising one arm and scratching his armpit. 'You think this girl's Mama's on the coast?'

'I think so.'

'By the sea?' said Eulalia through a mouthful of banana.

'But you don't want to get noticed. So eat up and follow me. And bring the rest of the food and the coffee with you, dumb ass. You, little lady, you stay in here a minute and change out of your clothes. You put on the stuff I just bought you, bring your pyjamas in the bag. C'mon, out of the shed you guys, out of the shed, give the lady some privacy!'

401

They waited a couple of minutes until Eulalia reappeared, wearing a white t shirt with a dolphin on it and a brightly multicoloured skirt and the pink flip-flops, bulging bag of pyjamas clutched in her hand. She looked quite pleased.

The man led them across the yard, but when he saw Nicholas about to pick her up and carry her again across this battlefield of shattered glass and twisted metal and rainbow pools of motor oil, he shoved him out of the way and picked her up himself, carrying her under one arm. She closed her eyes, wishing she could close her nose too.

He stopped and set her down near the remains of a white taxi by the gate.

'Does that actually go?' said Nicholas.

'Course it goddamn does. Goes like a bird. And you won't get noticed by the cops so much in a taxi.' He tapped his head.

'That's true,' said Pepito.

'For sale, three hundred dollars.'

'I … I can't, I'm running so low…'

'Or you can hire it for fifty. That's a special deal. And don't fucking thank me, I hate people who fucking thank me. You can have it for fifty, plus you put gas in it, and bring it back when you're done. If you don't bring it back I will come and find you and rip your head off and –'

'OK, *OK,* not in front of the girl, *please.*'

The man turned and glared at Eulalia so hard that she stepped back. Then he grinned suddenly for the first time. It was almost worse than the glare. He had more gold than teeth in his head. He ruffled her hair and said, 'Sorry little lady.'

She glared back at him and smoothed her hair straight again.

The taxi, a heavily smoking Hyundai, made a terrible grating noise and wouldn't go above third gear or thirty mph. So it fitted in quite well on the roads of the country. It had a hole the size of a manhole cover in the footwell of the passengerside, so both children sat in the back and addressed

Nicholas as their chauffeur.

The first road block they came to, on the way out of the city, Nicholas held out a ten dollar note lightly between index and middle finger and said he was a doctor and the note was plucked away and they were nodded onwards.

'I've got oily marks on my new t shirt,' said Eulalia. 'Where that dirty man picked me up. And I'm *hungry*.'

They ate bananas and some fried beans, but a proper plateful would be good, if they didn't attract too much attention. After half an hour, still amid the decrepit outskirts of the city, they pulled into a roadside diner and sat at a table in the corner and ordered three plates of eggs and sweet potato. The children devoured it. Nicholas felt too anxious to be hungry.

There was a TV on in the corner and Pepito stared up at Nicholas as he swallowed his last mouthful. Then he twisted round and watched the TV and then twisted back.

'Do you see that?'

The colour had drained from Nicholas's face. 'Of course I see that,' he said.

'What?' said Eulalia, still eating.

'So *now* what do we do?' said Pepito.

He stood. 'I'm going to make a phone call.'

69

Maria was still working in the field when one of the overseers called her from the end of the row.

'Hey, lady! Your kid's in trouble! Back in the main block.'

She ran almost without breathing, gripped with fear and wild imaginings, only to find Héctor sitting peacefully in the TV room with a wad of bloody tissues pressed to his nose. She almost collapsed over him, hugging him, panting and perspiring. He was trying to speak.

'What happened?' she demanded. 'What happened? Who did this to you?'

'It's just a nose bleed. But Mama –', and he kept pointing back towards the television.

'Your nose just started bleeding?'

Héctor looked uncomfortable. 'Well, no. Me and this other boy, we were playing lions and tigers, and he –'

'Which other boy?'

'This *other boy*.' He stared at her stubbornly.

'For heaven's sake my pet, do be careful. Only last week you almost knocked yourself unconscious.'

'That wasn't me, that was the tree's fault,' said Hector. 'But Mama, on the TV –'

'Now put your head back,' she said, tilting it back for him. 'Have you swallowed lots of blood? Do you feel sick?'

'Blood tastes different to anything else,' he gurgled. 'Doesn't it? I never drunk it before.'

'Yes you have,' she said. 'Plenty of times.'

And then a word from the TV, a single word, made her head snap round.

'You see Mama,' said Hector, shifting to look round her. 'Lala's on TV! I told you!'

Maria stared. A moustachioed man in a shiny suit was reading out the news, and saying that there had been a dramatic kidnapping of a little girl at an adoption agency in the capital. There was a woman on the screen, very upset, saying that she had reason to believe that the little girl was in danger. They had been warned that there were those who might want to kill her. She wasn't sure why. The agency was a very secure compound, but somehow they had got in over the wall. She begged for those responsible to examine their consciences and bring the little girl back unharmed.

A policeman then said they were working very hard with the agency, and were determined to find the little girl. They were already following a number of leads. He held up some kind of Indian-style woven rug.

Hector gave a nasal squeal. 'Look, Mama! There she is again! That's the *third time*. Lala is really famous now!'

On the TV screen, there was a photo of Eulalia, her daughter. Her braids had been cut off and she was wearing a new dress that she didn't recognize. But it was her. *It was her*.

The overseer was at his desk with the air con humming peacefully, watching funny clips on YouTube, when the door flew open and his office was suddenly invaded by a human blizzard. A madwoman was standing there yelling at him, her eyes blazing, her long hair flying like some Mayan witch-goddess. Then she was snatching up the documents on his desk and ripping them to shreds and throwing them in his face. Behind her in the doorway stood a small boy with enormous wide eyes and a bloody wad of tissues pressed under his nose. The whole thing was deranged.

'My documents! My documents!' cried the overseer.

'My daughter! *My daughter!*' cried the mad woman. 'How could you? How dare you? How could you tell me such a lie as that?'

405

'What lie? Madam, please…' He cautiously got to his feet as it dawned on him who she was. That troublemaker. 'Madam, please, we have always done our best to –'

'I ought to strangle you with my bare hands! But what would be the point? Your heart has died within you already. You filthy liar. Now give me your telephone.'

She looked like she might spit in his face. The man kept well back from her. One of the guards would come soon. 'I, I…'

She was a mad banshee, leaning across the desk as he backed up against the wall, pressing her enraged face close to his, her wild eyes boring in to him. This one would need to be held down. Quaking, he handed her his mobile. Was she going to smash it? Perhaps she was possessed. They were very primitive, these people.

'Now,' she said, 'look up on your computer there the number I need. The Little Angels Adoption Agency in the capital. You find it.'

He sat down again, shaking, and tapped it in. She thrust the phone back at him.

'You dial it. Then give me the phone back.'

He did as he was told. It would be dangerous to do otherwise. Moments later she was holding the phone to her ear. A woman answered.

'My name,' said Maria, 'is Maria Chacach, the mother of Eulalia Chacach. Now listen to me very carefully.'

Only minutes after one extraordinary phone call, Felicia Veracruz had another. It was the weirdest, most garbled story, but nevertheless when she put the caller on hold and discussed it with the detective who was still going over the crime scene, they began to piece it together and the detective shrugged and she had to shake her head with relief. The little girl was safe.

She spoke down the line again. 'Well, her mother phoned us just a few minutes ago. And she would really like her daughter back.'

The next thing she knew, there was Lala's own voice coming down the crackly line. 'Hello Mrs Veracruz. I am with Doctor Nicholas now. He's taking me back to Mama and Papa soon.' Whispered voices. Then, 'And thank you for looking after me.'

The young Englishman again. 'So where do we go?'

'Have you got a pen?' said Felicia.

'Don't worry. I'll remember.'

When she put the phone down at last, she wanted to pray. But she didn't want to pray alone. She went and summoned all the children to the main room and the older ones grumbled and the younger ones fidgeted while she prayed. Only all she said really was thank you.

'So,' said one of the boys, 'she wasn't kidnapped really?'

'No, not really.'

'By bandits?'

'I'm afraid not.'

The boy's face was a picture of disappointment.

70

Nicholas took the borrowed mobile back to the woman behind the till and gave her a dollar and returned. Red in the face and almost *quivering*.

Pepito stared up at him over his Coke. 'Hey man, you OK?'

He looked like he might explode. He seized Eulalia and lifted her up and she squeaked indignantly, so he set her down again and he ruffled Pepito's hair wildly.

'Get in the car!' he said too loudly. 'We're going to the seaside.'

'To find my Mama?' said Lala.

He was grinning like a madman. Pepito was slightly worried, he'd never seen him look like this.

Back in the terrible taxi, Nicholas released the handbrake which didn't work anyhow and they creaked away down the road. After just a few minutes he said quietly,

'Children, I want you to cover your ears.'

They looked puzzled

'Come on, hands over your ears. Don't listen.'

They did as they were told, patiently.

He roared, 'FUCKING HELL I THINK WE DID IT! I THINK WE FUCKING DID IT!'

He was rocking back and forth violently in the car seat, holding on to the steering wheel and wrenching it so hard he looked like he might pull it free altogether.

Lala said, 'I had my hands over my ears but I still heard you.'

He was still redfaced and then he started laughing. 'I can't believe it. Not a clue, not a hope in hell, and then somehow it all came together. Just....' He shook his head.

The children exchanged looks in the back seat.

'Is he drunk?' whispered Lala.

'He's something,' said Pepito.

Nicholas's laughter subsided. And then he pulled slowly over and stopped on the side of the road and laid his arms across the steering wheel and laid his head on his arms and began to sob.

The children were very embarrassed now. Great heaving sobs.

After a bit he felt a small hand on his shoulder. It was Eulalia. 'Doctor Nicholas? What is it? We haven't been mean to you have we?'

He sat up again and wiped his eyes and he looked round and he was grinning again.

'No, it's fine,' he said. He gave a huge sigh. 'Phew.' He wiped his eyes again, blew his nose. He stared down at the huge hole in the passenger footwell. 'This is a really good day.'

He let off the handbrake and the taxi creaked forward once more.

He reckoned it would take them around five hours to cover the hundred miles to the coast. They should be there about an hour before sunset.

The heat was cruel. He could feel it coming off the tarmac through the hole in the floor. And the lower you turned the air con, the hotter it blew. But then the traffic thinned out and there was a breeze and Eulalia, who had hardly spoken all the while she was back in the adoption agency, chattered like a spring stream.

The last of the infernal city vanished behind them and they came down out of the mountains onto the steaming coastal plain. There were roadblocks and checkpoints and they came through them all as if protected by providence. Nicholas

wondered if all the cold days, all the misery, were like pre-
payment for a handful of days like these. Because what could
ever compare with the feeling of the living weight of her
flying into his open arms, back there in the night-time garden?
Or telling her that they were going to find her family, and
knowing it to be true this time? Nothing could ever again
equal that.

They stopped for petrol. The car drank fuel like a truck. They
bought drinks and went on. Both children slept a while.
Eulalia awoke to the smell of the sea, and a wide sandstrewn
road grandly named the Atlantic Highway.

Pepito came groggily awake to her prodding.

'What?' he grumbled.

'The sea!' she said.

And there was the sea, the Caribbean Sea, whipped up by
the wind and raked with cat's claws and white horses tossing
their manes, and out there lay the whaleback shadows of the
Islands in the Bay.

It made her feel wild inside. Her heart was a fluttering bird
in the bone cage of her ribs.

'You ever seen the sea before, Lala?' asked Nicholas,
looking in the rearview mirror. She shook her head, unable to
stop staring. Then she said, 'How big is the sea?'

'Um ... really big. This coast, something like five hundred
miles long or something. To the border.'

The sea was so huge and wild and beautiful and it looked
so lonely.

The Atlantic Highway was lined with tatty wind-whipped
palms, and almost lost under sand blown in from the beach.
There was sand in the footwells and standing up in the back,
leaning over the front seat, Eulalia could see the road lost in
sand running beneath them like a river.

There were black boys running barefoot among the palm
trees, shouting and laughing. Little huts thatched with banana
leaves, and big fat ladies sitting outside with babies. There

were fishing villages called things like Noche Triste and El Mar Dulce.

'Wouldn't you like to live in a village called Noche Triste, or El Mar Dulce?' said Nicholas 'Sad Night. The Sweet Sea.' He shook his head. 'What a country this is. Doesn't it break your heart?'

'It does too,' said Pepito, squinting out of the window. 'But don't you start blubbing again.'

'Bastard,' murmured Nicholas.

Eulalia put her hands over her ears.

Inland now was the great mountain of Pico Bonito, as steep as a pyramid, shrouded in mist and cloud, three thousand metres high and covered in dense jungle. Nicholas said that no one had ever climbed right to the top. He said it couldn't be done, even though there was the fabulous Lost White City still to be discovered somewhere up there.

'I'm going to find it,' said Pepito. 'One day.'

He daydreamed of the silent forests of Amazonas ... demons' heads carved out of stone ... strangler vines and a stone table and a silver cup....

They stopped for bottles of water on the edge of a small town. Pepito said he was just running down to see the sea.

Eulalia said, 'I'm coming too!'

But he said, 'I'm going for a pee. Stay there.'

She stood and sulked.

He looked back at her and grinned, hands shoved into his jeans pockets, torn Hawaii t shirt, wind in his hair. 'It'll be OK sister. Don't you worry.'

And then he vanished away among the dunes.

An hour later they still hadn't found him. Nicholas knew what had happened but didn't want to admit it, to himself or to Lala. Finally an old black boy in striped trousers, riding an ancient bicycle with a pineapple trailer, told them he'd given a lift to a boy in a Hawaii t shirt up back to Noche Triste, and seen him get in a truck there.

Eulalia cried. 'Why is he always running away?'

Nicholas squatted and put his arm round her. Holding in his own sadness, keeping his voice even. 'I think he's gone back to the city. It's his home. You understand?'

'There's only a tunnel there!' she cried.

'Come on,' he said. 'Maybe we'll see him again one day. Let's have something to eat.'

So they sat on a wall and ate tortillas.

'I wish Pepito was here,' said Eulalia, swinging her legs. 'He was very kind to me.'

She kept looking out for Pepito coming along on a bicycle but it was never him. Ancient men sitting high on shrimp carts drawn by tired and blinkered horses. Old painted fishing boats pulled up on the beach, paint blistered off by the sun. And far out to sea a tiny blue boat and a figure crouched in it, in the heart of the sparkle.

Nicholas went into the beach cafe to make another phone call. He came back and said,

'This place is called Zambo Creek. I like that.'

'But where's Mama?'

'Soon. Just you wait.'

They sat at the cafe on wooden crates. There was an old wooden barrel on end, half buried in the sand, and strapped to its side a rolled up canvas parasol, bleached colourless and stained with dried salt.

'The night life must be amazing here,' said Nicholas.

The wind was dropping as the sun started to go down over the Bay of Amatique. Just him and Lala. Lala falling asleep. Palm fronds stirring in the soft and humid wind.

That tiny blue boat came in at last. An old fisherman wading in through the shallows, pulling the boat after him on a rope. He wore nothing but a ragged pair of shorts and his skin was very ancient and wrinkly, his knees like knobbly fruit and his face like a turtle. Then he squatted down not far from them and lit a driftwood fire and laid an old car hubcap on it with holes drilled through and grilled some snapper on it and sold it to them and they ate it with their fingers sitting round the fire.

Everything was so strange and dreamlike today. Anything could happen.

A ship sailed away to the west and the low slanting sun made the sea sparkle more than ever. Blur and sparkle and dazzle of the sunlit sea. Lala gazed after the ship with her hand over her eyes, and then along the beach she saw a woman standing there. The falling sunlight dazzled. A bird cried out in the sky.

The woman stood still and looked back at her along the beach. She was in a light blue dress. A small still figure upon the sand, shimmering in the heat haze as if she might vanish.

Eulalia stared. A trickle of sweat ran down her forehead and over the back of her hand. Her eyes ached, her arm ached, she ached all over. The woman still looked at her. She began to shake.

Nicholas said something but his voice was very far away.

The shimmering figure of the woman held out her arms. Nicholas said something again but it made no sense.

She swallowed. She couldn't breathe.

The sea whispered, the sun laughed. The ground rolled beneath her. The woman held her arms out towards her.

And then she was up and racing over the sand and flying into her arms like a bird.

71

After a time, Maria looked up and gestured to Nicholas. He went over, almost embarrassed.

Maria wiped away her tears and bit her lip and smiled. 'I don't know what to say, I truly don't.'

'Well...'

Eulalia said, 'But what about El Pipón and Papa and Abuelita and the boys?'

Her mother stroked and stroked her hair. 'They are safe. We will see them.'

Lala clung to her so hard it hurt. With a free hand Maria stroked her girl's cropped and raggedy hair. It was beyond belief, beyond belief that she should have come to stroke her hair again. At night when she had lain awake crying for her daughter it was the touch and the smell of her hair, her skin, the sound of her chatter and giggle, the sight of her gap-toothed smile. Maria lay crying then and feeling like she was being physically trampled by her own memories of her.

'Did you buy her the new clothes?' she asked Nicholas softly.

'I, no ... this guy in a breaker's yard.' He felt so awkward, but couldn't stop grinning. 'There's a lot to tell you. We had some real adventures.'

Lala had a graze on her cheek and a sunburnt snub nose and insect bites on her legs – but she was alive and well. Her legs were so thin! She would blow away over the sand if she let go of her. But she would not let go of her.

'Did someone hurt you?' she said.

'No,' said Eulalia, 'he was very kind to me.'

'Who was very kind to you?'

414

'Pepito. Where is El Pipón?'

Her mother kept smiling and stroking her hair. 'I think he's grown up now and has gone to run wild in the forest. Hush child. It's for the best. You know he always had a wild streak and a little wolf in him.'

'Did he?'

'Certainly. Now Héctor is a little sick, he had a nosebleed, but he will get better again. Where we are staying there's a very good doctor. It's better than the village.'

'When do we go back home?'

'To the village? We shall see. All in good time.'

'You lost me,' said the child suddenly. 'Why didn't you and Papa come and find me?'

'*O niña*,' said her mother, 'the day the soldiers came, it was such chaos...' She took a deep breath to steady herself. 'Papa was gone. There was much misunderstanding. I am sorry even to remember it. Many of us were lost that day. Many of us were lost, many were separated. Many of our people are gone, and some were even killed, may God have mercy.'

'What happened to Abuelita?'

'I believe Abuelita has gone the way of the old, but our children have come back to us. Look at you!'

She stroked her hair.

'For a time I thought I would not see you again. My heart broke and I thought it would never mend. But now you are here. It is a miracle.' She wiped her tears away with the back of her hand.

'Will we go home?'

She said, 'I don't know when we will return. One day we may go back to the valley of San Antonio de las Flores. We have bought that earth with our blood. That's why it is red. They cannot steal it from us for ever. But we must have patience, *niña*. Patience and faith. *Dios es Amor*.' Mama smiled. 'Now we must say thank you to Doctor Nicholas.'

They sat at the Zambo Creek bar again. Nicholas bought them drinks. He had less than a hundred dollars left in the world.

Maria held Eulalia.

'I do not know why I am so rewarded. I can never give you enough thanks, never in a hundred years.' She wiped the corner of her eye with the back of her hand. 'When I saw what I saw on television, I went to the manager who had told me ... who had lied to me. Saying he had the documents to prove it. Now I told him that my daughter had been found, and I was so angry with his lies that I could have killed him. With my bare hands. But there was no need.

'Then I was all ready to walk out with our bags and with the boys to find Lala and then José, if it meant we should walk for the rest of our lives. From Mexico to Argentina, all over the world! They had lied to us, the most terrible lies, and we were stupid to believe them. I cannot believe how...' She paused, struggling for control.

After a while she said, 'The manager said, even after what I had told him, he said they were under instructions to await more news, and for someone else. I said Who? and he said An English doctor, Dr Nicholas Palmer. Your friend Doctor Nicholas is coming soon and there will be news.'

Nicholas's hands were tightly gripped. 'When was this?'

'The day before yesterday.'

He stammered, 'How did they know that?'

'I don't know.' Maria shrugged. 'They know all kinds of things. The real owners of the plantation are the army, you know.'

'The army?'

'The government and the army.'

He looked down at his own gripped hands.

'And then it was just as they said. As if finally they had stopped lying and were telling the truth. A call came and it was you – saying you were coming down to the coast with a present for us! I loved the way you said that very much. I cried and cried and could not believe what I was hearing. And the manager let me come, the swine of a man. Of course he could not stop me.' She wiped her eyes.

It was nearly dark now.

'Listen,' he said. 'You and the children will go back to the plantation, right? And I will go back and see what I can find out about José.'

She looked at him wide-eyed. 'You will do this?'

He nodded, pragmatic. 'It would be the most useful thing I can do now. The best arrangement.'

She nodded. 'Perhaps you are right. You know where we are. Perhaps José is even on another plantation, just down the coast somewhere, still trying to find us. Or having been told lies as well. It hurts me very much... So we should head back to the plantation soon. I do not want to leave the boys long, you can understand. We can get a taxi back and they will give me the money. They have some shame.'

Suddenly she stepped towards him and gave him a big hug. You take care now, Nicholas.' She stepped back again.

'When will I see Papa?' said Eulalia.

'He will come back to us. Or we will find him. I know we will.'

'But where is he?'

'Coming back to us. He is on his journey. But he will come back to us.'

'And we will go back to the valley and find El Pipón?' said Eulalia.

'One day,' said Maria. 'One day maybe.' Nicholas didn't know if she was quoting some old saying or song, but she added, 'When the rust eats the guns and the volcanoes lose their anger.'

Eulalia pulled her Mama's hand and took her down to the shore to paddle. Nicholas sat in silence and drank beer and watched the woman and the child on the shore.

He should go now. There was nothing more to say or do here. He should just go now, slip away, as gracefully as Pepito had done, without saying goodbye. He would in a moment. But he stayed a little while longer, just a little while longer. A few more minutes on that darkening shore, with Maria and Lala laughing in the small waves. Brilliant beads of green light surging around their bare legs like underwater glow worms.

The three boys would be sleeping soon, in their clean modern beds back on the plantation, with its resident doctor. Nicholas could just picture it. Who was he to say they should be living in a thatched *cabaña* in a highland village again?

And José was somewhere out there too in the darkness of that country, but coming back to them soon. He must be.

A pelican going by, noiseless pterodactyl against the sunset's afterglow. The warm tropical dark, the stars coming out. It would be the rainy season soon, when thick brown water would roar through the tunnel that used to be Eulalia's home, far away in the city, and the monsoon winds here on the coast would lash the lagoons to foam.

In the city the thieves would be coming out, and the soldiers would be on watch in the mountains for those mysterious insurgents. But there was no war here on the coast, looking northward out to the lovely Islands in the Bay and far beyond to the Yucatan Channel and to Cuba. Only frigate birds flying westwards, and green glow worms where the waves broke over Maria's and Lala's bare brown feet.

Lala sweeping her feet through the small warm waves, hands clasped behind her back, barefoot ballerina. Then raising her head and looking out with wondering eyes, seeing the pelicans slowly flapping west in the sunset. Big white herons stalking the twilight surf, parrots settling in the palm trees, frigate birds off Puntarenas. Cormorants sitting out on the mooring posts drying their wings. Saltfish drying stinky on the shore, the old black in his raggedy shorts raking them over, naked children still playing shiny as pebbles in the shallows. Soon to be called home by their mothers to supper and to sleep.

Vaya con Dios, Eulalia. Smiling up into the fathomless darkening blue with closing eyes. Hands clasped behind her back, barefoot dreaming ballerina. Her mother back up the beach now, watching her. Then the girl raising her arms up high for a moment and doing a little dance, skinny stick figure in silhouette against the setting sun. Her arms like the hands of a clock, foretelling a time yet to come.

72

Towards dawn, after sleeping all night in a truck, Pepito came back to the city and felt so lost and uncertain that he headed straight back to the tunnel. And the first words he heard fell on his ear like a blow.

'Hey – where you been? Marcello's looking for you.'

It was Osmin with his bag of glue. He snorted his toxic snot and bleared at him. He must have been up all night, full of some other shit as well.

'Why?' he asked stupidly.

Osmin shrugged. 'And you know about Catalina? She got fucked by half a dozen guys last night. Maybe a dozen.'

He was back in the city, amongst his friends.

'You join in?'

Osmin grinned.

'Did they rape her?'

Agustin said, 'She don't care.'

Pepito felt sick. He was nearly ready to head back out of town, find another truck straight back to the coast. Just go straight back. Sit on that beach there, look out to sea. Not move again, ever again. Just stay there forever, looking out to sea.

'You better go see Marcello,' said Osmin. He was enjoying it. 'He wants a piece a your ass.'

Pepito looked around at the muddy shoreline, the kites in the flat white sky. He felt ready to run but where could he run? He stammered, 'Marcello doesn't do early mornings.'

'He said if you want that little kid girlfriend of yours left alone, you go and see him. Or else...'

He was very afraid. His head flooded with wild schemes.

What if he went to the cops? Himself? Testified against Marcello? But Marcello was best friends with the cops, he had to be. What if he went back to see him and tried to kill him? But that was crazy. Marcello had all the power. He had none. There was nothing he could do. He was afraid, afraid for everyone. Maybe Marcello even knew about Lala and where she had gone. Maybe he even knew about the gringo.

'Be seeing you then,' he said, turning away.

'Hey,' Osmin called after him.

He looked back.

'You go carefully, *compadre*.'

Later he was very groggy, his hands were tied behind his back and he was very afraid. He lay on his side on a mattress and felt very sick and bloody and bruised because of the beating they had given him, his head very cold. But if they'd wanted to kill him they would have killed him by now.

The door of the windowless room where he lay was locked so there was no escape, and Marcello had said he would visit him again later. But he hoped that he was still valuable to Marcello and he wouldn't come to too much harm. He would not cry. They would not make him cry, not even now, and anyhow tears stung in your cuts.

It would not go well for him, his future, not for now, but he lay there stirring slowly and groaning and hurting like a bastard, knowing he had done the good thing. Lala had got away, and she would be OK with the loony English guy who was OK really, and she was going back to her Mama, it sounded like. He smiled to himself stiffly with his cracked and bloody lips as he thought about it. Because he had cheated Marcello of that much at least.

Later that night he fell asleep despite the pain, and he dreamt they were fleeing into the night. He was with Eulalia, and sometimes there was Nicholas there too and a woman, a mother. And the mother pointed and said, Someone should look after these kids.

They were with a group of people fleeing north, and he was falling asleep in a rumbling railway wagon with Eulalia and she had a pet animal like some kind of mouse, and she leaned against him in the wagon. Then they were climbing some creaking old wooden stairs, like something out of a hundred years ago, and it was cold but he was all excited like something really good was going to happen. He gave his coat to Eulalia, and he said to her, It'll be OK sister. Don't you worry. And she smiled with her little white gappy teeth and it was OK.

They came to a wooden door and pushed it carefully open and stepped into a small upper room. There was a fire burning brightly in the heart of the room. No smoke, just this golden fire, and around the side of the room there were people sitting peacefully, crosslegged, eating from bowls and talking quietly. They looked up and nodded and smiled, and someone said, 'Here at last.' And they had arrived and they were safe and the future was golden and it was America.

73

Nicholas stayed that night in a cheap hotel and in the morning he went out and knew that they had gone. The weather turned grey and a cold wind blew up. Dusty remnants of the unidentifiable gusted over the sand, plastic bottles aimlessly caught up and somersaulted and clattered into corners with a hollow clatter. It was the wind called El Norte coming out of the north and the mountains of Mexico.

Once there were three lost children. And then one of the children was saved. Maybe that wasn't so bad. In the world that was.

Suddenly he sat on the broad kerbstone of the sleepy sandstrewn road, his back to sea and the cold. Unmoving, unable to move. A black truck went by and someone shouted out at him sitting derelict there, Hey *puta* gringo! But he had known worse than that and felt no pang.

He was shaken back to the empty present by a phone's muffled ringing in his rucksack. He stared. He had no phone.

He delved inside and the sound was coming from inside the black plastic package of cocaine. He found his pocketknife. The phone still ringing. He sliced open the package and inside was a small transparent bag with a phone inside. He felt colder still.

When he finally answered he heard,

'Don Nicholas!'

His mouth opened.

'Where are you now, my old friend?'

His scalp was so cold. It was him. How could it be him? Lord of the Highland Clearances, Global Purveyor of Plant-based Stimulants, Sexual Dynamo, President-in-Waiting, Fruitcake.

'Say something!' That hearty roar. Rosy cheeks and manful dynamic moustache.

Nicholas heard himself saying from afar off. 'Thanks for calling.'

'How do I know? How do I know?' He was in a state of great elation. 'I know everything!' said the colonel. 'Perhaps I even let you escape from the airport, because I wanted to see what you would do, where you would go. What would become of you, in this dangerous country. Because you interest me so - perhaps! I watch you in the zoo!'

Nicholas nodded dumbly. But the colonel was in full flow.

'And then you have a mobile phone on you, and mobile phones can be tracked by GPS. It is always surprising how few people know this. And you have a package of mine. Oh Nicholas, do not be naïve. Of course we searched your bag when you were unaware, and a soldier heard you hiding something under the floorboards. So we hid a mobile in the package so we could monitor you, at least until the battery ran out. Smart, eh?

'This is a very small country. It is like you say, a small pond. And I am a very big fish in this small pond. I know everything.' He laughed. 'I *eat* everything!'

For a vertiginous moment, Nicholas wondered if the colonel could have orchestrated everything. Had scripted everything for his own deranged amusement.

The Colonel was still amused, and went on, 'So I know where you are, and I want my package back. It is worth quite a bit, but it is mainly the principle of the thing. I know about the family that you so love, from the village. The little girl, the mother, about everything you have done for them, about the sacrifices you have made. I know where they are too, and I shall keep an eye on them. You see? And if you do as I say and return to me, your loving father, I will see that they come to no harm. Do you understand?'

Had the moustachioed entrepreneur and military impresario really said, Your loving father, or was he now aurally hallucinating in his horror? He started to stammer.

'What about José? The father of the family? Do you know where he is? I said I'd –'

The Colonel interrupted.

'Calm yourself. Now this is what will happen. You will come back to me here, my friend and personal physician. Take the bus from the capital, it is running smoothly again all the way to Santo Domingo and the valley. Come and find me. I have built quite a place. You can ask anyone, they all know me. I am accounted quite a fellow in these parts! This whole backward forested department is becoming my seat of power, but from here my tentacles spread far and wide. Oh, life is sweet, dear Don Nicholas, and I want to tell you all about it and to share my victory with you. So: come.'

And then the burr of the tone.

He sat in the dust for a while and absorbed this new development.

He leaned over the mobile so he could see the scuffed screen in the glaring daylight. He thought he might as well use it to send a text to his beloved mother, even though it was uncertain she would ever get it. If this was still her number, if she still had a phone, if she had paid her bills, if she ever read her texts at all. If she was still alive and conscious and not lying comatose somewhere clutching a Lo-Kost gin bottle. Head down the lavatory bowl, maybe. Split ends turning blonde in the germicidal foam. Terminally undignified middle-aged middle-class drowned toilet drunk. That womb from which he wailing came.

Despite it being early morning, he texted, 'Darkness falling, heading home.'

74

It was evening of the following day when he came back to Chilitenango.

A jeep drove him up the valley and there was a new building going up fast. Nearly completed in fact. Wedding-cake gothic. Narco-bling. Very white and gold, with a lot of columns. It must have gone up in a matter of weeks. He might as well laugh and relax a bit now. Lala was saved, and José was not a child nor was he stupid. Nicholas would find him somehow, or José would find his family. The Colonel might even help him. He and José Silvestre Chacach would sit and drink beer at Zambo Creek yet.

They took him to some new barracks smelling sweetly of freshly sawn timber and they showed him into a room where he could stay.

'I am not a prisoner?'

'No of course not. We will try to help you. But you are free to come and go. Now please return the package that you stole from the aeroplane.'

Ha handed it over without a word.

They brought him a coffee and then in the last twilight he went out for a walk through the lost village.

He headed up the old familiar valley, a halting man in search of his people.

Bulldozers standing quiet, the trees stripped bare and laid for the logging trucks, huge swathes of brushwood set burning. The aid station itself looked like it was now the site office for the new plantations, for the growing of the lucrative and much-in-demand *erythroxylon coca*.

He looked up at the silhouette of the mountains, already dark against the fading sky. It would be a cold night.

Here had been the bar of the squawking Henrietta. He poked with his boot at nothing, and there on its face lay one of the white plastic chairs. The very same ones where, back in early January, just arrived from England, four eager, anxious volunteers had sat and drunk Cuban rum and talked rubbish and laughed. He set the chair upright. He almost missed them now. Blonde Lucy and her quick pixyish face, her homesick eyes, Caitlin strong and wry, Bridge and his yellow corduroy suit.

Oh it was burned and desolate, the diggers in their forest clearings, the beaten road, the vanished lanterns and hearthfires of those village evenings. He could not believe it was all gone. As if they had arrived just in time to catch the last few days of Chilitenango and the slow, closed, laborious life of the people that lived there.

Nor could he begin to calculate the balance sheet of profit and loss. Who had incurred what, who had paid what? But surely the people themselves had paid. The poor, as always. And what had been his role? Even now he could barely understand all that had happened, nor reckon what if anything he had learned from it, nor how it fitted with his former life and the undiscovered life yet to come.

Here was the stump that he would sit on some days in late afternoons on his way back from the clinic, taking a swig of water and wiping his mouth, still smiling to himself at the Sayings of Dr Hércules Menendez. Here was where he'd seen the great yellow and purple butterflies, and that tiny emerald lizard that ran over his boot. Uncertain of its way, uncertain even of how a lizard should behave, being still young.

Or he sat here with his back to this ceiba tree with its youthful prickles and vast roots, hat down over his eyes but still able to watch the people come and go in the village square. Grackles in the silk-cotton trees. The men on

427

horseback with bare machetes returning from the forest, clopping over the cobbles in the old square, rolled cigarettes in the corners of their mouths, eyes creased in the shade of their broad-brimmed hats. *Campesinos* in dusty jeans and boots, toothless smiles and soft greetings. Their *Adios* almost whispered, the gentle girlish handshakes of *los humildes*.

There stood a cottage and once he walked past coming back from the clinic and glimpsed a girl's face, bright with perspiration. She had come back from the river with water in jerry cans, and she still wore one of the traditional *huipiles*, and he glimpsed her in the darkness of the cottage, glowing beyond the shaft of sunlight that came through the door, and she was so beautiful his insides lurched. And then she turned away and he never saw her again.

There he had stopped once with Lucy to savour the smell of the freshbaked tortillas off the stone, sweet maize smell and ancient smoke, and the woman came out and smiled and insisted they take one each though they had only just had breakfast, and they took one each and they were so good.

There was where the drunk lay in the road, whom Lala had saved in her childish kindness. And there was the road up to the cabin and the clinic. Had they really killed Dr Menendez? Was it possible to kill him? He could well have been taken ill. Where did he lie buried, that obese wheezing form, was he decently buried? Yet he of all people, Doctor Hércules Menendez, in his blue suit and loud floral tie, would not have cared whether or where he was buried. Leave me to the vultures, he would have said, if they're damn fool enough to eat me. I hope they choke.

And down there among the trees had been the little white cottage of Uncle Uberto where he cooked up his home-made *tamales* with pudgy delicate hands.

There was where the house of Old Jorge had been. Jorge Rodriguez MacLellan, who even in his seventies used to drive mule trains right over the mountains and down to the Pacific coast. There was a path up into a stretch of forest yet untouched. How many times would Pedro Xom the *atzj'ib* have taken it with his little trotting steps, shawl splashed with moonlight. And somewhere up in that forest the little stone idol of Pascual Abuaj still stood, unworshipped now, unhonoured, the forest and time clothing him in outlandish and mocking lichens and the nodding fronds of ferns. In a few years' time he would be lost entirely, nameless as any other lost god.

There was the very copse where they had cut the saplings for the *bodega* and his spare bedroom that they had said they would build for him, because Lala had said that he should not be left out in his hammock on his own. That was the tree that Lala swung from and Héctor fell from.

Finally he came to where the cottage had stood. Well, he had promised Lala when he left the village for the airport that he would come back again. And he had kept his promise. But now that beloved home and the plot full of bright squashes and beanplants was but a scathed and blackened mountainside, crosshatched with caterpillar tracks. Here were the trees where he hung his hammock, here was where they built the *bodega* that day. Look, still a black outline where the walls had stood. Razed outline in the crimpled earth. The children squelching in the red trench, José's tired lined face. Héctor coming up grinning like a mud homunculus from his wallow. The doorway where the chickens pecked, the watertrough that José had sat in, the woodoven, and that time he and Maria sat on the bench there, and he had drunkenly longed for her. Then she had punched him.

And above it all the volcanoes of Santa Ana and Santa Miguel, impassive titans looking down on the lost village, mute guardians of nothing. And then San Salvador, always throwing up orange lava and a guide for sailors at night. The sailors blessed the volcano and called it the Lighthouse of the Pacific. And sometimes on very still nights, the moon on the mountains, a mighty column of smoke rose straight up from San Salvador to heaven, lit up grey and ghostly like the cloudy pillar that led the children of Israel when they were lost in the wilderness.

He went away and up the track a little further and turned off into the steep forest to the west. No shouts followed him, no bright birdcalls of children trotting after him. No one saw. There was only him and the forest, dark now and moonless beneath the canopy, with mossed and matted trees to embrace him, green grottoes to house him and keep him silent there. He stumbled and tripped and broke a stick from a tree and held it to his head and fired and reeled back laughing. A scuttling forest creature, far from the sun.

But even here there were clearings made by the diggers. He came into a clearing and by the starlight overhead he saw that he wasn't alone and he sat crosslegged near the body and bowed his head and wept. 'No, no, no!' For he knew that face, that body, even in this reluctant light.

At last he knelt up and scratched a hole in the dirt and buried the mobile that he still carried in his shirt pocket. Stamped it down into the dirt with the heel of his boot. Trod it flat again and dried his eyes and then turned and walked back down the valley.

75

'The Colonel wants to see you for dinner.'

'Now?'

'Now.'

He was led down a corridor at the back of the barracks to a door. The door was opened and there was a flight of stairs down to an underground level, and he could hear distant voices and laughter.

The soldier smiled to see his expression. 'There's a whole underground world down here,' he said. 'Come and see.'

There were soldiers with guns on every door. Doors opened onto more and more corridors, chambers, yet more stairs down still deeper into the earth. What was this place? Underneath the sweet valley of San Antonio, this vast underground bunker had lain unknown for years, shadowing the contours of the land above, awaiting rediscovery.

His footsteps echoed, the soldiers' boots resounded. The lighting was bright and hard and the sound of voice and laughter was nearer now. Reality was fading away, draining out of everything. He felt as light on his feet as a child, falling down a fractal tunnel of light.

There were men in black suits before a mahogany door inlaid with crescents and curlicues of brass, and a dark inner door similarly guarded, the sound of revelry within. Then that door too was freely opened to him, and he walked into a staggering debauch.

He took in an underground chamber like the audience hall of a mountain king, a long table, perspiring diners both military and civilian, bulbous bellies, bottles, music, a small stage for the wild-eyed music-makers, tasteful illuminations of smoked glass lanterns and candlelight. At least a dozen girls all slim and young, submissive and smiling, cocoabutter limbs a-gleam in the candlelight, and there were more exotic attractions too: a monstrous fat woman, a black man in a pink nylon wig and enormous wobbling moobies, a woman dancer in front of the band almost naked but for a g-string. A tumbler of iced rum being pressed into his hand. A short squat man, almost entirely bald, in a bowtie and a suit of shimmering silver. Another lightly-dressed girl, miniskirt and croptop, perched in the lap of a man who looked like a civil servant in thick-rimmed glasses and a moustache flecked with beer foam. The girl squirmed inscrutably, perhaps obediently, in the man's lap.

There was no sign of the colonel at first, so Nicholas was seated beside this unlikely couple. He nodded politely, not sure what else to do, nor what would become of him here. How far he might descend. The man stared at him. The girl looked slightly anxious.

He asked for rum and four bottles of Coke to himself so that he could get very drunk. It would surely help now. He said to those around him, 'My name is Bridge Kynaston!' He was smiling now but there was wildness to it. People shifted their chairs away from him if they could, even those who were drunk. He shifted his chair after them, beaming into their faces.

He explained in English, 'I came here to do good. To help this country if I could. You see? But I wouldn't say it really worked out. Not *really*. Although I did find Lala.'

Some wondered why this thin gringo fool was here. He was an embarrassment. He couldn't seem to stop himself talking.

'A girl once told me I was too high-minded for my own good, and old before my time. But I don't think she knew me very well!'

The girl in the man's lap at least appeared to find him funny. Or unexpected anyway.

'Nicholas!' cried a familiar voice. 'Come and talk to me!'

Colonel Maximo Inocencio was returned from doing battle and sat at the head of the table. King Arthur's shadow, janus-faced lord of discipline and chaos.

Nicholas stood and went over to him, and the colonel flung his arm around his sweating frame.

'The prodigal returns! I knew you would come back!' He was shouting above the din, but his voice was strong. 'I knew it! You are welcome, *Inglés*! But what timing! It is not always like this, you could have found us in a meeting. But come, come. We have much to discuss. Are you curious?'

'Full of curiosity. But I didn't have much choice, did I?'

'Ah, there is always choice. Sit. Eat. And drink!'

He did as he was told. Though he had zero appetite, minus appetite, yet he must keep his strength up for what was to come. There was chicken and steamed rice with spices and salad. He spooned a little onto his plate. Five a day. And he drank his rum. Sweet white rum, sometimes with fresh juice, extra sugar, a shot of lime, sometimes with more Coke. He raised his glass to the air and drank a loud toast to Bridge Kynaston. One or two around him uncertainly raised their glasses and drank too. The Colonel laughed. The girl in the civil servant's lap caught his eye again and giggled.

'Of course I knew where you were, I know everything!' The voice roared at him, that tremendous black moustache almost tickling his ear.

The Colonel drank water, but seemed drunk all the same. Drunk with success, with worldly accomplishment. His libido would be through the roof. Bursting up through the bedroom ceiling like a huge tumescent mushroom. There was a tremendously lawless and libidinous ambience tonight. Jesus Christ. Nicholas gulped more rum.

'The plantations, you see!' he was roaring. 'I always knew where you were, *Inglés*. Of course I did. I won't say all the time, but almost. I have my contacts. I was very angry with some of Marcello's people for maltreating you. So much so that I summoned him up here to see me, in my lair. My wolf's lair, yes? My *Berchtesgarten*. Ha! I wish you would shudder when I say things like that.'

'I get it,' said Nicholas. 'You're comparing yourself to Hitler. Splendid. He was great man. Much misunderstood.'

The Colonel laughed delightedly.

'And you're a teetotaller too.'

'Very nearly. Oh *Inglés*, it is good to talk to an educated man again. Even amid this…' he waved his arm. 'Swamp.'

'Why have you ordered me back here?'

'Ordered? No, *invited*. You do not have to stay. You think too ill of me. I would like you to be my personal physician.'

'How's your wound?'

'Silence about that,' said the colonel with a sudden scowl.

'OK, OK,' he murmured. 'I might want to give you one more shot of antibiotic tomorrow.'

'Enough of this now. Have more rum. More rum here!'

It was just him and his tormentor. The rest of the world was far away. The Colonel looking back at him and smiling. Just that equable, testing gaze, the taunting smile.

The Colonel twisted slightly in his chair. 'I know you, *Inglés*. I understand you to the depths of your noble young soul. You are drunk and disappointed, but you would still love to die a noble and heroic death. You are as plain as a sheet of glass to me, for all your shadows and silences. This is why you dislike me so much. But no – you walk out of here an ordinary man. How you will hate that! What a punishment for so noble a soul as yours!'

He slapped him jovially on the shoulder. 'Come on now, do not repine. Fill up your glass – and see how she looks at you! That one down there. My God, look at her. She would do anything for you. You must be hungry. Go to her. Because you can. You can do whatever you like here. I will only admire you the more for it if you do. Now come on.'

He drank one more glass and then he went along to the young girl took her hand very politely and she smiled.

434

He calmed down with her hand in his. His despairing mania subsided. He did not want to frighten her, the innocent. Her hair was a little tangled and frizzy and her hand very light in his. She led him away down a passageway to a small room with a bed in it and a quaint, smoky lantern. She leant against him in the doorway and that alone was enough, that touch of seeming affection. She must have been four or five years younger than him.

He was half the age of many of the men who had had her before, so it was like they were young together and hiding in here from the grown-ups. They lay on the bed and he did a funny impression of the colonel for her. When she wanted to kiss him he could hold back no longer and kissed her desperately. She started to unbutton his shirt, but then he stopped her.

She clung to him and asked him, didn't he want her?

But he just said, 'I have lost.'

'What? What?' Her brown eyes anxiously searched the room.

'I'm sorry. I have lost,' he said again. And he got up and buttoned his shirt again and left her there without another word.

'Come back,' she said after him. 'Please don't leave me here.'

76

He went back up to the forest with slow steps, like someone returning reluctantly to a house they know is haunted, and when he found the clearing he sat crosslegged there.

He had come to this country to learn and to help and even to heal where possible. Yet now he had no idea what he had really done. And the story wasn't over yet. Because tomorrow, he would have to choose whether or not to commit murder. Tomorrow he must decide whether or not to kill the colonel.

If the colonel allowed him to administer a general antibiotic, he might be able to do it that way. It would be most meaningful to kill him with a cocaine overdose, though how could he get any? A cocaine overdose by injection led to very rapid rise in heartbeat, a fierce rise in body temperature almost physically painful to the victim, profuse sweating, chest pain, feelings of panic and disorientation, organ damage, with the cause of death almost always heart failure. Or maybe enough of the anaesthetic lidocaine from the medikits would do it. Or he could just try and stab him in the heart with a knife or some scissors. But could he do that?

Or he could not kill him, because it was not his place, and how could he judge, and who was to say what the colonel would or would not do in the coming years?

He came back to the starlit clearing, and now there was a thin moon as well coming up. He looked over at the body nearby, and then he went and sat close. It broke his heart but it was not horrifying, it was beautiful.

He had seen a woman in the dissection lab, a homeless

woman who had lain three days and nights in a London park in winter. She looked just a little pale, her eyes sunk back, her jaw protruding, ribs prominent, but little else of note. Here, after only two or three weeks of the devouring tropics, there was little soft tissue left upon the face of his friend José Silvestre Chacach. Yet it was him, he knew his face still, and his clothes sunk down around his frame, and the seashell amulet around his throat. Which Maria had bought for him in the early days of their courting.

Nicholas knelt near him, nearer, as if in devotion. The musty odour of a cave, the fineness of his exposed bones. His jeans were bloodstained and there were two bullet holes in them, and some wild animal had been at his leg. His face was back to the skull now, facial tissue the softest of soft tissues, the least muscled. The skull beneath the skin just like the broad skulls on the stelae at Copán, the skulls of those long dead nameless Maya. Who went willingly to the sacrifice, for the sake of the tribe.

In his right hand José clutched a bright silver crucifix. It looked very like the one that had belonged to Pedro Xom, but how could that be? Perhaps José had found it somewhere and carried with him, clinging to it as he neared his end. Hoping it might save him. Or maybe he died more peacefully because he died clutching it in his hand. It would remain until José's own callused and hardworked hands were nothing but delicate patterns of bone, calcium lacework, darkening with algae and earth, the bright silver tortured man untarnished.

Then Nicholas lay down beside the dead man he had loved and closed his eyes and scooped armfuls of leafmould over his upturned face and stretched his arms out wide and lay breathing in the fertile darkness and was still.

After a long while he sat up again and shook his head and the leafmould fell away. Everything human must end soon. There was the bright moon and a new mist on the mountains and down the valley came the song of a guardabarranca.

Christopher Hart was born into a vicarage family in 1965. He was educated in Cheltenham, Oxford and London, where he completed a PhD on W.B.Yeats.

This is his tenth novel. His previous titles include *The Harvest* and *Rescue Me*, while his historical fiction, written under the pen name of William Napier, includes *Julia*, the best-selling Attila trilogy and the Last Crusaders trilogy. His work has been praised in both the *Times Literary Supplement* and the *Sunday Sport*, which is unusual.

He has also published numerous short stories, essays and reviews, in publications as diverse as the *Erotic Review* and *Trail Running* magazine. He writes regularly for the *Daily Mail* and the *Sunday Times*, where he is lead theatre critic.

He is married and lives in Wiltshire.

www.christopherhart.info

Lightning Source UK Ltd.
Milton Keynes UK
UKHW042054301218
334797UK00001B/129/P